Being an author has always been **Therese Beharrie**'s dream. But it was only when the corporate world loomed during her final year at university that she realised how soon she wanted that dream to become a reality. So she got serious about her writing, and now she writes the kind of books she wants to see in the world, featuring people who look like her, for a living. When she's not writing she's spending time with her husband and dogs in Cape Town, South Africa. She admits that this is a perfect life, and is grateful for it.

Raised in a small town on Vancouver Island, **Laurel Greer** grew up skiing and boating by day and reading romances under the covers by flashlight at night. Ever committed to the proper placement of the Canadian *eh*, she loves to write books with snapping sexual tension and second chances. She lives outside Vancouver with her law-talking husband and two daughters. At least half her diet is made up of tea. Find her at www.laurelgreer.com

Also by Therese Beharrie

Tempted by the Billionaire Next Door
Surprise Baby, Second Chance
Her Festive Flirtation
Island Fling with the Tycoon
Her Twin Baby Secret

Billionaires for Heiresses

Second Chance with Her Billionaire
From Heiress to Mum

Also by Laurel Greer

From Exes to Expecting
A Father for Her Child
Holiday by Candlelight

Discover more at millsandboon.co.uk

MARRYING
HIS RUNAWAY
HEIRESS

THERESE BEHARRIE

THEIR NINE-MONTH
SURPRISE

LAUREL GREER

MILLS & BOON

First Published in Great Britain 2020
by Mills & Boon, an imprint of HarperCollinsPublishers,
1 London Bridge Street, London, SE1 9GF

Marrying His Runaway Heiress © 2020 Therese Beharrie
Their Nine-Month Surprise © 2020 Lindsay Macgowan

ISBN: 978-0-263-27884-2

0620

MIX
Paper from
responsible sources
FSC® C007454

FSC
www.fsc.org

This book is produced from independently certified FSC™ paper to ensure responsible forest management.

For more information visit: www.harpercollins.co.uk/green

Printed and bound in Spain
by CPI, Barcelona

MARRYING HIS RUNAWAY HEIRESS

THERESE BEHARRIE

For Grant, because he's the reason I experienced Italy and its beauty and romance. I think—by law— that means I have to dedicate this book to him.

Also because he loves me unconditionally, which never fails to surprise and overwhelm me. Thank you.

CHAPTER ONE

IF ELENA JOHN hadn't known better, she'd have thought Micah Williams was simply being thoughtful. But she did know better. He wasn't being thoughtful; he was trying to charm her. Soften her up.

If they'd met before she would have told him not to bother.

Instead, she climbed into the limousine that had pulled up in front of her house with a resigned sigh. It was as luxurious on the inside as it was on the outside. In one corner a mini-bar packed with her favourite drinks—which couldn't be a coincidence since her favourite drinks were undeniably strange—and a basket of snacks in another corner. Music streamed through the speakers. Soft, unassuming, bland music no one could find offensive. Then there was the driver, who checked on her constantly, and the flight attendant, who took over from the driver once Elena reached the airport.

The longer she thought about it though, the more she liked the idea of Mr Williams trying to charm her. It wouldn't work, but the fact that he was trying reminded her of what she'd accomplished. Five years at her newspaper and finally, *finally* she'd got assigned an important story. A story about a powerful man. Now, the powerful man was trying to nudge her towards writing a good story.

She'd shadowed enough journalists, transcribed enough interviews, heard enough stories to know sometimes people did that.

She'd spent enough time with powerful men to know sometimes they did that, too.

Considering the situation she was leaving behind, the thought that Mr Williams was trying to manipulate her should have angered her. But this was for her job. She had prepared for this her entire career. And for once, she wasn't the one in the helpless position. So what if the limousines and private planes, the obedient and careful staff, and the access to her favourite things reminded her of the first sixteen years of her life?

It might be a precursor to the next years of your life, too.

The thought made her faintly nauseous.

'Ms John?' The flight attendant was staring at her, his spine so straight, his posture so poised, she wanted to know if he'd practised it. 'Through here.'

'Yes.'

She followed him through the blue velvet curtain into the plush luxury of Micah Williams's private plane. The design was different from her father's, which was mostly for efficiency and productivity. Here the open space was a balance of that and relaxation, with comfortable-looking chairs on either side of the aisle in front of a modern desk. The biggest difference though was the man standing in front of that desk.

Micah Williams.

He was handsome. She didn't bother tiptoeing around it. His skin was an awe-inspiring shade of brown, as if the heavens had opened and a stream of both light and dark shone on him. His body was clad in a suit that was made for his broad shoulders, his narrow waist, his long legs. His hair was dark and short, his stubble a length that told her it had been purposefully groomed that way. None of it was a surprise. Her research had prepared her.

What surprised her was the intensity of his gaze. The way he looked at her as if she had the answer to a question he'd had all his life. She wasn't prepared for how his mouth curved at the side when he realised she was staring. When she realised he was staring right back.

She resisted the urge to smooth down the red pants suit she wore. She still wore her black coat over it, but the red was visible. She'd purposefully chosen to wear the colour. It was *her* colour. That knowledge was one of the few things her mother had left her before she'd packed her bags to travel the world.

Having a colour made Elena feel good; being in her colour made her feel strong. Strength helped her accept that this man was staring at her so intensely.

'Ms John,' he said smoothly, stepping forward. 'Thank you for coming.'

'Did I have a choice?' she asked lightly. She gave herself a moment to enjoy his surprise. It flitted over the intensity, making it seem lighter. She knew it was an illusion. 'It's a free trip to Italy.'

Something twitched on his face. 'That's what you meant, is it?' His tone was dry. 'It has nothing to do with this being for your job?'

'No. It's all about a gondola ride.'

'You've been on a gondola before,' he said confidently.

'No.' She searched his face. 'Why does that surprise you?'

'For the same reason I don't believe you need a free trip to Italy.'

He knew who she was.

She schooled her face, trying hard not to give in to disappointment. It wasn't the end of the world. Her identity wasn't a secret. But—did this mean what she thought it meant? The only way to find out was to ask.

'Are you referring to the fact that my family owns the John Diamond Company?'

The intense look was back. Bemusement was there, too. 'I am.'

'Is that why I'm here, Mr Williams? Because of my family?'

The seconds ticked by. Eventually, he said, 'It is.'

She sighed. 'Wonderful.' Paused. 'Your attempts to butter me up were ridiculous, by the way.' It was an immature comment, and nowhere near an appropriate response to what he was admitting or the implications of it. But he didn't get a chance to answer her.

'We're about to take off,' the flight attendant said behind her. 'Can you please take your seats?'

She settled in a seat next to the window. Tried to steady herself by looking out at the city she loved. There was nothing on the tarmac besides a few other planes. Bright green grass was scattered beyond the tar, the dew of the brisk day settling on it. If she looked close enough, she'd swear she'd find ice sitting on the tips of the blades of grass. If nothing else, she was leaving a cold, wet South Africa for a sunny, warm Italy. If nothing else, she was leaving behind two men who thought they could control her life.

You're thinking about letting them though.

She exhaled slowly.

'I've upset you.'

They were in the air already, though barely, when Micah spoke.

'No.' She kept her gaze on the window. Outside it was all blue now, with white puffs of clouds around them. 'Why would you think that?'

'You insulted my attempts at cordiality.'

She almost laughed at the indignation in his voice. 'So try harder next time.'

A strangled sound came from the vicinity of his seat. She allowed herself to enjoy it, but didn't turn to look at him, or let him see her smile. It was a while longer before he said anything again.

'I didn't only ask for you to do this story because of your name, you know.'

So he had asked for her. Which meant that she likely hadn't earned this assignment as she initially believed. And she was more helpless than she initially believed. It smarted, and the sting of it coated her tongue, slipping into her words, her tone.

'I'm sure. It's those pop culture articles I wrote, isn't it? Speculating on who someone will end up with next truly does display the depth of my talent.'

'I did enjoy the article about the ex-rugby player bad boy who faked a relationship but fell in love for real.'

At that, Elena turned to look at him. He was sitting on the only other seat opposite her, lounging back in his chair, watching her as if he had nothing else to do. Elena knew that couldn't be true. The man ran an empire. His business had grown immensely in the ten years since he'd started it. His company sold luxury goods in Africa, primarily South Africa, and he'd recently partnered with two non-African brands worth millions to do that for. She suspected another brand would be added to that in Italy.

It was all part of why Elena's newspaper had selected him as their Businessperson of the Year. She was supposed to be writing an article about how amazingly busy he was. There was no way he had time to converse with her.

'You read that?'

'I did.'

He flicked a forearm out, rolled back his shirt sleeve. He did the same on the other side. She watched, stuck on the fact that he'd taken off his suit jacket. Also, on his forearms. His *forearms*. They were muscular, with lines of veins that looked as if they were pulsing. They made her want to trace them with her fingertips, then grip that swelling just before his elbow to feel the muscle there. She wanted to—

Nothing. She wanted to nothing.

What did Jameson's forearms look like? Did it matter? The marriage he and her father had proposed was purely business. Purely name. Which made what Micah had done sting sharper. She was there for her name, too. Not for his admittedly good-looking forearms.

Wait—Micah? When had she started calling him Micah?

'I have to admit, there was a lot of speculation, even in that.'

Okay, he was speaking again. Yes, right. She needed to reply. That was how conversations worked. If she remembered correctly, and honestly, she wasn't sure she did.

'Pop culture articles are speculative by nature. Unless you have a reliable source, but that changes things. The tone of the article. It shifts the attention. You have people focusing more on who the source could be as opposed to the content. Generally, I use sources for articles that are already more fact than opinion. Which, I guess, is the difference between having my piece in the entertainment section of the printed paper versus only the digital edition.'

The silence that followed her answer alerted her to how much she'd said. She'd surprised them both with it, but she refused to feel embarrassed. She knew what she was doing. Writing was not only her job, but her passion. She read articles and books on writing, did online courses, followed noted journalists on social media. All of this was over and above her responsibilities at the newspaper.

She was *capable*. It was part of why Micah Williams asking for her annoyed her. He shouldn't have had to ask; she should have been given this. She deserved it.

'This is exactly why I thought you'd do well on this article,' Micah said. 'There was something about your work that felt intentional. Even the fluff pieces, which I enjoyed immensely.'

'How could you not?' she countered. 'Everyone knows how much people enjoy fluff.'

He laughed. It was surprising and arousing. At that point, Elena should have known she was already in trouble. Then he said, 'Ms John, you'll quickly discover that my tastes aren't similar to most people's.' There was a slight pause. 'I'm going to enjoy showing you that.'

The fact that she *wanted* him to show her? That she thought she would *enjoy* it? Oh, yeah. Trouble.

Micah Williams hadn't expected the John heiress to be so...

Interesting.

The word seemed woefully inadequate to describe the woman sitting opposite him. As a result, he watched her more than was necessary. Her expressions were animated, her tone dry and sharp in equal measure, and she was surprisingly candid. Surprisingly attractive, too.

Not her appearance. He'd seen that in pictures. The wild, curly hair. The gloss of her brown skin and the dusting of freckles on only her left cheek, though that detail hadn't been clear in the pictures. He noted it now because it had a certain charm. As did the way her mouth was painted bright red. Her lips were full, plump, and he'd experienced plenty of people in his lifetime who would have been embarrassed by that abundance. Ms John seemed to have embraced it.

That peek into her personality was really the most attractive thing about her.

She embraced plenty of things, it seemed. The admittedly extra nature of how he'd brought her to his plane—not that he'd expected her to point it out. The fact that he knew who she was. That he'd requested her for the article. Micah hadn't expected it to be easy to get Elena on his side, but now he thought her honesty might aid him. Maybe that was why he offered her such honesty in return.

Either that, or those red lips. And that luscious body, tall and curved, clad in a red pants suit visible despite her coat. The white T-shirt she wore beneath it clung to ample breasts. And her heels, white as well, highlighted the most beautiful set of ankles he'd seen in his life.

He blinked. Ankles? Since when had he noticed a woman's ankles? Of all the things he'd been attracted to, ankles had never appeared on the list. His eyes lowered to her legs. She'd crossed them.

So maybe he simply hadn't seen the *right* pair of ankles. Interesting. Irrelevant, but interesting.

'Do you know, if you'd started our conversation with the fact that you've read my work, things would have been a lot less contentious?'

'Contentious?' he repeated. 'I don't know what you mean, Ms John.'

'Elena, please.' There was a slight pause. She hesitated. Undid her seat belt and stood, offering him a hand. 'I'm sorry. I didn't introduce myself properly. I am Elena.'

She didn't say her surname. He stored it into the vault of information he had about her, undid his own seat belt, and stood.

'Micah.'

'Good to meet you, Mr Williams.'

She took his hand. Shook in two quick pumps. It shouldn't have heated his blood. Shouldn't have had any effect on him whatsoever.

It did.

'If I call you Elena, you'll have to call me Micah,' he said, hoping to heaven his voice was normal and not tinted with the desire he suddenly felt.

'It feels…' she hesitated '…wrong to call you Micah.'

'Wrong?' Another interesting fact. 'How so?'

'Unprofessional,' she clarified.

'This is about the article.'

'Yes, of course.' She frowned. 'What else could it be about?'

This unexpected attraction between us?

'Nothing else. We're on the same page.'

He pressed the button that called the flight attendant, and when the man appeared ordered himself a drink. With alcohol. To shock his system into behaving. Elena ordered a water. There was that professionalism again. It obviously meant a lot to her. But why?

'I promise not to consider you unprofessional if you use my first name,' he said, accepting the glass from the flight attendant. 'I won't tell anyone at the newspaper either.'

'Thank you.' Her tone was somehow a mixture of dryness and gratitude. Fascinating creature, the John heiress. 'I'll call you Micah—' he ignored the thrill that beat in his heart '—for the duration of this week. Since we are spending it together, it might be strange to continue speaking to you so formally.' She didn't give him a chance to process before she was asking, 'Is the itinerary for this week finalised?'

She was putting distance between them, he realised. He kept his smile to himself. He wasn't sure what was amusing him more: the fact that she felt the need to put distance between them when they'd barely known one another for an hour; or how seamlessly she'd done so. He was being managed. Expertly. He hadn't thought much about how her being an heiress would affect this business trip. Well, other than his plan to endear himself to her. But now he was experiencing it.

A journalist had never put him in his place so skilfully before. Nor a woman. He barely felt that he'd been moved, let alone gently, if firmly, lowered to the ground. It was tied into the professionalism somehow. The attraction. He had no idea—and he wanted to know. Except that wasn't why she was here. He needed to remember that.

'It is. The one my assistant emailed to you is accurate, apart from two meetings that I have scheduled for our last day in Rome. It was the only time my client was available,' he added apologetically.

'You don't have to explain,' she said with a shake of her head. 'I know how it goes with business trips.'

'I imagine you do.'

Her brow lifted, but she didn't engage. 'Is there a reason Serena isn't joining us?'

'I wanted time to speak with you.'

'That's why you don't have your laptop open either?'

'I wouldn't have my laptop open when I have a guest.'

She laughed. It was a light, bubbly sound he found delightful. Again, not relevant.

'We both know guests don't get in the way of business, Micah.'

He lifted his glass to his lips thoughtfully. 'I'm beginning to think your experience of business and the way I conduct mine are different.'

She studied him for a moment, then reached into the huge white handbag she'd brought with her and pulled out her phone. She pressed a few buttons, and suddenly a large red dot was gleaming up at him.

'I'm beginning to think so, too,' she replied, despite the minutes that had passed. 'Why don't we start talking about those differences?' She touched her finger to her phone's screen. The device began recording. 'What inspired you to start this business, Mr Williams?'

An expert at managing, he thought again, and answered her.

CHAPTER TWO

Micah Williams was too suave for his own good. Or for Elena's own good. She wanted to get beneath the business-person persona. That wasn't part of her job, obviously. She was only meant to portray the businessperson. She had enough of the basics to write a good introduction. She could already see it.

Micah Williams is charming, but ruthless—a fact he wouldn't want you to believe. The latter, that is. He enjoys his charm almost as much as he thinks his audience does. And perhaps his audience does.

His eyes light up when he talks business, though there's always an intensity shadowed there, regardless of the business topic. He knows just what to say and he relishes saying it, knowing it's exactly what he should be saying.

But it's in that very fact that his ruthlessness lies. Williams has no qualms about telling you what you want to hear even as he uses what you don't want to hear against you. He's a lion, circling his prey, if the lion was tall and handsome, and—

Maybe she needed to work on that last line.

But the sentiment remained. Micah was giving her information she could have surmised from the handful of interviews he'd done before her.

She was good at reading people through what they didn't say as much as through what they did. It was what made her so good at writing pop culture pieces. She could deduce what people wanted the public to know and what they didn't. So she narrowed in on what they didn't; there was almost always a story there.

There was definitely more to Micah's success than 'hard work and good luck'. It had something to do with both his charm and his ruthlessness. If he so much as got a whiff of the fact that she thought him ruthless though, he'd protest. He was trying much too hard to get her to believe he was a harmless domestic animal.

He was definitely a lion. Nothing else.

She particularly knew it because of the way he was circling around her family.

She refused to indulge him.

'Can we take a break?' he asked after they'd been talking for an hour. 'I'm starving.'

Since they'd covered a lot more than she thought they would on the first day, travelling, she said, 'Sure. Will we be eating Chef Gardner or Ike today?'

He smiled. 'You've done your research.'

'I'm insulted you thought otherwise.'

'Wouldn't want that,' he purred. 'I apologise.'

She stared. 'You aren't as charming as you think you are, you know.'

His eyelashes fluttered. She mentally patted herself on the back for surprising him.

'I have no idea what I did to deserve that.'

'Of course you don't. You're on, all the time. It means you don't have time to reflect. Probably,' she added in the unlikely event that she was wrong.

His jaw tightened. 'Presumptuous.'

He wasn't trying to hide that he didn't like that comment. It was the first authentic reaction she'd seen from him—the first one that wasn't an acceptable reaction—and it made her heart thud.

'Journalists presume until they don't have to,' she said.

'Journalists?' There was a deliberate pause. 'Or heiresses?'

When threatened, a lion would attack. Micah had done just that to the elephant in the room.

An uncomfortable ripple went through her, but she was saved from replying when the flight attendant came in and took their orders for food. She was going to be eating steak on a plane, which was the kind of food she'd forgotten about eating on a plane since her parents had divorced. Her life had changed then.

If only it had changed enough for her to stop trying to please her unpleasant father.

'You're offended,' he commented after the flight attendant left. His expression was smooth again, as if he hadn't shown he was human minutes earlier.

'You implied my talents were a result of having a rich family.' She paused. 'You implied other journalists wouldn't have those talents unless they come from a rich family.'

'You're offended on behalf of other people?'

'It's called empathy. It's what makes me a damn good writer.'

And person.

She'd worked hard at that after her parents had all but abandoned her after the divorce. Granted, they hadn't been model parents before. Her mother had always been distant; her father an unyielding presence. That didn't stop her from trying to get their approval. Their love. A normal task for any child; a useless task for her. Her mother was travelling the world, living as though she had no child. Which was…fair. For all intents and purposes, Helen John *did* have no children. And Elena had no mother.

As for her father… Things were more complicated with him. The fact that he wanted her to marry someone for the sake of his business proved it. Especially when 'wanted' was a tame word to describe Cliff John's demands.

But indulging family issues wasn't professional.

'I…er… I shouldn't have said that,' she said.

Emotion flickered in his eyes. She had no idea what that emotion was, or why it felt dangerous. Alluring.

'I shouldn't have mentioned your family.'

'I'd appreciate it if you refrained from mentioning them again.'

The dangerous, alluring emotion flickered again. It gave her the distinct impression she was being toyed with. Everything inside her went on alert.

'Things aren't what they seem in the John family, then?'

She took a moment. Leaned forward. 'If you want to do this, Micah, you better be ready to do this. Because if my family isn't off-limits, neither is yours.'

A challenge.

Micah thought he'd learnt everything he needed to know about Elena during the interview portion of their conversation. She was sharp, insightful, compassionate. He wouldn't have thought her combative though. But how else could he interpret her challenge?

A fair response to you pushing the issue of her family?

That might have been it. Beyond wanting to know more about the John empire, he had no real reason to keep pushing. Did he *want* to provoke her, then? And if so, wasn't it fair for her to respond in kind? Except she wouldn't be able to if he didn't reveal how much of a sensitive topic his family was. He needed to pull back before he did.

This was part of why he never wanted to engage with people on more than simply a surface level. He didn't want to talk about his parents, or the distance they'd put into their relationship with him. He certainly didn't want to talk about his efforts to breach that distance. Efforts that had failed over and over again.

It made putting effort into any other relationship too exhausting to contemplate. So he didn't. Which wasn't entirely a problem since people who wanted relationships wanted to be engaged on more than a surface level. Even those who claimed they didn't want that. The women he dated always said they were fine with what he offered—at the beginning. As the months went by and he continued to dedicate himself to his business, to his relationship with his parents, they would express unhappiness. Eventually, they left. He no longer believed them when they said they wanted what he could give.

But he believed Elena. Believed that she would dig deeper into his family if he didn't stop her now. He couldn't afford to be intrigued by her. She might have been a puzzle of emotions he couldn't solve, but she was dangerous. He couldn't keep trying to put the pieces together, especially when he didn't have the full picture to work from. She wouldn't provide her picture, and he wouldn't provide his, and they would get along fine.

Why did that feel like a lie?

'I've already told you about my family,' he said, keeping his voice steady.

'You were "raised by a single mother, a lawyer with her own firm, and saw your father on occasion",' she recited. Tilted her head. 'Is that right?'

The side of his mouth tilted up. 'Yes.'

'That's what all the other articles about you said, too.' She pretended to examine her nails. 'It would be great to go into more detail. What was it like having a mother with her own law firm? Was it challenging? Inspiring? Did her success affect her relationship with your father? Did it affect yours?'

'Good,' he said after a beat. 'Great, in fact. Get all these questions out now, in the plane, so that when we get to Italy we don't have to waste time going through them.'

Her lips curved. 'Not fun, is it?'

It took him a moment. 'That was a trap.'

'It was and it wasn't,' she said easily. 'I would love to have that information for the article. But I also understand that you don't want it in the public realm. Because of my *empathy*.'

He studied her. Saw both triumph and sincerity on her face. She was slippery. Smart, too. He wasn't sure if he liked the combination. No—he wasn't sure what it meant that he *did* like the combination.

He didn't dwell on it. He needed to figure out what to do about her curiosity first. He didn't want to tell her the truth about his family. What would his parents say if they were included in an article about him? Would they even care?

His father had a brand-new family. Well, not new any more. His baby sister was twenty and his brother, seventeen. Regardless, his father had other things to worry about than what his thirty-two-year-old son said about him. Back when his father had had him, the idea of legitimacy still mattered. That was how his father had treated him. Like a mistake he didn't have to validate except on the rare occasion, when his guilt got the better of him.

And his mother? His mother would…not read the paper. She worked, hard, and that gave her little to no time for leisure. Elena had hit it on the head; his mother running her own law firm was both challenging and inspiring. But it was the inspiring part that mattered most. Perhaps, if he said something like that, Elena wouldn't speculate. And if his mother did ever see this, there would be no reason for her to be upset.

'Fine.' His tone was reluctant. Annoyed. He could see it in her smile. He cleared his throat. Hoped it cleared the emotion he didn't need her seeing. 'I'll answer one of your questions. We won't talk about family again after this.'

He didn't expect the agreement he got.

'Really?' he asked. 'It's that easy?'

'It's that easy,' she replied. There was nothing but sincerity in her tone now. 'I'm writing an article about you. I'm shadowing you for the next seven days to do so. None of that will work without a bit of give and take. From both of us.'

Those last words were heavy with implication. He barely refrained from rolling his eyes.

'We're in agreement, then. Family is off-limits?'

'Between me and you, yes,' she said brightly. 'I still want to offer my readers a good article.'

She'd told him he wasn't as charming as he thought; what would she think if he told her she was more charming than she could ever believe?

He stiffened at the thought. Told himself to get a grip. He was getting distracted from his plan. Elena herself—her personality, her looks, all of her—had already caused him to trip on some of the steps. But he would keep his goal in mind. That meant thinking clearly, strategically. No distractions.

'My mother is incredibly successful,' he said, keeping it concise. 'She worked hard, and was ready for the opportunities that came her way. That's what she taught me, too. To work hard and be ready. I did, and I was.'

'With Killian Leather and The Perfume Company?' she asked, naming the two clients he'd signed in the last year. Two of his biggest clients, who were part of the reason he'd been named Businessperson of the Year.

'Exactly.'

'She sounds like she inspired you.'

He tensed, but answered. 'She did.'

'Wonderful, thanks.' She switched off the phone he hadn't even realised she'd put on again. 'That was great.'

He nodded. Slowly let out the air that had been accumulating in his lungs. He'd survived it. He'd survived talking about his mother. Elena seemed content with his answer, which was great. She wouldn't ask any more. Or was he being naïve, believing her? He wasn't sure he would believe anyone else. But Elena was genuine in a way the other journalists he'd talked with hadn't been.

What if that was wishful thinking?

A sigh distracted him.

'What?' he asked.

'I can almost taste the steak.' She sank down in her chair, closing her eyes. Her hair pushed forward, framing her face with thousands of curly strands. 'I'm going out on a limb here, but I bet there'll be fries with it. Maybe a mushroom sauce.' She looked at him. 'Am I right?'

He lifted a finger of one hand and picked up his phone with the other. He relayed Elena's suggestions to the chef, who grumbled as neither had been on his menu. But he agreed. Micah did pay him a significant amount of money for that agreement.

'Yes, you're right,' he said when he was done.

'You didn't have to do that.'

'What's the point of having a private chef when you can't do that?'

'It's so…privileged, isn't it?'

She spoke thoughtfully, giving him a clue that he shouldn't give the startled laugh he wanted to.

'I'm sorry,' he said after a moment. 'I have no idea how to respond to that.'

'You aren't that out of touch that you don't know people don't live like this.' She gestured around them.

'Of course not. I used to be one of those people.'

Her pensive expression deepened. 'Not entirely though. I can't imagine the mother that owned a law firm left you struggling in your life.'

'A lot of my mother's money went back into the firm.'

'Are you saying you grew up poor?'

'No, I'm not,' he answered immediately. 'And since I seem to be speaking to a reporter, let me clarify: all of this is off the record.'

She lifted her hands in surrender.

'I didn't grow up poor,' he said. 'I had enough. My needs were more than fulfilled.'

'But?'

'But…my wants weren't.'

He wasn't talking financially, though it was true. He hadn't ever had the courage to ask his mother for something he wanted. He didn't want to be a nuisance or a burden. He made do with what she gave him, even when it meant he didn't have the things he wanted. He couldn't exactly complain about that when he had everything he needed, could he?

'Your wants involved a private plane? Private chefs?'

'Elena,' he interrupted when she opened her mouth to add something else to his list of faults. 'Is there a reason you're interrogating me like this? I try to use my money in a way that makes me as efficient as I can be. I also spend a significant portion of that money trying to help other people. I have no doubt we'll speak about that in depth in the coming week. So, why are you judging me?'

'I'm not judging you.' She shook her head. 'This is all just…familiar. But at the same time, it's not. It's like déjà vu, except in reverse. This has happened to me before, and I remember that it did, but I can't… I *don't*…feel like it's real.'

Faint lines appeared between her brows. It was adorable. It was concerning that he found it adorable.

'You don't live a life of luxury any more?' He didn't expect her expression to turn to stone. 'Wait—you don't live like an heiress?'

'No.' She straightened. It was as effective as her putting up a shield. 'I gave up the private planes and chefs a while ago. I even left behind the gold cutlery, diamond plates, designer cell-phone covers.' Her eyes sparkled with challenge. 'It's been a tough transition, but somehow, I manage.'

He couldn't help the smile, but he didn't know what to say. The research his assistant had dug up on Elena seemed woefully inadequate now. Or did it? He hadn't gone through all of it. He hadn't had the time. But he'd read her entire portfolio. Noted her earlier articles weren't as good as her current ones. Her personal information hadn't seemed important to him. He wanted a path to her father, not a relationship. It was foolishly naïve of him not to realise the personal information would have given him a clue to whether she was the right path to her father.

In fact, now it seemed embarrassingly clear that she might not be in her father's good graces. She was an heiress to billions, yet she was working as a journalist for a newspaper. As many other people had, he'd thought this was a flight of fancy; an indulgence. But now he saw she needed the job. It was her livelihood. She loved it, clearly, but it made her sharpness, her growth, the offence she'd taken at him attributing skill to wealth more nuanced.

He wanted to know how that would affect his plans. But he also wanted to know why. Why was Elena supporting herself when her father could do so without feeling it?

He needed to read the rest of what his assistant had dug up on Elena. For research purposes. For his plan. That it would maybe answer his other questions about her was irrelevant. No, those *questions* were irrelevant. There was only the plan.

There could only be the plan.

CHAPTER THREE

ELENA WAS BEGINNING to realise Micah's intensity came in different forms. Amusement. Concern. Hesitance. Annoyance. She wanted to know what other forms there were. Would he be that intense in a romantic relationship? In a physical one? The thought turned her skin into gooseflesh. It was probably best not to examine why. Not that she needed to examine why. That was pretty clear.

She blew out a breath.

Entertaining her attraction to Micah was a bad idea. She knew it. Yet she still thought those inappropriate things about his intensity. And when he offered her the bed at the back of the plane to rest, she wanted to invite him to share it with her.

Maybe she had altitude sickness because she was on a plane. That was what that meant, right? She'd lost her ability to think clearly because of a lack of oxygen or something. Except she was still thinking clearly. She knew Micah's intensity was dangerous. His power was dangerous. Her father had both, and he used them without a thought of the consequences. Even if those consequences were people's lives. His daughter's life.

Marrying Jameson will ensure your security for the rest of your life. Even if, say, you happen to lose your job.

What he was really saying was that if she didn't marry

Jameson, she would lose her job. Her security. After her father had used his money to control her for the first sixteen years of her life, she'd fought for her independence. Her job and security came because of *her* efforts. They had nothing to do with him. But she had no doubts he'd be able to strip away the fruits of those efforts. He was powerful enough that if he wanted, Elena would lose the job she loved. She would lose everything else she loved—her house, her car, herself—too.

She tried not to judge herself too harshly for considering her father's proposal then. She hated that she was, but she hated what would happen if she didn't give in, too. The entire situation turned her stomach. A work trip to Italy gave her the perfect excuse to escape the constant loop of thinking about it. Or so she'd thought. She hadn't anticipated her reaction to Micah. She hadn't anticipated that he would use the same tactics her father had to get her here. But they were cut from the same cloth. If she allowed it, that cloth would wrap around her face and suffocate her.

She stood. She was feeling too restless to sleep. She'd let Micah have the bed for the next couple of hours, and she'd get a start on transcribing the interview she and Micah had had before the conversation had veered onto steak.

She slid through the doorway that separated the bedroom from the rest of the plane. Then she stopped. Micah was there, pacing the length of the space. His shirt was open from his neck to midway down his chest, as if he'd started to change but had forgotten. He had papers in his hand, and he looked down at them at various moments during the pacing, his lips moving. He was clearly practising something. Based on the shirt, the way he ran his hand over his face, practice was not going as he wanted.

'Do you want some help?'

He whirled around, his eyes wide, and Elena thought it might be the only time she'd see Micah unprepared.

'Holy smokes, you almost gave me a heart attack.'

'Holy smokes? *Holy smokes?*' She couldn't help the laugh. 'I thought you were, like, thirty? Thirty-year-olds don't say *holy smokes.*'

'I thought you were in your twenties,' he grumbled back. 'People in their twenties shouldn't wear unicorns.'

She looked down. Well, crap. She'd forgotten to change. She'd pulled on her favourite nightshirt when she climbed into bed. It was raggedy, admittedly, stretched so it fitted over her shoulders loosely, skimming her thighs. It was perfectly modest otherwise, and the vest top she wore under pressed her breasts to her chest so hopefully, they wouldn't give him an eyeful. She absolutely didn't want that.

She cleared her throat. 'Unicorns are a magical species that appear when you open yourself up to the possibility.'

There was the briefest pause.

'Are you saying I don't believe in unicorns so they've chosen not to appear to me?'

'I think that's a question you have to answer for yourself.'

Don't suffocate, her brain reminded her. Yes. Yes, that was important. Why did it feel as if she wanted to forget it?

'So—do you want me to help you practise whatever it is you're practising?'

'It's Italian. You wouldn't understand.'

'Oh, we're jumping right to the patronisation then.' She straightened from where she'd been leaning against the doorway. 'In that case, I guess you don't want my help.'

'No, wait.'

She hadn't moved. The fact that he thought she had— and how much power that implied she had—shimmered through her.

'Can you speak Italian?'

'I can, actually.'

'Seriously?'

'Micah, stop this. You're embarrassing yourself every time you underestimate me.' She walked to sit at the seat he'd been sitting in earlier, and curled her legs under her. 'Okay, first give me context.'

He lowered to the seat she'd been in earlier, bracing his forearms on his knees. 'I'm supposed to speak at this banquet once we arrive in Rome. It's in honour of our partnership with Vittoria, which is—'

'The handbag company there were whispers about you signing with. Congratulations. But please, continue.'

'Thank you.' But he gave her a *How did you know?* look. 'I have to say a couple of words. But my Italian is…basic. I had a translator help me, but I think I'm screwing up.'

She held out a hand for the paper he had, scanned through it when she got it.

'There's nothing wrong with this. It's quick, to the point. Passionate, even.'

'I don't want my speech to be passionate.'

'Relax. The Italians will love it.' She handed the paper back to him. 'I'm listening.'

And she did, without comment as he went through the quick, to the point, passionate words. By the end of it, she thought she might deserve a medal. He was butchering the longer words, words clearly unfamiliar to him, though the easier ones he went through seamlessly. She took the page again when he was done, ignoring his questions, and tried to fix some of the words that had seemed too complicated for him. When she gave it back, he sighed.

'I have to learn this now?'

'Only if you want to sound better than you currently do.' She shifted forward, putting her hands in her lap.

'You don't sound bad. Your peers will appreciate the effort, I'm sure.'

He gave her a dark look. 'You like having this kind of power over me.'

'Not over you, over everyone. Must be the wealthy world I lived in as a child.'

Now he pulled a face. It was all very animated. Too animated for the smooth, charming millionaire. He was clearly frustrated.

'Fine, I get it. I overstepped. No need to rehash it.'

'Man, you cannot take being wrong.'

'I wasn't—' He stopped himself. Lifted the pages. 'Thank you for this.'

'You're welcome,' she said sweetly. Didn't move. When he stared at her, she shrugged. 'You don't want me to help you?'

'I'll call you in an hour.'

'Why? Just practise in front of me. I'll help you if you need it as you go along.'

He shook his head, giving her a forced chuckle as he did. 'I'm not doing that.'

'Why not?'

'You're going to make fun of me.'

'Me?' She put a hand to her chest. 'I would never.'

He didn't reply. She shook her head.

'You're serious? Okay, I promise not to make fun of you. I swear I don't deserve having to tell you that, but there you go. You have my reassurances nevertheless.'

'This is a very different side to you.'

'I can say the same about you.'

She'd already thought that. As for herself… He was right. She was relaxing into her personality, despite her own warnings to keep her guard up. She needed to stay professional. She needed to keep herself safe.

'I don't like it.'

'My side, or yours?'

His look was wry. 'Both.'

The way that made her smile told her staying safe was going to be hard work.

Micah had no idea how he could pay attention to what she said when he was still trying to get over the unicorn. But it wasn't *really* the unicorn. It was the body beneath the unicorn. Her legs, long and full, brown and possibly the best thing he'd seen in his life. Her shoulders, visible through the stretched material of her nightshirt. She wore a strappy top beneath the shirt, so he wasn't treated to the breasts he somehow knew would be free if she were home. Though the rest of the shirt was loose and gave him nothing else of her body, his own reacted.

Tightened, tingled, made him feel like a damn teenager with all the need. And now she was teasing him, helping him, seeing through him.

Seeing through him.

He didn't like it. Any of it.

'I'll practise. Let's practise.'

She gave a satisfied nod, her eyes displaying the same mood, and she took his breath away. The surprise of it didn't help either. He hadn't ever responded this way to anyone. The women he dated were always the same type. The women who moved in his circles. There was nothing wrong with those women; they simply weren't who interested him. It was easy to stay unattached from women who didn't interest him.

He'd learned from his father that attachments would put him in situations he didn't want to be in. Micah was his father's attachment, after all.

Whatever this was with Elena needed to stop.

'Are you going to start?' she asked.

'Yeah. Yes.'

He cleared his throat. Started saying what was on the page. It felt better now. More natural. He had no idea how she'd even known what would feel more natural coming out of his mouth. But he was grateful. He was grateful for her patience as he messed up, more times than he cared to admit. He liked the way she teased him as she corrected him, how there was no malice in anything she said. She wasn't making fun of him; he'd conflated the ease with which she talked to him with that. Maybe because he didn't know what banter looked like. What ease looked like. What friendship looked like.

He stopped at that thought. Erased the memory of it from his mind. There was no friendship. No attraction. *Nothing.* Hadn't he just told himself why there couldn't be?

'That sounds pretty good,' Elena said after what felt like the millionth time they ran through it. 'When do you have to do this?'

'Tomorrow evening.'

'Then you have about thirty or so hours to practise.' She sat back in the chair. 'Plenty of time to sound like a natural second-language speaker.'

'Second language? Not first language?'

She wrinkled her nose. 'I can't perform miracles in such a short space of time, sorry.'

He bit the inside of his lip to keep from smiling. 'If you had more time though, right?'

'Exactly.' She smiled. 'Seriously, you sound fine. Everyone there will love you.'

'You should be there.'

Immediately after he said it, he wished he could take it back. But then he saw her face. She…glowed was the best

way he could describe it. It was like being in a dark room
and having someone suddenly put on a light.

'I will be. Though I don't have this event on my itinerary.'

'That's strange.' Since he hadn't had Serena put it on
her itinerary, he was lying now, too. 'It should have been
there.'

'Hmm.' She took a second. 'Well, then, if it should have
been there...'

'I didn't realise you could speak Italian,' he added. 'It
gives me another reason to have you there.'

'Another reason?' she asked. 'What's the first?'

'Er... I... You're writing a piece on me. Of course.' He
swallowed. 'You should see this.'

'I will. I was just going to explore Rome anyway. It's
my first time in Italy.'

'You speak Italian fluently and it's your first time?'

Her expression closed, shutting in the light along with
it. 'I took it at school with some other languages. I thought
I would need it for...' She trailed off.

'But you didn't?' he asked, even though it was clear
what the answer would be.

'No.'

There was something so troubling in her tone that he
didn't push. He wanted to. The fact that he did told him he
was getting invested in...in *her*, he supposed. It wouldn't
benefit either of them to continue down that path.

'We're landing soon,' he said. Smoothly, because he
didn't care about troubling emotions.

'Oh. Okay.'

She looked lost for a moment. Vulnerable. He shifted
his weight between his legs. Reminded himself that he
didn't care.

He didn't care. He didn't care. He didn't care.

'I'll…er… I'll get changed.' She stood and walked towards the back of the plane.

You don't care. You don't care. You don't care.

'Are you all right?' he blurted out. Because he did care. No matter how much he wanted to believe otherwise. No matter how confused he was by it.

She stopped, only looking over her shoulder.

'Of course. I'm always all right.'

With that, she disappeared into the bedroom. Again, he told himself that he didn't care. This time, it was because she'd lied to him.

CHAPTER FOUR

As a rule, Elena tried not to be miserable in the morning. When her parents divorced, her father sent her to boarding school immediately. She'd fast learnt the value of mornings then. They were the only time of day she had in silence.

Her first year, she'd spent thinking about what she'd done wrong. Her father wouldn't have sent her away because of the divorce. She'd had nothing to do with that. It had nothing to do with *her*. Besides, she didn't bother her parents when she was home. Her efforts before—the tea or coffee she'd brought them; the baking she'd done; the dinners she'd made—had received ambivalent reactions at best, annoyance at worst. She was doing what the staff did. Did she expect recognition for that?

No, she'd expected love.

But as she'd grown older she'd realised that wasn't the way to go. She'd shifted gears. Tried to excel at school, or in extracurricular activities, because those were things people noticed. If people noticed, her parents would be more likely to notice, too. Maybe they would finally be proud of her. They hadn't been. Though she'd come close, once, with her father. She'd 'bested' one of his business rivals' children by passing her school year at the top of her grade. She'd carried around the approval he'd shown in that brief moment when she'd told him for years.

She suspected recreating that moment motivated all her future efforts to please him. Like considering a marriage that would stifle her.

It was silly. She knew it. His approval had come shortly before he shipped her off to boarding school without any reasons. It meant nothing. His punishment, however, could irrevocably change her life. That was what could happen if she refused to get engaged. That was what *had* happened after the divorce, when she'd finally realised, courtesy of an innocent comment from a schoolmate, she was being sent away because she looked like her mother.

Her father wasn't punishing her; he was punishing her mother. Or maybe he was punishing her, too, because she reminded him of his failure. That was how people like her father thought. Relationships were either successful or they failed. For reasons completely outside the effort they put into the person they were in a relationship with or the relationship itself.

Micah probably thought that way, too. It was a good reminder. She couldn't let how adorably insecure he'd been with his speech ingratiate him with her heart.

Elena took a deep breath and tried to stay in the present. It was early, the sun just lighting the sky, and she was standing in front of St Peter's Square, staring. She didn't have any desire to do anything but stare. Or simply *be*.

The Vatican wasn't first on the list of what she wanted to see in Italy, but she had been walking and stopped because of the peace and quiet. The early hour meant she'd beat out most of the tourists. As she walked to the square, pigeons scurried around, searching for food. They did so in the square as well, more of them, and that was the most activity in the place.

Elena walked between the stone pillars on the outer boundary of the square, wondering why they called it that when it was technically a circle. She imagined what it would be like when the Pope celebrated Mass there. She wandered aimlessly from one side of the square to the other. She took pictures, thinking about who she'd show them to. There were people in her life. People at the newspaper, mostly. Proximity friends.

It had been the same at school. Real friendships were hard work. Harder for someone like her. She'd experienced, more than once, people wanting to be her friend because of who she was. Those who didn't know her background almost always changed once they realised it. Once they realised she had money. When she started to refuse her father's money—it came at too high a cost—they treated her differently because now she had none. Kind of like how Micah had treated her once he realised she didn't live with her father's money.

Was that what he did?

She refused to dwell on the answer to that. She was in Italy. For work, yes, but this *being* wasn't work. She had the morning free because, according to Micah's itinerary, he had a business meeting until lunch. Most of the itinerary she received were hours blocked out for business meetings, actually. Which was fine. She didn't expect them to hang out as if they were *friends*.

But she did wonder why he wanted her in Italy if he was only going to spend meals with her. They could have done that in South Africa. She knew why the newspaper had agreed to send her to Italy though. She could watch him take over the world first-hand and take readers on that journey, too. It would hopefully lead to a boost in sales for the edition, which would make up the expenses of sending her on a seven-day trip to Italy.

Micah must have got involved to get the higher-ups to agree to that length of time. Most profiles, if they involved some sort of shadowing, were two or three days long. Why Micah got involved at all had been a question to her. She had her answer now. He wanted her to write about him because she was a John.

It couldn't be as simple as that, she knew. Still, she was intrigued by him. From a purely professional perspective. It was part of why she had woken up early that morning. She'd hoped to have breakfast with him, to ask him questions about his charity work, so she could get started on her article if she was bored. She had missed him, which didn't seem like a loss now that she was exploring. She certainly wasn't bored. In fact, she wanted to see more. And as she thought it, she noticed a group of passengers getting on a sightseeing bus some distance away.

She hurried towards them, but the bus had left by the time she got there. A couple of conversations later though, she had her own ticket to a different sightseeing bus. It was leaving in thirty minutes, so she ducked into a café while waiting. It was busy, clearly a place both tourists and residents visited. When she asked for a recommendation on a café speciality, she was offered hot chocolate. Literal, melted hot chocolate. By the end of it, she was convinced she was meant to live near a place that served the drink.

After a leisurely morning of sightseeing, she got off at a stop closest to where she was supposed to meet Micah for lunch. Or so she thought. Apparently, Rome had two streets named the same about thirty minutes from one another, and so she was thirty minutes late. She stumbled into the restaurant hot and sweaty.

'Oh, my word, I am so sorry.'

She wiped a hand over her forehead as she slid into the chair opposite Micah. He was watching her over his glass of champagne, looking cool and calm. Of course he looked cool and calm. He'd been in this air-conditioned restaurant for at least half an hour. She, on the other hand, must have looked like a troll. Maybe the look would have worked, had she had bright hair. But her boring brown hair would make her look like a troll without the mitigating cuteness.

'You're mad, aren't you?' she asked when he didn't reply. 'I'm sorry. I was on a bus, and I got off at the wrong stop, then I had to take a taxi to get here, which was ridiculously expensive, by the way, and—'

'Why didn't you just take the car I sent for you?' he interrupted her, his eyebrow quirking in a way she wouldn't have thought sexy on anyone else.

'The car? What car?'

'I sent a car to the hotel.'

'Ah.' A waiter arrived and poured her a glass of water. He disappeared as mysteriously. Or maybe not. She was too busy drinking the water to notice. 'That would have entailed being at the hotel, and, as I said, I was on a bus.'

'A bus.'

'Yes. Sightseeing,' she added brightly. 'It was wonderful seeing the city. The Colosseum is as gorgeous in real life as it is in pictures. From the outside, at least. I didn't see the inside because I didn't want to be late to this although I am now and what would it have mattered?'

'Elena,' he asked after a pause. 'Are you...uncomfortable by any chance?'

'I...' She faltered. Pressed a hand to her chest when she realised there was, indeed, a flutter of nerves congregating there. 'How did you know?'

His lips twitched. 'A hunch.'

She thought back over the last few minutes. 'Oh. It's because I was talking so much. Hmm. You're perceptive.' She emptied her glass of water before continuing. She was already speaking when the waiter refilled it and disappeared again. 'I hate being late. I hate contravening anything considered to be polite. Politeness was drilled into me for eighteen years. From the moment I was born, I'm sure, until I left school.'

'It sounds exhausting.'

His eyes were kinder than she'd seen before. Maybe that was why she said, 'It was. But it was part of being a John.'

'What happened when you left school?'

She barked out a laugh. 'A lot. This isn't about me, though I know you prefer it that way.' She let that linger. 'How was your meeting?'

He smiled, but not in a friendly way. It was satisfactory or knowing. It was also possibly both or something else entirely. The effect it had on her was distracting her from being able to tell. There was a fluttering in her chest and her skin was clammy. But then, she'd been late, and it was hot. Why did it increase after Micah smiled? She had no idea. She was considering an engagement to someone else. She shouldn't be noticing other men's smiles.

But she was. The wrong man's smile, because Micah wasn't a good match. He was too powerful, too intense, too distractingly handsome for her. It didn't matter though. What she felt for him was more than she'd ever felt for Jameson. Even though their marriage would be purely in name, that didn't sit right with her. Nor did the thought that Jameson would likely sate his physical needs with women outside their marriage. Heaven knew she didn't want to sleep with him, but she doubted he would be discreet about his relationships. How would that affect her as his wife?

'It went well,' he said, interrupting her panic. 'It was with the executive board of Vittoria. Just to iron out some details about the way forward.'

She waited as he gestured to the waiter, gave an order for a wine she would die to taste, before she asked her question.

'What does it feel like to be so successful in your thirties?'

She'd taken out her phone, pressed record while she'd been waiting for him to finish with the waiter.

'It feels...like a challenge.' He shrugged when she looked at him. 'It wasn't easy to gain success. It took ten years of eighteen-hour days, seven days a week. Most of the time, I pushed to see if I could. Now, of course, there's the pressure to continue being successful. Otherwise, I'm a fluke. It's a challenge.'

She leaned forward. 'That light in your eyes tells me you're up for it.'

Now his smile was catlike. 'I wouldn't be who I am, where I am, if I weren't.' There was a short pause. 'When people say "Do what you love and you'll never work a day in your life", I laugh. *Anything* you spend a significant amount of time on is work. Be that in your professional or personal life. The key is that when you find something you love doing, you won't mind putting in the work.' He sat back. 'Is that a good enough soundbite?'

She switched off her phone and mirrored his position. 'It would be an excellent soundbite—if I needed one. I don't. I'm writing about you.'

He narrowed his eyes. 'You know what I mean.'

She smiled. 'I do. But it's nice to see someone so easily confident get annoyed.'

'I wasn't annoyed.'

'I know.' But she smiled. Just in case it would annoy him.

He tilted his head, then shook it and laughed. 'You're something else, Elena.'

And you like it.

She startled herself. Those words were on the tip of her tongue. It sounded like...like *flirting*. She wasn't a flirt though. She chose her words carefully to avoid being one. Except in Micah's presence, apparently. Then, she spoke freely, and damn if that freedom didn't make her feel good.

'I took the liberty of discussing a menu for us with the chef, by the way,' Micah said. 'I thought it might be nice for you to experience full Italian dining.'

'Chefs must *love* you,' she said with a small laugh. 'Honestly, you realise you're not the only patron in this…'

She trailed off when she realised they were, indeed, alone.

He kept his eyes on her face as she realised it was only the two of them in the room. When she met his gaze, her confusion had the butterflies in his stomach scattering as if a stone had been thrown at them.

'There's no one here,' she said.

'I'm aware.'

She looked around again. What did she see? Sophistication in the wooden floors and accents throughout the restaurant? Class in the white and brown lines of the wallpaper on one of the walls, the brown and white paint on the others? Did she see romance in the white tablecloths, the candles adorning them? Or was it homeliness in the green leaves spilling over pot plants at strategic places; the framed pictures of the Italian family who'd created this wonderful place?

He'd seen all of it when he'd walked in an hour ago. He could do nothing about the décor, but he'd contemplated the candles. It was a warm summer's day outside. Why else would she think they needed candles?

For light, a voice in his head told him. He hadn't asked for the candles; they illuminated the darkness inside the restaurant. It wasn't overwhelmingly dark, but enough so that the candles were needed. He was probably being

overly sensitive. He didn't need a waiter to tell him that.
So he said nothing. Except now, as she looked around, he
thought he should have.

'Two things,' she asked, her gaze meeting his.

He agreed with a nod. He couldn't speak because he was
afraid of what his voice would sound like. Spellbound by
how he'd just noticed the brown of her eyes were lined with
some magical make-up thing. It made her eyes sparkle. It
turned him into an idiot who indulged fantastical thoughts.

'One: do you own this place?'

'No.'

'Okay, then, two: did you do this for me?'

'I did it for us.' He stood now, walking to the bar where
the waiter was standing and trying to be inconspicuous
as he readied their wine. 'This place is usually closed this
time of day, especially in the summer. I pulled some strings
so we could have…lunch.'

He almost said privacy. That would have sounded
dodgy. Luckily, the waiter offered him the wine to try.
He went through the motions of tasting it, though it was
one of his favourites and he didn't need to. With a nod of
his head, Micah moved to Elena and offered her the glass.
She did the same thing he had, but her eyes didn't leave
his. He had no idea how drinking from the same glass
could be erotic, but it was. Especially when Elena brought
the glass to her lips, parted them, and he got the quickest
glimpse of her tongue.

His blood got heavy, his skin grew tight, and heat spread
through his body as if a fire had been lit inside him. Elena
didn't help one bit. She was still staring at him with her
beautiful brown eyes, her hair wild around her face, her
lips red again, the colour mixing with the wine. The glass
she offered him now had the trace of her lipstick on it, and
it was the sexiest damn thing.

'Do you like it?' he asked, accepting the glass. It still had the tiniest bit of liquid in it, and he gave in to temptation by drinking it.

He placed his mouth on the outline of her lips.

'Yes.' Her voice was throaty. It did strange things to his body. 'Very much.'

The left side of his mouth lifted, and he lingered for much longer than he should have. But she was a magnet, and he was attracted to her, and he wanted, no, needed, to be as close to her as possible. Slowly, he turned around and walked to the bar.

'We're happy with this,' he told the waiter softly. The man gave him a knowing look, but it was gone before Micah could say something about it. All that was left was cool professionalism. Micah needed to follow his lead.

'Shall I get the starters ready, sir?'

'Please.'

He took the two glasses of wine the waiter poured to the table, offering Elena hers before settling in his chair.

'How was the sightseeing today?'

'You're deflecting,' she replied.

'From what?' he asked, because he was deflecting, but he didn't think she'd be straightforward about the chemistry that had happened between them.

Did chemistry happen? Or was it something two people experienced? Either way, they had it, they experienced it, and Micah wasn't happy about it. He had a plan. She was part of those plans. Except…suddenly that didn't feel right any more.

Maybe he *was* deflecting. Maybe he was deflecting so much he couldn't even tell what he was deflecting from.

'The fact that we're alone. You don't have to impress me.'

'I know.' Relief made him say the words with a smile. 'If it makes you feel any better, I had the restaurant for the meeting before this lunch, too.' He hadn't. This had been entirely for her, but he couldn't admit it now. She was entirely too observant and after the chemistry? He couldn't admit the truth, even though he hated lying.

'Really?' Did she deflate? Was he projecting? 'No wonder it went well, then.'

'It's part of it, I'm sure. Now, would you tell me about your day?'

She narrowed her eyes, as if she couldn't trust his interest in her. He was offended. Partly because she was right to distrust him—his plan included getting her comfortable with him. But that wasn't the reason he asked. He wanted to know about her day.

It disturbed him, the intensity he felt in that desire. He couldn't remember ever being interested in knowing about someone's day. Days seemed so mundane. When he spoke, even during small talk when things were supposed to be mundane, he asked about events. Events had purposes. The same couldn't be said for days. Wanting to know about Elena's day, wanting to know with an intensity? It rightfully worried him.

It didn't stop him from being engrossed in her descriptions.

'I don't know, Micah. I guess it could be because I haven't travelled in such a long time. Or that I'm here, one of the places I always wanted to visit.' The small smile on her face was an intimate glimpse into her mind. He tried to memorise it. 'It's wonderful. Every single thing. Even the pigeon who tried to bite my finger off when I tried to pet it.'

'You tried to pet a pigeon?'

Her cheeks pinkened. 'I know, I know. I got caught up in the magic!' she exclaimed, lifting her hands in front of her. Then she laughed. 'When I was standing in front of the Trevi Fountain, I was the main character of a fairy tale. I would have sung, if I could. Instead, I tried to pet a bird.' She laughed again, but this time, buried her face into her hands. 'I am such a dork.'

'Yes, you are.' When she looked up long enough to stick her tongue out at him, he laughed. 'I like it, Elena. It's…refreshing.'

'Well, then, if it's refreshing.'

And she rolled her eyes. Damn if that wasn't refreshing, too.

CHAPTER FIVE

HAD SHE THOUGHT she was in a fairy tale before? She must have been confused. Standing in front of a beautiful fountain, seeing people throw coins into it and make wishes was magical, yes. But getting ready for a fancy event, a dress waiting for her in her room along with fairies who did hair and make-up? It was something from her past. So far in her past she found it surreal.

She caught her breath at the elegant black gown. The material was soft and glossy, simple and sophisticated. Micah intended on her wearing it as it was, she was sure, but she had the perfect necklace to go with it. It was bright and African, the yellow, black, red and green of it mixing in a pattern perfectly representing her home. Her make-up and hair were flawless, and when she looked at herself in the mirror, she barely recognised the woman looking back at her.

It had been over a decade since she'd felt so luxurious.

She took a deep breath, pushed back the memories that were still coated with pain. Looked in the mirror again. She wouldn't be the woman missing a life where she had never been enough. Contemplating a life where the things that fulfilled her were gone, regardless of what she decided to do about marrying Jameson. She would be the woman looking back at her. The African princess from some fairy tale she'd created in her mind. For one night, she could forget the rest and be that woman.

She felt like that woman when she walked into the passage of the hotel and found Micah waiting for her.

His eyes widened, and his lips parted to such an extent that she wondered if it counted as his jaw dropping. Colour flooded his skin. She didn't think he realised it, or knew that he was clenching and unclenching the hand that hung at his side. His other hand was in his pocket, and she would have bet everything she had that he was clenching his fist there, too.

He wasn't the only one stunned by the other's looks, though she hoped she was controlling her response more than he was. She would forgive herself if she wasn't. Every fairy-tale princess needed a dashing counterpart and damn if he didn't provide the perfect one.

He'd shaved since their lunch. Got his hair cut, too. It made his face look more angular, his cheekbones more visible, that jaw more defined. His tuxedo accentuated every line of his body—which was magnificent, the muscles and softness she thought he might be a combination of. She would never know without touching him, and suddenly she understood what Micah's fingers curling and uncurling meant. He was fighting against reaching out and touching her. Now, she was doing the same.

Her heart pumped a little harder, more erratically.

'You look…' He trailed off before looking at her. The intensity was there, and this time she knew it was admiration, and maybe desire. 'I don't even have the words for it, if I'm honest.'

'I'd accept nice,' she said, her fingers curling around the yellow clutch she'd stuffed her lipstick and phone into. The latter was for recording the evening's events. And ignoring the calls from her father's office. She hadn't made her decision yet. He would have to wait.

'You don't look nice though.'

She gave a surprised laugh. 'I think you're supposed to pretend, at the very least.'

'No. No,' he said again. 'I meant you look…more than nice.'

Her laugh was more genuine this time. 'Thank you.'

His smile was sheepish. 'I told you I didn't have the words.'

'But you have the smile. And the general look of a man who likes what he sees. It's enough.'

Their gazes locked, lingered. She felt something intimate crawl up her spine. Her skin turned to gooseflesh in response.

'I bought you a plain dress for a reason,' he said softly, taking a step closer. 'I should have known you would take something plain and turn it into something magnificent.'

'You should have,' she whispered. 'It's exactly what I intend on doing with the story I write about you.'

He grinned. It was free, unrestrained. *Sexy.* She'd never seen him smile that way before. She felt as if she were seeing her dress for the first time again—that admiration, that longing—but more intense. As if she'd seen a million of those dresses at the same time. She had no idea what was happening to her, but she didn't care. She only cared about this man. The way he looked at her. The way he made her feel.

It wasn't how Jameson and her father made her feel. Small, vulnerable. Coerced. She'd met Jameson the day her father had called her to his office, outlining his plans for her life as if she had no say in it. Jameson had simply sat there, giving her a smile that was self-satisfied, though she was sure he thought he offered comfort. Her lungs had tightened. Her head had swirled. And she'd had to summon every ounce of strength to say she'd think about it. A month later, she was still thinking about it. Her time was running out, as her father's phone calls indicated.

But now, with Micah, everything felt different. Time was endless. She didn't feel small, and the vulnerability she was experiencing was *powerful*. She knew she had a choice here, standing in front of him. And that she'd made a mistake when she'd said he was just like her father.

He was more dangerous than her father. He made her feel strong. Desirable. Like a woman who wouldn't allow herself to be strong-armed into sacrificing her freedom for someone who wouldn't do the same for her.

'Micah,' she whispered, stuck in his gaze.

She all but felt him touching her. Her imagination made her shiver at the contact. She could only guess what would happen if he really did touch her.

'I know.'

He moved closer to her. Then swiftly, suddenly, she was pinned against the wall between his arms.

Micah was well aware that he was seducing Elena. He was as aware that it was a mistake. He had asked Serena to resend him Elena's personal information. In it had been plenty of clues to the state of her relationship with her father. Where she lived, how she lived. None of it came as a surprise after their conversations. What *did* come as a surprise was that she was about to announce her engagement. In a lavish party the day after they returned to South Africa.

As soon as he read it, he wanted to speak with her. Demand to know if it was the truth. But a cursory Internet search told him it was. It was the talk of every gossip site in South Africa. The elite of the elite had been invited. It soured his mood. Clung to his body as he got ready for a banquet he didn't feel like going to. Got heavier when he realised he shouldn't feel this way at all. He hardly knew the woman.

Then he saw her in her dress, and all rational thought flew from his mind, leaving only emotion. A possessiveness he only now recognised as the cause of his dark mood demanded he make her see that there was something between them. He fought against it, had managed enough to give her some harmless compliments. To tease. But something changed in her gaze, in her body, and fighting was no longer working.

Now they were pressed together against a wall.

There had been space between their bodies when he'd moved her there; there was none now. She arched against him, aligning their bodies so that he could feel how her breath was leaving her lungs in short, quick puffs. So she could feel how having her delightful, curvaceous body against his made him feel.

He didn't give a single damn.

'Elena,' he whispered, tracing the lips that she had painted red again. It made her lipstick smudge, and he had to resist the urge to press his mouth against the shadows of red. 'What are you doing to me?'

'Nothing.' Her hand touched his hip tentatively. Then her fingers sank into his flesh. It didn't matter that there were two layers of clothing between his skin and her hand. He felt the contact. Worried that he'd always feel the contact. 'I can't do anything to you, Micah.'

He stiffened, but didn't move. Couldn't move. He would despise himself for it later—for seducing her, for touching her, when she was someone else's—but he was caught in a spell. A curse. A curse that made the first woman he'd ever felt this way about be unavailable.

'Do you love him?'

She frowned. 'Who?'

'The man you're getting engaged to. St Clair.'

Her lashes fluttered seconds before the vulnerability that had been in her eyes when he'd first touched her disappeared. The heiress was back. He was a hundred per cent certain that the heiress wasn't who she was any more, but she was there nevertheless. She was there when she'd first boarded that plane, and she was here now.

It wouldn't have bothered him so much if he didn't know she wasn't the heiress. If he didn't know the heiress only came out when she felt threatened. He made her feel *threatened*.

He took a step back.

'I'm sorry. I shouldn't have...' He shook his head.

'No, I'm sorry. I just...' Her voice faded. She lifted a hand to her forehead, obscuring her gaze. 'You caught me off guard.'

'Because you're getting engaged.'

'Yes. No. I... I haven't decided yet.'

'You haven't—' He broke off. 'What the hell does that mean?'

When she looked at him, her gaze was dangerously blank. 'It means your background check didn't tell you everything.'

'I didn't need a background check. It's all over the Internet.'

Colour seeped from her face. 'What?'

She fumbled with her clutch purse, took out her phone, typed in hard, quick movements. He hadn't thought it possible, but she went paler as she read. Having just experienced the shock himself—though heaven only knew why *she* was shocked—he took a step forward. Her head snapped up, and the fire there kept him from moving any closer.

'You didn't know?' he asked carefully.

'That I'm announcing an engagement I haven't decided on when I get back? No,' she said in a cold voice. 'I didn't.'

CHAPTER SIX

HE WAS ON EDGE. He shouldn't have drunk all that coffee before his big speech. Then he remembered that he hadn't drunk any coffee that day. It wasn't caffeine making him jittery, but the entire incident with Elena. Her reaction had been…disturbing. Or maybe it was just nerves about his upcoming speech.

Yes, nerves. Not Elena.

He ordered a bottle of water at the bar and, when it arrived, guzzled it down like a man dying of thirst. It would make him need the bathroom, and was likely not a good idea, but he had to do something. He hadn't been this nervous since he'd…

Since he'd pitched his business to his mother.

Oh, great. This was exactly what he needed. A reminder of the woman who never thought he was good enough for anything, let alone a speech. He blew out a breath. That was a tad melodramatic. His mother thought he was a perfectly okay human being. She treated him as she would anyone else.

That had been a big part of his problem as a kid. He was *her* kid; he didn't want her to treat him as she would anyone else. But he hadn't realised that until one day, when he'd been nine or so, and she'd dragged him along to some benefit. It had only happened once in his life—she had no one to babysit him and even she wouldn't leave a nine-year-old alone—probably because she'd learnt her lesson and had back-up babysitters for her back-up babysitters. In any case, he'd gone with her, sat quietly at her table because he was so damn glad to spend time with her that he wouldn't do anything else, and watched her.

She'd smiled. At so many of her clients. She'd chatted and laughed and had turned into a person he hadn't recognised. And he realised what was wrong with their relationship: he hadn't given her an incentive to care about him. He was just her kid. She didn't love his father, or want a kid, so no wonder she didn't want him. But if he made her care? If he was important enough to make her care? Yeah, that would change things.

It had taken him two and a half decades to do it, but he finally had. Tonight was merely the beginning. One part of his plan to get his mother to notice him. Though the memories were painful, he needed them, and he was glad to have them.

So why was it Elena's face he sought in the crowd? Why did he feel confident and at ease because he looked at her? His mother was supposed to be his inspiration. Hell, he'd even take his father. What did it mean that Elena had burrowed her way into that plan?

Why did he feel guilty about the plans that involved her? And torn by the emotions he felt about her?

He set it aside and focused on his speech, which garnered him a rousing applause. He worked the crowd as he'd learnt to do over the years, before he realised Elena had disappeared. He gestured to Serena, told her to find Elena and bring her to him, and minutes later, she was at his side.

'Have you met Elena John, Lucca?' he said to the man he was speaking to from the executive committee for Vittoria. 'She's the reason I could deliver that speech this evening.'

Lucca exclaimed in delight. There were a few seconds of rapid conversation in Italian that he could barely follow, and then they were both laughing.

'Lucca says I should have let you make a fool of yourself,' Elena told him with a smile that didn't quite touch her eyes. 'He says I took away an opportunity for you to learn humility.'

'And you think I need it?' Micah asked in Italian. The bark of laughter he got in return told him all he needed to know. 'Well, now you have it,' he said good-naturedly.

Another quick sprint of Italian.

'You've endeared yourself to him,' Elena said.

'And it only took humiliation.'

'Do not worry,' Lucca said, patting him on the back. 'It happens to all of us at some time.'

'I sincerely hope to find it happening to you some time soon.'

Their laughter attracted a few more people, and before he knew it he was socialising with the executive committee of the company he'd just partnered with.

He had, of course, expected to chat with everyone. He hadn't expected socialising, with wine and laughter and teasing. He'd never experienced any of it before, at any of the galas he'd been to. He could have said it was the Italians, who had a greater desire for joviality than his other business partners. It would have been a lie though. The real difference was Elena.

She switched between Italian and English effortlessly, charmed easily, and ensured she spoke with everyone at least once. This wasn't her party—it wasn't even his—and he knew she was still distracted by what happened earlier. But she'd claimed the role of hostess as if it had been designed solely for her. He wanted to speak with her, to thank her, to give her a chance to breathe, but he couldn't get a second alone with her, she was so popular. In the end, he gestured to her with his head, and left the group under the guise of getting another drink. She joined him in the foyer.

'Your business parties are exhausting.'

'They are for the life of the party.'

She shook her head. 'That's not a role I want, nor deserve.'

'You might not want it, but you deserve it.' He offered her his arm before she could reply. 'Can we go somewhere private to talk?'

Elena hesitated, her expression tightening. But she placed her hand on his. They walked over the soft blue carpet of the hotel's foyer to the elevator. Elena didn't say a word when he pressed the button for the roof. When they got up there, she gasped.

'Why didn't they have the banquet up here?'

He looked around. Glass gave them the perfect view of a night sky that was, in his opinion, showing off. Stars twinkled brightly above them, enticing people to stay outside, to pay attention to their beauty. Beneath them, Rome showed off as audaciously, lights sparkling, people moving, music thumping. It seemed that Rome's night life was more active than its day life, which he understood. It was summer, the night was slightly cooler, though by no means cool. It was the perfect weather for parties or dinners on a terrace.

It was the perfect weather for seduction, temptation. For making mistakes. Even the prospect had him shivering. He set the desire aside.

'Thank you. For what you did down there.'

'It was nothing.'

'No, it wasn't,' he said. 'You're the reason those executives are looking forward to working with me. I seem like a great guy.'

'You don't think you are?'

He opened his mouth, but discovered he had no answer.

When she realised it, she gave a small nod, then walked across the stone-coloured tiles that lined the pathways between the rooftop garden the hotel had created on one side of the room. The garden was mostly made of potted plants and flowers, though large trees full of green leaves peeked over those pots. The side of the room he was standing on had tables and chairs, and he wondered why they'd chosen not to integrate the two so it didn't feel so disjointed.

'I can't quite figure you out,' she said, facing him.

His breath did something odd—tightened, caught, gushed out of his lungs. He knew it was because she made a picture in her black dress, her necklace gleaming bright against her almost gold skin with the backdrop of greenery behind her.

'What do you want to know?' He would tell her anything.

'Is it always about business for you?'

The question was more serious than she let on, he knew.

'It has been for the last decade or so. Since I went to university.' He walked to the edge of the room, leaned his back against the glass. 'It's given me purpose.'

'I understand that.' She was quiet for a long time. 'My work's done the same for me.'

'For how long?'

Her eyebrow quirked. 'Since I turned sixteen.'

'You wanted to work since you were sixteen?'

'No. I found purpose in work when I was sixteen. That's when my parents got divorced.'

He didn't answer, only waited for more. She was walking before she spoke, her gait smooth, elegant, as if she walked runways instead of streets. Part of him wanted to blame it on her upbringing. Wealth made people believe the world was theirs to claim, much as models did the runway. But something deep inside him resisted. Her upbringing might have taught her that, but somewhere along the way she'd learned to earn the world, too. At least her part of it. Everything he knew about her from the last two days they'd spent together pointed to it.

'I'm not the kind of person who almost kisses another man when they're supposed to be engaged,' she said. 'I need you to know that.'

He studied her. 'Then what kind of person are you?'

Her mouth twisted. 'A pawn in a powerful man's game.'

'What do you mean?'

She wanted to close her eyes and sink to the floor. The evening had taken so much of her energy. As had discovering her father and Jameson had planned an engagement party and invited the entire world before she'd even given her answer.

Because they think they already know your answer.

And why wouldn't they? Her father was used to using his power over her as a bargaining tool in her life. His money, when she'd needed something at school and he'd tell her to attend some event in return. To pretend the divorce hadn't changed their perfect little family, even though her mother was halfway across the world. When she'd got a scholarship that paid for university and accommodation and she no longer needed his money, he began to use her need for his love. He'd promised a dinner, to accompany her to a social event, to put in a good word for her at a potential employer. She needed his approval so much she would accept anything from him, despite how terrible it made her feel after.

Because she was compromising to get it. Her values, her independence, herself. This latest request was the biggest, and her father was pulling out all the stops to get her to agree. Threatening her job, promising her security, implying his approval. It wasn't worth it, she knew, but it was tempting. She didn't want to lose the life she'd spent almost a decade building. She didn't want to lose her chance of her father ever truly loving her.

Now there was Micah, complicating it all with his power over her. Because he had some. Why else was she there, trying to explain herself to him? Why else did she still want to kiss him? To let him hold her and make *her* feel powerful again?

It was a trap. It couldn't be anything else. And it was bound to make her feel as terrible as giving in to her father did.

'You're a powerful man, Micah. You know you play games. Use people.'

Anything she could have read on his face was covered by a blank expression. 'I don't know what you're talking about.'

That wasn't the reaction she had expected. She'd expected denial, or confusion. Genuine confusion, not this practised nonsense he was going for.

An uncomfortable feeling slithered down her spine. It hissed in her ears, saying *I told you so*.

'What are you hiding?' she asked softly.

'I'm not hiding anything.'

'Yes, you are.' She took a step closer. 'And it has to do with me.'

He didn't reply, only watched her with a guarded expression. She blinked, and stumbled back. It *did* have something to do with her. And if she took the rest of the conversation into account, it meant he was using her, too. But for what?

It didn't matter. The only thing that did was knowing she couldn't trust him.

She hated that it sent a crack rippling through her heart.

CHAPTER SEVEN

ELENA'S SECOND FULL day in Rome wasn't as exciting as the first. She spent the majority of it tailing Micah to his meetings. She'd expected it—that was what had been on the itinerary, and Serena had invited her to join him— and she'd brought her observation A game. She was quiet, discreet, and only spoke when spoken to. She was doing exceedingly well, actually, which was why Micah's stony expression whenever he spoke to her annoyed the hell out of her.

Actually, no. The real reason she was annoyed was because he was treating her as if *she* were the one keeping secrets. And she was sure it wasn't only keeping secrets either. His reaction to her questions the night before told her there was more there. She had set it aside though. She was a professional, after all. Except him showing everyone his disapproval of her made them both look *unprofessional*. She would have told him that, too, if she'd had any time alone with him that day.

But his meetings were back to back. When they had to change venues, they went in different cars, something she was sure he'd arranged. All of it made her annoyance grow. She stewed in it. Plotted her revenge. It wouldn't be sophisticated, but it would be satisfying. Like throwing her tablet at Micah. She would love to see his expression after that. But logic told her tablets were expensive—and so was Micah—so she settled for fantasising about his defeat instead.

They were supposed to have dinner at the end of the day, but Elena ducked out of it. She didn't want to socialise with him. She'd got enough information on his business habits during that day to write her article. Serena had sent her information about his charity work, and with the personal information Elena had got on the plane and in the restaurant, she could write a decent article. A *good* article. She didn't have to spend any more time with him. She relished that.

Her phone rang. Her finger hovered over the denial button, but it was Jameson calling now, not her father's office. He was the lesser of the evils. Besides, she had some things to say to him now that she'd processed the news of the party a bit more.

'Where have you been?' he said as soon as she picked up. 'We've been trying to get a hold of you.'

'Hello, Jameson. How are you?'

'Busy. Work and…' There was a pause. 'Stuff.'

'Yes, *stuff*,' she said slowly. 'Like the party you and my father are planning to announce our engagement at?'

'Elena—'

'It's a little presumptuous, don't you think?' she continued, ignoring what would surely be some form of manipulation. 'Or is it strategic? I'm not in the country, so you can plan your party without my protests.'

'Elena.' Jameson's voice was sharp now. 'Your hysteria is helping no one. Calm down.'

She almost swore at him. Barely caught the words before they jumped from her lips.

'We were merely moving things forward.'

'Moving me forward, you mean.'

'Your father assured me your answer would be in the affirmative.'

'I'm sure he did,' she murmured, her anger changing from sharp heat to something…cold. 'Is that why he's been trying to get a hold of me, then?'

'Having confirmation from you would be helpful.'

Not to me.

So say no, another voice said in her head.

And she wanted to listen to it. She wanted to say those words. But they wouldn't leave her lips, no matter how hard she tried. Something entirely different came out instead.

'I'm working,' she said woodenly. 'So you'll have to wait a little longer for that confirmation.'

He cursed. 'You're prioritising that man over me? Your future husband?'

'It's not about a man.' *And you might not be my husband.* 'It's about my job, and the fact that anyone could have got this assignment, but they gave it to me.'

'They gave it to you because you're a John. You don't have to prove yourself, if that's why you're doing this. You already have.'

She didn't bother to reply. Jameson would think that her worth was solely in her surname. It made Micah's assumption of the same on the day they met worse. She didn't indulge her thoughts about why that was. Accepted that she was raw when it came to Micah and left it at that.

'It's not a huge leap to assume Williams asked for you,' Jameson continued, apparently not caring that she hadn't responded. Though the way he hit the nail on the head felt like a whip against her heart. 'He probably thinks you're his key to partnering with the John Diamond Company.' Jameson laughed. 'Our engagement will secure my and your family's partnership though, so he'll quickly realise having you there was for nothing.'

For one horrifying moment, she thought she would gasp. Her head swirled, and she stumbled back to the bed, lowering so she had support for the knees that had gone shaky.

'Elena? Are you there?'

Her training kicked in. The sixteen years before the life she knew had fallen apart consisted of her parents coaching her in the art of vulnerability. That was, to never be vulnerable. People would use it against her. Powerful people would use it against her.

Micah had used it against her.

'Well, this has been lovely,' she said, her voice sounding odd, even to herself. 'We're travelling to the country tomorrow, so I'll be out of cell-phone range. Goodbye.'

She put down the phone before he could reply. She was about to switch it off for good measure when she saw a message from Micah.

Are you okay?

No. She wasn't okay. But she sure as hell wasn't going to admit that to a man who was using her. Just like every other man in her life.

What had she done to deserve this? To deserve feeling this alone?

She gave herself a few minutes to wallow, then went to her laptop to write.

Elena was waiting for him at breakfast. She wore a pink headband, curls spiralling around her head behind it, along with a pants suit—black this time—and a top that matched the headband. Her lips were painted the same soft colour, but she wore no other make-up that he could see.

She looked up when he arrived, took her cell phone out, pressed some buttons, then put it away.

'I emailed you the story I plan on submitting to my editor. It's only due when I get back, so feel free to add your comments and email them to me before the end of the trip. I'll apply them if they're reasonable,' she added with a warning glance.

'You're done?'

'I was inspired last night.' Her tone was flat.

'Serena told me you had a headache. That's why you didn't come to dinner.'

'I lied. I didn't come to dinner because you acted like a jerk the entire day. I didn't want to experience that for any longer than I had to.' She stood. 'Thank you for the opportunity to—'

'Wait,' he said, standing out of surprise. 'You're leaving?'

'I am.' Her spine straightened, as if she was daring him to argue with her. 'I'm going to Venice.'

'Why?'

'A number of reasons. None of which,' she added as he was about to ask, 'I'd like to share with you.'

'Okay, wait. Just…give me a second to catch up.' He looked around desperately. 'Coffee? Let's have one coffee together.'

Her expression was emotionless. 'Your driver is standing in the doorway, Mr Williams. If I remember correctly, your meeting starts in thirty minutes.'

'Elena,' he said sternly now. He softened his tone when her eyebrow rose. 'I'm sorry. Just…please. Coffee?'

He didn't know how long he waited for her to give the nod that eventually came. All he knew was he was offering to get coffee for them, even though a server could have done it. But he needed time to process. To ask himself why he hadn't expected her to stand up for herself. Why he'd wasted a day that he could have spent with her.

His emotions. He didn't know how to work through them. They'd shared a tense almost kiss; he'd seen her fit seamlessly into his world; and he'd discovered she was about to be engaged. He hadn't been prepared for any of it. Then she'd come dangerously close to figuring out his plan and his instincts had told him to shut down. To protect himself. So he did. He'd spent an entire day trying to ignore her and being unable to because she was so damn vibrant and beautiful and he was pulled to her in a way he couldn't understand.

Damn his parents, he thought suddenly, unexpectedly, *furiously*. If they hadn't all but abandoned him, if they'd taught him how to engage with people, he wouldn't feel so lost now. He would know what to do with his feelings. He'd be able to deal with them in healthy ways. He wouldn't have sulked at Elena like a teenager because he liked her and didn't want to.

He liked her.

Coffee slopped over the cup onto his hand, burning his skin much as that realisation burnt his heart. He set the mug down, gritted his teeth, though a part of him wanted to brace over the counter. But he wasn't helpless; he could handle some feelings. With that thought, he refilled the liquid that'd spilled onto his hand, grabbed the other mug and went back to his table.

Elena didn't speak, only watched him as she accepted the coffee, bringing it to her lips immediately.

He swallowed. 'Elena—'

Her sigh cut him off. His eyebrows lifted before he could stop them.

'I'm sorry, did my voice annoy you?'

She didn't even pretend. 'I don't want an apology from you, Micah, which I can already see on your face is what you were planning on saying. I want to catch my train to

Venice. I want to watch the green fields through the windows and enjoy the peace of not arguing with you.'

He studied her. There was something more going on.

'This is why you didn't reply to my message yesterday, isn't it?' he asked quietly. 'You're not okay.'

She closed her eyes. When she opened them, he sat back. He needed the support of his chair to understand what he saw there.

'No, I'm not okay. But you're part of the reason I'm not, Micah, so I don't have any desire to talk to you about it.'

CHAPTER EIGHT

IT PROBABLY HADN'T been her best idea to accept Micah's offer of coffee. Not when she was obviously in a fragile state—why else hadn't she controlled her tongue?

Oh, right. That look of complete and utter anguish on his face.

'You won't let me apologise,' he said, his voice low.

'Do you know what you're apologising for?'

His brow knitted. 'Yesterday. For acting like an inconsiderate, stubborn—' He exhaled. 'I was wrong yesterday.'

'What about the day before?' she asked. 'When you claimed you weren't hiding anything?'

His lips parted, but he didn't say anything.

'That's why I didn't want your apologies,' she said, pushing her chair back so she could stand. 'They don't mean a thing.'

'Elena—'

'No!' She slammed a hand on the table. 'I don't want to hear your excuses. I just want the truth. Did you or did you not bring me here because you want a partnership with my father?'

When he stared at her, the little hope she had that Jameson had been incorrectly speculating fluttered away, disappearing in the wind.

'Micah,' she said on what sounded like a hiccup, but

couldn't be. That would involve having emotions about the situation. But she'd prepared herself for this, so, obviously, she had no emotions whatsoever.

'I was going to tell you,' he said softly.

'Were you?'

'I…' He paused. 'Not if I didn't have to, no.'

She pressed her lips together and tried to control the emotions she did, apparently, have. Control was better than feeling them. That swirl of disappointment and betrayal that made no sense when she'd known this man for days. When she was, essentially, working with him.

'I didn't think it would come to this,' he continued in that same soft voice. 'I didn't expect for us to…' He frowned. 'I only wanted you to introduce us.' The frown deepened. 'You shouldn't have been hurt by this.'

But I am.

She didn't say it.

'You could have found a million other ways to be introduced to my father,' she pointed out, proud of how steady her voice was. 'You could probably contact him now and he'd agree to meet with you.'

'I've tried that.' Despite his frown, the sternness he spoke with, he seemed vulnerable. Why did *he* seem vulnerable when he was the one with all the power? 'I wasn't as successful then. He wouldn't take a meeting with me.'

'He will now.'

'How do you know?'

She gave a mirthless laugh. 'If Jameson knows about you, my father knows about you.'

'Jameson… Your fiancé?'

The repressed emotion in his voice had her pressing the heels of her hands into her eyes. This was…a lot to deal with. At least she hadn't put on eye make-up that morning. She'd been too tired. All the effort she'd been able to muster was to put something on her lips to distract from the rings around her eyes. She was aware that wasn't how make-up worked, but it was the best she could do.

She dropped her hands. 'He's not my fiancé. He's just the man my father wants me to marry to strengthen his company.'

'What? *What?*'

The outrage almost amused her.

'I'm a pawn to him,' she said simply. 'Not unlike how you intended on using me for an introduction.'

'That's not… It's not the same.'

She only looked at him.

'Elena, my intentions weren't malicious. I promise. I was just…' He took a deep breath. Then he met her eyes. Fierceness had woven itself between vulnerability, the result so captivating she couldn't look away. 'You're right. I should have tried to get in contact with your father through other means. But I was afraid that…that my mother would find out.'

'Your mother?'

'John Diamond Company is a client of hers.' He was continuing before she had time to process that. 'Partnering with your father has little to do with my business, and everything to do with her. We… We don't have a relationship. I was hoping to change that.' The pause before he went on this time was longer. 'But if she thinks I orchestrated this, the chances of that happening…' He shook his head. 'She wouldn't appreciate being manipulated.'

'I can understand that,' Elena said bluntly.

He nodded. 'That's fair. But… This is how I do business. I make plans. I follow them. I don't think about the people involved.'

'That sounds callous.'

His jaw jutted out. 'It is.' He paused. 'I thought about you.'

She wanted to believe him, but… 'Did that change how you treated me?'

'It made things more complicated.' He sighed. Continued speaking as if releasing the breath had also expelled his resistance. 'I struggled with it. That's what happened yesterday. Among other things.' His fingers curled into a fist. 'It's easier to pretend not to know how my plans affect other people. For many reasons. Most of all because being callous makes me—'

'Like my father,' she cut in.

'I was going to say like my mother.' He heaved out another sigh. 'I don't entirely know how I feel about that. I'm working through some things.'

'Clearly.'

The side of his mouth lifted. 'You seem to be, too, with your father.' He paused. 'He really expects you to marry this guy? Say no.'

'Easier said than done.'

'Isn't there someone who can intervene?' he asked. 'Your mother?'

'I haven't spoken to my mother since my parents divorced when I was sixteen.'

Surprised fluttered over his face. 'I'm sorry.'

'Don't be. We didn't have much of a relationship before. I wasn't losing out.'

'But…she's your mother.'

'That doesn't mean much if she doesn't want to be my mother.'

'But—'

She interrupted him before he could ask more intrusive questions.

'If you'd just told me you wanted to meet my father, things would have been a lot easier. Instead, you were manipulative. And now I'm wondering things like if I'm good enough at my job to be here.' *Or if anything that happened between us was real.* 'I don't even know if I should trust anything you say. Are you telling me about your mother because you want me to understand your motivations? Or are you doing it for some calculating reason I'll only discover once I trust you again? I won't do that to myself.'

She stood. 'Send me your opinions on the article if you want. Otherwise, I'll see you on the flight home.' She didn't look back when she left.

It took him the rest of the day to clear his schedule. Micah did it without hesitation. There was a high likelihood the executive committee of his company would have something to say about that, but he could afford to ignore them this time. He'd brought in several high-profile clients over the last year. And if he got John Diamond Company—

He stopped. It was exactly that kind of thinking that got him into trouble. Admittedly, it was hard to shut down. He was used to methodical thinking. He'd been practising it for over a decade. Probably before that if he was truly examining things.

His mother was an excellent businessperson. Sharp, motivated, strategic. He witnessed these characteristics before he could describe what they were, especially when she used them on him. There weren't many traditionally maternal things about his mother. She spoke to him as if speaking to an employee. If the employee was an intern. Or someone she didn't want to deal with but had to.

The easiest way of processing it was if he responded in the way she treated him. She'd appreciated that, in that she hadn't looked too annoyed at him. In fact, the more he became like her, the less annoyed she was at him. But she also appreciated creativity, a fact he'd come to know after he'd written an essay at school about what he wanted to be when he grew up. He'd got an A for the essay, had shown it to her proudly. After one look, she'd said, 'Micah, you don't have the skills to become a lawyer.' He'd never learnt what skills she thought that was. 'Show a little creativity.'

And so his trajectory had changed. When he was old enough to figure out where it was headed to, he did research. On the kinds of clients his mother represented, on the kind of business she appreciated. It led him to the affluent market, and soon he'd seen a path to getting what he wanted. He happened to be damn good at it, too.

He was less good at relationships. Turned out the characteristics his mother had inadvertently taught him—the ones that made him so successful—didn't work as well in his personal life. He should have known. His mother hadn't been there for him at all. Nor for his father, which was part of why things hadn't worked out between them. That was based on his father's point of view, which he'd been privy to before his father had married and started a family with someone else.

The one significant thing about his father's marriage was that it showed Micah there was hope relationships could work. He'd never cared about that before. He struggled with the fact that he cared about it now. But he did. He cared that he'd hurt Elena. That she thought he was like her father, who wanted to use her as though she weren't a person. That he was like the man who would accept her as his wife, but thought of her in the same way.

He didn't understand relationships, but he knew he wanted more for Elena. He wanted more *with* Elena. She was the first person in his life to make him feel…things. He would accept being her friend if that was the only relationship they could have. But he needed to prove that she could trust him first.

Which was why he was now walking the narrow paths of Venice to his hotel. Elena had told Serena where she would be staying and had given her all the relevant contact details. It had taken some convincing—unsurprisingly, Elena had inspired loyalty in the woman that had worked for him his entire career—but his assistant had got him a booking at the same hotel. He had no idea if Elena was out exploring, or if she was dining at the hotel's restaurant, or if she was simply sleeping. But he had to take a chance, and hope he hadn't crossed a line by coming to see her.

After he booked in, he called her cell. She didn't answer. He rolled his eyes. His annoyance was both because she hadn't answered and because he'd expected her not to. He sent her a message.

I need a moment of your time, please.

He got a reply within seconds.

You had a moment of my time this morning.

He could picture her saying it, her lips pressed against one another, her eyes daring him to contradict her. For some inexplicable reason, it made him smile.

We both know this morning didn't go well.

Whose fault is that?

His smile widened. He probably looked like a fool, standing in the foyer, staring at his phone and smiling. He didn't care.

Mine. That's why I'd like to apologise.

I don't want apologies.

You deserve them.

There was some time before the next message came.

I'm not answering your calls.

You don't have to. Just tell me your room number and we can talk in person.

What?

No.

You're not here?

Those three messages came in quick succession.

Give me your room number and check for yourself.

His bottom lip curled beneath the top row of his teeth as he waited for her to reply. He knew it was impossible, but he wondered if she knew how hard his heart was beating and was punishing him. But that didn't seem like Elena's style. She seemed more like the physical torture kind, not the psychological one.

As if confirming it, her message came.

Room 542

He almost ran to the elevator before he realised he'd refused the porter so he could contact Elena. In hindsight, he should have only contacted her after he was settled.

But Elena was angry at him, and it felt as if a sword were waiting above his head. It made no sense. It didn't have to. He would explain himself to Elena soon and that feeling would go away.

Ten minutes later, he'd thrown his bags into his room and was knocking on the door of room 542. An elderly lady answered.

'Well,' she said, after scanning him up and down. 'I didn't expect this as room service, but I can hardly complain.'

'Oh.' It took him a beat to realise Elena had duped him. 'No, ma'am, I'm sorry. This isn't—'

'Did you just call me ma'am?' Her accent became more pronounced.

'Yes. I'm sorry. It's something we use out of respect for—' He cut himself off. They didn't need to go into detail about what older women were called in South Africa. 'I'm not from here. Customs aren't the same. Please accept my apology.'

'You do like to apologise, don't you?' came a drawl from opposite them.

He glanced back to see Elena leaning against a doorframe with folded arms. Her hair was piled at the top of her head, her skim gleaming with what he assumed was sunblock, though it was evening and he was probably wrong. His brain quickly noted the other things about her—she wore a sun dress, lilac and simple, and nothing on her feet—before he shifted.

'There you are, darling.' He kept his tone even. 'I forgot my key card and went to the wrong room.'

'It must be because of all the alcohol you drank at the parade,' she said easily.

'Getting locked out of my room quickly sobered me

up,' he replied dryly, then turned his attention to the older woman. 'I'm sorry for disturbing you, ma'am.'

She didn't reply, only shut the door in his face. What would it have been like if he'd gone into her room for what she'd wanted? He shuddered.

'If you're cold, you should probably go inside.'

He turned. Noted her expression. 'You mean of my own room.'

'I do.' She smiled at him. It wasn't friendly. 'I have to admit when I didn't see you through the peephole after five minutes I thought you were lying.'

'That's why you told me the wrong room number?'

'No. I told you the wrong room number because I thought it would be funny.'

'Hilarious.'

Her smile was full of amusement now. 'Oh, I know.' There was a short silence after she sobered. 'What are you doing here, Micah?'

'I prefer not talking about this in the passage. Where I'm sure we have some eyes. And ears,' he added, easily picturing the woman who'd slammed the door on him eavesdropping.

'I prefer not talking about this at all, yet here we are.'

She wasn't going to make this easy, then. Okay. He expected as much.

'Can I come in? Please? Please,' he said again, for good measure.

She gave him a wary look, but stepped back to let him in.

CHAPTER NINE

SHE WAS EITHER the biggest fool in the world, or a sucker for
a man who was prepared to grovel. Perhaps both. Probably
both, she thought, as she stepped aside for Micah. Both, she
confirmed when he walked past her and politely waited for
her to close the door before he did anything else.

Both for him, a voice whispered in her head.

She shouldn't have answered his messages, or told him
where to find her, or let him into her room. He put her in
danger. He *was* danger.

'Your room is nice.'

'It's generic and dark, but clean and comfortable. I don't
know if that qualifies as nice.' She sat on the bed. 'You
didn't come here to compliment my room though.'

'No.'

He shifted, revealing his nerves. She shouldn't have
used the opportunity to check him out. He wore jeans
despite the heat, though he was dressed the most casually she'd ever seen; he'd replaced his usual shirt with a
T-shirt. It was tight over a body that looked muscular, but
had the softness of someone who had been buff once, but
didn't get to the gym as much any more. She had no idea
whether that was true, or whether Micah's body simply
looked like that.

What she did know was that she wanted to run her

hands over his broad shoulders, down the firm rounding of his torso, back up. She wanted to kiss the crook of his neck and make her way down to the firmness of his bicep. She wanted to—

She closed her eyes. She didn't need this attraction. It only reminded her that she couldn't afford to share it with Micah. She didn't trust him. But it also forced her to think about the decision she had to make. How could she marry Jameson when she felt this way about another man? Would she indulge in an extramarital relationship as he no doubt would? The very thought of it made her uncomfortable. And she doubted Micah would want a relationship with a married woman anyway.

She shook her head. She shouldn't be thinking about this.

'Sit down, Micah,' she said softly. 'You're making me nervous.'

'At least we'll be on equal ground, then,' he muttered, but sat. 'So… I'm…er… I'm sorry.' It was so sincere she didn't even feel tempted to interrupt the apology. 'For everything, but mostly because I made you feel used. That… sickens me.'

She looked at him for a long time. Saw that he was telling the truth. It shifted something in her brain. In her heart. 'Thank you,' she said.

Her acceptance drew a frown, but he nodded. Then blew out a breath. 'I'd like to tell you why I did all this. Please.'

'Okay.'

'I've just…never spoken to anyone about it before.'

She resisted taking his hand. Resisted comforting him. It took more strength than she would have liked. 'When you're ready.'

After another nod and a breath, he began.

'My parents never married. They were dating while at

university, found out they were having me, had me. They were about to graduate and they weren't meant to be serious. My mom already had a law firm she was going to do her articles at, and when they wanted to drop her because of her pregnancy, she threatened to sue them. They played nice, and she worked her butt off while my dad looked after me.'

He stood.

'They weren't happy together, but the arrangement worked for them, especially since my dad wasn't working and my mom was. But my mom was never home, and my dad realised he wanted more from life. When I was seven, they broke up for real. It was fine for my mom because she had a good job by then and she could send me to a school. My dad got a job of his own, and every semblance of family I had ended.' He walked to her fridge, took a bottle of water out. After he downed it, he said, 'I'll pay for it.'

She didn't care about that. She did care about the sad look in his eyes. It wasn't obvious. There was a resignation as he told the story, as if he were recounting something he'd told a million times before. Now she knew why he was so tight-lipped about his family. She also knew him telling her this was…significant.

'My point is,' he said suddenly, speaking fast, 'I don't know how to treat people.'

'You not having a family means you don't know how to treat people?'

'No.' He exhaled irritably. She preferred it to the sadness. 'It means I don't know… It means,' he said more deliberately, 'people are hard for me. Relationships are hard for me.'

'Who said anything about a relationship?'

'I didn't mean a *relationship*.'

'That's wh—'

'I know that's what I said,' he interrupted curtly. Exhaled. 'My mother raised me. But what she did wasn't really raising. I had food on the table, shelter, but I didn't have anything else. So, I followed my mother's example. I... I shut down the emotions. I was efficient and had single-minded focus.'

'That's why you're so successful,' she murmured.

'Yes.' He didn't blink an eye. 'But apparently, those characteristics don't do well when you're trying to befriend someone.'

Her lips curved. 'You're trying to befriend me?'

He heaved out a sigh and sat down next to her. 'Do you think I came here simply to torture myself?'

She thought for a moment. 'Thank you for coming here. For being honest.'

'I'm trying.'

'So I see.' Emotion swelled in her chest. She cleared her throat. 'I don't like being used.'

'I understand why.' He gave her another one of his intense looks. 'Does your father really expect you to marry for his business?'

She stood and walked to the window. 'Yes.'

'Will you?'

She didn't answer him for a long time. 'I don't know.'

Her considering marriage at her father's behest still sounded like a fantasy. It didn't belong in the real world. It didn't belong in *her* world. She was determined, independent, strong. Why would someone like that put themselves in that position?

'Why?' he asked eventually. He needed to know.

'It's a difficult decision.'

'You know that's not what I meant.'

She sighed, but didn't answer him. He stood and joined her at the window. It was night, and all they could see were shadows below them. Occasionally, the light from someone's cell phone would come along and given them glimpses of outlines of faces and walls and cobbled stones. But Micah wasn't paying attention to that. He was looking at Elena.

The light in her room was bright and clear, allowing him to see every nuance of her expression. Naked emotions stalked across her face leisurely, as if it were a hot summer's day and they were prancing around the pool. She didn't try to hide them, and he could see the battle between guardedness and a desire to tell him. She met his gaze, but didn't speak. The rawness in her eyes made him want to pull her into his arms and tell her it was okay. She would be okay.

'We don't speak much these days,' she started. 'Me and my father, I mean. Contact mostly came from me, anyway, and when I got old enough for self-preservation to win out over my desire to...' She trailed off. 'Anyway, he called me to his office. He never did that, and there was just this...hope inside me. Foolish,' she scoffed at herself. 'He wouldn't call me to his office to apologise for the years of neglect or for using me when he needed me. He only called to use me again.'

She leaned back against the window frame, her gaze now shifting to outside. 'When I got there, he told me about a mining accident that had killed two John employees. I already knew, of course. It was all over the news and it's my job to know the news.' She dropped his hand and folded her arms. 'He said stock was tanking and he needed something else for the media to focus on. And he'd found a way.'

'Marriage.'

She gave a curt nod. 'To the heir to a rival mining company. The company would be strengthened because of the combined power and the society wedding would be all anyone would talk about. Romeo and Juliet, minus the part where I kill myself.'

'But you'd kill a part of yourself.' He could see it in her eyes.

She tilted her head. 'It's meant to be a business arrangement. A publicity stunt. We pretend to be a couple, but we live as though we aren't married.'

'What does that mean?'

She shrugged. 'We would have to move to the same house, but other than that, everything would stay the same. I'd have my separate life. He'd have his.'

'He'd have mistresses.'

'So would I. Well, misters.' Her mouth lifted. 'Sounds great, doesn't it?'

'You're not married yet,' he reminded her. 'You're not even engaged. It's not too late.'

She didn't answer him for a long time. It made him wonder if he'd misinterpreted her 'great' as sarcasm. Maybe she *wanted* to marry this Jameson man. Why else would she agree to her father's suggestion?

Had it been a suggestion though? Perhaps it had been a command. But why would she obey it? What was the worst thing that could happen if she didn't?

'Elena,' he said softly. 'What are you not telling me?'

She looked at him, and what he saw there told him not to prod. So he waited. When the waiting spanned minutes, he reached out and took her hand. As the minutes ticked by, he shifted closer. By the time she spoke, they were standing a breath apart.

His heart was thumping, and he was afraid their proximity would mean she could hear it. Or worse, feel it. Either way, she would know how much this was affecting him. How much the fact that she'd taken the last two steps towards him meant to him. They were sharing an intimacy he hadn't shared with anyone else in their conversation. He was drawn to her physically unlike anyone else. He wanted to kiss her. To share *more* with her.

He didn't want her to marry that man.

'He threatened my job,' she said hoarsely. She was staring up at him with big brown eyes that told him as much as her words did. She was scared. 'He didn't say it outright, but he didn't have to. My father… He's powerful.'

Anger pulsed through his body. 'So am I. I'll get you another job.'

'I don't want another job.' She bit her lip. 'I want this job. *My* job that I worked for, for years. The job that brought me here.' Her voice caught. 'It's not fair.'

He slid an arm around her waist, taking great care to be gentle and not give in to the emotion that told him to throw her over his shoulder and run away with her.

'And now there's this stupid engagement party in four days. *Four days*, Micah. I didn't even agree, but my father's invited everyone to it and the media's latched onto the whispers exactly as my father intended.'

'He's trying to strong-arm you into doing this.'

'Yes.' She let out a shaky breath. 'Along with threatening the one thing he knows means the world to me, he's pulling out all the stops to get me to agree.'

'Has he done this before?'

'Not to this extent.'

'That's why you stopped using his money. Why you put distance in your relationship.' She nodded, though he was really confirming more than asking. 'Why did you go to his office that day? You said hope, but for what?'

She rested her hands on his chest. 'If your mother called

you and asked you to do something for her, without warning or context, would you do it?'

And finally, he saw. He understood. She'd hoped for a relationship, for the love of a parent. She worried that if she didn't do this, she would lose not only her job, but that chance of love. As someone who'd spent his entire life searching for that love, doing what he thought he had to in order to get that love, he couldn't judge her. It was an impossible situation for a child. His heart broke for her even as he hated her father for putting her in that situation in the first place.

She cracked the first real smile she'd given since they started talking. 'You understand now why I jumped at the chance to be here. To escape it.'

She gently pulled away from him and walked towards the bed.

'Besides, you know, it being a wonderful opportunity. Writing a cover story is career gold for me. Or it was,' she said, narrowing her eyes at him. 'Now that I know I wasn't asked because of my skill, the ask has been tainted.'

He winced. 'I'm sorry. But regardless of how the opportunity came about, you're here, right? You do a good job, it won't matter how you got here.'

She opened her mouth, but no sound came out for a while. 'That's a good point.'

'That hurt, didn't it?'

She smirked. 'Maybe.'

He studied her, but her expression was as closed a book as it had been open earlier. He thought about pushing, but it didn't feel right. So he simply said, 'They wouldn't have agreed for you to write the story if you hadn't earned it, Elena.'

'I believe you. What?' she said in response to his surprise. 'You have pull with a demographic we've been struggling with for some time. Millennials. A solid portion of who will find you attractive. They need this story to be good.'

His face burned. 'We weren't talking about me.'

'No, we weren't.' She smiled. 'It's cute that you're flustered by people finding you attractive.'

'Why couldn't you just take the compliment and leave it at that?' he grumbled.

Her smile widened. 'Thank you for your compliment.' She put a hand on her hip. 'You know, I came here to forget. Not to rehash all of this.' She shook her shoulders. 'I needed an Italian escape with a tycoon, not an Italian confession with one.'

'You're strange, you know that?' Her laugh warmed the parts inside him he hadn't realise had gone cold during her story. 'But you have a point. I can't do much about your decision, but I can distract you. Have you made any plans for Venice yet?'

'Some.' She closed the space between them. 'Nothing that can't be cancelled.'

'I'll work around them.'

Tentatively, he opened his arms. She immediately stepped into them. Rested her head on his chest. It was comfortable. Warm. It felt exactly right.

'We'll make these the best days of your life.'

'Thank you.'

He couldn't resist the kiss he pressed to her forehead in reply.

CHAPTER TEN

WHEN ELENA WOKE the next morning, she asked herself whether she'd dreamed the night before. Micah had apologised and opened up to her about his family. In turn, she had told him about the impossible situation with her father. Now, they were going to spend the remaining days in Italy exploring Venice.

It was wild. But her life had, over the last month, been wild. Unrecognisable. One day she'd been living the life she created for herself, the next day she was contemplating marriage to a stranger. She hadn't paid attention to how little she'd liked the disruption. She had simply been focused on getting through it.

Micah forced her to think about it though. Spending time with him, being attracted to him, talking to him. It made her think about how she didn't like what her father was doing. It made her realise the full capacity of what Cliff was asking her to sacrifice.

It wasn't so much marriage itself, since the institution was easily escapable, as her parents' marriage had shown. If the marriage was based on normal things, that was. Love or respect or mutual admiration. Things that might fade over time. But *her* marriage would be a business contract. Those were harder to get out of. Business contracts with her father would be impossible to get out of. Was a job, however much she loved it, worth sacrificing her freedom for? Was the chance—the *chance*—of her father's love and approval worth giving up her future?

It caused her chest to ache, that thought. The *knowledge*. She knew that her father wouldn't change simply because she'd done what he'd asked. She'd had years and years of experience that told her that wouldn't happen. He would go back to ignoring her—or, worse, using her again and again because she was more accessible to him. It would break her. But now the question was whether giving up the hope of a proper relationship with her father would break her more than that would.

The emptiness and hurt echoing in her body reminded her why she hadn't examined her feelings about the situation. She shut them down, took a shower, and prepared for her day with Micah. He would ensure that she'd forget her problems, at least for the next few days. Her eagerness for him had nothing to do with *him* though. Things might have shifted slightly between them the night before, but this? This was all about forgetting her situation. It had nothing to do with him.

Her heart begged to differ when she got to breakfast. It skipped a beat when Micah looked up from his tablet and smiled. His teeth were white against his brown skin, bouncing off the white of the linen shirt he wore. When he stood, she saw he'd paired the shirt with dark blue chinos and white sneakers that could have been brand new, they were so immaculate.

'You look pretty hip,' she said, taking a seat opposite him.

'I had to look decent since I was spending the day with you.'

She pinched her thigh under the table so she wouldn't swoon at those words. 'What did you look like before?'

'A businessperson.'

'Ah, yes, and we both know businesspeople don't look decent.'

He narrowed his eyes. 'I wanted to look appropriately tourist-like.'

'You absolutely succeed.' She gestured around them. 'As you can see, most of the tourists here look as if they've walked off the catwalk.'

'Elena,' he said, expression pained, 'would you like me to change?'

'I was teasing.' She shook her napkin out and set it on her lap. 'You should have known that, since I was clearly complimenting you. Are you nervous about how you look or something?'

'No.'

He said it too quickly. He *was* nervous, so much so that he didn't want to talk about it. She had questions: Was it because the clothes were new? Did he never dress casually? Had he never simply been a tourist before? Were all his experiences overseas business?

She asked none of it. Because he'd clearly tried, for her benefit, and that was sweeter than she knew how to articulate.

'I think there was a compliment in there for me, too,' she said instead. 'Clearly you're aspiring to my fashion sense and I appreciate that.'

She wondered if he knew how much relief was in his smile.

'You do look…er…decent today. I like the crown.'

She smiled and touched the arrangement of flowers on her head. 'I bought it in a shop nearby. It's ridiculously extra, but I like it. Plus, it makes me look like a silly tourist and I kind of like that.' She rolled her eyes. 'I know it's silly. Who wants to look like a tourist? It's like putting a target on my back. Or on my forehead. But I don't know, I guess…'

She trailed off at the way he was looking at her. 'What?'

'You're rambling.'

'Micah,' she said slowly, 'I know you're not an expert on social interactions, but pointing things like that out isn't polite.'

'I thought you wanted me to be honest?'

She had nothing to say to that. Because yeah, she wanted him to be honest. But how did she tell him there was a thing like being too honest?

His chuckle drew her out of her confusion.

'Oh, you think this is funny?'

'It is.' He grinned. 'Payback is always fun.'

'Payback… Oh, for your clothes?' At his nod, she laughed. 'Haven't you heard the phrase "Revenge is a dish best served cold"?'

'I've never been a big believer of that. Personally, I think revenge is best served as soon as possible so neither party forgets.'

'Your brain is a wonder,' she said, shaking her head.

'Thank you.'

She rolled her eyes at that response. 'So. What's on the agenda today?'

She stole his coffee as he went through their day, interrupting occasionally to ask a question or tease him. He made it so easy. He often said something that could be understood in several different ways, and she would purposely understand the wrong meanings. That frustrated him, or annoyed him, which made her laugh, then he would laugh, and it all made her breathe more easily than she had in a long time.

It was leaps and bounds away from how she'd perceived him before. He was still charming, but that charm came from him being himself. From his mistakes, his laughter. The way he wasn't performing a persona. She didn't think he'd appreciate if she announced it to the world, but he didn't mind being that way with her. She felt touched. And warm. That warmth was so precious that she held it close, like the only light in a room of darkness.

That metaphor was alarming, even to her.

'I know that I shouldn't be this excited to go on a boat since I've done it before, but this makes me so happy.'

Elena did a little stomp with her legs, before twirling in a circle. It made the skirt of her dress whirl around her. Micah tried to focus on the top half of her, but there was a delay in the shift of his gaze—he couldn't help it—and he got a glimpse of full brown flesh. It was as enticing as the rest of her. She wore a bright yellow dress, as if she'd realised how much sunlight she'd brought to his life. With her flower crown, she looked like a summer goddess.

It worried him how badly he wanted to worship her.

'It isn't a boat. It's a gondola.'

'My mistake,' she said blandly, and made him smile. She did that a lot. And he was smiling more than he ever had before. That worried him, too. But it didn't stop him from smiling at her. Or from thinking about how different she was now, when she wasn't thinking about the decision she had to make.

What if she didn't have to make it?

He couldn't pay attention to the thought when the gondolier called for them to get in. He did, using the man's help, then gently nudged him aside to help Elena. She smiled brightly, and it became obvious why he'd wanted to help her. Apparently, he would do anything to get that smile. To keep it there, too.

It stuck as they sat down and the gondola began to float

down the canal. It was a bright, sunny day, and the blue-green of the water around them sparkled as it stretched between buildings. A gentleman began to sing, rich and deep, and Elena sighed at his side. She snuggled closer, not intentionally, he didn't think, but it made him hold his breath.

That might not have been the right description of it. It was more like someone was squeezing his lungs, so he had less capacity to breathe. He'd felt that way the entire day. When they'd been exploring the stores around St Mark's Square. Or when Elena had insisted on feeding the pigeons, then got alarmed when more and more of them came.

'What is it with you and pigeons?' he'd asked. 'I told you this wouldn't end well.'

'I thought you were exaggerating. You exaggerate.'

'You live in Cape Town, Elena. You've been to the Waterfront. You know what pigeons are like.'

'I thought European pigeons would be different.'

He'd laughed, harder when she hid behind him. She'd ended up giving the bag of seeds to a kid before running away, causing the pigeons to scatter. They'd eaten pasta and chocolate crêpes and taken pictures. Once, Elena had photobombed another couple, then apologised profusely and taken about twenty pictures of them alone to make up for it. Now they were here, on the canal, having someone sing to them.

It was a lot to process. Not the experience, but the emotions that accompanied it. And the thoughts. Those insidious thoughts that had popped into his mind all day, then scurried away before he could put his finger on what they were suggesting. They all pooled together now though, growing into an idea that stole his breath.

It was based on never wanting to see Elena as tortured as she had been the night before. To keep her as happy as she was now, as she had been all day. It was built by the memories of how she'd elevated his business banquet that night in Rome because she fitted so perfectly into his world. She went head to head with him when he did something stupid, forced him to think about the way he treated people, and made him feel more like himself than he ever had. If he'd ever encountered his equal, she was it.

She was it.

'This is so nice,' Elena said at that moment, as if sensing his confusing thoughts. And his body, as if confused itself, responding by putting an arm around Elena's shoulders.

He froze. Until she rested her entire body against him. Then he melted.

It was like the hug from the night before. Warm and comfortable. Except there was more now. She was looking up at him, smiling, and he felt himself stumble. Whatever part of him had been standing steady in the face of the onslaught that Elena was unknowingly waging against him broke down. Whatever sanity he had left that told him not to indulge his ridiculous idea fled.

The proposal spilled out of his mouth.

'Marry me.'

CHAPTER ELEVEN

ELENA DIDN'T HAVE a moment to process before the clouds of celebration broke above her and it began to rain.

'A proposal!' the gondolier cried. He shouted in Italian to another gondolier close by. 'A proposal!' he said again.

'Oh, no,' Elena started to say, shaking her head, but the man had stopped steering.

He reached out to take Micah's hand, then grabbed both of Elena's and kissed them. When he saw she had no ring, he clapped, shouting about spontaneity and romance in Italian to his colleagues. There were two women who squealed happily, and another who wished them well quietly. All the while, Elena couldn't say a word. Micah replied to them weakly, accepting the congratulations as more gondolas drew near.

By the time they reached land again, Elena had regained her composure. She smiled her thanks and waved at the women who'd squealed earlier. She let Micah help her out of the boat and even managed a smile for him. Their gondolier was still looking at them with pride, and she allowed him to hug her.

When they were walking away from all the commotion, Elena felt herself deflate. She almost stumbled down a set of stairs, but a steady arm snaked around her waist. It seared through her clothing, and, despite the drama he'd caused in the last hour, reminded her they had something.

But that didn't mean she wanted to marry him. She was still working through the situation with her father and Jameson. How was she supposed to marry Micah with that going on? And what had provoked his proposal in the first place? They had spent a lovely day together, yes, but a day didn't make a marriage.

Or was it the *more* that could make their marriage? She'd felt connected to him from the moment they'd met, after all. She'd been comparing her relationship with Jameson to him ever since then. Oh, no. This...this *thing* he'd done was making her lose her mind. She didn't appreciate it. Not one bit.

Micah had the wisdom not to try to talk to her until they were back at the hotel. Wordlessly, he followed her to her room. She stepped back to allow him inside, then closed the door and leaned her back against it. Neither of them spoke for a long while.

'What just happened?' she asked eventually.

'I... I proposed.'

He looked as stunned as she felt.

'Yes, you did. I suppose that question was too vague, then. *Why* did you propose?'

'I don't know.' He looked at her. Ran a hand over his head. 'No—I do know.'

She waited for the rest.

He sighed. 'I wanted to save you from marrying someone you didn't know.'

He seemed genuine. And his motives were...she didn't want to say pure, because that had implications she didn't want to think about. He was well intentioned.

Still.

'You can't just propose to someone, Micah.'

'I know.'

'I mean, it's one thing if we were dating and this was a surprise. In which case, a proposal on a gondola would be appropriate.' Perfect, actually. Because if she removed the fact that he'd put her on the spot, and that they weren't dating, she would have been thrilled with the proposal. 'But obviously this isn't a romantic proposal. It's a business proposal.'

He didn't answer for a beat. 'It's another option. From a...' he hesitated '...a friend.'

Friends. That description didn't seem right to her. It seemed inadequate. But at the same time, she'd rather he call her a friend than try to figure out what other label fit.

'I don't know what to say, Micah. We've only known one another for days. We spent a solid portion of that time not speaking.'

'But when we spoke, it meant something, didn't it?' he asked quietly. 'And days might not be long, but it's longer than what you've spent with the man your father wants you to marry. Isn't it?' he prodded when she didn't reply.

She nodded. Not only to his question, but to the rest of what he said. She knew him better than she knew Jameson. She trusted him more than she trusted Jameson. Which wasn't saying much, considering how little she trusted Jameson. Relief rippled through her. She quickly realised it was because the notion of trusting Micah...was nerve-racking. Thinking that she didn't trust him *that much* felt safer than thinking that she did. After what he'd done to her, the games he'd played, she was right to be cautious.

But he'd also apologised for doing that. He'd had a sincere motive, which she, of all people, could understand. He'd tried to earn back her trust. Told her the truth about his parents and cancelled all his plans to spend the last few days in Italy with her. She felt comforted in his arms; she felt alive in his arms.

But did that mean he was a safer choice than marrying Jameson?

'Why marry you?' she asked, a little desperately. 'Shouldn't I just say no to my father?'

He walked over to her refrigerator and took another bottle of water. He downed it as quickly as he had the bottle the day before.

'According to my understanding, if you say no to your father, you'll be punished,' he said long after he finished drinking. 'You'll lose a job that's important to you. I assume that puts you in a difficult position with your financial responsibilities. And you obviously won't be offered help from your father. Not that you'd accept it.'

She angled her head, accepting all his presuppositions.

'I can keep you from losing your job.'

She blinked. 'How?'

He gave her a wry smile. 'The same way I got you to do this story on me.'

'You can...you can really do that?'

'I can.'

'No,' she said, shaking her head. 'My father is powerful. He has connections. Friends. He'll buy the paper if he has to.'

'I'll buy the company that owns the paper,' Micah said patiently. 'I can arrange for it before we go home.'

'Wh—why?'

'If you're my wife, I'll do anything I have to in order to protect you.'

And he had the power to, she realised. He could fight her father on his level. He could *beat* him. She would never have to do anything her father bid her to do again if she had Micah protecting her.

It removed the fear of her losing her job and security from the equation of the Jameson situation. But what about the rest? She paced the floor, silently thanking Micah for giving her a moment to think. The media would go wild for a marriage between her and Micah. She was an heiress; he was a self-made millionaire. And they got married after she was assigned to write a story about him? It was a romance novel in real life, and the press would portray it as such. The focus from the tragedy at the John diamond mine would shift, and the John image would be elevated.

Her father would love it.

As for the business… Her father would love that, too, if she was honest. He would love to hitch his wagon to Micah's star. Micah was a fresh, young businessperson who would invigorate John Diamond Company's image—and potentially the business itself—and make Cliff John look like a visionary.

Had Micah thought about that, too?

'What's in this for you?'

'Beyond helping a friend?' She narrowed her eyes. He smiled. 'Fine. I can't deny the business advantages our partnership will have.'

'You mean a partnership with my father.'

No, I mean *our* partnership. You were magnificent at the banquet, Elena. Your presence there is part of the reason Lucca and the rest of the Vittoria board are looking forward to working with me.'

'You could have achieved that without me.'

'I would have mangled my speech, annoyed people with my bluntness, and had them whispering about me learning humility if it wasn't for you.' The ends of his mouth tilted up. 'You make me look good. You make my business look good. Advantages.'

Stunned, she swallowed. 'This has...nothing to do with my father?'

'I've been planning to pitch to him for years,' he said, smile disappearing. 'That won't change if we marry. It can't.' His eyes pleaded with her to understand.

She did. Even if it stung a little.

'Of course.'

'I can make sure whatever business we do together doesn't affect you in any way.' He moved closer to her, but didn't touch her. 'I can protect you from him.'

'Can you stop me from wanting his love, too? No,' she said quickly. 'That was unfair. I'm sorry.' Her legs were shaking, so she sat down on the bed. 'This is a lot to think about.'

He came to sit next to her. 'I know. And I'll give you as long as you need. As long as is feasible, considering your father wants to announce your engagement to another man in a matter of days.'

She nodded, but didn't speak.

'I'll give you every assurance you need to feel safe,' he said softly. 'Not in the form of promises, but in a contract. We can stipulate everything legally. If I do anything to break that contract, you can take me to the cleaners.'

Her lips curved. 'I don't want your money.'

'I know. It's part of the reason I want to marry you.'

'Worried about gold-diggers?'

He gave a surprised laugh. 'No. I was thinking that your reasons for marrying me are nobler than money.' He paused. 'But come to think of it, it would be nice not to worry about gold-diggers.'

She snorted, but her mind was already wandering. Past all the business stuff, past her father, both of which they agreed on. It settled on the more dangerous things. The emotions that sat in a tight little ball in her chest marked with Micah's name. If that ball ever unfurled, it would cause untold damage. It was more likely to unfurl if they were married. As would the physical attraction she had for him. That ball sat *much* lower, felt like fire whenever he touched her, and begged her to touch him.

'You joke now,' she said, desperate to get away from the thoughts that made her heart pound, 'but what if you want a real relationship one day? What if you fall in love with someone and—what?' she asked at his smile.

'I barely managed to keep this friendship alive, Elena. I have no hopes that I'll be able to keep a flirtation alive, let alone a real relationship.'

'If you speak with them the way you've spoken with me—'

'Let me rephrase,' he interrupted. 'I don't want to flirt, or date, or marry. For real, I mean.' His smile was wry now. 'It's too much time and effort. I won't be missing out on anything by marrying you. But if you feel like you will be—'

'I don't.' She sighed. 'I just want to focus on work and—' She stopped herself. 'Children. What about children?'

He frowned. 'Never thought about them.'

'But do you want them?' she pressed.

'Do you?' he countered.

She shook her head vehemently. 'If I have my parents' genes in me, it would be better for both me and the non-existent child if we didn't cross paths.'

'You would be a great mother.'

'We'll never find out,' she told him.

'Agreed.'

'So easily?'

'I've never thought about them, and you don't want them. Seems pretty easy to me.'

She studied him. 'You're being pretty cool about this. Too cool, for someone who's about to be married.'

'You haven't said yes yet.'

She almost said it then, but thought better of it.

'I need time to think.'

To figure out if saving myself from this situation I'm in with Jameson is worth risking you hurting me some day.

'You have as long as you need.' He stood. 'Just remember this.'

She looked at him. 'What?'

'There could be worse things than being married to someone who respects you. Who you respect. Hopefully,' he added.

'I do,' she said softly. And knew he was right.

Micah called his lawyers immediately after he left Elena's room. He paid them a lot of money for the privilege of their advice, though he did feel bad about the hour. Not bad enough not to call them. He wanted to be ready if Elena agreed to his proposal. And he had a feeling she would. Which meant he might be married soon.

He should have been worried. Anxious. Something along those lines. He shouldn't be feeling…whatever he was feeling now. A hum, a buzz inside him. As if he'd consumed a swarm of bees and they were making their way through his body. He wouldn't call the feeling excitement. More anticipation.

He couldn't deny the advantages to marrying Elena. Everything he told her was true. She was the perfect business spouse; her linguistic skills were more helpful than he could have imagined; it would make a potential business partnership with her father easier. But he hadn't only been thinking about business when he proposed. He'd been caught by her. In the way the sun glinted off her hair. The smell of the salt of the canal and the perfume on her skin. When she was tucked into his side, he felt fortified. He felt whole. An illusion, he knew. No one could make him whole besides himself.

But that was it. Elena made him feel as though he *could* make himself whole. He hadn't even known the version of himself when he was with her existed, to be frank. He laughed, relaxed. His brain turned off, not constantly calculating or devising his next steps. It was different from how he'd been in the thirty-two years of his life and he liked it. He liked who he was with her.

And *that* should have worried him. That there was more than business involved in his decision to propose. That he was considering marriage at all when it hadn't appealed to him in the past. His parents hadn't married, so he didn't have anything to—or not to—emulate. And the people around him who were married treated the institution cavalierly. Adultery and disrespect were as much a part of marriage for his peers as their spouses were. Micah had no doubts, considering what his research revealed about the man, that Elena's would-be fiancé would follow that custom if they did marry.

It highlighted another alarming reason for his proposal: he wanted to protect her. From her father, who seemed callous and uncaring of the woman Elena was. From the man her father wanted her to marry, who would likely find ways to erase Elena's personality. He couldn't bear the thought of it. She was too vibrant, too vital.

Marriage might not have appealed to him, but being in Elena's presence did. Being in a partnership where they could treat one another as equals and respect each other for who they were? He could get on board with marriage for that.

Why did he just become aware of a slight trepidation kicking with every beat of his heart?

He went to the bar and took out a tiny bottle of brandy. He poured half of it into a glass and drank it, then poured the other half into it and added ice. He took the glass to the sliding doors, and opened them to Venice.

Laughter and music from some far-off place drifted up to him. He couldn't see much, but he could hear the water of the canal. It lapped against buildings, lightly, so that the sound was barely more than a whisper. The light breeze was likely the cause of it, but as it touched his face Micah couldn't fault it. The balcony he stood on was small, about five steps away from his hotel room, but it was enough to house two small chairs. He settled into one, and tried to figure out that trepidation.

Downsides. There had to be a downside to marrying Elena. *Everything* had downsides. There would be legal complications that came with being married, wouldn't there? But he had a team of competent lawyers and both he and Elena would stipulate the terms of the agreement. That didn't seem so much of a downside as it was admin. He could handle admin.

Children. He had never thought about them. To him, that said enough. Children deserved parents who wanted them. At the very least, parents who thought about wanting them. He had no desire to repeat the mistakes of his parents. Elena didn't want children either. That solved the problem easily, if making prospects for the physical part of their relationship less exciting.

Well. That posed a problem he didn't think could be easily solved. He couldn't see himself dating if he was married to Elena. Not only because the thought made him slightly nauseous for reasons he'd rather not examine, but because no woman had appealed to him the way Elena did. He had no interest in discovering if someone in the future could appeal to him in that way. It complicated sating his physical needs. But could the same be said for Elena?

If she wanted to go outside their marriage, he would have to respect it. He didn't own her; he didn't believe marriage or any relationship would change that. But he didn't want her to go outside their marriage. He wanted her to turn to him if she needed…that.

And *that* was a downside that made things a hell of a lot harder for the both of them.

CHAPTER TWELVE

'Do you unpack your belongings when you're staying at a hotel, or do you keep things in your luggage?'

Elena thought it was a strange morning greeting from a man who had just proposed to her, but she answered. 'I keep most things in my luggage. Generally my toiletries go in the bathroom and I have to pack those up. Good morning, by the way.' She slid into the booth opposite Micah. 'Did you sleep well?'

'I had a solid three hours, yeah.'

'Three hours?' She lifted her brows. 'Did you have something to think about?'

He smiled. It was teasing and a little sly, and it made her stomach jump. Or was that her hunger? In the whirlwind of the night before, she hadn't eaten. She'd drunk numerous cups of tea as she'd sat up and thought Micah's proposal through. She'd exhausted herself, but she thought she had an answer. That smile was making her doubt it though. Could she be his wife if his smile made her—?

Hungry, she interrupted her thoughts. She was *hungry*. *I bet.*

It was as if her thoughts were punishing her for interrupting them.

No, she told them firmly. *Stop misbehaving.*

'Yes, I did, which you know.' He eyed her. 'How much sleep did you get?'

She pretended to count. 'Oh, about three hours, too. They weren't solid though.'

'I'm sorry.'

She waved away the apology. 'You weren't in bed keeping me awake. Oh, you ordered me coffee?' she exclaimed when the waiter put a cup down in front of her. 'You're a lifesaver.'

He didn't reply, but his eyes had gone intense again. Not that it said much; that was his normal state. Although he had seemed lighter recently. Lighter compared to who he usually was, which was saying something, what with the proposal.

'What's wrong?' she asked when she'd taken a drink of her coffee and he was still staring at her.

'Nothing. You said… Never mind.' He picked up his menu. 'I'm thinking full breakfast this morning. It's going to be a long day.'

'Hold on. I'm still…'

She trailed off, replaying her words. When they caught up with her, she nearly dropped the cup she was bringing to her lips again. Not at what she'd said—that was perfectly harmless if Micah didn't have such a dirty mind—but at his reaction. It told her they needed to talk about that *thing* she'd thought about at several points of the night.

'Why…er…why is today going to be a long day?' she said, drinking her coffee as she intended to. It had nothing to do with the much needed caffeine and everything to do with hiding her blush. It also distracted her from having to talk about sex with her future husband and she was looking forward to that.

Not looking forward to that. *Not*.

In response to that correction, her mind offered her the

memory of Micah pinning her to the wall. Heat flooded
her body and, instinctively, she pressed her legs together.
Then she cursed both her body and her mind for betraying her, and tried not to think about how sensitive every
part of her body had suddenly become.

She took another gulp of coffee.

'I...er... I thought we could go to Tuscany.' Micah took
a sip from his coffee, too. Were his motives the same as
hers? 'There's a small town there that would be perfect
for today.'

'Oh, I don't want you to go out of your way to show me
Italy. Venice is plenty.'

'But we've done Venice,' he said with a small smile.
'You've seen most of it. Of course, we can spend more time
finding the jewels of the city. But wouldn't you rather go
to the countryside? Sip wine in the vineyards? Eat home-
made pasta?'

She stared at him for a long time. 'You're a hell of a
businessperson. I'm pretty stubborn, but I swear you can
talk me into almost anything.'

'Almost anything?' he enquired gently.

She opened her mouth to tell him what she'd decided,
but the words wouldn't come out. She frowned. Was she
being cautious? Or did she feel hesitant?

'It's okay, Elena.' His eyes were softer than usual. 'We
don't have to talk about it now.'

'But we have to talk about it,' she insisted.

'We will. After the wine and pasta.' He smiled.

'You already know me so well,' she teased, though a
part of her meant it. 'But yes, wine and pasta it is.'

That was how Elena found herself in the beautiful town
of San Gimignano later that morning. It took them some
time to get there by train, but the journey was beautiful.
Green stretched out through the windows for kilometres

as Micah told her about San Gimignano as if he were a tour guide. That was how she knew that the town was in the heart of Italy's wine country, and that it had narrow streets and old architecture much like Italy's cities.

But his descriptions couldn't prepare her for the feeling she got once they were there. It felt like history and peace, an uncommon combination, yet somehow it captured the atmosphere perfectly. The buildings were tall and old, as promised, but they felt rich with culture and were beautiful. They stretched up like stone trees to the sky, with ivy creeping up them as if wanting to see the sky, too.

They stopped at a rustic restaurant Micah had been to before, and were guided to a terrace that overlooked the vineyards. The terrace itself was beautiful. Flowers were planted in a large square in the middle of the space, and terracotta pots with flowers stood on the boundaries of it.

They were seated at the edge of the terrace and had the best view. Then the wine and the pasta came, and Elena thought it was the best day.

'Are you trying to persuade me to marry you, Micah?' she teased when their meal was done. She wouldn't have done it, but it was her third glass of the delicious wine, and she was in a teasing mood.

'You'll have to tell me if it's working before I admit that,' he said with a small smile. He was as tipsy as her, unless he could hold his wine better than she could. She doubted that.

'It might be.' She sighed contently. 'I've been more relaxed yesterday and today than I've ever been in my life.' She thought about it. 'In fact, this entire trip has done a world of good for my mental health. Despite those unexpectedly tense moments between us.'

'Tense moments?'

'Oops. Probably shouldn't have said that. But don't pretend like you don't know what I'm talking about.' She wagged a finger at him, then used the hand to count down the tense incidents. 'In the plane, when you looked at me in my unicorn shirt. At the banquet when you pinned me against the wall. After the banquet when we fought about—' she waved her hand '—something. Our conversation in my hotel room. The proposal.' She waved her hand at him. 'We need to stop it now or I'll run out of fingers to count on.'

'You have another hand.'

'Good point. Though that's not *my* point, so maybe it isn't.'

'Are you drunk, Elena?' he asked, this time with his annoyingly sexy smile on display.

'Of course I'm not drunk.' She said it a tad loud. She knew that because the people at the table next to her looked over in amusement. 'Hmm. Maybe I should switch to water.'

She studied her wine glass, drank the last drop then filled it with water and downed that.

'At least it has the same taste as the wine.'

'You're cute when you're drunk.'

She snorted. 'Please. We both know I'm cute when I'm sober, too.'

His smile went from his lips to his eyes. Somehow. He wasn't smiling at her, but she could tell he was still amused, and it had something to do with his eyes. Hmm. He could definitely hold his wine better than she could. She would have to remember that for their marriage.

Their marriage. She was marrying him. And she hadn't told him yet. She should probably tell him.

'We need to talk about sex,' she said instead.

And the shock of it sobered her right up.

* * *

'Do you want some dessert?' the server asked, oblivious to the tension between him and Elena.

'No,' he said quickly.

'But coffee, please,' Elena added.

'And for you, sir?'

'No. Yes. Yes,' he repeated. He could do with some coffee if they were going to be having this conversation.

The server disappeared, but Elena didn't say anything. She poured herself another glass of water and drank it, though slower than she had before. He suspected it was to delay the conversation, but he would wait as long as he had to. It was a skill he'd mastered in business negotiations, waiting. There was no way he would speak before she did. Let alone on this topic.

'I'm sorry,' she said, clearing her throat. 'I shouldn't have been so blunt about it.'

Micah drank from his water glass, too. He didn't want her to think he was panicked at her bringing this up. In fact, he was elated. It meant they were on the same page in terms of what they were trying to prepare for with their marriage. It meant she was probably thinking about saying yes to him. It meant he wouldn't have to bring it up.

'It's fine. You want to talk about it, we can talk about it.'

'Are we calling it "it" like we're two teenagers?' she asked lightly. '"Are we going to do 'it', Micah?"' She was shaking her head before she even finished. 'I am so sorry I did that. The fact that it went through my filter tells me I should have stopped after that second glass.'

'Elena, it's okay. You're just nervous.' He couldn't help his chuckle though.

She gave him an unimpressed look. 'If I was—and I'm not saying I am—the only thing I'd want from you is your laughter. So, thank you.'

He lifted up his hands, and shut his mouth. But she was so adorable. Her cheeks were red from the wine or the sun, he didn't know. Both, he decided. Her hair was an intricate web of curls at the top of her head, slightly off balance because of the hat she'd replaced the flower crown with. She'd brightened as soon as she'd put it on, and walked around with it all day until now, despite the bulk it created on her head.

She was wearing another charming summer dress, white and red this time, and had paired it with her signature red lipstick. It was faded from the food she'd eaten and wine she'd drunk, but he could still see. He wanted to kiss her lips.

'Okay, before I get there, I need to say that I'm… I'm going to say yes to marrying you.'

Her words didn't have the lyrical cadence they'd had earlier, and he thought the water was working fast. Then he realised she'd told him what he wanted and he wasn't processing it. The server arrived before he could and, after he thanked the man, Elena began to speak again.

'I need to talk to you about two things first though. One is sex, but we'll get to that. Not to the sex. To the topic.' She frowned and stared at the black coffee. 'I should have ordered an espresso.'

He didn't speak, half amused, half entranced by her words. By everything about her.

'Look, you've never had a personal…friendship, or whatever, like this before. I don't mean physically—' she blushed, but pressed on '—but emotionally. You've never had someone who wants to spend time with you. Not the business you, or millionaire you or whatever, but *you*. I…um…care about you, and I guess you sense that, and I just wanted you to know that you don't have to marry me because I'm the first person to do that.'

She bit her lip at the end of it, as if keeping herself from adding to what she said. What more could she add? He almost asked her, but now he was thinking about whether she was right. Was he offering to marry her because he felt obligated to? Was this a response to someone who cared about him?

He had no means of comparison, so he struggled to answer that question. He didn't know what a personal friendship—or whatever, he thought wryly—was like. His relationship with his parents was non-existent, so he wasn't sure how he responded to love. Which sounded dramatic since he knew his parents loved him. In their way. So if he was responding to love, it was to his brand of love. The fact that someone loved him in a way that he could actually feel.

Wait—not love, care. Elena cared about him. He was responding to how she *cared* about him.

'How would I know if I'm doing that?'

Elena tilted her head. 'I'm not sure.'

'How do you know you're not accepting me because you don't know what any of that looks like either?'

Her lips parted, then formed an oh. She gave a little laugh. 'I guess I don't know that either.'

He brought his coffee to his lips. 'It's not exactly something I hoped you and I would have in common.'

'We have plenty of other things in common,' she said with a shake of her head. She continued, but he made a mental note to ask about those things later. 'And I came up with an answer. Kind of.' The knit in her brow deepened. 'We know how we felt when our parents treated us the way they did.' She paused. 'The not great stuff, and the way it made us feel. I don't feel that way now, with you.' She swallowed. 'But there was one time my father...almost acted proud of me.' She looked down, as if she were ashamed. He barely stopped himself from reaching out to her. 'And it made me feel…warm. Valued.' Now she met his eyes. 'Kind of how you make me feel.'

He had no idea what to do with the feelings that admission awoke in him. It felt as if a volcano had burst. He tried to focus on something else; *anything* other than the hot lava of emotion spreading inside him. Logic chose her relationship with her father. What she told him helped him understand why she was so eager to please the man. She wanted to feel warm and valued again. He couldn't blame her for that. Especially not when he wanted to feel that way just once with his parents.

Especially not when she made him feel that way, too.

Something skittish skipped through his chest.

'I'm sorry. I didn't mean to make things so sombre.'

'You didn't.'

Her eyes softened. 'I appreciate that lie.'

'Elena,' he said slowly, trying to get his thoughts in order. 'There are many reasons I asked you to marry me. Many logical reasons that have nothing to do with the fact that you…care about me.'

'Oh. Yes, of course.' She gave a quick shake of her head. 'I didn't mean to imply—'

'But,' he interrupted, 'the fact that you're concerned I might be doing this for less straightforward reasons, if you will, is also a part of why I asked. You're a rare breed of person,' he continued carefully. 'I would be honoured to be your husband.'

Their eyes met, held, and he was reminded of the lava again.

Which he promptly fell into when she said, 'Even at the cost of what you want to achieve with your mother?'

CHAPTER THIRTEEN

'WHAT DO YOU MEAN?' Micah asked once he resurfaced.

'What if my father chooses to punish me for going against his wishes by refusing to partner with you?' Her voice was low. 'You said that plan had something to do with your mother, didn't you?'

'Yes,' he murmured, realising he hadn't told her the details of it. 'She cares about her career more than anything else. I thought she would care about mine, too, if I partnered with your father. He's her biggest client.'

'And if she cared about your career, she might start to care more about you, too.'

He gave a curt nod. She studied him for a while.

'Is it worth it, Micah? Am I...? Is *this* worth the risk?'

It was a damn good question. And the fact that she was asking it meant more to him than he could comprehend. It told him it was worth the risk. Despite her deliberate rephrasing, he thought *she* was worth the risk. His gut agreed. It also told him she would care about him even if he didn't do anything to make her care about him.

She wasn't like his mother.

It was a confusing realisation in the context of everything that was happening. His mother was the reason he and Elena were even having this conversation. His desire to get her attention had put him on this path. Now he was considering throwing that away? Why? Because someone was offering him a relationship he didn't have to work so damn hard for?

Yes.

The lack of turmoil he felt at that was refreshing.

'I don't know what it means that I'm saying this.' He spoke slowly, in case something changed. It didn't. 'But I'd still like to marry you.'

'Micah,' Elena breathed. She reached out and covered his hand with hers. 'Are you sure?'

He turned his hand over and threaded his fingers through hers. 'Yes.'

Elena studied him. Seconds later, she shifted to the seat beside him, then grabbed his hand again.

'There's no shame in wanting a relationship with your mother. Even at the cost of this.'

'I know.' Because he couldn't resist it, he cupped her face. 'But I think my life will be fuller with you in it. My life will just be…different, with my mother in it.'

Emotion flooded her eyes. 'I'm sorry,' she whispered, clasping her hands around the wrist of the hand that held her face.

He could tell she meant it. She wasn't controlling her facial expressions. She was showing him her heart and, in it, he could see her sincerity. And more. So much more. More than he'd ever thought he could hope for when any-one looked at him.

'You don't have to be sorry for something outside your control,' he said.

'Not marrying you is *inside* my control.'

'It wouldn't make a difference to my relationship with my mother.' Somehow he knew that with certainty. 'I have no guarantee working with your father would either. I do know that marrying you would make a difference to my life.'

She bit her lip, her eyes not leaving his. 'Are you sure?'

He nodded. 'If you are.'

She nodded, too. 'I am.'

'Then let's get married.'

'We need to talk about something else first.'

He dropped his hand and groaned. 'I think we've talked enough.'

'You're right.' Her eyes sparkled. 'Maybe we should try a kiss, then?'

She didn't care that she was being forward. Micah's actual proposal had been clumsy—romantic, but clumsy—but this? This admission of what he thought his life would be with her in it? It was swoon-worthy. It was movie-worthy. It was romance-novel-worthy, kiss-you-until-you're-breathless-worthy. She wanted to be breathless.

'Are you sure?' he asked, though he'd already shifted forward, bringing their lips close together.

'I wouldn't have suggested it if I weren't.'

'Ah, yes. I forget you say what you mean.' He put his hand at the base of her neck. It sent a shiver through her. 'It's refreshing.'

'So you keep saying.'

Now she moved closer, running her index finger around the button at the top of his shirt. It was another white shirt, like the day before, except this one was short sleeved instead of rolled up. It revealed round biceps, and, before she'd fully thought it through, she was running her finger along the veins she could see there.

'You know what *would* be refreshing?' she said lazily. 'If you stopped talking and kissed me.'

She only had a flash of his smile before his lips met hers.

The sensation was other-worldly. A foolish description.

A fanciful description. It fit. Not once in her lifetime on earth had she felt so consumed by a kiss as she did now. The world around them ceased to exist. Only the heat that went from her lips down to her core, trailing a path that pulsed with desire, existed.

Then he slipped his tongue into her mouth, and she realised that existed, too.

It was probably a good idea to establish that both their bodies existed on this plane she was on. Her hands had somehow found both his biceps, and were holding on for dear life. His hands were resting on her thighs, squeezing her flesh as if anchoring his fingers there. Their mouths moved in union, giving and taking, enjoying and lusting.

There was more to the lusting than the physical. It felt deeper. It felt as if it touched her heart. It raced as Micah kissed her; a testament to his skill and his words. He kissed as intensely as she'd imagined he would, but with a hesitance that told her he was paying attention. To her responses, to her body. To what gave her pleasure so that he could continue to give it.

All of it told her he was a good man. And that, really, was what her heart was reacting to. He made sure she wanted to kiss him before acting on her suggestion. Even now, he was being careful. If his hands ever moved from her thighs, it would be after a question. Either verbally, or through a subtle touch that asked for permission. When she gave it, he would pay attention to her body as thoroughly as he was currently doing to her mouth. He would ask her for guidance, she knew, and would obey when she offered it to him.

He would torture her in all the right ways. His kiss—this simple kiss—told her so. Now, more than ever, she was glad she'd broached the topic of sex with Micah. The sooner they clarified their positions on it, the sooner they could act on those positions. She was certain of what he wanted. She knew what she wanted, too. She had never been as eager to sate her needs with anyone else.

'Micah,' she said, the shock of it forcing her to pull away.

Her breath took a long time to catch up to that shock. As it did, she lifted trembling hands to her mouth. It felt swollen. It felt used. Both felt like triumphs.

'It was too much too soon,' Micah said hoarsely. He reached for his water and emptied the glass in seconds. Then, seemingly having a handle on himself, he poured another glass and handed it to her.

'No, that's not it,' she said, accepting the water.

'Then what?'

Or maybe that *was* it. Not the kiss, but the realisations. The emotions. Too many too soon. But she couldn't tell him that.

'I was just thinking… I'm glad it's you. Not Jameson, I mean.' She tucked a stray curl behind her ear. 'We wouldn't share that.'

'Did you…er…?' He cleared his throat. 'Did you try?'

She gave him an amused look. 'Did I try to kiss a man who saw me as only a business arrangement? No.'

'Good.'

'Is it?' she asked casually. Colour touched his cheeks. It was the first time she'd ever seen him blush. He shifted, telling her he didn't like it as much as she did, and she took mercy on him. 'Honestly, I don't think Jameson would have ever been interested in me. I don't think I'm his type. Too mouthy.'

She'd been joking, but he didn't crack a smile. He didn't even reply. It wouldn't have been a conversation if he didn't shift, avoiding her gaze.

'What?'

'Nothing,' he said quickly. Too quickly.

'Then why are you acting so weird?'

'No reason.'

'Micah.'

'It's not relevant any more.'

'So you should have no problem telling me then.'

He narrowed his eyes. 'You're just as formidable as you say I am, you know that?'

'Thank you,' she said. 'Now spill.'

After a long pause, he answered. 'I had Serena send me over some information about the man you were going to marry.'

'Did you?' she asked lightly. 'Any particular reason?'

'I was…interested.'

'Hmm.'

'In any case,' he said quickly, 'there was a story from this week that… Well, I'm sure you've seen it. You're a journalist.'

'I don't see *every* story.'

'No, I suppose not.' He cleared his throat. 'You probably have an alert for the man you're thinking about marrying though.'

'Surprisingly, no. But,' she said conversationally, 'if you keep stalling, I might reconsider marrying you. Or spill this glass of water on your pants and tell everyone you've had an accident. Probably the latter. Less dramatic.'

Micah frowned. 'Those are both dramatic options.'

'Micah.'

'Fine.' He cleared his throat for the millionth time. 'There was a photo on a gossip site. It was purely speculation, in light of, I think, the news of your impending engagement. They claimed the man was Jameson St Clair.' He paused. 'With another woman.'

Elena took a second. 'Do you have the link to the story?'

He studied her, but took his phone out, typed on it for

a moment, then handed it to her. The headline was sala-
cious, which she expected, but she focused on the picture. It showed a man walking into a hotel with a woman.
She was dressed in a sophisticated black dress that was
tight and ended above her knee. The man wore a distinc-
tive suit—bright blue, with white pinstripes. It was what
Jameson had worn the day her father had suggested their
marriage. The shock of the suggestion had every detail
embedded in her mind.

Jameson had been with another woman the same day
he said he would marry her.

'Well. I guess mouthy has nothing to do with it. It's
because I'm brunette,' she said, handing the phone back
to Micah.

'It's him?'

'It is. And that's the same day he and my father said
they wanted us to marry. The suit,' she answered when his
brows rose. 'It stuck in my mind.'

'I'm sorry.'

'Don't be.' She shrugged. 'This would have been the
reality of my life. You've given me another option.' She
reached for the coffee they'd both forgotten, finding it
lukewarm. Still, she drank it. She needed the kick for the
question she was about to ask him. 'Unless there'll be pictures of you coming out like this?'

His gaze didn't waver. 'Heavens no. I prefer brunettes.
Mouthy brunettes, to be specific.'

She sat back in her chair and grinned. Couldn't help
it. 'We should probably start planning our wedding, then,
huh?'

CHAPTER FOURTEEN

THEY LEFT SAN GIMIGNANO that night. They'd spent the afternoon discussing their plan, and they'd both decided going back to South Africa a day early would only benefit them. They could go to Micah's lawyer's offices, sign a prenuptial agreement, and tell her father.

At least, that had been Micah's suggestion. Elena's was more radical.

'We should get married before we tell my father,' she said matter-of-factly. 'There's no point rushing on the prenup unless we're getting married soon. And getting married soon will put us in a better position when we see my father.' She glanced at him. 'If you need to buy the parent company of my paper, you can do it for your wife, not your fiancée.'

'I trust you,' he said once he could form a coherent reply. 'I'll do it for my fiancée, too.'

'Yeah. Yeah, it's too fast,' she said, shaking her head. 'Sorry.'

The expression in her eyes had him saying, 'There's more to this, isn't there?' She bit her lip. It tugged at his heart. 'Elena, you can tell me.'

It was a while before she did. 'I'd feel safer—more protected—if we were married when we speak to him.'

It did him in, her vulnerability. He nodded. 'So let's get married before we see him.'

The first half of the plane ride, they spoke about every possible condition they wanted in their pre-nup. Elena's professional independence was assured—at Micah's insistence—as was Micah's wealth—at Elena's insistence. They added clauses about business commitments and personal functions, birthdays and special occasions. They stipulated that neither of them wanted children, and if they did it, both parties would have to agree on it and put it in writing. There would be a probationary period where both of them would have to display the behaviour they wanted to see in a parent. Essentially assuring the other they could do work/home balance.

'Just in case,' Elena said.

'Just in case,' he agreed, but he was sure it wouldn't be necessary.

After they repeated all that and more to their lawyers, who recorded it with their permission, they ended the call and sat staring at one another.

'That was interesting,' he said.

'It was.' There was a beat of silence. 'We didn't talk about sex.'

He paused as he reached for his drink, but continued when he realised he couldn't delay any longer. 'No, we didn't.'

'We'll need to tell them if they need to put an infidelity clause in the contract,' she said nonchalantly. 'I know what you said after the Jameson thing, but if you've changed your mind, we should be prepared for that.'

The way she was picking at her trousers told her she wasn't as relaxed as she was pretending to be.

'I haven't changed my mind,' he said, watching her. 'But I've already had the clause inserted.'

'Yeah?' Her fingers stopped moving. 'What did you say?'

'If I cheat, you can leave.'

She frowned. 'What about me?'

He cleared his throat. 'I told them I would confirm later.'

There was a long pause. She reached over and took the drink from his hands. Unlike him, though, she drank it. He watched her swallow. Only she could make it seem like an action that belonged in a seduction. She pressed the glass to her lips before handing it back to him, as if she'd realised it wasn't hers.

'You know, it's not cheating if we both agree we can go outside the marriage for sex,' she said, watching him closely.

'No, it's not.'

He drank the remaining liquid in one quick gulp.

'We haven't made any decisions about that. Why would you involve the lawyers?'

'I went into this knowing that I didn't want to—' He broke off to clear his throat. Actually, he was giving himself time to figure out what he wanted to say. It wasn't working, so he stopped trying. 'I don't want to go outside our marriage. I know it's not strictly a real marriage, but it feels disrespectful. What if someone saw me and this other woman? The speculation in the media would be as bad as with Jameson.' He shook his head. 'I'm not him.'

'Yet you're telling me *I* can choose that?' She stood and came to sit down next to him. His seat wasn't meant for two, so he ended up half sliding off it. It didn't help; Elena still ended up sitting on him. 'What about the speculation if the media sees me with another man?'

He tried to ignore how wonderful she smelled. How his skin was getting hot and every cell was becoming more aware of her proximity.

'There wouldn't be as much attention on you if you wanted to do that.'

She studied him. 'Stop being so careful, Micah. Tell me what you feel.'

What would it be like to trail a finger over the skin near her collarbone? It looked so smooth, so silky. When they'd been kissing, he hadn't had the benefit of touching her the way he wanted to. He wanted another chance, but in the same breath, he wanted—

'Micah.'

Oh, yes. She was talking to him. 'What?'

She snorted. 'You're being so careful. It's working on my nerves. I'm sure my questions are doing the same for you.' She didn't wait for an answer. 'I'm going to tell you what I think. Honestly. You might not want to hear it.'

She waited for an answer now, as if he would have one. Should he have one? He tried to ignore the allure of her skin, her collarbone, the memories of that kiss with her, and thought about what she said. She wanted to tell him what she thought about fidelity in marriage. Right. And she wanted to do so honestly because she thought he was being cautious.

He frowned. 'I'm not being careful.'

'You're not saying what you want to say either,' she countered easily, unsurprised by his delayed response.

'I… Elena, I don't know how to say what I want to say.'

'Because you're trying to think like a businessperson. Don't. Think like *you*. A man, a husband, or whatever the hell role will help you to be honest.'

'You really want that?'

'*Yes.*'

'Fine.' He didn't let himself think. 'I don't want to go outside our marriage for sex for a number of reasons. I've given you a lot of them. The most important is that I find you incredibly attractive, Elena.' His voice dropped. 'I feel…something for you that I have no interest in feeling with anyone else. I doubt I could.' He couldn't help the caress he gave her, starting at that pulse in her neck, tracing the soft skin to her shoulder. 'I don't want to cheat because I don't think I'd want anyone as much as I want you.'

Elena's lips parted, but he didn't think it was only surprise. He had been terribly candid. But the quick breath that pushed through her lips when he skimmed her collarbone told him it was lust, too. She cleared her throat.

'Why would you want me to find someone else then?' Her voice was barely above a whisper.

He put an arm around her waist. When she leaned into him, he pulled her onto his lap. She immediately locked her arms around his neck.

'Did I give you the impression I wanted that?' With her closer now, he could let his lips do the work his fingers had done. He brushed them over that spot at her collarbone. She arched her neck. He kissed the exposed skin. 'Elena, what I want is for you to come to me for your physical needs. But I believe in your independence and your ability to choose what's right for you. If you don't believe in what I believe, I can't fault you for that.'

'Hmm.'

It was all she said. He didn't blame her for the lack of response when he was the reason she wasn't responding. He assumed. His hands were skimming the sides of her breasts now, his thumbs brushing over the light padding of her bra. He didn't linger there—he would lose his mind if he did—but there was no lack of places to touch. She wore a wraparound shirt with her trousers, perfectly respectable as it ended right where her pants started. It was less respectable if someone pushed the end of the shirt up to expose her skin.

He was up for the task.

Her skin was glorious. Soft beneath his touch, the faint

strip of brown he'd revealed. She shivered as he touched her, all around her waist, and when he looked at her again, she was watching him with hooded eyes.

'You know,' she said lazily, 'I was going to tell you pretty much the same thing. Not the things about finding you attractive—' she paused to give him a saucy smile '—but that I don't think going outside our marriage for something we could get inside it would be productive for either of us. Of course,' she continued, shifting so that she was straddling him, 'there's an argument that could be made for sex making things murky between us.'

Plump flesh peeked out at him from the V at her chest. He dragged his eyes up.

'Will you be making that argument?'

'I can keep a clear head when it counts,' she told him. 'So, no?'

Her lips curved. 'No. How about you?'

'Please,' he said with a snort.

'Wonderful. Personally, I don't think we should include lawyers in this.' She opened the buttons at the top of his shirt. 'They already know too much about our relationship as is.'

'If you're sure.'

Quite frankly, he didn't care. Not when she was kissing the skin she'd exposed in some sensual tit for tat that he was looking forward to exploring. She sat back at his answer though.

'The way you've handled this whole thing…makes me sure,' she repeated. 'I believe what you say. And I promise I won't cheat on you. I won't break your trust.' She shimmied off his lap, giving him a mild look when he made a noise of protest. 'We should keep things respectable between us until we're married.'

He smiled despite the lust travelling through his veins. 'Should we?'

'Yes.' She sniffed. 'I'm a respectable woman.' She straightened her top and then her shoulders. 'A respectable woman who knows the value of delayed gratification.'

He rested his forearms on his legs, watching her as amusement and dark desire tangled inside him. 'You should tell me more about that.'

With a reflection of his amusement and desire sparkling on her face, she did.

The ethics of marrying a man when she was supposed to announce her engagement to another confused Elena if she thought about it too much. But she was sure it was the right thing to do. If she and Micah didn't get married before they went to speak with her father, she was afraid they never would. She couldn't risk that. This marriage had become a shiny light in a darkness she hadn't realised she'd entered into. It made her feel strong again. She had no idea when she'd lost that feeling, but she had, and to have it back was heady. Especially when she didn't know if it was permanent.

It might be, Elena comforted herself. She might hold on to her strength, her power when they saw her father and told him the news. But the fact that she wasn't sure was enough to make her feel unsteady. Looking at herself in the outfit she was going to get married in didn't make her feel that way though. Nor did the fact that she was about to get married.

Elena stared at herself in the mirror of the hotel suite. They'd arrived in Cape Town hours before, had gone straight to Micah's lawyers and signed their papers. Something had come up for Micah's attention while they were there, and they'd parted, agreeing to meet at the hotel they'd booked a suite in until things were finalised.

She had no idea what that meant, or how it would look, but for illogical reasons it felt like the right thing to do. A part of her expected paparazzi to be at her home, taking pictures of her before she could speak with her father. Or worse, Jameson would be there. Or her *father*. None of that was likely, but she didn't want to worry about that, too. So she accepted Micah's offer of the suite, went to a store and bought herself something to get married in. Then she got ready to get married.

Her outfit of choice was a white suit and lace vest. It was pretty much like the other suits she wore, but fancier. The material was softer, more expensive because it was her wedding day. It was also much sexier than any suit she wore. The lace vest was to thank for that. It covered everything it had to, but it clung, and, with the material like a spider's web, seemed created for temptation.

She felt more comfortable in it than she would a wedding dress, she was sure. And it meant something to her that she wasn't giving up a part of herself to marry someone for her father. Although strictly speaking, she *was* marrying someone for her father. She wouldn't be marrying at all if it weren't for him.

But at least this way he can't weaponise the fact that you aren't married against you. At least now you're safe.

She hadn't realised how much she'd needed that security until now. She hadn't realised how powerful the threat of her father's presence—the threat of his demands—was in her life. Her heart pained that this was her reality, but it was time she faced it. Just as she had to face that she would rather have the peace of no longer being threatened by her father than the hope of being loved by him. Facing it made her smart. Accepting it would make her happy. At this point, she could only manage the first.

A knock on the door brought her out of her head. Thank goodness. She went to open it.

Micah stared at her dumbly. Shook his head. 'Wow.'

'Hello to you, too,' she said with a smile. It lightened the darkness inside her. Reminded her why she'd agreed to marry him. The light grew when his eyes kept dipping to her outfit. 'You know I have a face, right?'

'Right,' he said, his head snapping up. His eyes widened then, too, and if she didn't think he'd tease her for it, she'd thank him for the reaction. It soothed any remaining shakiness thinking about her father had brought.

'I thought you looked beautiful that night at the banquet. No—I thought you couldn't look *more* beautiful than you did that night at the banquet.' He blinked. 'I was wrong.'

Good heavens, this man was a charmer. She wanted to be annoyed by it, but she couldn't be. The gooeyness slid into her bloodstream, carried to her heart before she could even try.

'Thank you. I'm glad this non-wedding wedding has some wedding wedding elements.'

His eyes grew concerned. 'You know we don't have to do this today.'

She stepped back so he could walk into the room. 'You know we *have* to do this today.'

He brushed a hand against hers as he walked past her. 'Fine. We can have another wedding. A *wedding* wedding.'

'I appreciate the offer, Micah, but I don't want a wedding wedding. The elements of a wedding I want, I have. A man I respect is marrying me. Also someone so completely enthralled by my good looks that he's aware of how lucky he is.'

Micah smiled. 'I guess you do have it, then. But we can talk about it later. The business thing took longer than expected. We have about twenty minutes before we have to leave for Home Affairs.'

'It's unlikely a government-run department is going to require us to be there on time,' she replied, rolling her eyes.

'Only if you don't have connections.' He winked. 'I'm going to have a shower.'

On his way to the bedroom with its en-suite bathroom, he pressed a kiss to her forehead. Elena spent much too long thinking about the casual gesture. It was just so… *easy.* She didn't completely trust it. Not because she didn't want to; precisely because she wanted to. Whenever things seemed too good to be true, they usually were. At least when it came to Elena and relationships.

She was trying not to think about it when Micah walked into the living room of the suite wearing only a towel. It was like an advertisement, but it was anyone's guess for what. Cotton, for the towel? He was clean-shaven, so it could have been anything to do with shaving. The scent trailing after him was powerful, but not overwhelming, so perhaps he was selling some perfect combination of men's cologne. Or perhaps he was selling nothing. Perhaps his intention had always been to make her salivate.

When they met, she remembered admiring the muscle that was clear in his frame. Now, she could do it first-hand. She'd been right to think there was a layer of softness insulating that muscle. It made Elena wonder why only perfectly sculpted men were used as models. Micah's build made it clear that he was strong and human; he had a life beyond the gym.

As it turned out, that build was *exactly* her type.

And Micah knew it, too.

'Should I worry about the way you're looking at me?' he asked casually.

'Why did you come out of the bedroom if you didn't want me to look at you like this?'

'I'm looking for the suit bag with my clothes in.'

'The one you took into the bedroom?'

He smirked. 'Did I? I must have missed it.' He paused. It felt as though he was giving the electricity between them time to spark. 'I'm not mad about it.'

'I don't imagine you are,' she said in the same mild tone he used. 'Now, get ready so we can go.'

He was smiling when he went back into the bedroom, and when he emerged again minutes later, he looked exactly like the models she wanted to see in fashion campaigns. His suit was tailored to fit his broad shoulders and lean hips, and the navy colour was perfect against his brown skin.

'You look nice,' Elena said when he reached her.

His eyes danced with amusement. 'If that's what your face looks like when I look nice, I might have to call an ambulance to check your heart on days I look gorgeous.'

She rolled her eyes. 'The ego on you.'

'It's not ego when it's the truth.'

'I can't believe I'm marrying someone who said that.'

He offered her an arm. 'Let's make it official anyway.'

She took the arm with a firm grip and a nod that was just as firm. 'Yes. Let's.'

CHAPTER FIFTEEN

MICAH'S CONTACTS ENSURED they were in and out of the Home Affairs office in exactly forty minutes. Married.

They were now married.

Elena refused his offer to get dinner to celebrate. She was worried someone might recognise them and take photos. Those photos would almost certainly reach her father, and they wouldn't have the opportunity to surprise him with the truth.

'It'll be easier if we surprise him, trust me.'

That was all she said until they reached the suite.

He hadn't thought to book two separate rooms for them. Not based on the way they had responded to one another when they'd kissed, or on the plane. Their kiss after they made their vows to one another hadn't been as hot as either of those occasions, but it had lingered, and he'd felt a promise in it. Perhaps that had been presumptuous, but Micah thought he could be on the night of his wedding. Now, he doubted it. Elena had all but curled into herself, and nothing he said lured her out of it.

'Do you want something to eat?' he asked, loosening his tie.

She kicked off her shoes and shook her head. 'No, thank you.'

He didn't think she'd eaten anything since that morning, so he knew she wasn't denying it because she wasn't hungry. He was about to ask when she grabbed her phone and disappeared onto the balcony.

He didn't follow immediately. She needed time and space, clearly. Otherwise, she wouldn't have taken it. But he wanted to follow her. He wanted to demand she talk to him. They were married now, for heaven's sake. He didn't want their marriage to start off on this foot, where they didn't speak with one another.

He had enough of that growing up.

He swore at the reminder.

He'd been avoiding thoughts about his parents since he'd had that revelation about his relationship with his mother. It had been easy to do with everything that had happened in the last few days. But it was still there, as it always was. Lurking around the distractions he offered himself, waiting for an in. Apparently, he'd given it one now.

He threw off his suit jacket and tossed the tie on the bed. He undid his cufflinks and set them on the bedside table. He rolled up his shirt's sleeves, kicked off his shoes, then headed for the minibar in the living room. It was fully stocked, and he grabbed a brandy as he had the night he'd proposed to Elena. Now though, it wasn't to celebrate his actions; it was to clear his thoughts.

His mother would never know about his plan to gain her attention by partnering with Elena's father. That simple fact anchored him. If she knew, he would feel more pathetic than he already did. He was a grown man, and he thought he could get his mother to pay more attention to him through a business transaction. If he had his mother's attention, he wouldn't feel so bad about not having his father's. It would still smart, there was no doubt, but at least he wouldn't feel as abandoned as he did now. Because at least his father had left him for a reason—another family. The kind his father had always wanted, no doubt.

His mother though? She'd left him for a business. For work. Something that had no value in the grand scheme of things.

That very thought told him how much things had shifted in his brain. He'd felt the same way about work as she had for the longest time. Up until this trip to Italy, in fact. In Italy, he'd learnt he could be himself. Have his interests, and still be cared about. He didn't have to twist into impossible shapes for that to happen either. It had just happened, naturally, and it had put a lot of things into perspective.

He was still processing all of it, but he knew this: Elena was his family now. Their marriage might be a business agreement, but their relationship had more emotion in it than anything he'd experienced with his real family. He trusted her, and she wouldn't hurt him the way his mother did. He knew it.

The thought had him stalking to the balcony and opening the sliding doors. He found Elena sitting with her feet against the railing, her phone in her lap.

'It's beautiful, isn't it?' she said before he could talk. 'I will never forget Italy and everything we saw there, but this? This is…' She trailed off with a head shake. 'This is home.'

Slowly, he took a seat next to her. The hotel was in Cape Town's centre, and looked out on the buildings and streets of the business hub of the city. They were up high enough that they could see the ocean during the day. Table Mountain loomed above it, dark and steady at night. It didn't have the quietness or the quaintness that Italy had, but the sounds were familiar, the stars were brighter and, as Elena said, it was home.

'I sent Jameson a message telling him I'm not marrying him.' She wasn't looking at him, so she didn't see his head whip towards her. 'Then I messaged my father to tell him there wouldn't be an engagement party tomorrow, and that I'd see him at eleven a.m. to explain why. Figured I'd give us some time to have breakfast, at least.'

No wonder she'd gone quiet.

Even as his instincts congratulated themselves on knowing something wasn't right with her, his heart chastised him. He'd forgotten about the party. He should have known saying no to it, to the engagement, would be hard on her. She was worried about disappointing her father, about sacrificing what she wanted from him. Their wedding hadn't only been about them, not for her, and he should have known that.

'How do you feel?'

There was a long silence.

'Good.' She laughed, but it didn't sound free or unburdened. It sounded as if it was wrenched from somewhere deep inside her. 'I feel good. I'm so relieved I made the decision—the right one—and I don't feel like I'm betraying him.'

Her voice changed as she spoke, getting higher and less steady, and he stood and gently pulled her into his arms so she could lean on him.

'No, no, I'm fine,' Elena assured him, but her face was pressed into his chest and he could barely hear her. He was also fairly certain his shirt was wet. 'I'm glad it's you,' she said with a hiccup. She leaned back. She was crying, but she didn't seem to know it was happening. Perhaps she was refusing to acknowledge it.

'I'm *so* glad it's you.' She pressed her lips together. 'This feeling in my chest that used to be there isn't there any more. It feels weird. Empty. Which I know makes no sense because it also feels right.' She curled her hands into his shirt. 'We feel right.'

Now she lifted to her toes and kissed him lightly on the lips.

'I'm so glad it's you,' she whispered again, before wrapping her arms around him and hugging him more tightly than he'd ever been hugged before.

Maybe that was why it felt as if something clicked inside him.

She'd just fixed something broken.

Elena was sure there were rules about not blubbering all over a spouse on the night of a wedding. Too bad. She hadn't paid attention to the rules before when it came to Micah. Though it might have been more accurate to say their relationship hadn't followed the rules since she hadn't actively willed it that way.

She wasn't supposed to feel as though a man she'd met a week ago was the only person she could trust in the world. Trust. It terrified her that she even thought it. There were still parts of her that worried Micah would turn out like her father. Or like any of the powerful men she'd come to know in her life. But she also knew that was unfair. He had proved to her that he was different. Ever since he came to Venice to find her, he'd offered her honesty. He was protecting her. He'd held her when she cried. And when he touched her, he made her head spin and her heart fill.

It was that filling heart that was the *really* scary part about trusting him.

She tried to talk herself out of the fear. Things weren't too good to be true. It was okay to feel safe with him. She didn't have to worry about her father or Jameson or losing her job any more. She would be okay.

'I'm sorry for messing up your shirt,' she said as she

pulled back and saw the damage. Smeared make-up and wetness didn't do anything for what she was sure was an expensive piece of clothing. 'I'll pay to have it cleaned.'

'I'll take care of it,' he said. He didn't move closer to her, but it felt as if he wanted to. She had no idea how she knew it. 'Just tell me you're okay.'

'I'm fine.' She walked back into the room. 'It was residual stress from the last few days. Or the last month. I'm fine,' she said again.

'If you're sure.' He was watching her intently. 'Tea?'

'Please.' She watched him go through the motions for a second, then said, 'Who told you to give someone tea when they're feeling shaky?'

He glanced over his shoulder. 'That's a thing?' He smiled when she gave him a look. 'It's part of pop culture. I'm not completely oblivious.'

'Thank goodness for that,' she murmured. She went to the bathroom, washed her face and tied her curls up. She was still wearing her wedding suit, but she had her Italy suitcase with her. She could change into a sleepshirt.

When she left the bathroom, her tea was steaming on the table in the little lounge of their suite. The sleepshirt could wait, she thought, but took off the jacket of her suit and draped it over the back of a chair.

'Thank you,' she said to Micah, who was sitting in the seat opposite the one she'd taken.

'It's a relatively simple way to make you feel better.'

His eyes pierced hers as she took a sip from her tea. She sighed as the warmth soothed the remaining unsteadiness. Then she sighed when she found Micah still looking at her.

'I feel a lot better, I promise. It was really just tension. And all the stuff with my father and Jameson.'

'I understand.' His drink was brown liquor. He sipped it slowly. 'I also understand that you don't always deal with your feelings when they come up, which means something like this happens, I'm betting, quite frequently.'

'No,' she said defensively. 'It's never happened before.'

'Guess I'm wrong then.'

'Not entirely. I mean, I could be better about...' She trailed off. 'This is not a therapy session.'

'It's a hell of a lot cheaper than a therapy session,' he said with a small smile.

'Yeah, I only had to sell my singledom to you. Ooh,' she said when he opened his mouth, 'was that too far? Did I make you feel uncomfortable?'

'No.' He narrowed his eyes. 'I *am* wondering about your sense of humour. That was...dark.'

She laughed. 'Best you know that now before we really get stuck into this marriage thing.'

He smiled, but didn't reply, and they sat drinking their beverages in companionable silence.

'I'm sorry I worried you,' she said softly. 'I wasn't thinking about you... It'll take some time, but I'll get there, I'm sure.'

'If it makes you feel any better,' he said in the same tone of voice, 'I wasn't thinking about you either. I should have known marrying me when you had telling your father hanging over your head would be hard.'

'It wasn't—'

'You didn't want to sit on my lap yesterday because of it.' His eyebrows rose. 'Wasn't the respectability about that?'

'Well,' she said, frowning. 'I was doing a little more than sitting on your lap, Micah.'

'I don't remember that.'

There was a challenge in his voice that switched the atmosphere in the room from comfortable to...something else. She couldn't describe what it was, exactly, but it felt dangerous. Not in a *you might get hurt* way, but in an *adrenaline makes you see life differently* way. Suddenly she was aware of the breeze fluttering through the sliding door he hadn't closed. It was a warm night, uncommonly so for the season, so the wind only felt seductive.

She could have been projecting since she also just noticed Micah had unbuttoned the first few buttons of his shirt and rolled up his sleeves. It exposed delicious skin that she wanted to touch. And if she touched, she was certain she would end up wanting more…

'Well,' she said again, setting the empty teacup on the table, 'I can't blame you. I hardly remember it myself. Not the way you touched or kissed me here—' she traced the skin at her neck as he'd done with a finger '—or here.' She touched her midriff, and felt the lace material beneath it.

She wanted to take it off, to offer Micah this piece of her she'd kept guarded for as long as she could remember. But that felt too rash, too brazen. Especially after she'd exposed her emotions to him.

Except that made her feel *more* connected to him. It made her *want* to be rash, brazen. In the end, she settled for loosening her hair and fluffing the curls. His eyes followed the movement, and his fingers twitched. He wanted to touch them. She wanted him to touch them.

'I don't remember that at all,' he said, setting his own glass down. He stood. Began unbuttoning his shirt. 'I should probably get ready for bed. It'll be a long day tomorrow.'

He pulled the shirt off, revealing the body she'd drooled over earlier that day.

Damn him. He was winning.

'We both should.' She stood and unbuttoned her trousers. Heaven only knew where the modesty she'd felt seconds ago had gone to. Her competitiveness had consumed it.

Her lust had devoured it.

Rash and brazen indeed.

'Is there just this one bed?' she asked, walking past him as she shimmied the trousers over her hips. She'd worn the appropriate underwear for white trousers. She hadn't realised how appropriate it would be for her wedding night. Was that by sheer force of will or ignorance?

'I…er… I didn't think I needed to…'

His words were slow, stammering. She turned around. 'Is something wrong?'

'No.'

But his eyes were sweeping up and down her body. When they rested on her face, the hunger there threatened to steal her breath. The only reason it didn't was because she felt the echo of it inside her. She was playing a game with him, but the truth of it was that she wanted him. Not because of the way he looked without a shirt on, or because of how he wore a suit, or because he looked like the models she'd never had the common sense to conjure.

She wanted him because she wanted to be close to him. She wanted to feel that trust they'd built in a new way. He thought about her as no one had before. He was considerate and cautious, and he wanted her to be independent, to keep her own mind and make her own choices. Despite what he wanted.

It was hugely different from the conditions they'd met under. Or was it? Micah hadn't known her then. He'd been on his own for the longest time, and he didn't know how to think about other people. He hadn't learnt that from his mother since she hadn't shown that to *him*. So he'd emulated what he saw and did what he had been taught. Then Elena had come along, and communicated that honesty, that respect, were important. He'd immediately adhered to that. Though no one had taught him how to consider someone else, he'd done it for her.

That was the man she wanted to make love with. And suddenly her hesitancy, and perhaps even her shame at wanting it, melted away.

'Elena,' he whispered. 'You're so beautiful.'

She bit her lip. 'I don't think you're supposed to say that. Not if you want to win.'

He closed the space between them, his arms resting on her hips. When she didn't shift, the grip of his hands tightened. 'I don't know what competition we were in, but I'm pretty sure I'm winning doing exactly this.'

She circled her arms around his neck. 'I used to think your charm was annoying.'

His head reared back slightly. 'What?'

She chuckled. 'You always knew the right thing to say.'

'And that was annoying?'

'Yes. Because it didn't seem genuine. It seemed…practised.'

'I do *not* practise my charm.'

Again, she laughed at his indignation. 'Of course not. I just meant… It felt like something you had to do. It didn't sound like something you wanted to do.' Her eyes dropped to his lips. 'Now, I know that everything you say comes from you.' She brushed her thumb over his bottom lip. 'The real you, not the person you think you have to be.'

'Elena,' he whispered. 'Let me kiss you.'

She lifted her head to his in response.

CHAPTER SIXTEEN

HE WOKE UP as the sun hit the curtains, the thin material barely keeping the rays of light out. But he didn't mind. He was waking up to a new life, a new world, it felt like. The reason for it lay with her head on his chest, her curls tickling his chin.

Micah ran his finger up and down her spine, his body responding to the touch as much as it did the memories of the night before. He couldn't help but to think about it. To think of her, beneath him, as they made love for the first time. The complete trust on her face, flushed with pleasure. He liked to think he'd earned that flush with the attention he'd lavished on her. The worship of her body—her breasts, her thighs, what lay in between.

When she stirred beside him, he was ready to make new memories.

'Hmm,' she said as he shifted to face her. 'Morning.'

He pressed a kiss to her neck. 'Good morning.'

Her head fell back. 'I think I read an article about this once.'

His kisses made the trail back up until he was kissing behind her ear, a spot he'd discovered she enjoyed quite a bit.

'About this specifically?' he whispered.

'No,' she said with a hoarse laugh. 'It was about marriage. About being careful about what you start your marriage with because your spouse might come to expect it. I think the article was directed at traditionally female roles in the household—don't iron shirts if you don't want to keep doing it, those kinds of things—but it definitely applies now.' Her fingers slipped under his chin. 'Unless you plan on waking me up with seduction every morning, don't do it now.'

'In that case, I should probably give you more realistic expectations.'

He didn't give her a chance to reply before he kissed her. She immediately opened up to him, pressing her body close to him. He gave himself a moment to process the onslaught of sensation. The feeling of her breasts pressed against his chest. Of her skin heating against his. Of the heat of more of her—of *all* of her.

Then he focused on kissing her. He wasn't ever going to tire of it. Good thing, too, because the more he kissed her, the more responsive she became. The hand that wasn't caught beneath her trailed down his back, lingering, caressing. When it moved to his front, reaching between them, he heard the groan as if it came from outside himself.

The touches, the kisses, the intense intimacy. The emotion, the connection, the feeling of only *them*. All of it made him feel as if he were floating above his body. Then she welcomed him into hers, and he dropped back to earth, overwhelmed by pleasure and gratitude for his wife. His partner. His…equal.

After, Elena told him to shower first so she could call down for breakfast. As the water beat down on him, he pondered his thoughts during their lovemaking. Explored how they made him feel. It was strange, but there was no alarm. Only an odd kind of acceptance. This was his life now. Elena was his wife, his partner, his equal. It was a life he'd never contemplated, and now, he couldn't imagine it being any different.

He left the bathroom with a bemused smile—which immediately faded when he saw Elena. She was standing in a hotel robe, phone in her hand, a tight expression on her face.

'I put it on to check if my father called.' Her voice was disturbingly detached. 'He did. I didn't listen to the voicemails, but I have a message that says I'd better have an explanation.'

He walked over and pulled her into his arms. 'We knew this was going to happen, Elena. Your father was never going to accept the embarrassment of cancelling an engagement party without an explanation.'

'Even *with* an explanation he might not.' She was chewing her thumbnail even as her head rested on his chest. 'I know we expected this. I just…'

She didn't finish her sentence, only pulling away from him to look out through the sliding door.

'Elena?'

She took a deep breath. 'This is going to be hard.'

He shoved his hands into his pockets. She'd moved away from his physical offer of comfort, and he didn't know if he should keep trying. He didn't know if he had the right to. It was a confusing thought to have after what they'd shared the night before, that morning. After his thoughts in the shower. But he didn't know if a spouse or partner or equal meant… Well, this. Emotional comfort, he supposed, though that didn't feel like an adequate explanation.

It was all clouded, muddled, so he focused on what was clear.

'It is going to be hard.'

She gave him a shrewd look. 'I'm pretty sure you're supposed to say something more supportive than that.'

He curved his lips, but it wasn't a smile. 'I *am* being

supportive. If I tell you it'll be easy, you'll know it's a lie. At least this way, we can prepare for hard.'

'We?'

He shrugged, though her question felt as if it clouded things even more. 'We're partners, aren't we?' He didn't wait for an answer. 'I'm expecting this to be like a business meeting. A particularly difficult one, but a business meeting nevertheless. We're offering him the reality of our situation. The way he engages with that is his problem.'

She kept biting her nail. He took a step forward. Stopped.

'Elena, look at me.' Her eyes lifted. 'You don't have to be afraid of him.'

'Don't I?' she asked in a small voice.

'You're married to a man who's just as powerful as your father is. Maybe more. Externally,' he clarified. 'But *you're* the person who's dealt with him your entire life, despite being afraid of him, and come out on the other side.' He couldn't resist walking to her now, or tipping up her chin. 'That takes courage. You've built a successful career outside him. That takes strength. You're kind and sharp and annoyingly quick-witted—' he smiled when her eyes narrowed a fraction '—and that makes you just as powerful as he is. More.'

Her eyes filled, and she bit the bottom of her lip when it started to tremble. Then, in movements quicker than he could anticipate, she rose to her toes and gave him a passionate kiss. She pressed her body into his, wrapping her arms around him and tightening them so much he thought she was trying to become a part of him.

But she already has.

The thought had him breaking off the kiss, pulling away. He was panting, but he didn't know if it was from her or from the shock of that thought.

She gave him a little nod, acknowledging his response

in some knowing way, before disappearing into the bathroom. Micah stared after her for a long time.

What did she think she knew? And why did he feel as
if that would change things more than any realisation he
had about their relationship?

It was hard to imagine that once upon a time, she'd lived
in this house with her parents. She'd thought she had a
good life. A normal life. But she hadn't known then that
mothers didn't tend to be as cool with their children as her
mother had been with her. She hadn't known that most
children didn't feel as though they needed to earn their
parents' love and approval. That fathers didn't treat their
children as objects.

Her parents' divorce had changed many things, but most
of all, it had opened her eyes. And when she'd started seeing, something had cracked open inside her. Nothing had
been able to fill that crack. Not friendships, though she
didn't have enough of those to judge. Not her job, though
she'd tried her hardest for it to. But this morning, when
Micah had been tenderly outlining all the things that meant
she could take on her father, Elena had felt the crack fill.

She was forced to face it then. Forced to face what she'd
been running from since Italy.

She was in love with him.

It was concerning in many ways. They'd known one another for just over a week. A *week*. She scoffed at people
who claimed to fall in love so quickly. Now, she wanted
to talk to them all and ask them how it was possible. Did
they fall for the other person's sincerity? Their willing-
ness to change? Did they fall for the efforts their person
made *to* change?

Or was it the quiet determination their partner vowed

to protect them with? Or the passionate tenderness they made love with?

Was it just that Micah was this way? That he was the person she was meant to be with? That falling in love with him was simply inevitable?

She couldn't deny they'd had a connection from the moment they met. Getting married had sealed that bond. Sleeping together had solidified it. Deepened it. In between the pleasure and sighs, Elena's world had changed and she didn't know what to do about it.

Especially when she was sure Micah's world had stayed the same.

Micah squeezed her hand. She looked over, realised he'd been watching her. He thought the turmoil on her face was because they were about to see her father. Tension skittered through her body. Yes, this meeting was more pressing than her feelings. She'd have to put off dealing with falling in love with her husband until *after* she'd dealt with the first man whose love she wanted, but would never receive.

She stilled. Then nausea welled inside her and she had to exert every ounce of control to ignore it.

They walked to the large house that had been painted from white to grey since she'd moved out. She hadn't been here since. Then her father summoned her to his office and now here she was. She should never have answered the call.

The area in front of the house had been designed around a circle. Trees and bushes formed the inner and outer circle, with gravel filling the spaces in between. There was already a car parked on the gravel when they arrived, and it took her all of two seconds to recognise it as Jameson's. Her father's cars would be parked in the garage at the back of the house. Something rebellious inside her had almost guided Micah there as well, but she resisted. She didn't understand why she felt disappointed that she had.

'You okay?' Micah asked as they rang the doorbell. He spoke under his breath, as if he was worried someone would hear. Clever. She wouldn't put it past her father to put a camera at the door so he could watch unsuspecting guests.

'Good.' Her voice cracked.

'Do you want me to do this alone?'

At that, she turned. Gave him a faint smile. 'I have to do this. I have to.' She spoke as much to herself as she did to him.

He opened his mouth, but the door opened before he could.

'Elena,' the woman at the door said when she saw them, her eyes going wide.

'Rosie,' Elena said, not quite believing it. 'You're still here.'

She walked into the open arms of the John housekeeper, feeling a warmth she'd missed since they'd started preparing for the meeting. Rosie had always been kind to her, though professional—her parents wouldn't accept anything else—and Elena hadn't seen her since she'd left either.

'Of course I'm still here.' Rosie's voice still held the traces of her native country. 'You would have known that if you'd come to visit.'

'You know why I haven't,' Elena said, the warmth dimming. 'It wouldn't have gone well for either of us.'

'I see,' Rosie said, her eyes tight. 'Well, child, you've grown up well. I am happy about that, if nothing else.'

'And I'm happy you *are* still here. I thought your sharp mouth would have got you into trouble.'

Elena was teasing, but it was a legitimate concern. Rosie meant well, but she was too honest. She spoke her mind even when she wasn't asked, though that had been reserved for Elena's ears. But with no one else listening, Elena had wondered if her father had been a recipient of

Rosie's comments. If he had been, there would not have been the same indulgence.

'My mouth is not so sharp these days.' Her eyes were, though, and they told Elena Rosie had learnt that lesson the hard way. Her heart beat painfully, but she managed a smile.

'I hope it'll still be with me.'

'Child, you are supposed to announce an engagement today. Your husband will have a sharp mouth to put you in your place.'

'There it is.' A relieved laugh tickled Elena's throat, but despite the reprieve from her tension, she wasn't in the mood to laugh. 'Actually, that's why I'm here. To introduce my father to my husband.'

She gestured to Micah. He held out his hand, smiling as charmingly as he'd been taught. But before he could speak, a voice thundered from the top of the stairs.

'What the hell did I just hear?' A tall, stately man descended, but stopped after three steps. 'Did you say this man is your husband?'

Elena's breath left her for a second. Somehow, despite it, she managed a small, 'Yes, Dad. This is my husband.'

Micah wanted to throttle the man who made Elena's voice change like that. From warm to cool; from strong to almost broken. He'd hated everything about the last hours they spent together. She'd barely spoken to him, the fire that was essential to her nowhere to be found.

If he thought it was only because of her father, he would have understood. But something about the way he caught her looking at him—the way she quickly looked away when he did—made him think this had to do with *him*. It was easier to blame her father. Easier than examining everything he'd done, trying to figure out what had made her respond this way.

He forced himself into the present. Elena's father was coming down the stairs, followed by a man Micah recognised as her would-be fiancé. The man's gaze was on him: a sharp, accusatory stare that didn't bother Micah a single bit. If looks had any effect on him, he wouldn't have been the man he was, nor the businessperson.

'Please explain to me why you're saying you're already married when we're supposed to announce your engagement tonight?' Cliff John asked stonily.

Elena's shoulders hunched slightly. Rosie inched forward, as if to comfort Elena, but Elena shot her a look and the woman left the room, shaking her head. Micah shifted closer to Elena, just a fraction, so she could feel him by her side. No matter what was going on between them, he would show his support. That was what their marriage was about.

She cleared her throat. 'Dad, this is Micah Williams. He's the man I was doing the story on for the newspaper.' Elena turned to him. 'Micah, this is my father. Cliff John. And this is…' She faded, then shook her head, her shoulders straightening again. A fierce pride shot up inside him. 'This is Jameson St Clair.'

He waited until both men were level with them before moving over the gleaming white tiles to offer his hand.

'Mr John. I've heard a lot about you.'

He left it at that. Cliff John stared at him for a moment, but took his hand. Micah turned to Jameson. He didn't offer a hand, but gave the man a slight nod.

'Mr St Clair.'

He moved back to Elena's side immediately.

'Elena, is it true?' Jameson asked before Micah got there. 'You're married to him?'

'Yes.'

Elena stared at him in a mixture of defiance and

strength. Micah resisted his smile, but welcomed the enjoyment. *This* was his Elena. This was his wife.

'Explain yourself, Elena,' Cliff said. 'I won't ask again.'

Micah ground down on his teeth to keep from responding. He waited for Elena—they all did. She was quiet for a long time, though her defiance and strength didn't falter. She didn't need his protection, he realised. Perhaps externally, as he said, but not where it mattered.

'I didn't want to marry Jameson,' she said eventually. Simply. 'You didn't give me much of a choice, so I had to create one for myself.'

'So you married *him*?' Jameson snapped. 'The man I told you was using you to get to your father?'

Micah did his best not to look at Elena, but he understood why her anger had been so fierce now. She had every right to be angry, regardless of how she had found out, but finding out from Jameson? From another man using her? It must have stung. Micah would have done anything to go back and change his motives. He didn't want to be on the list of men who'd tried to use her.

'It isn't so different from how you wanted to use me, is it? At least Micah had the decency to care about me.'

'I can't imagine why you thought you didn't have a choice, Elena.' Her father's voice was disinterested, as were his eyes, but Micah wasn't fooled. His lips were thinned under his white moustache, the skin between his eyebrows furrowed. Micah was good at reading people, and Cliff John was upset.

No, not upset. Livid.

He could feel Elena tremble at his side, but her chin lifted. 'You threatened my job.'

'Did I?' Cliff asked, edging forward. Elena moved back, without realising it, he was sure. Micah shifted, too, but he wished with all his strength he'd stood behind her so she would have backed into him and realised what she was doing.

'I thought I was merely offering you something you've always wanted: to make me happy,' Cliff continued.

Micah felt the change in Elena's body at that statement. The trembling stopped; *everything* stopped. She didn't move, didn't blink, didn't breathe. Just when he thought he would have to intervene, she exhaled sharply. Her inhalation was just as sharp. She looked at Micah, and the emotion there, along with everything else he'd witnessed over the last few minutes, handed the baton over to him.

'And she still is, Mr John,' Micah said smoothly. 'Elena conveyed your intentions regarding the marriage you proposed.' Disgust coated his tongue at that line, but he continued. 'We believe we can still reach those ends with different means.'

Micah didn't spare a glance at Jameson when the man snorted. He had Cliff's attention. And if he had it, Elena didn't. She could process whatever was happening in her brain.

He angled his head. 'You've probably already heard of me, Mr John, but I'll assume you haven't and tell you who I am.' He didn't pause at the slight rise of Cliff's eyebrows. 'I sell a lifestyle to all of Africa. Recently, I've expanded to Europe. I don't have to tell you what a partnership between my business and yours could mean for both of us.' He let it linger. 'But mostly for you.'

'You're arrogant.'

'Confident,' Micah corrected. Then smiled. 'Perhaps arrogant suits, too. It's semantics, honestly. Would you like to discuss semantics, Mr John, or would you like to discuss how I can make John Diamond Company the talk of the diamond industry? Not only in Africa, but the world?'

'You can't do that,' Jameson said, speaking for the first

time since Micah started his pitch. 'John Diamond Company existed long before you and your business. What can a partnership with you do for their profile that they couldn't do themselves?'

'I imagine it's the same thing a partnership with your family could do for them.' He still didn't look at Jameson directly, because he knew it would annoy the man and impress Cliff. 'Except on a much larger scale. I just signed a contract with the second biggest jewellery store chain in Italy. The contract was based on me providing them with diamonds from Africa that are reliable, well known and ethically sourced. I was hoping you'd be my supplier, but, if not, I'd be happy to offer the opportunity to someone else.'

Micah experienced the stunned silence with the same satisfaction he did every successful business deal. He was certain he'd won Cliff John over. He wouldn't need to secure Elena's job—although he'd already put out feelers to do that, if necessary—because Cliff had come over to their side. His daughter's disobedience had brought damn near world domination for his company right to his doorstep. He wouldn't dare do anything to make her unhappy now.

It wasn't the emotional support Micah wanted to offer her that morning, but it was the best he could do.

'Mr Williams—may I call you Micah?' Cliff's tone had eased into a charm he was willing to bet was Cliff's 'closer' voice.

'Of course. We are family.'

'Micah.' Cliff's smile was all teeth. 'Why don't you come up to my office and we can discuss this in more detail?'

Micah turned to Elena. Her expression was closed, but that wasn't unsurprising if she was still processing. 'Would you like to come with?'

'No,' she said softly. She smiled at him, but it didn't reach her eyes. Alarm fluttered through him. 'No, thank you. I don't have anything to add to that conversation.' Elena waved a hand. 'I'll see you at home.'

'You're leaving?'

'Only because it's business.' She leaned forward and brushed a kiss on his cheek. Then she turned to her father. 'I assume this is fine with you?'

Her voice was cool and, again, pride filled him. She was fighting back. He knew it cost her, but they would deal with that together.

'Perfectly fine.'

'You asked me to be here, Cliff,' Jameson said, all rage. 'You told me we'd get to the bottom of this misunderstanding. How am I supposed to explain this to everyone? What am I supposed to do with everything we've bought and planned for today?'

'I'll cover any financial costs you've incurred,' Micah said, looking away from Elena to Jameson. 'It's the least I can do.'

'You son—'

'Jameson,' Cliff interrupted. His voice was a mirror of the coldness of Elena's, and stopped Jameson in his tracks. 'I think it's clear there hasn't been a misunderstanding. I'll make sure people believe the engagement was only rumours. When they announce the marriage to the world, all will be forgiven.'

'Wh—what about me?' Jameson asked, eyes wide. 'What about my family's company?'

'This is business,' Cliff said, his smile shark-like. 'Deals fall through every day.'

Jameson stared at them, stunned. Elena broke the silence.

'I think I'll get Rosie to call me a car.'

She left all three men with that. Micah stared after her, willing her to look back, to acknowledge their win. She didn't.

CHAPTER SEVENTEEN

ELENA SPENT THE ride to the hotel wondering what she was going to do next.

The suite was booked for another night, but she couldn't bear to stay there again. She cherished the memories that had been created there. She'd got ready for her wedding there. She'd talked and laughed and made love to her husband there. She had never felt closer to another person than she had in that room.

It would be a constant reminder that she was in love with Micah and he would never be in love with her.

She might have been overreacting. But as she'd watched him go to bat for her she'd realised two things. One, she loved him even more deeply than she first thought she did. He protected her exactly as he said he would. More importantly, he supported her. His steady presence, his proximity... All of it had given her the courage to finally stand up to her father. To finally see, *truly* see, the extent of how her father was using her.

Cliff knew that she wanted his love and approval and he'd used that against her. A man like that didn't deserve Elena's love and attention. It hurt more than she could possibly express, but she had been clinging to her father for too long. To the hope that he would love her because if he didn't, who else would? Not her mother, who had forgotten Elena existed years ago. Elena didn't have friends, or other family members. She had a husband, but her second realisation told her he wouldn't love her either. Because as she watched him handle the situation with her father, she knew he was perfectly happy with the arrangement they'd made.

Their *business* arrangement. Not a marriage, but a partnership. She couldn't live with him, sleep with him, love him knowing that he would only ever see it that way.

She'd spent her entire life trying to get one man to love her. She couldn't spend the rest of it trying to do the same with another.

She pressed her lips together as she packed her belongings into her bag and called a car. She was about to grab her wedding outfit in the garment bag in the closet, but stopped. It would only hurt her to see it. For it to remind her that she loved her husband and needed him to love her back, but he didn't. Without a backward glance, she left the room and went to her home.

When she was there, she opened her laptop to check her emails. She'd been avoiding work and the implications of her marriage for much too long. Micah hadn't replied to the email about her story, so she assumed he had no notes. Not that it mattered. There was no way she could write the story as his wife.

Her heart broke as she outlined the information for her boss, attaching what she had written so whoever got assigned to the story would benefit from her trip to Italy. She'd come back the day before, yet it felt like a dream. The exploration, the privacy, the newness. Now she was back home, feeling more exposed than she ever had, by a situation she shouldn't have put herself in.

The response from her editor—that was somehow a rebuke, congratulations, and request in one—told her to focus on work. It was reliable. And with Micah as her husband, her job was safe. She closed her eyes. Shook her head. Focused. She might have messed up her old assignment, but she wouldn't mess up this new one. She would write about her whirlwind courtship with Micah for the newspaper. It would be more fiction than fact, but the readers would never know. And they would love it. If they did, this could still be a way forward for her.

She wrote back, then got up to make herself a cup of tea. She was nursing it on her couch when the knock on the door came.

She'd been expecting it. With one last sip of her tea, she set it on the coffee table and opened the door.

'Elena?' Micah walked in, moving in for a kiss. She assumed. She stepped back before he could touch her. She wouldn't torture herself with more memories. 'Are you okay? Your things weren't in our room when I got back.'

'You found me,' she said easily, closing the door behind him. 'Do you want tea? Coffee? I don't keep alcohol in the house. I'm sorry about that.'

'No.' His brow was creased so deeply she was sure there would be indentations once it smoothed. 'I want to know if you're okay.'

'No.' She went to sit on the couch again, bringing her tea with her and crossing her legs. 'But I will be.'

He didn't move a muscle, just kept standing there. She could almost see inside his brain. He was trying to work out what to say. Going through everything that had happened to check whether something had gone wrong.

He wouldn't be able to see it. He hadn't done anything wrong; she'd been the one to change. She was no longer happy with their arrangement. She needed him to love her. She needed the person she was in love with to love her. The fact that he didn't would torment her every day.

She'd do everything in her power to try and change his mind. She knew she would because that was what she'd done with her parents. With her father. And look where that had brought her.

Micah didn't deserve that. He didn't deserve her trying so hard to please him she lost herself. He'd made his arrangement with her; not the version of her that she thought he wanted.

Beyond that, Elena finally saw that *she* didn't deserve it. She deserved to be fulfilled and happy. She deserved to be herself.

'What's going on in your head, Elena?' Micah asked eventually.

'We made a mistake,' she said softly.

'What do you mean?' He moved now, sitting on the chair opposite her. His body was stiff.

'Last night,' she forced herself to say. 'Sleeping together. We shouldn't have done that.'

'Why not?'

She fortified her heart at the curt words.

You expected this. But if you don't do it now it'll be worse.

'I was right. It made things murky.'

'Is that supposed to make sense to me?' He stood. She merely lifted her chin. She wouldn't get up. Her knees wouldn't hold her. 'What are you saying? What are you *really* saying?'

She didn't know how to respond to his anger. She was already feeling vulnerable, and every word he said battered against her defences. She wanted to tell him that she loved him, that she wanted him to love her, but she couldn't stand to be rejected. Not after hearing her father use her love for him against her. Not after figuring out her feelings for Micah. It was all too much.

But she could do this. She could get through this. She had with her father, and she would now. After a few more breaths, she said, 'We have a business arrangement, and it works. We both got what we wanted from my father today. We'll likely continue to be successful working together in the future. But sleeping together adds a dimension to this relationship that…that won't work.' She took another breath. 'Business, Micah. Let's keep it that way.'

It was clawing at him, the familiarity of this situation. But the claws came from a dark place. He couldn't afford to shine a light on it when he needed all his attention to understand Elena. Her posture was stiff and cold, worse than it had been when they'd been at her father's. Her face was beautiful in its aloofness, he could admit, but he didn't like it. He preferred the beauty of her smiles, the animation in her eyes. When she was teasing him, or gazing at him with lazy pleasure. He wanted *his* Elena back, not the one who brought the claws and destroyed the light. The one he didn't understand.

'Why?'

'I told you—'

'You gave me some rubbish diplomatic answer,' he hissed. 'I want to know *why*? What changed between last night—this morning—and now?'

He realised he sounded desperate, but he couldn't help it. Panic had joined his complicated emotions, spurring the words.

Slowly, she set her tea down on the table in front of her. It was a round glass table held up by metal spirals painted gold. What a strange thing for him to note. Especially when his eyes shifted to her hands and he could see them shaking.

'I'm doing this to…to protect us.'

'From what?'

'From me.'

She blinked rapidly, showing emotion she hadn't given him since he'd come to find her. He thanked the universe for it. Emotion was what made *his* Elena, and if she was showing it, even in this form, it meant that she was coming back. If she came back, maybe this wasn't some warped repetition of his childhood.

He didn't have a chance to process that thought.

'I spent my life trying to get my father to love me because he's the only person I thought would.' A tear ran down her cheek, but her gaze was steady on him. Strong. 'A mistake. He showed me a fraction of approval once and I mistook it for love. I based all my hope on it.' She shook her head. Cleared her throat. 'I... I can't do the same thing with you, Micah.'

Her words paralysed him.

His thoughts kept running though. The panic kept fluttering. But now he saw it was for a completely different reason. Before, it had been because he was worried she would reject him—them. Now, he was worried she was about to change them. For ever.

'You're happy with the way things are between us.'

'I... Yes. It's *us*,' he said, his voice cracking towards the end.

'I'm not,' she replied softly. 'I want more from you. I *need* more. Can you give me more?'

He opened his mouth, but the claws were back, threatening to shred his tongue if he replied.

'It's okay,' she said, voice hoarse. 'It wasn't a fair question. I shouldn't have asked it.'

'Elena.' He shook his head. 'What are you saying?'

'You know what I'm saying.' She stood now, squaring off with him in a raw way that broke his heart. 'I can't say it. I won't say it, and complicate the arrangement we have.' She continued without letting him speak. Which was good. He had nothing to say. 'I'll keep to the agreement. I'll attend social functions, or business functions. Have Serena sync our social diaries and send me information and I'll be the perfect spouse.'

'I don't…expect you to do something you don't want to do.' He spoke slowly. Heard the emptiness of it. 'I won't use you like they did.'

'You won't be using me,' she said, shoulders straightening. 'We have a contract.'

'I won't keep to the contract.'

She stiffened. 'I'm a woman of my word.'

'If you were a woman of your word, you wouldn't be changing the terms of this relationship on me,' he spat. He knew he'd regret it later. Didn't care.

'Do you think I want this?' she demanded, ice melting into fire. 'I want to focus on healing after this whole thing happened with my father. I want to stay your friend, or whatever the hell we are, Micah. That's what I *want*. But the one thing isn't possible with the other. I can't be your friend if I want to heal.'

'I'm not your father.'

'No, you're my husband. But you can't love me in the same way he can't love me, so what does it matter? I can't live the rest of my life like that.' Her tears reappeared, but she ignored them. 'How can I live the rest of my life wanting someone to love me *again*? How does that help me heal?'

He took a breath, wanting to say words that would make them both feel better. But he couldn't. He was afraid, and the fear pulsed so loudly, he couldn't hear what words they were. He could only hear the warnings, could only feel the alarm. He said nothing.

'See?' she said softly. 'I was trying to protect us by giving you an easy way out. Now we're just in pieces.'

Slowly, so slowly, he walked to her door. 'Elena,' he said, turning around. 'I'm sorry. I want to—'

'Don't,' she interrupted. 'I understand. You can't love me because if you do, it makes you as vulnerable to me as you are to your parents. They've caused you enough pain. At least this way, you don't have to worry that I'll do to you what your parents did to you.'

His world stopped for a second. As it did, the darkness overtook his senses and he saw she was right. But it didn't matter because, now, *he* wanted to protect himself. To fight back the darkness, the fear, and crush the claws. He couldn't do that with her. She would remind him that he wasn't as strong as she was. She would remind him of a light he could never possess.

With one last look, he walked away from his wife.

CHAPTER EIGHTEEN

ELENA MIGHT HAVE got married, but her life was as normal as it had been before her wedding. Apart from the fact that she had to pretend to be living a blissful, married life, of course. Her editor had read her piece on her and Micah's marriage, had decided it would be a great companion piece to the profile Elena had done on Micah, and printed both. One on the front page of the business section; the other on the front page of the entertainment section.

Separation from her husband had no part in that. So Elena lived the lie.

No one would know it wasn't the truth. Micah's profile was high enough that no one expected him to carpool with her to work or pop in for lunch. Micah certainly wouldn't tell anyone. Things would become more complicated if there was an event Micah was at and Elena wasn't at his side. But it had been six weeks and that hadn't come up yet. She would worry about it if it did. In the meantime, she would enjoy the boost those articles had given her career.

After some adjustments, apparently. Her new workload had been a welcome distraction from her emotions, but it had left her feeling run-down. She was tired all the time, even when she woke up, and she had no appetite. It was more or less the same way her body had responded to the adjustment of boarding school, and then the school nurse had done some tests and prescribed some vitamins. She'd felt so much better afterwards though, so she forced herself to go to the doctor even though she had no time for it. She wasn't as understanding when they called to discuss the results.

'Doctor, I'm sure you have a lot of things to do today other than tell me my iron is low.' Elena offered the woman a winning smile. 'We can make this quick.'

'I appreciate the offer,' Dr Jack said dryly, 'but it's a little more complicated than an iron problem.'

'Oh?' She sat up straighter. 'No anaemia? Some other vitamin deficiency, then?'

'None of the above.' Her expression was kind. 'You're pregnant.'

'I'm—' Elena broke off with a laugh. 'Please. There's no way I'm...'

She trailed off when she realised there was a way. A very logical way, really, since she wasn't on anything and condoms were...

'Are you sure? I haven't had unprotected sex.'

'I am sure. This indicates you're about seven weeks pregnant?' Dr Jack showed her some page with levels of hormones, which she honest to goodness couldn't take in. 'If you tell me when your last period was, I'll be able to tell you more accurately. I also have an ultrasound machine in my examination room. If you'd like more certainty, we can do that?'

Elena nodded numbly. She did everything numbly after that. Except when the doctor smoothed gel over her belly, pressed the wand against her stomach, adjusted some things on the machine, and a heartbeat sounded in the small room.

A heartbeat. That was coming from inside her.

'That sounds good,' Dr Jack said, examining the machine. She tilted it towards Elena. 'This is your baby. They're still a small little thing at this point, which is normal based on how far along you are. Seven and a half weeks now that I have that information about your period.'

'But...the sex was...'

She couldn't finish that with the heartbeat still pumping. It was so fast. Was that normal?

'Well, we count based on the first day of your last period, though conception might take place later. Don't tell anyone I said so, but it's hard to say accurately.' There was a pause, and then the sound disappeared. Dr Jack set the wand back at the machine and sat down beside her. 'I can tell by your reaction that this is a surprise. I can talk to you about your options. I can also give you a copy of this so you can listen to it later when you're deciding about your options.'

'That seems a bit harsh, Doctor,' Elena managed to say. 'Am I supposed to make a decision while listening to...to that?'

Dr Jack smiled. 'You don't have to listen to it. I just want you to have the option of listening to it. Now, let's get you cleaned up here and have a conversation about what's going to happen next, shall we?'

'Mrs Williams? Mrs Williams, please.'

For a moment Micah wondered what Serena was doing calling his mother. But Elena was already in front of him before his brain could figure out the calling was happening inside his office.

'I'm sorry, Micah. She wouldn't listen to me.'

'I have to talk to you,' Elena said, looking a little wild.

He took her in—greedily, though he would never admit it—and made sure she was okay. Then he gave a little nod to his PA and waited until the door was shut.

'Wait, why did Serena call me Mrs Williams? She calls me Elena.'

'You've let the world know we're married, haven't you?' He clung to the coolness, though everything inside him yearned to hold her. 'Why have you barged into my office in the middle of a workday?'

She frowned. Shimmied her shoulders. 'I have to talk to you.'

He merely lifted his eyebrows.

'It's important.'

He tried not to let his concern show. It was tough, particularly since he'd spent most of the last six weeks wondering how she was. Even when he managed to bury it by burying himself with work, it popped into his thoughts. When he was in a meeting, or walking to one. When he got home and headed to bed and wondered what it would have been like to come home to her. To have her waiting in his bed.

Those thoughts flooded his mind more and more as the days passed. It would have forced him to face what was keeping them from being together even if his parents hadn't suddenly contacted him. His mother had reached out when she'd heard about his partnership with Cliff John. It had been less than he'd hoped for, but more than he'd expected. She'd arrived at his office, primly asked him out to dinner. When he'd accepted, she'd spent the evening talking about work. They had nothing else in common, he supposed, and still he'd longed for more. He hadn't heard from her since, and he had no desire to reach out from his side either.

It took a while to accept it, but he realised it had been in motion from the moment he'd proposed to Elena. He knew then already that the reunion with his mother would underwhelm him. It had tempered his expectations, hence the surprise at her offer of dinner. He'd been even more surprised when his father had congratulated him on his marriage. Micah hadn't read the profile Elena's newspaper had done on him, uninterested in reliving Italy when his memories of her feistiness, her laugh, her kiss there kept him awake at night.

Apparently, the article had been combined with an article on their whirlwind courtship and marriage. His father had relayed that fact; Micah hadn't read that article either. When his father asked if Micah and Elena wanted to join him and his wife for dinner some time, Micah told him he would get back to him. He never had. One, he and Elena weren't doing anything together any more. Two, if his father only wanted him to join his family for supper when he was a married man… Yeah, he could stuff that invitation.

His dream about reconciling with his parents had come true in the last weeks, and he was unhappy. Because he saw how damaging that dream was—how damaging *they* were. They'd taught him that opening his heart would only hurt him. Even when he wanted to open his heart, fear of disappointment kept him from doing so.

Screw them.

'Are you going to tell me this important thing?'

'It's better if I show you.'

Elena didn't seem deterred by his sharpness. He was annoyed that he wanted her to be. That he wanted to affect her in the same way she affected him.

She wanted a real relationship with you. What more do you want?

Anger and frustration—at himself—kept him from answering that question. It didn't stop his inhalation when she came to his side of the desk, putting a flash drive into his computer. He was a masochist, probably, but he

wanted to see if he'd remembered her smell correctly. He
had. It was still as soft and tempting as it had been that
week in Italy.

That night in their hotel room.

'I have no idea what this is, but—'

A rhythmic sound stopped his words in their track. It
was fast, loud—a *da-da,da-da,da-da* that went on and on
and on. His eyes lifted to the screen of his computer. It was
black and grey, but the grey was in a strange shape that—

Oh. His brain put the sound and the screen together
and… Oh. *Oh.*

'What are we going to do about this?' Elena croaked at
him. He looked at her. She was watching the screen, looking as helpless as he felt. 'It's a…a…'

'A baby.'

Now she looked at him. 'Yeah. A baby. That we made.'
She laughed in a way that clearly indicated she didn't find
it funny. 'Micah, we made a *baby.*'

A string of questions ran through his mind.

*Are you sure? How sure? How did you find out? Are you
okay? Is the baby okay? How are we going to be parents?*

He got stuck on the last one, mainly because he thought
Elena was, too. The other questions were kind of already
answered by her appearance there. Of course she was
sure—she wouldn't have been there otherwise. She'd found
out from a doctor; he was looking at the evidence of that.
And he was sure she would have told him by now if they
weren't okay. She wouldn't have asked what they were
going to do about it if they weren't…would she?

'Are you both okay?'

'Yeah, we're fine.' She exited the window on the computer, as if she was done watching the grey and black and
hearing the *da-da,da-da,da-da*. 'I'm tired, and eating's
a problem, which is why I went to the doctor in the first

place, but I'm fine otherwise. And things seem normal with the...you know.' She shrugged. 'It's early.'

He got stuck on one piece of information. 'You're nauseous?'

'No. I just...don't want to eat. I doubt that has anything to do with the pregnancy. I forgot to ask, actually. I guess I'll have to read up on it.'

'What else could it have to do with?'

She quirked a brow. 'Really? That's what you want to talk about?'

'I'm still processing the other thing.'

Her expression softened. 'Stress. I've been working a lot. The...um...the articles about you helped.'

Are you working a lot because of me? Because you're trying to forget me the same way I'm trying to forget you?

It was presumptuous, but he was sure that was why.

It wasn't only presumptuous though. It was unfair. She was the one who'd taken a risk. She had put her feelings out there, hoping for something more. He couldn't give her more.

Except apparently, he had. If she was keeping the baby, they'd be as linked by their child as they were by their marriage contract. More. They could ignore their marriage contract. They'd been doing that for six weeks now. They couldn't ignore their child.

They were going to have a child.

'Can I help?' he asked, a little woodenly. 'The stress probably isn't great for the baby. So. Can I help in some way?'

'Oh. No. Not unless you can write my stories for me.'

'I can get you an assistant to—'

'It's okay, Micah. I can manage.'

'With the baby?' he asked. 'Are we keeping it?'

'We?'

He looked at her. She didn't show any emotion, and he realised she was protecting herself. 'You don't need me, I know. But this is *our* responsibility.'

'When did I ever say I didn't need you?' she asked, a flicker of angst crossing her face before it was gone. 'I'd like to keep it. I… I don't know anything beyond that, but I'd like to.'

'Me, too,' he said softly. Unexpectedly. He had never thought he would be in this situation, so any answer he gave would have been unexpected. But wanting this child? He needed a moment to process because he did. He wanted this child.

'Look, I know things are…weird between us, but this child is going to need us. Both of us. We need to give them the best that we can, and we'll need to work together.' She moved away from him, clutching her handbag closer to herself. 'I can put my feelings aside so our child can have the kind of parents and family we didn't.'

He should have thought about that. About being a parent, about his parents, about himself. He didn't want his child to have the same life he had. He wanted better for them.

'You're right.'

'I know.' Her lips curved into a small smile. 'Why don't we take the day to…process? We can meet tomorrow morning to talk about things.'

He nodded again.

'I'll send you a message with the details,' she said. Then she was gone. As if she'd never been there at all.

But she had been there. Today, and almost seven weeks ago now when she'd come with him to Italy. She'd changed his life. She'd shown him what it was like when someone cared about him. She'd helped him grow. She'd offered him love and understood even when he couldn't offer it to her in return. At least not in the way she needed it. Now, she was giving him a family.

With one glance at the door, he opened the file with the video of his baby. Watched it for a long time. Knew he'd hear the sound of the child's heart beating in his dreams that night. And the next. Maybe for ever. It wouldn't be such a bad thing.

The longer he listened to it, the more grounded he felt. The more courageous he felt. This child gave him hope. He'd have an opportunity to do things the way they were supposed to be done. He would give his child the things he didn't have. Love, support, a family. His child would give him the same, if he allowed it.

Elena would have given him the same, if he'd allowed it.

He sat back, the truth of it hitting him over the head. Of course, he already knew on some level that he was in love with her. Why else would he be so terrified of letting her in? He compared her to his parents even though she didn't deserve it. He compared her to his parents even though, in Italy, he'd already known she wasn't like them. She'd offered herself to him unconditionally, and he'd been too cowardly to accept. Or to offer himself to her in return.

It didn't mean that he didn't feel the same way about her. He loved her, but telling her would mean risking rejection. He was tired of rejection. He was tired of working so hard not to face it, but having to face it anyway. It was a fine thing to worry about after he'd rejected his own parents. After he'd rejected her.

Now they were having a kid, and he felt so stupid it had taken that for him to be brave. But that little heartbeat asked him to be brave. Even if it was too late, he needed to try. If there was a chance his child wouldn't have to witness a broken relationship as he'd had to with his parents, he had to take it. If there was a chance he could be with the woman he loved enough to have a family with, he had to try. Elena had every right to reject him now, but he wouldn't let that stop him. This was the final step to freeing himself from his past with his parents. And freeing himself would mean fullness. Happiness. Love.

He'd known about Elena's pregnancy for all of thirty minutes, but it had already changed him. And *that* was what love from a parent to a child should look like. Courage. Growth. Trying. His child would never know what conditional love would feel like. There would be no hoops for them to jump through; there would only be love.

He hoped he had the opportunity to treat Elena the same way.

CHAPTER NINETEEN

ELENA KNEW HAVING a child was a life-changing experience. She hadn't expected finding out she was pregnant would be as dramatic.

After leaving Micah's office the day before, she'd gone home and cried. Not because she was pregnant—though heaven knew there was some of that in there, too—but because she missed him. She wanted him back in her life. She wanted them to raise their baby together and be a family.

It took her a while to realise she would have all of those things now that she was having their baby. Not in the package she wanted, but she would have them, nevertheless. For it to work, she would need to set her feelings aside. Her desire to not be around Micah so he didn't remind her of what she didn't have no longer mattered. Her biggest responsibility now was her child. And since she'd told Micah it was possible for her to ignore her feelings, she wiped up her tears and faced her reality.

Still, she didn't sleep much that night, her mind too busy processing. The one good thing was that it helped her realise her child deserved the love Elena didn't have in her life. All things considered, it would be nice to explore that with a child. Special, too, because she'd made that child with someone she cared about. It wasn't a perfect situation, but that was okay. She would focus on her baby and let that heal her.

The doorbell rang promptly at eight the next morning. She expected nothing less from the man she'd married.

'Hey,' she said when she opened the door. 'I thought it would be easier to meet here. More private, too. There's been some interest in our relationship since the article.'

'I heard,' Micah said. 'Can I come in? This is heavy.'

She nodded, letting him pass. He was carrying a box, which he set on her kitchen counter. It was strange seeing him in her space. It obviously wasn't the first time he'd been there, but she hadn't been paying attention then. But seeing him between her brown couches and cream walls and her various gold accents caused something in her chest to swell.

'You heard? I'm sorry,' she said with a wince. 'You've probably been teased about it.'

'No.' His expression told her that was the most ridiculous thing he'd heard. She resisted her smile. 'My father told me.'

'Your father?'

'He seemed to think marriage solicited a dinner invitation.'

She waited a beat. 'Your tone tells me little else solicited dinner invitations.'

'Nothing else,' he corrected.

'Well. I guess it's good that he's trying.' Again, his expression told her it wasn't good. 'How did the dinner go?'

'I didn't accept.'

'Why not?'

He shrugged. 'I'm done jumping through hoops for people who should love me unconditionally.'

'Oh. Wow.'

They stared at one another for a few seconds, then both started laughing softly.

'It's a good realisation,' she offered.

'It could have come a bit earlier,' he replied with a small smile.

'We all learn things at our own pace.'

'Yeah, we do.'

The amusement faded, but their eye contact remained. They were communicating on some level. Since she didn't know what level that was, and he wasn't offering anything more, she gestured to the box.

'What, er...what's in the box?'

He turned and looked at the box as if he hadn't brought it. She went to his side while she waited for an answer.

'It's for you,' he said after a long pause.

'It is?' She frowned when he pushed it towards her slightly. 'What's inside?'

'A care package.'

'A...'

She stopped speaking when she opened the box and saw what he meant. The box was filled to the brim with items. Herbal teas, crackers, ginger biscuits, books about pregnancy, movies about pregnancy, chocolate, chips, cocoa butter and stretch mark cream, a framed photo of their baby that he must have got from the video she'd shown him the day before. There was much more, but her hands faltered as she felt a strange tightness in her throat.

'You put this together?'

He ran a hand over his head. 'I looked up things that would be helpful to you. I didn't know about the creams and stuff, but a woman at the nature store helped me. She also said a cup of peppermint or chamomile tea would help with stress. That could help with your appetite thing.'

'I thought I said that wasn't a part of my pregnancy.'

'It can't make it any easier, can it?'

'No. It can't.'

She sat down on the kitchen stool in front of her counter and rested her hands in her head. The tightness in her throat had progressed to a burning at her eyes. She didn't think she'd cry, but she was pretty close to it. She spied a glass bottle of lemonade in the box—lemonade? Why?—and she reached in and took a sip. The sourness distracted her from the way her body was reacting. It helped her get her emotions under control.

Or not.

'You can't keep doing this.'

'What?'

'Reminding me that you're a great guy.'

'Oh.'

He looked as if he wanted to say more, but he didn't. So she said, 'I'm sorry. I shouldn't have said that. We should talk about the baby, right? Okay. I think—'

'Elena.'

'No, Micah. I can't… We can't do this.'

'Elena.'

She felt the tears falling down her cheeks. 'I'm sorry. I just… I need more time. I'll be okay with how things are between us soon. I promise. So let's just—'

'Damn it, Elena, look at me.' His voice was edged with desperation. It was reflected in his eyes when she met his gaze. 'I was a fool for pushing you away. That has nothing to do with the baby, and everything to do with me.' He hissed out a breath. 'I guess what I'm trying to say is that I love you. I love you, and I want to try again.'

In his dream the night before, Elena had fallen into his arms and told him she wanted to try again, too. But he was wide awake now. He knew that because now she was simply sitting, staring at him. He deserved it, he told himself, his heart thudding. He deserved the torture of waiting for her to say something.

'I think I misheard you,' she said slowly.

'You didn't.'

He reached over and took her hand. Prayed she wouldn't pull away. Then got distracted by the way she felt. Even in his dreams, he hadn't been able to capture what it was like when Elena touched him. The heat, the need, but, most importantly, the rightness that settled inside him.

'You're right, I pushed you away. I was scared. Scared you would be like my parents and reject me.' His grip tightened on her hand. Still, she didn't pull away. 'I don't know what it's like to love someone and have them love me back. I *do* know what it's like to love someone, and have them not love me the way I need to be loved.'

'Yeah, it sucks,' she said sullenly.

His lips curved. 'I know. And I'm sorry I made you feel that way because I didn't want to trust that first part. The part where I love you and you love me back.'

'You hurt me,' she said in a small voice. 'In the same way my parents hurt me. In the same way your parents hurt you.'

'I know. I know,' he said for the third time in as many minutes. 'I'm so sorry, Elena. If you'll let me, I'll spend the rest of my life making it up to you.'

She didn't speak for a long time. At first, he struggled against his instincts. He wanted to pull her into his arms, tell her they could be a family, kiss her, then take her to her bedroom and make love to her. But none of what he wanted mattered. It was only her, and her choice, and whatever that was, he would respect it.

But she was still holding his hand. That had to mean something.

'Do you really love me?' she asked. 'Not the baby—*me*. Would you have come here and told me this if it wasn't for the baby?

He took a breath. 'Yes. But probably not for a long time.' At her frown, he explained. 'I was already on my way to realising how stupid I'd been. I didn't only speak with my father, but my mother, too—later—' he said when she opened her mouth '—and I realised that they weren't worth the effort I was putting into them. They'd taught me to fear love, but they weren't worth what I was sacrificing with you.'

He pushed her hair back.

'But realising it didn't mean I had the courage to come here and tell you that. I would have needed time to, and maybe a knock over the head. Or a pregnancy surprise.' He gave her a small smile. 'But I would have told you regardless, I promise. Because I love you, and I have, probably since I saw you in that unicorn nightshirt and you told me I didn't see them because I didn't believe.'

'I'm not sure that's what I said.'

'We can argue about it later,' he teased, but sobered quickly. 'If you still want me here later.'

'I'll always want you here,' she said softly. 'My love for you isn't conditional. Even when you're being dumb, I still love you.'

'You know exactly what to say, don't you?' he asked, but before he was even done talking, she was hugging him so tightly he could barely breathe.

'I'm scared, too, you know. But I love you. I love you.'

His arms folded around her. 'I know you're scared. But you're braver than me. You're stronger than me. Our baby is going to have a wonderful mother.' He lifted her chin. 'You don't have to be scared any more. Your love is safe with me. Believe me.'

Her lips curved. 'I do. And yours is safe with me. You're safe with me.'

Her expression told him she would make sure he knew it for the rest of their lives.

And he would do the same for her. That understanding, their love, meant more to him than he could express. So he leaned forward and kissed her instead.

EPILOGUE

Four years later

'WHO THOUGHT BRINGING two children to Italy was a good idea?'

'I believe that was you,' Elena said easily, lifting her son's ice-cream cone when he tilted it to the side to lick his fingers. 'You said something about bringing them to where our love was established, or something equally corny.'

'You used to think that was charming.'

'Now I think you carrying a baby girl in a carrier at the front of your body is charming.' She brushed the hand she didn't hold her son with over the head of the baby gurgling against Micah's chest. 'It's also very sexy.'

She leaned forward and kissed him, lingering even though she probably shouldn't have.

'Hmm,' Micah murmured when she pulled away. 'How long until naptime?'

As if answering, Kai shouted, 'Bird!' at her feet. It startled his sister, and Ellie immediately gave a loud cry.

Elena laughed. 'Two children in Italy is not as romantic as two adults in Italy.'

'That's for sure,' Micah said, comforting Ellie.

Elena followed Kai to the pigeons, warning him against

feeding them his ice cream. She'd learnt that lesson the hard way her first time in Italy.

She'd learnt a lot since her first time in Italy. To be fair, it had been almost four years ago. She'd got married and had two children since then. Her job was still important to her, though a little less than her family was, and her recent promotion seemed to prove it. The newspaper was undeterred by her family planning, which she knew made her lucky. She also knew she had a unique angle on many of the stories their readers were interested in. The wife of a South African businessperson who wasn't afraid of telling the truth.

Fortunately, she had a husband who supported her.

They'd taken their time to build the foundation of their marriage. It was a strange approach considering they were married within a week of knowing one another and pregnant after their wedding night. But they'd both been hurt by their families. They'd made progress, even before they'd decided to try a relationship, but it still took work. And they put in the work. In between pregnancy and caring for an infant. In between caring for a toddler and finding out they were pregnant again.

Relationships took constant work, and neither of them was afraid of it. In fact, they welcomed it. Because working meant they still wanted to be there. They still wanted one another. It was a damn good feeling to be wanted.

'I don't suppose we could take them on a gondola ride,' Elena remarked later that day. 'No—what am I saying? Kai would be in the water within minutes.'

Micah laughed. They'd swapped children, both of whom were asleep, exhausted by the excitement of the day. She and Micah were walking back to the hotel, but lazily, the summer's day not dictating haste.

'Last time I was in a gondola I spontaneously proposed. Perhaps this family is not made for gondola rides.'

Now Elena laughed. 'Ah, we were such babies then. Could you imagine being where we are now, then? You, dominating the luxury goods industry. Me, dominating childbirth.' She shook her head. 'What powerful parents we are.'

'One more powerful than the other.' Micah made sure Kai was secure, then put an arm around Elena. 'I watched you give birth. It was…wild.'

'A euphemistic way to put that.' She leaned into him. 'I think this is the happiest I've ever been.'

'You say that all the time.'

'I mean it every time. More so today.' She stopped walking and turned to him. 'Our first family trip is to Italy. I wasn't this lucky. You weren't either. But we're doing it for our kids. There's a lot to be grateful for.'

'They won't remember this, you know,' Micah said, but his expression was soft. 'It didn't matter where we took them on vacation.'

'That's obviously not my point.'

'I know.' He lowered and kissed her gently. 'You're what these kids will be most grateful for some day. I know that because that's how I feel.'

'Right back at you, Daddy.'

'I thought we agreed you wouldn't ever call me that in public.'

'I thought you would keep a sentimental moment sacred, but you didn't. You used logic. So I guess we'll both just be disappointed then, won't we?'

Micah laughed and they resumed walking. It was companionable and quiet. It was perfect.

'Remind me to ask Kai about the pigeons when he wakes up,' Micah said suddenly.

'What about the pigeons?'

'I want to know if he thinks the ones in Europe are different from those in Africa, like his mother.'

She slapped him lightly on the shoulder, and his laughter echoed in the dusk.

* * * * *

THEIR NINE-MONTH SURPRISE

LAUREL GREER

To my critique partners—Ashley, Bee, Deana, Kelly, Stacy and Tiana. I couldn't do this without you (or the carbohydrates and bubbly). Thank you for your love, support and brilliant feedback.

Chapter One

Marisol Cardenas's car was only the second one in the lot when she pulled up to the Sutter Creek Veterinary Clinic. *Excellent.* She'd purposefully planned to arrive ahead of opening hours, before Lachlan got busy and found yet another excuse to blow her off. When she'd left him a voice mail back in January, she'd told him they could talk later.

She hadn't meant five months later.

But after he hadn't called back, she tried the clinic. And wow, his receptionist. A peach, that guy. The snarky "He's in the Andes"—she'd laughed at that one. As if Lachlan would be traveling given how committed he'd been to starting his dog training facility. The subsequent "He's in Australia" and "Why don't you fly to Korea and see him there instead of clogging up my phone line" excuses had been equally creative, but not nearly so funny.

And she'd been too busy throwing up to test what the fourth song and dance would be.

Message received, Lachlan.

But have I got one to give to you.

He could use his receptionist as a human shield all he wanted, but couldn't avoid her in person. And yeah, it had taken her months to get her life together enough to be able to come back to Sutter Creek. But now that she'd arrived, she was here for good.

Her second-hand maternity clothes and mismatched dishes and many, many textbooks were now stacked in the living room of her new apartment, a tangible—and heavy—reminder that her life was in Montana, now.

And with it, her child's life. *Lachlan's child, too.*

She'd driven past his apartment building on her way into town yesterday, and his truck had been right out front. Only the boxes and suitcases stacked to the roof of her ancient hatchback had prevented her from ringing his buzzer until he acknowledged her existence for the first time since December.

"We going to do this, baby?" she murmured, laying her hands on her round belly. "Yeah, I know. It's time."

Time to get out of her car and tell Lachlan he was

going to be a daddy. Even though he wasn't going to like it.

Acid burned her throat. He'd been honest, at least, when they'd been in the tangled sheets of their passionate, vacation-only fling.

I'm not looking for any kind of commitment, Marisol. I don't want strings.

Nor was she upset that he didn't want a relationship with her. She didn't want that, either. A failed marriage during her undergraduate years had taught her that finishing a degree and having a relationship did not mix.

But parenthood was different. Hopefully, with time, Lachlan would come around to the idea of being a father. As a vet tech in his sister's practice and a search and rescue handler, he was incredible with dogs and other animals, so she knew he had the capacity to care. He was well loved in Sutter Creek, too, or at least it had seemed so based on the sheer volume of hugs and conversations he'd been dragged into the few times they'd emerged from his bedroom while she'd been here on holiday in December.

And unless she stopped staring at the cheery blue clapboard building, one of the tiny ski town's well-meaning residents would spot her, correctly guess her child's paternity, and pass on the news to Lachlan before she mustered up the courage.

She could grip her steering wheel and deep

breathe all she wanted, but no relaxation exercise would make this easier.

Rejection, here I come.

She hoisted herself out of the car, groaning at her lack of grace as she reached in to snag her satchel off the passenger seat. Her third trimester belly—she'd passed that marker last week—guaranteed she'd be waddling until she gave birth.

The sun promised a warm June day, but it still hadn't managed to take the morning chill off. She wrapped her thin cardigan over her ever-expanding bump and headed for the door. If Lach's shifts were the same as they'd been six months ago, he'd be working seven to four, so would have gotten here over an hour ago. His truck wasn't in the parking lot, but that didn't mean anything. He'd told her he usually biked to work in the summer months. And as much as she'd wanted to forget about Lachlan Reid, her brain had collected facts about him like a crow with shiny objects.

She shut her car door and walked along the cement sidewalk to the front entrance. The renovated rancher had pretty white shutters and planter boxes filled with geraniums and marigolds. The bright dots of color swam in her vision as she momentarily held her breath. She inhaled deeply—not far off what she'd been learning in labor and delivery class—and tried the door handle. Locked. Damn.

She knocked as loudly as she could in case Lachlan was off somewhere feeding animals or something. Her PhD focus on canine psychology meant she'd visited a fair number of animal clinics, and they usually had similar floor plans, with kennels in the back.

A lock snicked from the inside, and the door swung open.

Marisol's heart raced.

It needn't have. The person standing there had Lachlan's dark blond hair and the same cheek dimples, but was about a head shorter and female.

"Maggie," Marisol croaked at the veterinarian. The woman was dressed in purple scrubs, and still had the same pink-on-porcelain complexion as when Marisol had briefly met her in December. Not like Maggie's brother's outdoorsy tan. His skin had been almost as brown as Marisol's, though her complexion came from her Colombian dad. She spent way too much time holed up in university libraries to get any color from the sun. "Uh, nice place you have here. I like the blue paint."

Maggie crossed her arms and cocked her head. She took a step back. "Looking for Lachlan, I assume?"

Marisol swallowed down her panic. She hadn't gotten much of a read on the vet the last time she was in town. She'd been too busy kissing Lachlan to pay much mind to his family.

Keep it casual. "Yeah, I thought I'd stop by and

say hi." *Before nine on a Monday? Like that's going to throw her off the scent?*

Judging by Maggie's laser gaze on Marisol's belly, veterinary school covered simple arithmetic. "*Just say hi?*"

Marisol pressed her lips together. There was something sacred about learning about becoming a parent, about that knowledge transfer. She couldn't violate it, no matter how much Lachlan's avoidance stung. She'd been lying to her own brother since she realized she was pregnant, claiming her child was the result of a New Year's Eve date with a fellow doctoral student. And she'd dodged the "Are you, uh, expecting a roommate at some point?" question when she'd accepted her keys from her new landlord yesterday. The woman, Mackenzie Dawson, worked for the ski resort and knew Marisol's brother well. Not exactly the person to be spilling secrets to. But Marisol had to handle Maggie carefully. Now that she'd moved to Montana, a good relationship with her child's aunt was critical.

"I got to town yesterday and was exhausted. Crashed the minute my brother finished helping me unload my car," she said quietly. "This is my first chance to speak to Lachlan."

"Sweet baby jelly beans," Maggie murmured. She backed up until she rested against the waist-high counter of the reception desk. An odd mixture of anger and hope stretched her mouth. "I'm going to be an auntie?"

"I need to talk to your brother."

The derision darkening Maggie's brown eyes made Marisol's stomach lurch. Apparently, neither Reid sibling was going to be excited about a new addition to their family.

"You should have talked to him months ago," Maggie said. "I know you haven't yet, because if you had, and if you're going to tell him what I think you're going to tell him, he would have filled me in." She waved a hand at Marisol's stomach. "It's not like this is new information for you."

Holy crap, were the halogen pot-lights overhead emitting solar flares? Sweat beaded on Marisol's brow, and she shucked out of her cardigan, then held it in front of her bump. "He blew me off."

"He wouldn't do that," Maggie insisted.

No, sorry, he had your receptionist do it for him.

Holding in the sarcastic response, Marisol spread a hand over the cotton of her maternity blouse and aimed for a neutral smile. "Maggie, I really don't feel right confirming or denying anything with anyone except Lachlan. Is he here?"

The other woman shook her head. "He's starting late." She checked her watch. "He'll be here in ten."

Marisol gritted her teeth. "Mind if I wait?"

"You'd better." Maggie's lips flattened, but she motioned for Marisol to enter and have a seat in the waiting area. "You're going to let him be involved, right?"

"If he wants to be." Marisol winced. *Ack.* There went not confirming anything. Sure, it was a technicality at this point, but still. She mentally kicked herself as she eased into a seat in the space adjacent to the reception desk, filled with pet-friendly vinyl chairs and stunning wildlife photography.

"If he *wants to be*?" The exclamation nearly rattled the front window. "You clearly don't know Lachlan very well."

How could she have? She'd come in December to visit her brother, Zach, and his fiancée and child, and had spent a good chunk of the vacation in a passionate fling with Lachlan. Hours before catching the plane home, she had brought up the impossibilities of a long-distance relationship. It had been nice to have that as an excuse instead of having to explain her feelings about commitment. Lachlan had saved her further, though, throwing out his "no strings" line. He'd explained that everything in his life had to focus on expanding Maggie's clinic with a training facility for working dogs.

She could thank her divorce for teaching her to appreciate Lachlan's kind of clarity.

She'd understood his single-minded priorities, too. She'd delayed her academic goals when she married young. Her husband had been a grad student, and she'd reduced her course load to part-time so that she could work to pay a bigger chunk of their bills. They'd planned for her to go back full-time once he finished his degree. But he'd accumulated more bills than she'd known about.

Even though the judge presiding over their divorce had ruled that her ex was responsible for payment, he defaulted on the payments, and the creditors had come after her. Settling his debts in a desperate attempt to avoid bankruptcy had made it even harder to finish her degrees in the ideal amount of time. Working part-time, scrambling for scholarships and grants, borrowing from her parents—she'd been playing catch-up for close to a decade. She'd learned to bury her pride, to scrimp and plan.

And when she realized she was pregnant, she came up with a new plan. One that she loved, no matter what Lachlan decided to do. Living in Sutter Creek meant she was blocks away from her brother and his family. That was more hands-on support than she had in Vancouver, given their parents and sisters lived a couple of hours outside of the city. And she'd even been able to arrange to complete her PhD prospectus and dissertation research at the university in Bozeman. She'd been lucky to find a professor who was experienced in canine psychology. God, given how involved Lachlan was with avalanche dogs, he probably knew her supervisor. His interest in canine behavior had been one of the reasons Marisol had started flirting with him in the first place.

Now that she was set for support and her degree, it didn't matter if he was too busy building a dog-training empire to get involved with their baby. She wouldn't be left in a hospital, grieving alone…

There won't be any grieving this time. Just joy.

Swallowing down the memories threatening to emerge, she glanced up at Maggie, who was still standing by the reception desk with a perplexed look on her face. "I know your brother as well as he let me know him."

Maggie's brow crinkled. "Are we talking about the same Lachlan?"

"Given your nose scrunches up identically when you're confused? Yeah."

"Oh." White teeth tugged on a lipstick-free mouth. "You know a few things about him, then."

I know a lot *about him.* Mainly things to do with his naked body, though. Nothing useful for figuring out coparenting.

Instead of trying to turn any of that into something shareable, she shrugged.

Maggie's throat bobbed, and her eyes grew damp. "He's going to be elated. He's wanted a family forever."

Elated? That didn't make any sense. "But—"

Marisol's phone chimed in her satchel. "Excuse me, that might be Lach. I texted him yesterday." Yet another unanswered message, but at least she could say she'd tried.

She pulled out her phone. Just her brother, a text

asking her to call. "Crap, I need to make a call, but my phone isn't set up with US minutes yet—sorry to impose, but is there one I can use?"

"Behind the reception desk. Dial six to get out. Just make sure you vacate the seat by eight fifty-nine, or face my receptionist's wrath."

"If that's the only wrath I face today, I'll be golden," she muttered as she crossed the room to the reception counter.

Maggie caught her wrist. "What do you mean?"

Heat rose up Marisol's neck. "It was a joke. Poorly timed, maybe, but let's be honest—you've been edging on laying into me since I got here, and I wouldn't be surprised if your brother did the same, so..."

"He's not going to—" Short, sun-streaked curls bobbed as Maggie shook her head and released Marisol's arm. "Crumb cake. I shouldn't get involved in this."

Without a parting greeting, she disappeared down the short hallway and behind a door, which promptly slammed.

Marisol flinched, and the motion made the baby shift. She rubbed a hand over her stomach and sat behind the reception desk. "Shh, everything's under control."

Or, rather, she thought it had been. Arrive in Montana safely—check. Move into apartment—check. Complete degree requirements—underway. Love baby with entire being—check, check, check.

She loved a well-crafted list.

But *he's wanted a family forever…* If Maggie meant family in the sense of wife, kids and dogs, that wasn't an item Marisol was prepared to even think about, let alone write down.

Lachlan Reid swung open the side door to his sister's veterinary practice and the high-pitched bell tinkled, as per usual. The walls of the rear hallway were still hurting for a fresh coat of pale blue paint. His German Shorthaired Pointer, Fudge, ill-mannered as hell when not working as an avalanche dog, pushed past him and headed for her food dish as she always did.

Nothing else was the same.

The blueprint roll in his hand, the one he finally had the savings and financing to see come to fruition, canceled out everything familiar this morning, from the well-loved laminate on the floor to the faint barks signifying breakfast was being served in the kennels.

He'd spent five months working his ass off teaching other SAR dog handlers abroad, which had provided extra seed money to make this blueprint come to life. That, plus the grant he was a shoo-in to receive, meant things were a go. Success didn't smell sweet, it smelled like kibble and disinfectant and the dirt floor of the ancient barn out back that he'd finally renovate into a dog training facility.

He wiped his sneakers on the mat and traded his hoodie for the lab coat hanging on a hook in the staff room. Grabbing a coffee from the gurgling machine, he headed down the short hall behind the front desk, toward the head of long, chestnut-brown waves tied in a no-nonsense ponyt—wait, what?

He froze in his tracks. Coffee slopped on the floor.

Their receptionist was a guy.

Who did not have a ponytail. Especially not *that* ponytail.

Lachlan knew that ponytail. Intimately. And it, and the woman it was attached to, was supposed to be in Vancouver, not Sutter Creek.

Lach had spent a good deal of time under the mistletoe with his hands in Marisol Cardenas's hair.

On her shoulders, hips… Hell, all over her curvy body.

His stomach heated and palms tingled at the possibility of getting to repeat the experience.

The reception desk ran parallel to the hallway, forming a T. And why she was sitting behind it, well, he wasn't ready for the answer. His feet refused to move forward.

I'm seeing things. Got affected by the altitude on the glacier yesterday. But two long blinks affirmed he wasn't suffering from delayed-onset hallucinations. Maybe his sister let Marisol in?

Who cares? He could think of far worse ways to spend a Monday morning before the literal animal hordes arrived. Or rather, he would have back in December before Marisol had preemptively cut off any possibility of a relationship by asking, "this is just a fling, right?" He'd stammered out some sort of response, saving his pride by telling her he was too busy with work to get involved with anyone.

And when he'd gotten a last-minute invitation to work out of the country after the original trainer had backed out, jumping on the offer had been about distracting himself from his memories of Marisol as much as the welcome financial opportunity.

He'd only returned a week ago, and adjusting to no longer living in a hotel room was taking longer than he'd expected.

The dog, finished with her meal, pranced past Lachlan to greet Marisol. Not with her usual wiggle-ass maneuvers, though. Fudge gave Marisol a few tentative sniffs, and let out a whine before sidling up and putting her brown-and-white head in Marisol's lap.

"Hey, baby," Marisol crooned, scratching the dog behind her ears.

Affection warmed his core, but he shut down the response. *She's talking to the dog, not you, idiot.*

"Hey, Lach."

Yep, no endearment for him. She didn't even turn around, kept her focus solidly on whatever book she was holding.

"Hey, baby," he mimicked. Not to the dog, and by the way Marisol sat straighter, she knew it.

He closed the distance and hitched a hip on the desk. "Mari—"

Holy. Jesus.

His lips went numb. He gripped the counter with both hands to stop himself from sliding to the floor.

And she gripped her textbook to her abdomen. Her very *round* abdomen.

Marisol's golden-brown skin paled. Her throat bobbed once, twice. She muttered something in German that couldn't be anything but profanity. "Lachlan…"

A thousand responses bounced around his head, but all he managed to get out was one crude word.

Burying his fingers in his hair, and unable to control his gaping mouth, he stared at her stomach. He was versed in domestic animal gestation, not human, but that bump had to be around the six-month mark. He didn't need to count backward to know what that meant.

Her lip started to wobble and indecision swam in her green eyes. "Say something."

Get it together. He coughed, then croaked, "Is it— I mean, did we— But we used—" He ended the nonsensical half sentences with a blitz of expletives.

A nervous smile kissed the edge of her full lips. "Not quite sure if I caught what you meant, but I think it was along the lines of 'yes, it's yours.' We made a baby. And we did use condoms. But that one time, we started without…"

"Without," he echoed, dropping his hands to his sides. "Weren't you on the pill?"

"Yep. And I'll save you from asking—I used it correctly. The chances of pregnancy were miniscule. And yet…"

He coughed again. The desk creaked as he let it take more of his weight. "And you didn't say anything? It's *June*, Marisol."

He dealt with distress all the time. Pet owners and ranchers, pale and shaking when their animals were in need of care. Idiot hikers, defensive and cranky when they had to admit they should have taken a compass instead of relying on their now-dead cell phone's GPS. But nothing he'd run across in either job quite matched the mix of ire and dread flashing in Marisol's green eyes.

"You have got to be kidding me." Her clenched teeth muffled her words.

"Am *I* kidding *you*? Try the other way around."

"I'm clearly not." Mouth tight, she waved a hand at her stomach.

Son of a… He'd run his hand over her abdomen dozens of times before. Back when it had been flat. And now it *wasn't*. His *baby* was in there. "Last time I checked, 'mind reader' wasn't anywhere on my résumé."

"So learn how to return a goddamn message!"

His tongue lay useless, thick in his mouth.

What was she talking about? None of this made sense. He massaged his still-numb lips with his fingers, stopping himself from reaching out and touching the bump, so damned foreign. Something niggled in his gut. The need to learn her new form until it was familiar again.

And whatever she'd just shrieked at him, too, about returning his—

Oh. Oh, *Christ*.

"What message?" he asked quietly.

Twisting her hands, she fidgeted with her clothes, straightening the summery blouse and skirt. "The ones I left you in *January*."

January, when he'd been in the mountains outside of Santiago. "I was having a hard time getting service, so there were a few times I went a few weeks without checking. They must have gotten automatically deleted."

"Deleted." She mouthed it more than spoke it.

"Why didn't you call back? Once I left Chile, reception was way better."

Thank God she was sitting down—she started shaking hard enough he'd have worried she'd lose her balance.

Concern jolted through him. He could deal with being pissed off later. Right now, her rapid breathing ranked as way more important.

He knelt on the floor in front of her and turned

her chin to catch her gaze straight on, and pressed a fingertip to the notch in her wrist. Her pulse fluttered, way too fast.

Then again, his was about the same.

"Deep breaths," he said.

"Chile… As in the Andes?" she murmured. The regret braided into her dawning understanding sucker punched him. "And Australia? And Korea?"

"And New Zealand," he said. "But if you knew…"

"I didn't. I thought he was lying."

"Zach?" Who else but Marisol's brother would have told her where Lachlan had been?

"No, whoever answers the phone here."

Evan. Evan, who had no qualms about enforcing a "no personal calls on my phone line" policy, and did so with his patented level of sarcasm.

He reached out to pull her into him, one hand on the base of her skull, the other at the small of her back.

Holding her again was a goddamn gift. Holding her while she was pregnant with their child… Indescribable.

The child she didn't manage to tell you about for half a year. His brief haze of amazement evaporated.

"What about online?" The question came out a snap.

She startled and stepped away, falling back into the desk chair before he could get a hand out to steady her. "What about it?"

"I'm on Facebook. And checked my email regularly."

"Facebook? I'm supposed to send you a message about this on social media?" she said, pointing to her belly. "No way. You were avoiding my voicemails, so what was the point? I figured I'd have to do it face-to-face the first chance I could get."

"I *wasn't* avoiding you," he emphasized.

Though the set of her jaw suggested she was having a hard time adjusting to the knowledge. "I thought you had instructed your receptionist to lie to me. I wasn't up for being ignored electronically, too. I was puking my..."

She slammed her lips shut.

The dog plastered herself to Marisol's side. She flattened her liver-brown ears and glared at Lachlan. Fudge clearly didn't need the adjustment time that Lachlan did. She seemed to have appointed herself Marisol's protector.

And Lachlan understood that. The need to ensure Marisol's safety seeped into his bones, into every corner of his soul. It didn't erase his questions, though. Even if he did extend her the benefit of the doubt, understanding why he was finding out she was pregnant when she was six months along was only a glimpse of the trail they were now going to have to hike together.

"How long are you here for?" he asked.

"Here...in the office?"

"Uh, no, in town."

"Right. Baby brain," she whispered, closing her eyes.

"Do you expect to raise our child in Vancouver? Away from me?" he prodded. "I can't just up and move my business before the shovels even break ground."

"Lachlan," Marisol cut him off softly. "I know we have lots to talk about—"

"You *think*?"

A warbly throat cleared from behind him, on the other side of the half wall that separated the reception desk from the waiting room. "Lachlan Reid, that boarding school your parents sent you to may have been lax on manners, but your grandmother did not allow you to speak to ladies like that."

Damn it. The last thing he wanted was for half the town to be up in their business before he'd had the chance to discover exactly what that business was. Lachlan cocked a brow and turned to regard Gertie Rafferty, the silver-headed dynamo who'd been keeping the Sutter Creek gossip chain going for most of her eighty-plus years. Mrs. Rafferty's Russian blue peered up at Lachlan from her perch in the woman's arms.

He didn't bother to remind Mrs. Rafferty that his workplace wasn't the most appropriate of places for a dressing-down. He'd dated her granddaughter one teenage summer, and had stolen too many cookies off the trays in the back of the older woman's bakery to ever be considered fully grown.

"Boarding school was fifteen years ago, Mrs. Rafferty," he said.

"So you've had plenty of time living here to lose those entitled habits." She turned her attention to Marisol. "Hello, dear. You look as pretty today as you did when you last visited. That baby's all out front. Must be murder on your back. And thank goodness Lachlan is finally home so you can bring him to task."

Marisol blushed. "Oh, well, we're not together..."

He cringed. Was Marisol even going to want to publicly acknowledge him as the father? He sure as hell was going to insist on it, but until they'd had the conversation, it wasn't any of Gertie's business. "Mrs. Rafferty, it's not what you think—"

"A handsome devil like you, dear? It's exactly what I think. I had four children. I know how reproduction works."

"You're making assumptions—"

She cut him off with a piercing look, punctuated with a *mew* from her cat. "And you're making your grandmother roll over in her grave, letting your sweetheart walk around without a ring on her finger."

His brain scrambled to get caught up. Sweetheart? Ring? Both words he could get used to when Marisol was on the receiving end, but the flat look on her face indicated she did not agree.

"We need a little time," he said.

"Doesn't look like you have much left," Gertie said with a pointed glance at Marisol's belly.

He coughed. "Well, we—"

"He didn't know about the baby," Marisol said between gritted teeth. "He didn't know I was coming." She looked at Lach with all the honesty in the world in her eyes. "Talking to you was my number one priority, though."

"Instead, everyone's been talking *about* her all morning," Gertie added. Marisol groaned, and the older woman's pale cheeks flushed. "Just curiosity, dear." She eyed Marisol from behind thick-lensed glasses. "The buzz in the bakery is that you've signed the lease on Mackenzie Dawson's old place. And Lachlan's name has come up a few times, too, given how he was squiring you around before Christmas."

Marisol sighed and splayed her fingers on her stomach in what looked like an unconscious gesture. Her cheeks reddened. "We've had all of ten minutes. Surely Sutter Creek can extend us a few hours, days maybe, before people start calling caterers and booking churches? Because I don't want to—"

He put a hand on her shoulder, and she stopped talking. Good. Because for some reason, he didn't want to hear that she didn't want to marry him. Especially not with an audience. Not that he was going to suggest that. Marriage wasn't something to jump into, even with a baby involved. But having her confirm she'd already written off the idea… It was as if a handful of the mealworms they kept in the supply room were inching up his spine.

The room had filled up some during Mrs. Rafferty's questioning. Two more people with their animals sat in the waiting area, and shoes squeaked on the floor down the hall. Maggie called Mrs. Rafferty into a treatment room, but the older woman's pointed observation of him made it clear he should expect more of the same during Kittay's appointment.

Evan, their twentysomething receptionist, came behind the desk and shooed them out of his space with a flick of his wrist. "You're a minute late already, Lach. You have a presurgical exam on Petunia in room three, and after Dr. Mags does her thing with Mrs. Rafferty's cat, you're up with her vaccinations."

"Evan," Lach said gruffly.

The willowy man paused. "Yes?"

"Marisol tried to call the clinic while I was away."

"Lots of women called, as per usual. I told them exactly where you—" Evan stopped talking as his gaze landed on Marisol's stomach.

Lachlan had seen Evan dangling by one hand from the underside of a cliff overhang. The guy was fearless.

Except in the face of an irritated pregnant woman, apparently.

His face turned whiter than his platinum blond hair, and he scrunched his nose apologetically. "Oh.

Well. You should have told me why you were calling, honey."

"What, announce I'm knocked up to someone I don't know?" she said. "I wasn't going to tell anyone before I told Lachlan."

The explanation stilled some of Lachlan's shaky parts. He wanted to be mad. Wanted to wallow in having been kept in the dark. But the reasons for her silence made that hard.

"Besides," she continued, "you were cranky, sure, but you were being honest. I was the one who didn't believe you, because Lachlan hadn't…" She didn't finish the thought. Nice of her to hold back from blaming him in front of an audience.

Even if it was starting to look like he deserved some of it.

But no—how would he have known?

"There was no way for me to call back given I didn't get the message," he said testily. The last thing he wanted was for it to get around town that he'd actually sloughed off the mother of his child.

"Right," she mumbled.

"Uh, truly sorry if I complicated things." Evan petted Fudge, who was mooching for treats. "Try again, dog. The only being in these parts who's allowed to have a round belly is Marisol. Or should I say, your mommy?"

"I'm not Fudge's mommy. Lachlan and I aren't…"

Marisol closed her eyes. Her previous blush was turning into a green tinge.

Lachlan took her hand and pulled her down the hall. "I'll correct everyone."

"I think the cat's out of the bag. Or rather, the cat's in the treatment room with a cell phone–wielding senior citizen."

"You don't look well," he said. "Do you need to sit down? Water? Crackers?"

"I'm fine. Just overwhelmed."

He snorted. "I know that feeling. I have more questions than I can count, but they'll have to wait."

"I should have waited until this evening to come tell you," Marisol murmured, leaning into him a little.

You should have persisted and told me months ago.

The mental picture of Marisol suffering from morning sickness and hurting because she'd assumed he was avoiding her kept him from spitting out the retort.

She glanced at her flip-flop-clad feet. "I have a plan."

"You don't think I should have a say in that plan?"

"No. I mean, yes, but… I honestly didn't think you'd want to." Her posture slumped. "We don't need to make any decisions today. We have until September. The sixth, to be specific."

So two and a half months, give or take. He blew

out a breath. "I *want* to make decisions, Marisol. I'd prefer to do it without everyone and their dog—or cat—interfering, but—"

A throat cleared, and he spun toward the noise. His sister stood in the doorway to the operating room, knuckles white around a tray. "You found out, then."

"I thought you were waiting to tell me first," he said to Marisol.

Marisol let out a sound of throaty regret. "I was. But Maggie let me in this morning. She guessed."

Maggie eyed Lachlan. "Are you going to be okay?"

"Yeah— No— I mean—" He swore again, and his profanity-averse sister cringed.

Marisol's mouth tugged down at the corners. But he knew her displeasure had nothing to do with his language.

His heart sank. "We'll figure this out, I promise."

"I have it figured out."

He blinked, irritation heating his neck. If she already had everything solved, her definition of talking did not line up with his.

"Lach, Petunia is not going to dictate her medical history herself," Evan called from down the hall. "And, Dr. Mags, you have the Franklins' Weimaraner waiting for you after you're done with Kittay. Do not throw my schedule off today, folks."

"On it, Ev," Maggie called, whirling into the exam room to a waiting Mrs. Rafferty.

"I don't know who looks more miserable, you or my sister," Lach said.

"Go," Marisol said firmly, ignoring his observation and pushing on his shoulder with a finger.

"You won't leave town before the end of my shift?"

Her expression turned thunderous. "I'm not leaving *ever*. I've *moved* here, in part so that you can be close to the baby. So I'd appreciate less asshol- ish snark!"

Frozen in place by the magnitude of her announce- ment, it was long after the side door slammed behind her that he realized she'd mentioned him being close to the baby, but not to her.

Chapter Two

"Don't even think about lifting that box."

Marisol froze at her brother's command, then ignored it, toting the offending collection of pots and pans into the galley kitchen. "It's light. Calm down, Zach."

Her brother scowled at her through the pass-through of the wall connecting the kitchen and dining area, and resumed assembling the desk she'd had delivered this morning. No way was she kneeling on the floor for an hour with a screwdriver—her back would be furious from the strain. So she owed her brother.

But she bristled at the suggestion she didn't know her limits.

Not that Zach didn't have plenty of reasons to doubt her judgment. She only needed to look as far as her credit history for a reminder that she'd made her fair share of terrible decisions in her life. But she would not trust so easily this time. She'd get a co-parenting arrangement set with Lachlan and would be well settled in her new apartment by the time the baby arrived. She'd have her PhD prospectus presented and approved by then, too.

Panic teased the base of her skull, and she gripped the counter as a grounding exercise.

One step at a time. Kitchen first.

The lack of space—she only had the dining-living area and two bedrooms to fill—made for easy unpacking. With a little elbow grease, she'd have all her boxes emptied by the time Lachlan came over after his shift ended. Not that she was in a hurry to resume that awkward conversation.

Only to be outdone by the one I have to have with Zach.

Ugh. Would he understand her reasons for telling him someone other than Lachlan was the father of her baby? Zach *was* more forgiving than most, and before finding love with his fiancée, he'd kept secrets himself…

Yeah. Secrets. Not dishonesty.

Probably best to wait until after he'd finished building her desk, though. She wouldn't want to knock him out of his construction groove by announcing she'd been lying to him about her child's paternity since she found out she was pregnant in January.

Shoving down the guilt, she bent over awkwardly to load frying pans into the drawer under the oven. Her new apartment had come mostly furnished—with some of her brother's furniture, given he'd lived in the same unit for a few months with his soon-to-be wife. Knowing Marisol would be taking over the lease, they'd left behind some essentials that didn't fit in their new house. They'd moved in the spring so that Ben would have a yard to grow up in. Zach was going through the process of adopting Ben, Cadie's son from her first marriage. Cadie had been widowed, and her son wasn't yet two, so Zach would be the only dad the boy remembered.

Watching Zach love someone else's baby as his own had been one of the reasons Marisol had believed Lachlan might come around to parenthood.

So why are you upset that it's something he's apparently wanted all along?

Good question. Maggie's assertion that Lachlan had wanted a family his whole life had been jostling around Marisol's brain since this morning. She wanted him to have a connection with their child.

But I don't want him to want one with me.

She shoved a stack of bowls into one of the cabinets with too much emphasis, and the porcelain clattered.

Right. For all the effort she intended to put into

helping him establish a bond with their baby, she'd put the same into making sure he *didn't* form one with her.

He doesn't want strings. It'll be okay.

"Everything under control in there?" her brother mumbled around the couple of screws he had sticking out of one corner of his mouth.

"Mmm-hmm. I have all of three cupboards' worth of crap. Once I'm done in here, all that's left is loading my books onto the shelf you've yet to build," she said.

He looked at the ceiling in exasperation. "No better way to spend my day off."

She cringed. She'd been in town all of twenty-four hours and was already a burden. "Never mind, I can do it."

Shaking his head, he spat the screws into his palm. "Marisol." Their parents had prioritized speaking their first languages around the house—Spanish for their dad and German for their mom—and Zach was hands-down the best linguist of their generation. He always pronounced her name with perfect Spanish inflection, unlike their sisters, who anglicized the hell out of it. "I want to help you make this place a home. Some of my best memories are from this apartment, and hopefully it'll be the same for you."

"I do want that." She'd do her best with what she had. Renting a house was out of the realm of student-budget possibility. And the apartment wasn't huge—an open-plan dining-and-living area and two bedrooms—but there was a park nearby.

Plus, she could take the kid to her brother's yard for playtime.

Zach growled at the sheet of directions, then leaned back against the dining room wall. He stared through the rectangular space in the wall, suspicion written in his green eyes. God, he looked like their dad sometimes. Acted like him, too, which usually brought on the waves of younger sibling inadequacy...

Marisol's stomach turned, and she focused on unpacking her plates instead of making eye contact.

"Cadie said she saw your car at the vet clinic this morning," Zach said.

Spectacular. Talk about a fishbowl. Maybe she wasn't up for small-town life. As fast as she'd unpacked, she could repack—

No. This move was a good one for her PhD candidacy, and a necessary one for her baby. She couldn't chicken out now.

Not with staying in Sutter Creek, or with apologizing to Zach for having lied.

"Mari?" he prodded. "Thought you and Lachlan were a onetime thing. Especially given..."

"We were." The baby chose that moment to shift, as if in communion with Zach. She laid a hand on the tiny foot kicking her navel and cocked an eyebrow at her brother. "You have some major uncle vibes, you know that?"

"The kid and I are going to be best friends." His smile faded. "I promise, okay? I want him or her to know nothing but love from our family. Father or no father."

Oh, frick. There was the guilt again, snaking its way up her spine. *Family can have many definitions.* She'd tried the traditional route once before, and look how that turned out—she'd had to sign divorce papers before receiving her bachelor's degree. She'd just managed to pay off her parents last year. They'd bailed her out when her ex's creditors had come after her. And even though she thanked the universe every day that he was no longer in her life, she'd never forget the pain of him walking out on her post-miscarriage. She wasn't up for another epic fail. Finishing her PhD and raising her baby were going to take her all.

"I appreciate the help. I moved here for that."

Would need the help, in fact, depending on how much Lachlan wanted to contribute. He'd seemed surprised when she'd told him she had a plan.

Be fair—you dropped a lot on him.

"So if you aren't wanting something permanent with Lachlan, why would you go…" Zach's mouth fell open.

Marisol's throat closed over.

"Oh. No goddamn way, Mari."

She crossed her arms between her breasts and her bump, the anatomy of being pregnant still so unfamiliar at times, especially now when the only thing that mattered was the betrayal darkening her brother's face.

"Zach. I—"

"Choose your words carefully," he warned, rising stiff-shouldered from the floor.

"I can explain—"

A knock sounded at the door, and she jumped so high she almost knocked the bar of halogen lights from the ceiling.

"That's Lachlan, isn't it?" Zach said through gritted teeth.

"Probably."

He swore. "He's the father?"

"Yeah," she whispered.

"You told me it was another grad student."

"I did." Holy Mother, it was hard to talk around the lump in her throat.

"You lied."

"I did."

"You didn't have to lie."

"I—"

"Do *not* say 'I did.'"

"—did."

Zach dragged both palms down his face. *"Why?"*

"I couldn't get a hold of him. I tried, and I thought… Well, that's not important, crossed wires and all that."

"The guy's one of my SAR buddies, Mari. We messaged every week or so while he was away."

Damn it. Maybe Lachlan had been right about trying Facebook. Maybe she'd let her fear guide her decisions too much.

And lay my heart out for a guy to stomp on again? No, thank you.

The framed psychology degrees still in a box on the floor taunted her with the point that she might have some teensy-weensy commitment issues.

Damn right, I do. And she wasn't going to apologize for them. Nor was she stupid enough to set herself up for another failed relationship. Not with a baby involved.

"I couldn't ask you to contact him for me, because then you'd have guessed, and he needed to be the first to find out," she said.

Zach's chin dropped a fraction and he closed his eyes in resignation.

"I'm sorry," she said.

Another series of raps sounded.

"Answer it," Zach mumbled.

"Okay." She made her way to the door, wincing as one of her hip ligaments pulled. Hurray for carrying around a soccer ball on her front. At least all the super attractive—*eye roll*—pregnancy stuff would keep Lachlan's hands off her.

Her brother followed. His hand landed on her shoulder, a wordless gesture of always having her back, no matter how much she screwed up. When she hesitated, hand hovering near the knob, he yanked it open for her.

Lachlan stood in the hall. He took his hands out of his pockets and straightened. He pinned her with a questioning gaze, then lifted his chin at her brother. "Zach. Hey." Nerves flitted across his face as he attempted a smile. "Seems we're going to be family."

Zach let out a noise so close to a growl that Marisol planted an elbow in his gut.

"Ow." His grip on her shoulder tightened. "Real talk, Reid. I get you not knowing was a misunderstanding. And that this is new to you. But now you're aware. And if you screw up here—" he shuffled around Marisol and jabbed Lachlan in the chest with a finger "—it won't matter that Fudge is a skilled-as-hell cadaver dog. No one will ever find your body."

Skirting past Lachlan, her brother started down the hallway.

"Hey!" Marisol yelled. Her brother's protective streak was legendary, but she could tell the threats were bravado. "You didn't finish my desk!"

"You have bigger fish to fry than a desk, little sister," he called back before disappearing into the exit staircase.

She did. Six-feet one-inch of muscular male "fish," To be specific. And the life they'd created together.

"You're off early."

Lachlan nodded. He gripped the sides of the doorjamb with both hands, standing on a bit of an angle and making his T-shirt stretch across his tall, lean frame. Any attempt he'd made to finger-comb his hair had only made the thick, caramel-colored strands messier. His eyes hooked into her core, threatening never to let her out of their deep brown spell. But the crooked smile that usually lit up those eyes was nowhere to be found. Had she ever seen his mouth set so grimly?

"I can build your desk," he said.

"So can I. That's not the point. Zach just found out about…you…and he—"

"Pretty familiar with that feeling."

"I… I'm sorry." A knee-jerk apology. But hell, she was Canadian. Came with the territory. And something about those flat lips demanded it.

One side of his mouth curved up. "For what?"

"This hasn't gone well."

Relief crossed his face. "Ah. Not sure there was a good way to go about it, Marisol. But I'm just glad you're not apologizing for the baby."

"Of course not."

His fingers whitened on the wood frame. "You didn't consider termination?"

"I did. Decided it wasn't right for me." After losing one baby, choosing not to have this one hadn't been an option.

"Okay. Then it's not right for me, either." He tentatively reached toward her stomach, catching her gaze in wordless supplication.

It's about touching the baby. Not me.

She nodded.

Lips parted, his breath caught audibly as he rested his big hand on her belly. The air hitched in her own lungs. He shifted forward a little, until they were only a foot apart. Placing his free hand on the other side, he framed her bump.

The warmth from his palms seeped through the thin cotton of her blouse. God, her skin was too sensitive there. The heat of the caress spread downward, pooling between her legs. She bit her lip. Hopefully he wouldn't want to touch her often. They'd gotten into this because they couldn't keep their hands off each other.

It was tempting to pull away, but the awe on his face… He was clearly having a moment. She wasn't going to take that from him.

"How often does it—uh, he? She?—move?" His hands shifted, little circles of torture that necessitated she swallow to get any words out.

"A lot in the middle of the night. Or when I'm sitting. And I don't know what the sex is."

"You want to be surprised?"

She shook her head. "I'm dying to know." Had gone so far as to have the ultrasound tech mark it on the file. But she'd never asked her doctor for the information. "It didn't feel right to find that out without you."

He straightened, hands falling to his sides. Dark doubt clouded his expression. "If you thought I was avoiding you, why would you want me to be involved?"

A hundred reasons clogged her thoughts. She waved him inside to the living area, currently populated by Zach's worn, corduroy couch and the Ikea coffee table she'd jammed Jenga-style into her hatchback. "Getting involved with the baby is different from getting involved with me."

"Getting involved with the baby *will* mean getting involved with you."

"Not how we were."

A breath hissed between clenched teeth. He flopped on the couch, challenging her with his gaze. "It pisses me off that you've been alone in this, Marisol."

She sat on the edge of the sofa, leaving a chunk of distance between them. Safety in inches. Or feet. "All you missed was puking and naps."

"And ultrasounds. And first movements," he said softly.

"I didn't think you'd care about that, to be honest."

His head tipped back, exposing a strong column of tanned skin over strong neck muscles. "I shouldn't have fed you that line."

"What line?"

"Whatever I told you about being too busy for a relationship. It was self-preserving nonsense, and I almost lost out on knowing my kid because of it."

Her pulse drummed in her chest, racing hard enough for her to feel the rapid, irregular beat at her wrists and under her jaw. "I don't want strings."

"Yeah, I get that, but what if *I do*?"

Her stomach knotted. "No, that's what you told me. That's what you said."

He swore. "And you believed me."

"Why wouldn't I have?"

"Because I was lying."

Information that would have been useful yesterday.

The bastardized quotation from one of her favorite films, *The Wedding Singer*, popped into her head, but she kept it to herself. Hell, she wouldn't have been able to speak if she tried. Her heart hammered in her throat. What was she thinking, moving to a new town, a new *country*, making all sorts of adjustments and arrangements with her doctoral program for the sake of a guy she'd had a fling with for a couple of weeks? Had she lost her mind?

No. I'm doing this for the baby, not for Lachlan. And my plan is going to work.

"We have time to figure each other out." His voice rasped, still at half volume.

He had to stop with the suggestion that they were a "we." They didn't have anything to figure out beyond visitation days and parent-and-tot swimming lessons and whether or not to baptize the baby Catholic. Getting closer to each other was just asking for trouble. She coughed, clearing her throat. "That's why I came now. So we can decide how we want to coparent."

Glancing around the half-unpacked apartment, he shook his head. "And you've moved here?"

"I did. It's a boon for my degree—there's a professor in the psych department at the university in Bozeman who's a canine behavior expert. She's willing to supervise me. You might know her. Jennifer Wiebe?"

His brows shot up. "I've heard the name. But hang on, you're switching schools?"

"Yeah. I have just enough time to finish and present my prospectus before my due date. I'm going to be lecturing this summer—some freshman psych courses running in July and August—and starting again in the winter session. I won't teach for the semester after the baby's born. And with moving here—I'm closer to Zach and Cadie. We're planning on sharing a nanny."

"I don't get a say in that?"

"Do you want one?"

"Yes." He coughed. "What if I *hadn't* wanted to be involved?"

Defensiveness ran up her spine. "I know! I gambled, okay? I get that. But the thing is, dogs don't lie. Fudge loves you as much as I've ever seen a dog love. I was hoping that loyalty would transcend your claim about not wanting 'strings.' And getting to be around my brother, and working with Dr. Wiebe... Even if you wanted nothing to do with the baby, I was still better off." She smiled. "Minus the loss of universal health care. That's a bit hard to take."

His eyes widened. "Do you not have health insurance? Do you need to get on mine? Damn, I wonder if it counts as a preexisting condition, or if it matters that we're not married. Should we get married—?"

"Take a breath, Lach. I'm covered through the university," she assured him. "I was joking."

His laugh came out forced, jagged. "Sort of."

"Sort of." She settled into the back of the couch and drew her knees up as best she could. "And no, we shouldn't get married. Been there, done that."

"Huh?"

It appeared today was the day for owning up to all her flaws. Awesome.

"I got married when I was in second-year university."

"You did?" He scrubbed a hand through his hair and blew out a breath. "Wow. I, uh, assume you're divorced?"

"Years ago." She could have offered up details, but they hovered in her throat, refusing to come out. The years it had taken to process the grief of her miscarriage, and her ex's lies...

She wasn't up for risking that kind of devastation again.

Lach was just going to have to redefine what "family" meant. He could have the kid part. Hell, he could have a wife, too. Just not Marisol.

She crossed her arms over her breasts. They'd been full before pregnancy, and now they were ridiculous. Credit to Lachlan, he hadn't checked them out yet. Or maybe he just wasn't interested in her anymore. That would save a lot of time and angst. "I have a bad track record. It's a good thing we're going to keep this platonic."

"We are?" He blinked, clearly bewildered.

"Yeah, Lach. We are. We need to be friends, make sure we're functioning as parents." Not giving in to the monkey-sex urges they'd had back in December. If they did, they'd flame bright for a few months, and then crash and burn, screwing over their chances to coparent.

"Friends." His gaze, purposeful now, landed on her lips, and flicked down to the rest of her body before returning to her face. He crossed an ankle over a knee and spread his arms wide on the corner of the couch. Jeez. He looked more at home in her living room than she felt. "You really think we can keep this platonic? Isn't it a bit of the cows already getting let out of the barn situation?"

"Come up with all the cute analogies you want, but these barn doors are staying shut." She closed her eyes, not wanting to give away any hint of the desire she felt for him. It was all physical. Just dregs from their fling. And pregnancy. God, as soon as she'd gotten over her morning sickness, she'd gotten all needy and it hadn't gone away.

"Okay, sweetheart. If you say so."

"You think you're that irresistible?"

"I think we have a spark."

"Then we need to put it out."

Bemusement flickered on his lips.

"What?"

"You let me know when you figure out how to do that."

She stiffened. "I think I know how to control my thoughts. Might have read a book or two about cognitive processes over the years. And don't try to tell me you're going to convince me otherwise. We need to focus on getting ready for the baby, not trying to cobble together a romantic relationship that will invariably fall apart."

She'd never trust someone so blindly as she had her ex-husband. His financial dishonesty was almost mild compared to the scars he'd left when he accused her of getting in the way of his goals and ambitions. Lachlan shook his head and gripped his knees hard enough to make the tendons rise on the backs of his hands. "Given I've known about the baby for all of five hours, I don't think it's unreasonable to ask for a little processing time."

"True." The word wobbled on her lips.

What if processing meant deciding he'd push for something she didn't want?

He looked at her sharply. "I'll *always* respect what you want."

Oh. She'd said that out loud. *Oops.*

"And we will focus on getting ready for the baby," he continued.

"Thank you," she whispered.

"Nor am I going to try to coerce you into a relationship. I have no interest in being with someone who isn't wholly into being with me."

"Okay." Frick, why couldn't she get her voice up to its normal volume?

His gaze pierced her again. "I'm a good guy, Marisol. I'm not like my—"

She blinked at his abrupt cutoff. "Like your…"

"Nothing." Bitter regret edged his words. He cleared his throat and smiled.

The dim replication of what was usually a megawatt grin took her aback. She didn't know what to do with any of that—not the shadows in his eyes, nor his insistence he was a good guy.

Talk about a recipe for temptation.

Her stomach growled audibly. "I need a snack." Or a second lunch. She'd been on the six-meals-a-day plan lately given she could only eat about half what she normally could. "And I'm sorry, I'm not set up for company yet."

"Let me take you out."

"We're not going on a date."

He rolled his eyes. "It's not a date. I'm feeding my kid."

My kid. Hearing someone else speak in possessive terms was super weird. And sexy.

No. Not sexy.

"If we go out, it's going to be this morning all over again, isn't it?" she asked. "People up in our business?"

He sent her a wry smile. "Pretty much."

She shook her head. Running into more nosy neighbors didn't appeal. She'd spent the last six months contemplating what it was going to be like to be a single parent. And after she'd figured out how to make it work to come to Sutter Creek, she'd had the thought that people would make assumptions. Even so, she'd underestimated how interested people would be in her pregnancy and her relationship with Lachlan.

"I'm not up for that particular level of intrusion this afternoon."

"Order in, then?" he suggested.

Staying in her apartment and sharing pizza, having to keep her eyes off his "I lift large dogs for a living" chest muscles? Yeah, not up for that, either. "I don't think so."

A hurt expression clouded his eyes. God, she couldn't look at him when he started to resemble one of the puppies he treated. "I just need to be alone. But maybe tomorrow—oh! Tomorrow. I have a doctor's appointment. Would you like to come?"

His face lit. "Abso-goddamn-lutely."

"I wasn't sure."

He caught her under the chin with his thumb. "You can be. When you need me, I will be there for you."

Which was a big part of why she'd come here. So now that she knew he'd help, why was she scared as hell to accept?

Because I'm being logical, keeping my distance.

"You'll be there for the baby, you mean." She'd absolutely include him in that. But when it came to things that only involved her—she'd have to stake out space.

Chapter Three

"You are ruining my schedule," Evan griped as Lachlan stripped out of his scrub shirt and pulled on a T-shirt in preparation to head to Marisol's appointment late the next morning. "We're going to end up working after hours, aren't we?"

"Well, I will, with the Johnsons being okay with me cleaning Flick's teeth at the end of the day instead of now." It was the second day in a row he'd had to ask Evan to do some last-minute switching, and the guy had been grumbling all morning because of it. It wasn't a habit Lach wanted to get into—he wanted to be an asset to Maggie, not a hindrance—but today was a special situation. "Head out at your usual time, though. I can shut everything down and lock up."

Evan placed a protective hand on the computer monitor. "Risk you messing up Lucille? That's a big no. I'll stay. Deon and I can kick our dinner plans out a little. But only because this is monumental for you." His cheeks reddened. "And because I played a *tiny* part in keeping Marisol's message from finding you."

Lachlan held out a finger and thumb with a fraction of space between them.

Evan winced. "Sorry."

"Enh, it was as much technology—and me—as you. And that aside, I still hate messing up the schedule."

Evan's sigh fluttered the papers on the new-patient clipboard sitting on top of the desk. "If it's a boy, you can name him Evan in honor of all the crap I put up with."

"I'll keep that in mind." Lach shook his head and put on his bike helmet. The veterinary clinic was a mile out from the town center where Marisol's doctor's office was located, an easy trip on his road bike.

The sun beat on his forearms and wind whistled in his ears, waking him up a little. He made a habit of never watching the clock whenever he struggled to fall asleep, but there had been a definite sunrise glow around the curtains before he'd managed to nod off last night. This morning, rather. Ugh.

His thoughts had flitted around faster than a hummingbird. He hadn't been able to settle on how he felt. He loved kids. And screw following his parents' pitiful example.

But aside from the sheer shock of learning he was going to be a father, it was the mother of his child who had him tied in knots. Marisol wanted to be platonic? How the hell was he supposed to manage that? He'd been infatuated with her since the moment they hooked up.

He'd met her while sharing nachos with his SAR buddies at the end of a long day on the hill. She'd been ski-rumpled and adorable, and had pulled him in with jokes about hockey and an encyclopedic knowledge of dogs. And man, there was nothing better than colored Christmas tree lights picking up the green in her eyes, or splashing a rainbow glow on her golden-brown skin. For the rest of her vacation, she'd spent more time in his bed than on the mountain.

With some permanent repercussions.

Gripping the handlebars, he gulped warm, early-summer air into his lungs. *It was more than a roll or ten between the sheets. I cared about her.*

He had. Still did.

And the baby… God, he would love the kid.

Could love Marisol, too, but she clearly didn't want that. And he'd meant what he said—he wouldn't convince her otherwise. He'd keep his feelings out of it. Doing his job sometimes meant having to compartmentalize for the sake of being objective. He'd have to do that with Marisol. Jam the emotions down deep.

Yeah, 'cause that's healthy.

Maybe not. But necessary.

He locked his bike, shoved his helmet in his backpack and pushed through the doors of the Sutter Creek Medical Clinic.

The waiting room was half-full—he nodded at the owner of a Siamese patient of Maggie's and at one of the local ranchers, who smiled knowingly. But Marisol wasn't there.

He scanned the room again, wiping his damp palms on his thin cargo shorts.

"Head to exam room three, Lachlan." The receptionist, a high school classmate of his oldest sister's, pointed to a hallway. "Dr. Matsuda took your partner in about ten minutes ago."

The announcement tripped him up. "What?"

Sympathy crossed her face. "It's okay. You probably haven't missed much."

He was late? How? He checked his watch. Eleven thirty-five, and Marisol had told him her appointment was at eleven forty. His gut rolled, and he hustled toward the corridor.

Knocking on the door labeled Three, he waited to be let in. The door swung open, and Caleb Matsuda's smiling face greeted him.

"Hey, doc," Lachlan said.

"Reid. Congratulations. Marisol tells me this was a bit of a surprise." The doctor, a few years older than Lachlan's thirty-three, ran a hand through his short, dark hair and clapped Lach on the shoulder with the other as they stood in the entryway.

"Uh, yeah…" He didn't want to throw Marisol under the bus—with her moving to Sutter Creek, it would be crappy if her decision not to tell him about the baby right away clouded people's opinions of her. He wished things hadn't played out the way they had, but he also didn't want her to have any reason not to like living here, or for the local contingent not to accept her. Then again, Caleb was a recent transplant himself. He probably understood the ins and outs of adjusting to small-town life better than most. "We're figuring things out, though."

"You'll do great."

"I hope I haven't missed much of the appointment. Didn't think I'd be late."

"Thanks for understanding. Garnet and I are heading out camping for a few days—and we can use any head start we can get."

Lachlan had become good friends with Caleb in the last six months—the doctor was madly in love with one of the women Lachlan volunteered with on the county search and rescue team. Come to think of it, the doctor had a shared history with Marisol's brother, too. They'd been involved in an avalanche a couple of years back.

He motioned between Caleb and Marisol. "I guess you two know each other because of the…uh…" He never was sure whether Caleb felt like talking about the tragedy. The guy was open about his PTSD, but bringing it up still made Lachlan's gut twist.

"Yeah, Marisol was in Whistler after the slide," Caleb said calmly, waving Lach into the room. "We've met a few times. And I'll be honest, I'm still getting used to treating people I consider friends, but it's not a conflict of interest or anything, so let's just keep things casual, okay?"

"You got it," Lachlan said.

"Marisol and I have just been going through her history," Caleb said. "Saved the good stuff for you."

"Oh." Caleb probably assumed Lachlan knew Marisol's medical information. So not the case. Hell, he hadn't even known she'd been married before. And he didn't feel like admitting his ignorance. If Caleb brought anything up that would make Lachlan's lack of knowledge obvious, he'd just have to fake it. Breathing in resolve, he scooted around the doctor to get his first look at Marisol, half reclined on the exam table in her street clothes. The pink of her short-sleeved T-shirt highlighted the healthy glow in her cheeks. His chest tightened. Damn, she was beautiful.

"I texted you," she murmured.

"Phone's in my bag. I biked over."

The quick swing from thinking he'd let her down to realizing he hadn't added to the magnitude of walking into a doctor's office for a freaking prenatal appointment weakened his knees. He sat down in the chair next to the exam table with a thud.

He swallowed, fighting the sudden onset of dry tongue.

Marisol rolled to her side and reached out to squeeze his shoulder. Warmth spread from her palm. Oh, man, he enjoyed her touch too much.

"You'll get used to it," she said. "Appointments become boring after a while."

"I don't think so, sweetheart."

Uncertainty crossed her face, a hint of pleasure covered by a whole lot of will to resist it. At the endearment? At his wonderment? Who knew?

Her expression blanked as quickly as it had slipped. She withdrew her hand and refocused on Caleb, who was typing something into the computer attached to the counter. "You saw my blood pressure history?"

"I did. Your doctor in Vancouver included a record." Caleb cleared his throat. "It's something to watch. The family medicine team here is well prepared to provide care and to ensure your pregnancy remains uncomplicated, and I know you want to stay local for your appointments and delivery. But if complications pop up, we may need to refer you to an ob-gyn in Bozeman."

Both Marisol and Caleb glanced at Lachlan. Crap, he was breathing too fast. Noticeably so. He forced a shrug. "Complications. Not a pleasant word to hear."

"Perils of being in a medical profession." Caleb's nod was sympathetic beyond usual bedside manner. "Being a vet tech, you know too many ways that conditions can go sideways. Even if the chances are low."

"Don't get me wrong, I'd lie down in the road for my patients. But there's a big difference between Mrs. Rafferty's cat and Marisol."

"I dunno," Marisol said lightly. "That cat was pretty cute."

"You're more than cute. And our baby…"

Biting the inside of her lip, she studied her hands. A hint of red colored Caleb's tawny cheeks, and his smile went mushy.

Well, crap. Way to stay objective, Reid.

Was he really being fair to himself, though? He could bury his feelings for Marisol, but not for the baby. And given they were intrinsically tied through gestation… Damn. How was he going to do this?

He fisted his hands. He'd have to. For her to trust him, he had to stick to his word. And he'd promised to respect her limits.

Focus on the science. On finding a way to coax out answers on Marisol's blood pressure without giving away that he knew nothing about her medical history.

"What's the probability of her numbers worsening?" he asked.

Caleb shrugged and wrapped a cuff around Marisol's arm, then studied the display as the electronic device inflated, then deflated. "They're not in the danger zone right now. And it's not something we can predict. Home monitoring, regular appointments to check for protein in the urine, exercise, a balanced diet—hopefully we never get to the point of doing more."

Lachlan's heart skipped a beat. If something happened to Marisol or the baby... This was too much to process, learning about the baby a day ago and now having to contemplate complications—

"Lach." Marisol cut off his thoughts. "I'm healthy. So's the kid. I'm taking care of things."

"I know." He screwed his mouth up. How to say the right thing... "I just want to help where I can."

Clearing his throat, Caleb effectively broke the tension in the room. "Have you heard the heartbeat yet, Lach?"

He shook his head. No pretending on that one.

Caleb brought over a fetal Doppler and applied gel to the wand. Marisol scooched up her T-shirt. One swipe of the device, one faint, rapid *lub-dub*, and Lachlan was a goner. His jaw went loose, and he stared at Marisol's bared belly, the rhythmic beat of their child's heart filling the room. Filling his soul.

"One-forty-two. Nice and strong." Caleb withdrew the wand and handed Marisol a small towel. He gripped Lachlan's shoulder for a second. "Take a minute if you need it. And make an appointment for two weeks from now, Marisol."

"You got it," she said, cleaning the gel off her belly.

Good thing Caleb had addressed Marisol, because Lachlan couldn't make his voice work. He'd have to text his friend to have a good camping trip later. Wow. He would not have predicted he'd react this strongly—he listened to heartbeats on an hourly basis at work, would have expected to be at least a little desensitized. Apparently not.

Caleb left the room with a smile and a wave.

Marisol fixed her T-shirt and sat up, legs dangling off the high bed. She patted the table next to her, crinkling the paper. "Come here. Baby's moving. You should feel it."

He hitched himself from the chair to the space next to her, and braced a hand on the table so he could reach across and palm her stomach.

A little pop tickled his palm.

His heart skipped again.

"It's okay to be affected by it. It's a lot to absorb in twenty-four hours," she said.

He shifted his hand lower, following the pattern of bumps and nudges as the baby wiggled. "Twenty-seven hours."

"Right." Marisol splayed her hand across his.

"The kid's active."

"The Doppler always gets her going."

He did a double take. "Her?"

"Better than 'it.'"

"Could we find out?" he croaked, vocal cords straining with yearning.

"Let's ask at my next appointment. If you want to come."

"Of course," he said.

The scent of Marisol's body lotion cut through the odor of sanitizer. Last time he'd caught a whiff of that sugary confection smell, it had been fading on his sheets as he woke up alone after she returned to Vancouver. He swallowed down the urge to nuzzle the crook of her neck. Withdrawing his hand from her stomach, he gripped his knees.

"Hey." She slid her fingers along his jaw and gently turned his face to her. "Don't worry. I have this under control."

"You've mentioned."

Worry muted the green in her eyes. "I need that control, Lach."

"Okay. I—" He ran his teeth over his lower lip. "I haven't figured out where I fit into your plan yet."

"I haven't, either. Not entirely."

The truth stung, but he appreciated it nonetheless. Honesty mattered. How many times had he and Maggie borne the brunt of his parents' lies? Getting pulled between their mother's guilt trips and their father's ambivalence and living in the no man's land of constant parental battles. Their half sister, Stella, had escaped it some by living with her mom in Sutter Creek. But their dad had been a jerk to her just as much as to Maggie and Lachlan. Thankfully, their grandparents had filled the parental gap some before his grandmother passed away. And if he was lucky, he'd find a woman who looked at him the way Grams had smiled at Pops for close to half a century. A woman he'd go to bed wanting to please and wake up next to with a grin on his face because she was snuggled in his embrace.

Love's a joke, son. Don't be weak.

Ignoring the echo of his father's voice, he jammed his hands in his pockets. "Parents need to be a team, Marisol."

"Sure. And I'll work with you on that. But there's not much you can do while the kid's still uterus-bound. Beyond getting the nursery ready, preparing my prospectus presentation is my biggest priority until I deliver."

Frustration tingled along his spine and he hopped off the table. "I know you're used to doing things yourself. But you don't have to be alone. I'll come along to appointments, help you get the baby's room ready. I'll need one at my place, too." Though where he'd put a baby in the tiny apartment he rented to maximize how much he could save for his dog training facility, he didn't know. He'd figure something out, though. "Hell, I can help you with your prospectus if you like. You know my background with avy—avalanche—dogs. And Maggie's been training assistance dogs since she started college."

She slid awkwardly to the edge of the table and he caught her elbow, easing her down to the floor. Her gaze shifted to his hand and her lips formed a grim line.

"What? You can't tell me I didn't make that easier for you right there."

"Things haven't worked well for me in the past when I tried to share my life. And I have too much on the line to screw up again."

"Then you didn't have the right partner."

"No, I did not."

But clearly, she didn't believe he deserved that title, either.

Well, for the sake of the feisty little being who'd punched the heck out of his hand, he'd have to show her he did. That even if they weren't a couple, they could create a kick-ass life for their kid. He'd been the ten-year-old abandoned at boarding school. The fourteen-year-old who'd pieced together a birthday party for Maggie because his parents were somewhere in Europe on business and forgot to call. The fifteen-year-old who'd provided Kleenex and company when his half sister, Stella, had miscarried and her high school boyfriend had been long gone.

No child of his would go through anything similar. He and Marisol had to learn to communicate and work together.

So she didn't know how to share her life?

Well, he'd share his with her until she believed she could do the same.

"When do you start at the university?" he asked.

"Tomorrow. I have to maximize my time."

"You'll be tired. Let me cook dinner for you."

She bit her lip. "Give me a few days before you act as the welcome committee, okay?"

He frowned. "Okay, but I don't like the idea of you sitting alone all week."

"I'll be fine. Tell you what. If you're meeting the SAR crew after work on Friday, I'll come join."

That was usually the routine. *Won't be for long. I'll be dealing with diapers and feeding routines on the weekends.*

Jarred by the thought, he shook his head. That was going to take some getting used to. Maybe a few days to adjust wouldn't be a bad idea. He'd wait until the weekend, and then make sure he helped her get acclimated to Sutter Creek.

And to having him in her life.

Chapter Four

By the end of the workweek, Lachlan was climbing the walls to make contact with Marisol. But he forced himself to be patient, waited until he was about to dig into his lunch before he called.

"Hey there," he greeted, stomach warming as he absorbed her "hello" for the first time since he last saw her. Tuesday felt like a lifetime ago. Every second pet owner that walked into the clinic had reminded him of his impending parenthood. But the flood of congratulations and curiosity only made him want to be around Marisol more.

"What's up?" she asked.

"It's Friday," he pointed out.

"I noticed." A hint of humor tinged the word. Tiredness, too.

He'd know better why—adjusting to a new university? Or just the pregnancy?—were it not for her insistence on space. This whole "you can be connected to the baby, but not to me" thing she had going on was, in his mind, impossible.

And in his heart, undesirable.

As promised, he'd tolerate her drawing that line. But he didn't like it. And he'd jump on any opportunity he had to develop their own relationship, hence dialing her number instead of mowing down his burrito the minute his lunch break started.

"You'd mentioned coming out with me and the SAR crew after work this evening."

"I did."

Yep, definitely tired. But also mildly amused, so maybe she would still be up for getting together. Provided she didn't mind a change of plans. "So, it seems it's the one week where everyone's off doing their own thing. We had a call last night. Got sick of each other's company after being up until the wee hours together."

"Oh—you sure you shouldn't be catching up on sleep, then?"

"I'm used to it," he assured her, keeping the phone pressed to his ear as he leaned back in one of the mismatched rolling chairs that surrounded the table in the clinic's staff room. "Can I convince you to do something else? When will you be back from Boze-man? We could grab a bite. Pie, maybe. You can't call yourself a real Sutter Creek resident until you've had a hand pie from the Aussie place. It's only a few blocks from your apartment."

"Uh…" Lead-heavy doubt weighed down her pause. "Sure. I've been sitting a lot this week. I could use a walk."

"Perfect. Text me when you're home and I'll pick you up."

He worked the rest of his shift and then split for home to shower off the dog slobber and cat hair. Fudge, still tired after their late night spent tromping through the bushes searching for—and successfully finding, thank God—a man with Alzheimer's who got away from his nursing home, sacked out on her dog bed. He almost envied her nap, but going for a walk with Marisol beat out sleep any day. After his shower, he didn't shave—she'd mentioned liking his stubble one night when she'd been kissing her way up his throat. He took an embarrassingly long time settling on the right shirt to pair with his shorts. His choice needed to give her enough to look at, to enjoy, without coming across as trying too hard. He picked his nicest golf shirt, counting on the thin material catching her eye.

Much like her curves and long limbs were *his* fa-vorite flavor, she'd once made it clear she appreci-ated his body. And if reminding her of that helped to weaken some of her defenses? He wasn't above making sure his shirt showed off his pecs a little. Not going-to-the-club tight—that wasn't close to his style, either the tightness, or clubbing. But thin, technical material didn't hide anything.

And he was okay with that.

He threw on a pair of shorts and his stainless steel watch, decided on his canvas slip-on shoes—he had a feeling Marisol wasn't walking anywhere quickly these days, not with that cute pregnant sway she had going on—and sat down at his kitchen counter. Was she going to make him wait long? He was liable to sweat through the shirt it just took him twenty damned minutes to pick out.

Christ, if Maggie heard that, she'd never let him hear the end of it. Evan, too. The two of them never passed up a chance to harass Lachlan. Though the receptionist had been unusually demure this week, hadn't even corrected Lachlan's technique when they ran into each other at the bouldering gym yesterday. Evan probably still felt guilty for not helping Marisol out more when she'd called in the winter.

That made two of them.

If he never missed another call from her again in his life, it would still be too many.

Tonight, however, it seemed she was going to make him wait for it. The minutes ticked by on the microwave display, and he did the circuit of his small-as-anything apartment. Flipped through a magazine sitting at the Formica kitchen bar, moved to the bed and made it through a comedy special he'd been meaning to watch on Netflix, and spent a good ten minutes giving Fudge a belly rub while scrolling through his Facebook and Twitter feeds.

Damn, had she stood him up? It was almost seven; surely she was home by now. Maybe he should call her—

His text notification went off, saving him the decision.

Sorry. Got held up. Give me ten, and I'll be ready.

Suppressing the concern that she'd worked late on a Friday when her yawns made it sound like she should have cut out early, he replied that he'd be there ASAP. He confirmed his dog was snoring and out for the night, then hoofed it over the elementary school field and down one of the trails that followed the creek that gave the town its name. The trip between their apartments took nine minutes at a quick pace. Good to know. No matter what, he'd always be close by whenever she needed him.

Though where he was going to put a baby in his tiny home, he had no idea…

He didn't need to buzz up; she was waiting for him outside the front door to her building.

Her back was to him. Couldn't tell she was pregnant from that angle. But when she turned… What had Mrs. Rafferty said the other day? Marisol was all out front?

Whatever the term, she was adorable. She wore a summery, dark-blue dress and flat, leather walking sandals. Simple, but hinted that she'd put some effort in, too. His chest warmed a little.

"Hungry?" he called, jogging the rest of the way up the sidewalk.

She smiled, twisting her hands in front of her.

"Relax, Marisol," he said, slowing as he got within a few yards. He held out his arms for a hug.

She didn't reach back.

Discomfort ran through him, and instead of forcing the embrace, he squeezed her shoulder.

Not awkward at all, champ. Nice going.

She bit her lip, which was painted a bright pink. Familiar, that color. He'd washed it off his abs the morning after the first time she slept over.

"So…pie?" he said, mouth dry from the memory.

"You're not the first person to tell me it's required eating."

He jerked his head in the direction of the town center, back along the path in the opposite direction from where he'd come. "Follow me."

She did, bracing her hands against her back and kneading her thumbs into her lower spine as she walked. "I'll be honest, I was really tempted to go straight to bed. It's been quite a week. But I need to move. I'll seize up if I don't."

"I could—" *Put a pause on that.* No way would she take him up on a massage offer. Not even a therapeutic one. "I mean, I could put you in touch with someone at the holistic health center. Caleb's girlfriend—you remember Garnet, right? You met last time you were here—anyway, she's an acupressure practitioner. Cadie's sister swore by the treatments when she was pregnant."

She looked a little dazed, stared at the asphalt-paved trail. "Uh, okay…"

"I know. Sutter Creek is a lot to take in. I can help with that. I didn't grow up here, but I lived with my grandparents every summer after I turned ten, so it was close enough." He'd literally crossed off the days on a calendar during the school year, waiting to return to Montana.

"Where were you during the rest of the year?"

"Boarding school."

She shot him a sympathetic look.

"Enh, it wasn't awful—better than being in Chicago with my parents. But it wasn't as good as being here. Eating care packages of my grandma's brownies was a world away from digging into a tray fresh out of the oven. And the boys' dorm was all the way across campus from Maggie, too far for my liking. She and I shared bunk beds during the summers at my grandparents—I loved that."

"Really? I'd have killed my sisters—or Zach—if I'd had to share with them."

He shrugged. "Maggie and I have always been close. We're only eighteen months apart, and we share an outdoor gene. We have an older half sister, Stella. Spent summers with her here. She moved to New York after she graduated, rarely comes back. She's...ultradriven. Citified."

Marisol put a hand to her chest and gasped in mock horror. "God forbid."

With a sheepish grin, he laid a hand between her shoulder blades. "I forget you're a city girl."

"I wasn't until I went to university. Whistler's small. But I found living in the mountains suffocating. Wanted nothing but to get away and bury myself in books."

Concern rang in his chest. That reminded him of Stella, too, though his sister was more about making money at her hedge fund firm than succeeding in academia. "You're sure you're okay moving here?"

She bit her lip. He steered her toward the staircase that led from the path up to the pedestrian-only Main Street. Their footfalls echoed on the wooden treads, driving home her silence.

"Priorities change," she answered finally.

"That they do."

"Why didn't you live with your parents?"

Startled by the question, he cleared his throat. "Bit out of left field."

"You brought it up."

"Guess I did." They exited the staircase through a

short lane that led to the street. He pointed down the block, to one of the clapboard, two-story buildings that couldn't decide whether it belonged in a Bavarian village or on an Old West film set. "Pie's there."

She shied away from his hand and picked up her pace along the wooden sidewalk. Her wary gaze locked on him.

Damn. He needed her to trust him, and if she heard about the abysmal parenting he'd been treated to, she was bound to get the wrong idea about the kind of father he'd be.

"My mom and dad—"

"Lach!" An open-armed blur of auburn curls and freckles flew out of the outdoor goods store.

"Garnet." He caught his SAR colleague's offered hug. "Your ears must have been burning. I was just recommending to Marisol that she come see you."

"Oh, you should." Garnet smiled, wide and guileless, at Marisol. "First session's on me. Welcome to town—Caleb tells me it's for good. Zach must be over the moon."

Marisol tugged at her thin cardigan, tucking it over the straps of her sundress. "He's happy, yeah. And thanks for the offer. I'll call your clinic."

Garnet smacked Caleb in the abs with the back of her hand. "Look at you, Daddy. That, and getting your doggos up and running—quite the year for you."

"It is."

"You still going to have time for SAR?"

"Of course."

She tilted her head toward the store she'd just exited. "Just spoke to Jack. He's still going to give us all our personal equipment at cost. Winter stock'll be arriving within the next month or so."

"Mine'll do me for another year." His bank account balance, tenuously hovering between black and red with all he was squirreling away for upcoming operating costs, blinked like a strobe light in his mind. And now he'd have to factor in support for Marisol and the baby, especially while she was off work.

His shirt felt a little tight around his neck, and he flicked open a second button. "We'd better get going, Gee. I'm starving, and I'm betting Marisol is, too. She was in Bozeman all day."

They said their goodbyes, Marisol promising again to call for an appointment, then resumed their stroll down the sidewalk.

"You've got a lot on your plate," she murmured.

He lifted a shoulder. "We should figure out expenses, how much you're going to need from me."

"Now there's a fun conversation," she said, gaze on her pink-painted toenails as she walked. A muscle ticked in her jaw.

"I want to make sure you have a cushion."

Taking away his own, but providing for his child mattered the most.

She grabbed his elbow, halting him in his tracks. "What's entailed in your business expansion?"

"We're renovating the barn out back of the clinic. I'll be transitioning to training search and rescue animals—I get funding from outside agencies, who then donate the dogs to various SAR organizations. Area-search, cadaver, trailing, avy… Of course, then the dogs have to train and cert with their handlers, but it speeds up the process. And I'll teach courses for established teams, too." Adding a baby to that mix—well, there wasn't anything to do about it. He'd have to manage all of it. He wasn't giving up on the dream he'd been working toward for a decade. Nor would he be anything less than a fully involved father.

"Sounds pricey," she commented.

"Any new business is. That's why I was away this spring—saving up money, and also putting myself in an organization's good books in hopes of being a shoo-in for a grant I'll be relying on."

"Ugh, *that*, I know. Grants, that is. Not saving up money. Being a student—I'm on a bit of a shoe-string." Her eyes widened. "Not that I won't be able to support the baby. I can. I'm not expecting a check from you."

"You should."

"That's not why I'm here. I don't want to be a burden."

"You're not." Her coming to town, having her job lined up and plans for a nanny and an apartment—

he was more worried that she wasn't going to involve him at all rather than relying on him more than he could handle.

"And you'll still be working at the clinic?" Worry rode her tone.

"Some, yeah," he said. "It'll be a balance."

"Start small, okay?"

"With the expansion?" As if a person could do anything other than dive headlong into a new business endeavor.

"No, with the baby. I'd rather have you commit to help out a little and stick to that rather than taking on too much and backing out."

The words whipped at him, stinging, leaving welts. "I'd never..."

She started to walk again.

"Marisol."

The wounded expression she laid on him when she stopped and turned flayed him open. "I can survive being let down, Lachlan. *Have* survived. But I won't let it happen to my child."

His mouth gaped and he scrambled for a reply. Christ, her ex must have done a number on her.

"Whatever happened in your marriage? I won't repeat that pattern."

"I never thought this was possible, but I am too full of pie. I miss eating normal-sized meals," Marisol complained.

Lachlan was showing her around the town square, and between dinner and the baby, she was full-on waddling.

He sent her a half smirk and tucked her bangs behind her ear. She tilted her cheek toward his palm, then caught herself.

Gah! Instinct was a pain in the ass.

"Can't say I thought I'd get the chance to stroll around the gazebo with you again," he said.

"Gotta agree with you there." Her hand brushed his. Okay, how had she ended up walking so close to him? Was he magnetized or something? Crossing her arms above her stomach, she scrambled for a neutral topic. "Summer looks good on the town."

Eventually she'd get used to Sutter Creek in greens and browns instead of white and holiday decor, but today, it seemed incongruous. Back in December, she'd soaked in the few romantic, Christmas-themed dates they'd gone on, assuming she'd never see him again.

Arching a brow as if to challenge the inanity of discussing the seasons, he checked his phone quickly, then the cloud-streaked sky. "How tired are you?"

"Somewhere between ready to fall asleep and needing to prove I'm not boring. Why?"

"Let's go get my truck. I want to show you something, and it's a bit of a drive."

"This isn't a date, right?" she blurted.

"Of course not. I just want to show you the best the area has to offer."

"Can't say no to that," she said. Sadness tinged his smile, and her heart panged. *Don't let those puppy dog eyes get to you. He works with them. He can't help the similarity.*

Puppies. Focus on puppies. "Tell me more about your business plan."

Discussing floor plans and training techniques worked as an excellent diversion on the walk to his apartment. But the second he helped her into the car, and the strength of his hand against her forearm zinged straight to her core, reality rushed in. She'd agreed to be stuck in a close-quarters cab with his shirt tugged tight across his hella-hot pecs. Making her mouth water. And even if he kept his hands firmly on the wheel, she didn't want him to. She wanted him to reach over and link fingers with her.

He'd developed a habit before, drawing little circles with his thumb on her wrist and the back of her hand.

She missed it.

I can't miss it.

He'd confided his goals about the training center. She'd no more stand in the way of those than she would her own. She had to focus on her degree, her dissertation, and he needed to focus on his plan. Not push it aside. But starting a small business—the financial risk in that made her stomach turn. She was glad she wasn't depending on him for money, because if he was already relying on grants and loans, anything he gave to her would have to come from somewhere less reliable.

"I don't remember you being this quiet, Marisol." He pulled up to an old-fashioned diner and cut the engine.

"I didn't have as much on my mind when I was on holiday." Lies. She'd totally been consumed by the way he filled out his shirts. Then it had been the undershirts he wore to go skiing, but still.

"I'm going to get us a treat. To go, though."

"I'll stay in the truck," she said. "Too much effort to get in and out."

Too much chance you'll touch me again.

He jerked his head in confirmation and headed for the glass front door. With the diner's wide windows and fluorescent lighting, watching him was easy. He sidled up to the front counter and leaned to whisper something to the middle-aged waitress pouring coffee for a pair of senior gentlemen wearing cowboy hats.

The waitress tossed her head back in a laugh, and disappeared through a set of swinging doors.

Lachlan turned his head, grinned when he caught Marisol staring.

Crap. She dropped her gaze, stared at her phone and skimmed through her Instagram without really seeing any of the posts.

A couple of minutes later, movement flashed in the corner of her eye, and the driver's door opened. Lachlan leaned in and set two lidded soda cups in the console between the front seats.

"Hello, dear." A slate-gray head poked around from behind him.

"Oh, hello, Mrs. Rafferty," Marisol said.

With a beleaguered look just for Marisol, Lachlan climbed in. "Gertie was just telling me she's moving in a few weeks."

"My grandson finally convinced me it's time to downsize. A place came up in the independent-living building, and I'm making him a trade."

"What's that?" Marisol asked.

"He'll work on getting me grandchildren, and I'll work on worrying him less."

Pain flashed across Lachlan's face, which seemed out of place for what Mrs. Rafferty had just said. Marisol raised a brow at him. He shook his head quickly and forced a smile. "I'm sure you'll get into more trouble—er, I mean, be busier—if you're at Sutter Gardens, Gertie."

She grinned and put a hand on the edge of the truck door, preventing Lachlan from closing it. "If you're needing more space than that shoebox you're living in, my house would be perfect for you."

"I'm not looking to upsize," Lachlan mumbled, taking a sip of whatever was in his condensation-frosted cup.

"Oh, but you'll have to. I know the apartments in your building. They're made for chairlift operators and seasonal staff, not people about to welcome a baby."

An audible grind filled the car as Lachlan clenched his teeth, and Marisol couldn't decide whether to laugh or groan.

"Vet techs don't make much more than lifties," he said.

The older woman pressed her lips together. "I'd charge you excellent rent."

"Thanks, Mrs. Rafferty, but I don't think I'm in the market. Marisol has her own place, so it'll just be me and the baby on the days I have him or her."

"Hmph. You young people…" She narrowed her eyes at them. "I've half a mind to call up your grandfather and Carol, tell them to knock some sense into you."

"Please don't," he said, voice low.

"*Half* a mind." She harrumphed again. "Well, you two go on your date—"

"It's not—"

"—and think about the house. There's plenty of space for a couple and a child. More than one, in fact."

Before either Marisol or Lachlan could protest the audacity of that statement, Mrs. Rafferty slammed the door.

"Wow," Marisol croaked. "The woman has force."

"Oh, she's something, all right. Sorry about that. She was just finishing up with her bridge club as I was putting in my order. Followed me out of the restaurant."

"No worries." Except now she was extra worried he'd overextend himself. She wasn't going to judge him for not having a substantial salary—she was glad he did what he loved—but was he promising financial support he didn't have? She had just enough to make ends meet.

Having this baby was her choice. But that didn't remove his responsibility… Would this put him in debt, though? Being beholden to monthly payments beyond one's means was something she'd experienced for too many years.

But didn't you come here in part so he could step up and be a father?

Argh.

He passed her the second soda cup. "Sutter Creek's finest."

Popping off the top, she peeked in. A scoop of vanilla ice cream bobbed in brown soda.

"I made sure the root beer didn't have caffeine."

She took a sip of the sweet, creamy drink. "Caleb would chastise me for drinking this because of the sugar, and I don't know where I'm going to put it— I'm still stuffed—but holy crap, it's delicious."

"It's the perfect accompaniment to the show I'm going to take you to."

"A show?" She didn't know if she had it in her to go see a movie. Sitting in a darkened theater, brushing against Lachlan's built biceps in that mouthwatering shirt… She kept from groaning, but barely. "Not sure how much longer I'll be able to stay awake."

"I'll have you home by dark."

"Deal." She poked at the foamy layer on top of her float. "You're really patient with Mrs. Rafferty. Even if she seems to say stuff that doesn't sit right with you."

"Yeah." He turned the key and the truck roared to life. The tires crunched as they turned out of the parking lot onto the road. "Lot of history between my family and the Raffertys. Not mine, Stella's. And being the only veterinary practice in town, we have to interact with them. Maggie and I work with the sheriff—Mrs. Rafferty's grandson—a lot with SAR, too. I've made my peace with him."

"So mysterious."

"Nothing that needs to be dredged up."

There were those sad eyes again. More unresolved-past-hurts than puppy-dog, though.

She plunked her drink in the cup holder and laid a palm on his shoulder. "Not your story to tell?"

"Nope."

She rubbed a slow circle, trying to release some of the tension from his posture. A soft smile crossed his face, and he kept his right hand on the wheel, reaching across his chest with his left to cover her fingers. "You have a magic touch, Marisol."

You make me want the magic back.

The tires hit gravel again as he turned onto a dirt road that bisected wide swaths of grassy ranch land.

"Uh, where are we going?" she asked.

"You'll see."

They drove for another twenty minutes. He plied her with questions about her prospectus and the intensive summer courses that would start in a few weeks. And she kept her palm on his shoulder, his big hand blanketing the back of hers, unable to bring herself to pull away.

The soft stroking of his thumb along the tendons of her hand soothed, mesmerized.

He only let go when he stopped the truck at a gate, hopped out, opened it, pulled the truck forward onto an even narrower dirt road and exited one more time to close the gate behind them.

Driving slowly, he grinned. "Hopefully we don't bounce the baby out early."

"If I end up going overdue, I'll ask you to bring me out here and play NASCAR driver." They hit a pothole, and she grabbed the holy-crap handle on the truck ceiling. "Where is it we're going?"

"Best view in town."

"View of what?" The road veered west, putting them in the glare of the sun, which was almost kissing the horizon.

"The sunset."

She held up her hand to shade her eyes, and he flipped up the console and rummaged, then handed her a pair of aviators. "Thanks. When you said show I thought you meant a movie."

A corner of his mouth crept up. "Nah, we did that already. That's a cold-weather activity. I want to show you all the glory of a Montana summer."

Yeah, long days and short nights could lead to a whole lot... Anticipation fluttered behind her breastbone. *Easy, killer. Not that kind of glory.*

Though the man had a way with his mouth...

And the only thing I'm going to enjoy about his mouth is the conversation that comes out of it.

He pulled the truck into a makeshift parking lot of sorts, a round patch of dirt big enough for a few cars to park.

"What, did someone do donuts repeatedly with their dually until there was a clearing here?"

"Pretty much." He put on a false twang. "Where'd a city girl like you learn about our country trucks?"

She rolled her eyes. "You've clearly never been to Squamish." The little community, between her recent home in Vancouver and where she'd grown up in Whistler, was as quintessential a British Columbian small town as you could get.

"Can't say I have." Reddening, he coughed and gripped the steering wheel. "Think you might take me up there one day? To meet your parents?

I wouldn't mind knowing my kid's grandparents. They're the only decent ones…"

What kind of home life had he had as a kid? Her heart ached for him. "Lachlan—"

"Look," he interrupted. He pointed at the sun, a glowing red ball dipping behind the horizon. "Perfect night for this. Mother Nature's giving you a good welcome."

"Wow," she breathed as the sun dipped to half and then a quarter and then disappeared. Streaks of pink and crimson shot through the wispy clouds, which stretched as far as she could see, until orange became yellow became lavender, the promise of approaching dark kissing the edges of the sky. "That's so pretty."

She glanced at him.

His gaze seemed fixed on her, and a corner of his mouth twitched up.

"The prettiest," he said.

Reverting back to the sunset, her cheeks heated. God, they probably matched the clouds. One silly little compliment—assuming he was talking about her and not the colors on the horizon—and she melted. Ugh, she needed some self-control.

"You're flirting," she scolded.

"Am I?"

"You know you are."

"I know I'm having a good time with you. Whether we call it flirting, well…"

She sighed. "You made a good point, though."

"About you being pretty?"

"No! About my parents. And you meeting them one day. That makes sense. They'll want to meet you, too. I'm sure they'll be down here the minute the baby's born, but once she's bigger and can travel, I'll want to take her up to Canada now and again. And if you want to come... I won't say no."

"Thanks." He ground out the word, as gritty as the tires had been against the road. "Appreciate that."

She shrugged. "It's nothing."

Such a lie.

It was a lot.

A big, tangled mess of a thing.

He reached over and threaded his fingers through hers and they watched orange fade to navy.

And she couldn't untangle their hands any more than she could their lives.

"It's everything, Marisol."

"Well..."

"Don't minimize it. Please."

"I'm not. It's just... It's the least I can do. You're stepping up, exactly how I asked—"

He brushed a thumb down her jawline, stealing her words. "Of course I am. When it comes to family, I don't do small."

Chapter Five

Marisol glared at the line ahead of her at Peak Beans. Apparently, two weeks of being in Sutter Creek hadn't been enough for her to learn the rhythms of the place. She hadn't anticipated a crowd, and she really wanted to get on with her Saturday. But the seven people who were also waiting for coffee had a similar plan, interfering with her good intentions. With how busy she was preparing her prospectus, her weekends had to serve a double purpose—getting extra research done and taking care of all her personal stuff, too.

And none of that personal stuff was going to involve thinking about how Lachlan had referred to her as family, or how she'd invited him to meet her parents. She'd successfully avoided getting stuck in that particular emotional quicksand since he'd dropped her off after watching the sunset, and wasn't going to let herself get mired in it today.

Today's column in her day planner was a rainbow of coded pen marks, and she'd already checked off the first item, an acupressure appointment with Garnet James. Wow, the woman had gifted fingers. Marisol owed Lach a thanks for that recommendation. Her shoulders were almost what someone would call loose.

Well, loose-adjacent.

Now it was on to Bozeman to hit up the second-hand stores for some apartment things, and hopefully an evening finding journal articles to back up her nebulous hypothesis.

She inched forward in the lineup. The ticking minutes were a palpable weight. Pulling up a journal article on her phone, she started reading.

"Hey there." The gruff, masculine voice wrapped around from behind. Heat settled low in her belly. Having Lachlan murmur in her ear was no different than having his hands all over her. "You look way too tense for someone who just came from an acupressure appointment."

Her back cranked another notch. She jammed her phone in her purse and turned to flash him a benign smile. "You knew I had an appointment?"

"Garnet mentioned it at SAR training a few days ago."

"Fricking fishbowl, this place."

"Yep," he said cheerfully. His gaze dropped to her tapping foot, and he cocked a brow. "Your 'I'm used to putting in a mobile order at Starbucks' is showing."

"So?" she grumbled. "I didn't know ten o'clock was coffee rush hour."

"What's the hurry? You're not working on a Saturday, are you?"

"Uh, I will be after I run some errands. I have a ton to finish before the baby's born."

"So you've said." The corners of his mouth turned down. "Canceling on dinner on Tuesday said a lot, too."

Guilt kicked her in the throat. She'd love to say she'd bailed on the impromptu plans because of school, like she'd told him. And she had stayed late in Bozeman that night. But she could have come home, gone out for dinner with him. Casual, like he'd promised. But the more she thought about everything they'd discussed in his truck last Friday, the more she was nervous about the next thing she'd agree to. And she'd been too afraid to risk making more of a connection than they already had. So she'd hidden behind schoolwork. "I hope me canceling didn't say anything other than 'I have a crapload of work to do.'"

"It…" He leaned close to her ear. "Gotta be honest, I spent the rest of the week trying to convince myself you weren't avoiding me."

She winced.

"Were you avoiding me?"

He stayed close, likely to ensure they had a modicum of privacy as they inched toward the counter in the packed café.

All it did was ensure every pore of her body hummed with energy. She could try to tell herself that nothing good would happen if she closed the space between them.

To a large extent, that was true.

A broken heart, having to parent with someone whom she'd loved and lost, that would be devastating.

But a whole lot of awesome tended to follow him and her and touching bodies.

Adrenaline and oxytocin. Chemicals, not reality. Don't be fooled.

She had enough of those to do with pregnancy— add in any more and she'd be a blithering mess.

Backing up a few inches in an attempt to stifle the electricity still zapping between them, she forced a neutral expression. "Like I said, I have a crapload of work to do."

His strong shoulders deflated a little. "If I learned anything from my parents, working hard and avoidance can coexist."

The psychology student in her twigged on the residual trauma under his words. "Lach…"

He lifted a corner of his mouth, a little "nothing to see here" shrug of lips.

She hated anything other than joy there. If she went up on tiptoe, pressed her mouth to his, could she erase that sadness?

In the middle of gossip central? Talk about giving everyone the wrong idea.

Including him.

And herself.

In no world would a relationship bring joy for either of them. No matter how delightful it would be to revisit their kisses.

"We're up!" He ushered her forward and frowned as he got ready to place their order. "I don't know what you prefer."

"We never went out for coffee," she said gently. "And I wasn't pregnant at the time, so I'm not drinking what I used to anyway. Caffeine and all that." She turned to the barista and ordered a decaf iced latte.

"Right." He stepped to the other end of the barnwood bar and waved for her to follow.

"Hey." She couldn't be responsible for the disappointment in his eyes. Yeah, getting close scared the hell out of her. There was so much new going on. Familiarizing herself with a new department and advisor while jumping into the summer semester of teaching left her with barely enough energy to drive home and eat something with vegetables in it let alone figure out Lachlan Reid.

But getting to know him was just as important as figuring out school and an unfamiliar town. She wasn't going to be able to be a good coparent if she kept him entirely at arm's length. There had to be a balance. Surely she could adapt to the new without forgetting the old.

"You're still good to come to my doctor's appointment on Monday, right?" she asked as he put an arm around her and pulled her closer.

Not out of affection, but because she'd been so lost in her own head that she hadn't noticed a mom with a stroller was trying to get past.

"So sorry," she said, shifting farther away from the woman and out of Lachlan's hold. She looked up at him. "I make a better door than a window, eh?"

His mouth finally stretched into a real smile. "That'll be you in not too long, pushing a stroller. It'll be me, too, for that matter."

"That it will."

He bent his head to her ear. "It's going to look good on you. Just like this does."

He ran a quick palm over her T-shirt-covered belly, and her knees got downright close to dissolving.

Sweet Mary, did he purposefully work to smell so good? But how? It wasn't cologne. A little soap. And lemon laundry detergent. And man.

Her impatient hormones gave her a poke again, reminded her that six months was a very long time to go without appreciating how good a man smelled. And all the enjoyable things that tended to follow burying her nose in Lachlan Reid's neck.

Which she wasn't going to do. No matter how tempting that tanned notch at his collarbone became.

"Flatterer."

"Never. And of course I'll be at your appointment," he said. "Also, I'm off today, which is why I was giving you a hard time about working too much. If I can take the time off, you can, too. You've been here for two weeks, and I bet you're still living out of boxes."

Her cheeks flared hot. "School's busy. But I'm planning to head into Bozeman today to get a few things I'm missing."

"Sounds like something you need a truck for. I have one of those."

"I'm not getting anything big."

His face fell.

"But I'd love the company, if you're offering."

They hit up a used furniture store and found what Marisol declared to be the perfect bench for the foot of her bed.

"I've never had to sit to put on my socks before," she explained, blushing adorably.

He almost teased her for the admission, but she

seemed a little on edge today, so he didn't want to push her in the wrong direction. So he let her guide him from store to store, playing bag-carrier in her wake.

A discount department store was good for towels—cheapest way to make a small bathroom feel lux, according to her—and a runner for the entryway.

At an antiques store, she rooted out forks and knives from a pile of assorted cutlery.

But none if it was baby stuff. Disappointing. Which was weird. Was he nesting? Did men nest?

All he knew was the urge to create safety and calm for this woman and their child burned like a damned inferno inside him.

"This dresser would make a perfect change table if it was painted white and distressed a little," she said, running her hand along the top of a long, wooden piece, currently a drab brown. She made a face. "Who am I kidding? I don't have time to be refinishing furniture."

Neither did he, but he'd find some if it meant bringing her nursery vision to life. He committed the identification code to memory and made a mental note to buy some white paint at the hardware store. And to watch a YouTube video on making a piece of furniture look stylishly worn instead of dilapidated.

"Have you thought of a crib?" he asked.

Her jaw dropped. "Have I thought of a crib?"

"I didn't mean it that way—"

"I'm carrying fifteen pounds around on my stomach. And ten on my ass and thighs. You really think I haven't thought of a crib?"

"Should have stuck to the hand towels," he muttered.

"What?"

"Nothing." Hopefully the sun he got when he was out training with the SAR crew yesterday would hide the warmth in his cheeks. "What, uh, are your thoughts on a crib?"

"I'm borrowing one from Zach and Cadie for now. Ben's moving into a big-boy bed."

"Handy timing."

"Yeah." She fussed with a stack of crocheted doilies on the table in front of her. "Will you want to have the baby at your place? You'll need a crib, too."

He'd need a new place was more like it. Gertie Rafferty had not been wrong about that. But how was he going to swing the expense? He doubted her offer of cheap rent would be as low as he was paying on a studio apartment. Her house had to be a four-bedroom, at least. "I definitely want to share custody."

His stomach twisted the minute he spoke. *Custody.* He looked away.

"Are your parents divorced, Lach?"

"Huh? I mean, no. They've been married since right before Maggie was born." His dad had cheated on his first wife with Lachlan and Maggie's mom.

And now their union was fueled on spite and making money off other people's misery. "They work together, too. The law firm of Reid, Reid and Travers—building the coffers thanks to collapsing marriages since 1982."

Her eyes widened. "The way you said 'custody' made me think you had a history with it."

"Not with being shuttled back and forth or anything." With having parents who liked to use each other—and their children—as verbal-trap bait? There, he was familiar.

"But with being neglected."

It wasn't a question.

Did she expect an answer? He didn't intend to give one.

Being ignored interspersed with brief spurts of lavish attention had been jarring. No need to revisit the specifics, except for the parts that affected them now. "Not a pattern I intend to repeat."

"Lach." Her eyes glistened, and she discarded a lacy scrap of fabric on the table. She threw her arms around him.

Hugging her back, he smiled. Both at the gesture, and at how her belly was big enough to get in the way. "It's okay, Marisol. I've worked past it, really. Found what I needed elsewhere."

She stepped back, leaving a void in his chest, an echo of the emptiness he'd felt when she'd left after her winter holiday.

"But our pasts always leave scars," she said.

"You're the psychology expert. Isn't the general principle that scars fade with time?"

Picking up a teaspoon that had been turned into a bracelet, she studied the tag. "Some dogs never manage to heal from trauma. God, we had a rescue mutt when we were kids. Sweetest guy. But the minute a man with a hat stepped on the property? Pandemonium. Total Mr. Hyde."

He laid a hand over hers. "Look, you're never going to get me to say that dogs can't experience complex emotion, or that they can't empathize—"

"Technically, we don't know they can. That's what I'm studying in part. But I wasn't talking about empathy, I was talking about how someone with a bad childhood might never get over it, and that's okay—"

"Childhood, Marisol?" As if she was still talking about him. "Or a marriage?"

Her throat bobbed, and her gaze flew around the store, wild and searching. "Look! There's baby stuff over there! Ohhhh, an antique pram…"

She strode away from him, and started flicking through garments on a rack with shaky hands.

He lingered back by the doilies for a minute longer, calming his breathing. Having never met Marisol's ex, not knowing his name, even, would complicate his attempts to locate the dude and destroy him. But Lach was resourceful. If he could find a small child in a thick forest during a snowstorm, he could find one asshole and—

Okay, enough fantasy time.

Marisol was the one who was here, the one who needed his attention. Her troubled frown erased his earlier desire to look through tiny clothes and soft blankets. Once he was certain any murderous intent was erased from his expression, he ambled over to her and placed his hands on her shoulders from behind. He fully expected her to shrug off the affection. She didn't, and his heart gave a victory kick.

Christ, her back was knotted. He pressed his thumbs into a few of the tense spots, rubbing at the rigid muscles.

Her hands landed on the handle of the pram she'd exclaimed over, a navy, leather-sided number that reminded him of the baby carriage in a picture of his grandmother and his father from the early '50s. Veins rose on the backs of her hands as her fingers tightened.

"Hey, now," he said. "You're making my job harder. And erasing all Garnet's good work, to boot."

She took a deep breath, and a fraction of her tension dissipated. "There. All relaxed. Happy now?"

"No, sunshine. Not at all."

"The 'sol' in my name doesn't mean sunshine, you know. It means 'Mary of solitude.'"

"I know. I looked it up. But your smile is pretty damn sunny." When she wasn't lost in whatever past garbage her ex-husband had tossed on her, that was.

She turned. There wasn't anywhere for her to go,

though, not in the cramped store. The pram rocked as she bumped against it. But she didn't look upset that they were in each other's personal space, so he didn't take a step back.

"Mine means warlike. Or something to do with lakes," he threw out. "Scottish, of course, given my mom's from there."

Her expression softened. She reached up and ran a hand down his stubble. "Didn't know you were into anthroponomastics."

"Say what?"

"Name meanings."

"Such an academic, showing off your ten-dollar words."

She blushed.

He leaned in. "I like it."

The pretty rosiness warming her light brown cheeks deepened. Her lips parted.

Christ, it would be so easy to close the distance, taste that mouth again.

She'd been too delicious to forget.

And had felt too good in his arms to bother to try.

He mentally slapped away the thought. She was just stuck on how to reply after he'd flirted with her with all the grace of a high school freshman.

Don't take it as an invitation. A massage could be explained away as a friendly gesture. A kiss, not so much. A kiss lay over the line she'd drawn, and he wasn't going to violate that line without clear permission.

Thumbing the center of her lower lip, the tiniest of caresses, he waited for a response.

She lost all the color in her face and whirled around.

His hopes sank to the bottom of his stomach.

Not the answer he wanted, but at least it was clear. He stepped backward, giving her space.

She picked up the tag hanging off the pram. "Damn. Way too expensive. My parents are buying me one of those top-of-the-line mountain-going strollers, so there's no point in splurging on a second."

And if he was going to surprise her with that dresser, he couldn't also justify the carriage, no matter how much it made her eyes light up.

No matter how much he hated not being able to give her the world.

Chapter Six

*C*lunk.

Marisol let out a squeak and gripped the wheel tighter, startled by the sudden noise coming from under the hood of her car.

Thwap, thwap, thwap.

The wheel wasn't pulling, but even so—not a good noise. Crap. She'd really wanted to be on time this afternoon. She was supposed to be meeting Lachlan and Maggie to go to the corn-and-burger fund-raiser the search and rescue crew was hosting as part of the town's Fourth of July celebrations. They'd both given her a hard time and pointed out that she was acting like a Canadian by not taking the day off.

But days off didn't exist in her world right now, not until the sixth of September.

Not after it, either.

Sighing, and thankful she had roadside assistance, she pulled off onto the wide shoulder. She rolled down her windows to prevent the car from getting too hot and cut the engine. A belt was probably on the verge of snapping. Too bad she didn't have leggings on, she could fix it.

Provided leggings worked the same as nylons did as a makeshift belt on a car engine. Actually knowing how to replace a belt on the engine of a car would be kind of key, too. One of those moments where being an academic was less than useful. Having read a random fact in a book was not the same as actually being MacGyver.

She called for a tow, but there was only one Triple-A affiliated facility in Sutter Creek, and apparently there were delays. It was going to take a good forty-five minutes for them to get to her, given it wasn't an emergency.

Tell that to the large club soda I had at lunch.

"I'm pregnant," she threw out. Never knew when that would help.

"Oh, been there, honey," said the female voice who'd answered the call. "How far along?"

"Six—I mean, seven months." Caleb had reminded her of that when she and Lachlan had gone in for her now biweekly appointment last week.

The call center woman clucked her tongue. "I'll do what I can to get someone your way as soon as I can. But the holiday means we're short a truck."

Damn. Thanking the woman, she hung up and tilted her seat back a few inches. At least she had a full bottle of water. Not that drinking was going to help with the tiny baby elbow digging into her bladder, but at least she wouldn't get dehydrated. The sun angled through the passenger window of the car, catching Marisol's right side. Sweat dotted her temples, and she scrounged for an elastic, then twisted her rapidly curling hair into a hasty bun.

She should text Lachlan, at least, apologize for being late.

Car trouble, she typed. Probably won't make it for the BBQ.

Three dots appeared immediately, and then Where r u?

About twenty minutes down the highway.

His reply came within two seconds. B there in 15.

She was about to tell him not to bother, but God, she had to pee.

K, thx, she replied, adding, Don't speed.

About twelve minutes later, a dot of forest green appeared in the distance on the winding highway that hugged the Gallatin River. So much for her insistence that he not speed. He passed her, then pulled a U-turn and parked behind her.

She could have gotten out to meet him, but watching him stride toward her through the side mirror kinda had the feel of a sexy-police-officer fantasy, which, hello. Sure, he had on a gray T-shirt and navy plaid shorts. But she could pretend he was plainclothes…

Stop objectifying your child's father.

She snorted at herself. Objectifying Lachlan was exactly what had gotten her into this mess.

"What seems to be the problem, miss?" he drawled. He braced his hands on the open window ledge and smirked.

"So I wasn't the only one thinking officer-and-damsel-in-distress. Nice touch with the aviators," she teased. Except it wasn't a joke. Those sunglasses, plus his wind-mussed caramel hair and crooked grin, made him look like a fricking model. His grip on the car making his biceps bulge didn't hurt, either.

Her mouth went dry.

I'm just thirsty.

One of his eyebrows rose above the dark frames. "You've got water right next to you."

Crap, there she went thinking out loud again. "I didn't want to risk having to use the facilities even more."

He snorted. "Good thing I came to get you." He opened her door and offered her a hand. "Grab what you need and leave the key under the mat. Freddy'll call when he gets the car to the shop."

Taking his fingers, she stood, way less gracefully than she would have liked. Her ears went hot. "I swear, I'm going to have the poise of an elephant once I'm full-term."

Smiling softly, he kissed her cheek. "Stop it. You're beautiful."

"You have to say that. You're the one who did this."

Except, he didn't have to say it. Nor did he have to shift closer to her and scrape his teeth along his lower lip. Or tighten his fingers on hers.

A thrill of heat coursed through her limbs. He was under no obligation at all to want her. Nor should she *want him* to want her. But…did he still?

She couldn't see his eyes. His sunglasses were too mirrored.

Uh, you don't need to see his eyes. Those predatory shoulders? They say it all.

"Lachlan?"

He shook his head slowly, amazement flirting on his lips. With his free hand, he palmed the side of her belly. "I did do this," he said lightly. "And just when I think I'm used to it, I get reminded… And I'm thrown for a loop all over again."

"You always throw me for a loop," she murmured. Okay, why had she said that? Stupid.

But the way he was caressing her stomach, it

wasn't a bonding-with-the-kid touch like he'd done before. His jaw was too slack for that.

And the flicker of a pulse at his throat—that said *I love touching your body.*

Maybe a little *I want to touch it some more.*

She reached behind her and swung the car door shut, then leaned against it. Their linked fingers meant she brought him with her.

Lifting his sunglasses to the top of his head, she stared into his questioning eyes.

And damn it. It was hot, and she was bothered, and she was too tired to pretend it had to do with her broken-down car or the July sun or anything except the six-plus-feet of masculine perfection waiting with his head tilted slightly.

"Want me to grab your briefcase?"

"After."

His eyes were hope and need and melted chocolate. "What's first?"

"Kiss me." She ran her hands up his chest. God, she'd been wanting to do that for weeks, and the hard muscles did not disappoint.

His mouth teased the skin by her ear. "Where?"

The drawled question fluttered in her hair. Anticipation shimmered along her skin.

Everywhere.

But that was impossible.

So she settled, caught his jaw with a finger and pulled his lips to hers.

Settled. Ha.

As if kissing Lachlan Reid would ever be settling.

With nips and brushes, a hand along her neck, one at her hip, he laid a mesmerizing kiss on her.

Sweet Mary, his mouth.

How could it get better?

She didn't want to think about how much he'd practiced on his trip across continents. But who cared? She had him here, now, and he was the key to everything locked up inside her.

No.

She had critical reasons for her walls. They needed to stay intact.

No matter how blissful it was to dig her fingers into his back and press every part of her against his hard body.

"Lachlan." She turned her face to the side.

He held her head to his chest, which rose and fell rapidly.

"Mari," he croaked. "Forgot you taste like sunshine, too."

She exhaled, shifted out of his embrace. She didn't know how to reply to that. Or how to get across the reasons why any more kisses would lead them further into stupidity.

"We should go. I really— Well— I mean— The kid's using my bladder as a trampoline."

A couple of minutes later, Lachlan had Marisol ensconced in his air-conditioned truck. She looked marginally less pink, but entirely still flustered.

He got that. His heart sprinted, could probably keep up with the truck were it to sprout legs and run on the shoulder.

He wasn't stupid enough to believe she'd let him kiss her again. No, her shuttered eyes blinked "permanently closed" more effectively than a damned neon sign.

Could he live off the memory of nuzzling her ear? Of the jolt of arousal that had slammed through him when she turned his face and kissed him?

Driving to Bozeman would remind him of her melting in his arms on the side of the road for the rest of his damned life.

She shifted in her seat, and he glanced at her. Her gaze focused on her hands, and she toyed with a delicate trio of gold rings on her right middle finger.

"We need to stay friends," she muttered.

"You're telling me friends kiss like that?"

"Hence not kissing."

He suppressed a laugh, but it huffed out through his nose. "Kind of broke that rule."

"That we did." Her expression shifted, a battle between resistance and yearning.

"You look torn."

She rolled her head along the headrest, tilting her face to look at him. "I *am*."

Since when? She'd been the one to make the rules in the first place. Rubbing his mouth with a hand, he covered up the I-told-you-so that was flirting with the corners of his lips. "Sounds like a dilemma."

"It is." She frowned. "I…"

He waited.

"I really like kissing you, Lachlan."

His jaw dropped. There was no covering the shock from that. Not that she enjoyed making out with him. He'd felt that in her pliable body, in her eager kiss. But that she'd admitted it? Where was the full-on, that-was-a-terrible-decision litany he'd been anticipating?

"Well, let me know when you want to do it again," he said.

She grimaced.

"Or not." Yeah, that was more in line with his expectations. He really needed to figure out where her head was at. Probably wrapped up in her past. He could head her off at the pass, there. "Tell me about your divorce."

"God, why?"

Keeping his eyes on the road, he reached over with one hand to stroke her forearm. "I want to understand."

Damn, silence could be loud sometimes. The truck rumbled and the radio played, but not loud enough to cover Marisol's breath hitching.

"He left me in the hospital. And in a hell of a lot of debt, to boot."

Uh, what? Money troubles, he was familiar with.

And that explained all her questions about his business and her hesitance about him getting involved financially in her life. But an illness of some kind? That was a surprise. He snuck a glance at her. She was staring out the side window, face completely turned from him. "When were you in the hospital?"

"After a miscarriage."

Tick, tick, boom. The word landed like a time-release grenade.

Heartache and clarity throbbed in his chest. "Oh, sunshine…"

She shrugged.

He almost pulled the car over—his arms clamored to hold her—but she was folded into herself, clearly needing physical space. "Sorry's never enough, Marisol, but even so, I am."

"Thanks."

"Were you worried you'd miscarry our baby?"

"Uh, yeah. And not exactly past tense."

Fear flickered behind his breastbone. Too fragile, life… But at the same time, not. He clenched the steering wheel instead of reaching over and touching her bump, confirming the solidity, the reality. "Seems like something that would have come up at a doctor's appointment."

"It has. Caleb and I talked about it before you arrived at my first appointment. He, like my doctor in Vancouver, isn't worried. My previous miscarriage was just chance, not because of a recurring risk."

"You don't sound reassured."

She shrugged. "You're in the medical field. You know how things can go wrong."

"I know how they can go right, too." He cleared his throat. "Same thing with relationships."

Yeah, he tended toward idealism. His sisters harassed him about being a romantic all the time. But he had no interest in being miserable like his parents, or lonely like Maggie and Stella. It wasn't taking the risk to be with a person that caused problems, it was not being willing to put in the work, or being too selfish to be a team. He'd seen his grandparents celebrate their fifty-third wedding anniversary because of teamwork. And after Grams died, his grandfather had found love again, was happy living with his new wife under the Palm Desert sun. Love was worth it. He had to believe that.

Wanted to convince the woman currently worrying the edge of her seat belt of that, too.

He could love her so easily.

"I just want things to be platonic, Lachlan. Kissing proved me right—any physical intimacy confuses things. And parenting's going to be confusing enough on its own."

"You're wrong, Maris—" The phrase stopped him. *You're wrong, Lachlan.*

Christ.

The last thing he wanted was to echo his father.

The man had a trademark on being an overbearing jerk.

He shot her an apologetic look. "I mean, I don't agree. But if your ex left you at such a critical time *and* left you in a bad place financially, I can see why you're wary."

That earned him a little smile of relief.

The lengths he'd go to get her to smile… Could get dangerous, really. But if she needed him to be patient, well, he could do that for her. Sometimes, being a team meant letting the other person take the lead for a while. Which, fine. He had no problem with that, and hopefully she'd one day want to kiss him again.

Sharing their lives still seemed too tall of a sell. He'd have to work up to that.

Chapter Seven

"Hello?"

The Monday after the long weekend, Marisol stood in the empty veterinary clinic waiting room at the end of the workday, hoping to bend Lachlan's sister's ear. The woman trained therapy dogs, and given Marisol's proposed research surrounded canine empathy, she was curious to get a variety of perspectives. She'd scheduled a prospectus presentation date for mid-August, and the thing wasn't written yet. Running a freshman psychology course was seriously cutting into her time. Also, napping. She felt guilty every time she passed out on the couch, but couldn't help it. The baby demanded naps. And being exhausted had an adverse effect on her blood pressure.

"Hello? Anyone here?" she asked, peering down the hall behind the reception desk. Evan was nowhere to be seen.

Maggie's curly blond head poked out from the staff room doorway at the end of the corridor. "Is someone out— Oh."

Marisol smiled, despite Maggie's dull tone. "Got a minute?"

"I guess." She waved Marisol into the staff room, but didn't look too pleased about it.

Nerves jangled in Marisol's stomach. It didn't seem right to dive into "can you help me with my research" with someone wearing a scowl worthy of the Grumpy Cat poster on the wall.

"My brother's out back," Maggie said, turning away to clean the coffeepot at the sink under a wide double window. Back when the building had been a house, this room must have been the kitchen. Marisol smiled at the old-school, harvest-gold appliances, nearly facsimiles of the ones still housed in her abuelita's kitchen in the basement suite of her parents' Whistler home.

"I'm here to talk to you, actually."

"Ah, you've finally decided to get to know your new family?" She put the coffeepot down in a drying rack with a thunk.

Oh, great. How was she supposed to ask a favor

now? She settled into one of the mismatched chairs ringing the pristinely clean Formica table. "I'd love to."

Maggie plunged her hands back into the dishwater. A muffled clatter of cutlery against stainless steel rang out. "Wouldn't have thought that, given you bailed on us on the Fourth."

Hadn't Lachlan explained why Marisol hadn't been able to make it to the barbecue that night? Marisol frowned, not that Maggie could see her face with her back turned. She made sure to keep her voice level. "I was sitting in the waiting area at the mechanic's, signing away my—"

Okay. A firstborn child joke seemed harsh. Nor did she feel like admitting how much the bill for a new serpentine belt was eating into her incidentals budget for the month. She had a stipend from the university, and a decent grant from a group supporting women in STEM, but no cushion to speak of. A car repair expense was no small potatoes, especially since she couldn't revert to eating ramen noodles like she'd done while finishing her master's. The baby needed protein and veggies.

"Yeah, he mentioned something about that." Maggie's shoulders drooped, and she turned. A world of worry pooled in her eyes.

"I wouldn't cancel without a reason."

"Reason or not, people still end up disappointed."

Marisol stiffened. She was not here for a lecture

on behavioral consequences. "I didn't mean to let you down."

"It's not about me. It's about my brother." Maggie dried her hands and sat down across from Marisol. Her fists clenched on the table. "He might be the youngest, but you'd never know it. He's been taking care of me since we were kids. And he would have with Stella, too, had she let him. Nothing fazed him. Needed tampons? Send Lach to the store. Boyfriend troubles? He was the best listener in the family. But…"

Silence dragged. Apparently, the therapeutic techniques class she'd taken was wrong—people didn't always elaborate if you waited quietly. Marisol cocked her head. "But…"

"He's fazed, Marisol."

Huh. She settled back against her chair. He hadn't seemed bothered when he came to retrieve her from her car on Friday. No, wait, he had. He'd admitted to feeling thrown. "Shouldn't he be, though? A baby and all that?"

"He could have used more time, which he would have had if you'd put in a modicum of effort to find him and tell him."

"I did, I called, and—" God, what was the point in finishing? Maggie knew the extent of Marisol's efforts, and clearly found them lacking, and was still stewing about it weeks after the fact.

"Came to see me at work, sunshine?"

Marisol jolted at the intrusion, and glanced over her shoulder.

Lachlan stood in the doorway. The comfortable, slow, hot-as-anything smile stretching across his face had nerves dancing on her diaphragm again.

"I was here to see Maggie, actually..."

His smile flickered for a second, like a light bulb loose in its socket. "That's good to hear. Gotta keep Auntie Maggie on our good side, right?" He strolled next to Marisol and settled a casual hand on her shoulder.

An urge rose to rub against him. *Which is just wrong. I'm not a dog begging for a back scratch.* Plus, he wasn't coming on to her. He was just a toucher.

"You should have asked me out for coffee," Maggie grumbled, staring at her brother's hand as he rubbed absentminded circles around Marisol's shoulder blade.

Funny, Marisol swore she'd put on a shirt this morning. But by the heat seeping from his hand to her skin, it was as if the cotton of her blouse didn't exist.

"I— What?" Her brain couldn't simultaneously make sense of Maggie's words and Lachlan's touch.

"Instead of coming here, catching me in scrubs and dog hair. It's not exactly a getting-to-know-you locale." Maggie shot Marisol a suspicious look. "If that's why you came."

"It was." An image of the cursor of her word processing program blinked in her mind. She couldn't move forward on her proposal without bouncing her ideas off an expert. "Of course it was. And I was also wondering if I could run a few questions by you about a study I'm going to need to set up if my dissertation plans get approved."

"Right." Maggie shot to her feet, sending her chair screeching back a few inches on the tile floor. "Figured it wasn't just about me. Otherwise you'd have come before now."

She stalked out of the room.

Marisol closed her eyes, a curse hovering on her tongue.

"Hey." Lachlan pulled a chair around and sat, knee brushing hers. "Do you need a veterinarian for those questions, or would a tech do?"

The hopeful lift of his mouth set off alarm bells. But why? Lachlan was just as qualified as Maggie in terms of working dogs. He'd for sure have ideas and contacts for her. But she couldn't get her lips to form the words. Enlisting his help was one more tie she couldn't afford. Neither the closeness nor the risk she'd start depending on him only to have him get busy with the upcoming training facility construction and no longer be able to help her. She didn't want him getting ideas, either, that this would lead to the depth of connection and vulnerability that he

seemed to want. She'd never be able to open up like
that again.

"That's okay. I'll figure it out. I was just hoping
to use the topic as a way to thaw out your sister," she
lied. "Which backfired."

A tawny-blond brow lifted. "She's gone a bit
guard dog. I'll talk to her."

"Because that would go over well. Something
tells me Maggie's not going to like you coming to
my defense."

"As long as I'm happy, she'll be fine."

Fear snaked down her spine, and she stared at
her knees. Would he be happy, coparenting the way
she wanted?

*Better to try that than being together. Together
will eventually come apart.*

It would be bad enough to face that on her own,
but she didn't want to subject her baby to that kind
of rejection. She had another heart to guard now,
not just her own.

He shifted his hand to the base of her neck and
massaged a knot.

She swallowed a moan.

"Want to come over for burgers?" he asked.

Her hesitation must have struck a nerve because
he grimaced.

"Come on, Marisol. Work with me here. We're
going to need to be friends if we're going to raise a
kid." He pulled his hand away, held both in the air

like a bank robber was pointing a gun at him. "Is that the problem? Me touching you? I'm sorry. I'm an affectionate guy. I didn't mean anything by it."

I wish you had.

He had a point, though. They would be around each other a hell of a lot. Which meant she needed to get desensitized to him. And a zillion psych textbooks told her the best way to do that was through exposure. "Burgers sound great."

Lachlan backed his truck up to Maggie's double garage Tuesday evening. Fudge was a liver-brown and white blur as she hopped out of the car and surveyed Maggie's front yard with her nose to the ground, making sure no squirrels had dared set a toe on the premises since their last visit. He let himself in with his spare key and managed to hit the automatic door button before his sister noticed. She came into the garage from the inside entrance right as he was shifting the dresser to the end of the tailgate.

"Uh, Lach?"

"Yeah?"

"Whatcha doing?" Fudge bounded over, and Maggie bent down to snuggle the dog before standing and adjusting her headband. The pink strip held her hair off her face, and her Darth Vader pajama bottoms and bought-it-in-high-school sweatshirt broadcasted she was in for the night.

"I'm unloading a dresser. Come help. Climb up and lift from the top while I lower it down."

"What?"

"Climb up and lift—"

"Yeah, I heard you." She rolled her eyes and snapped her fingers at Fudge to lie down on the dog bed in the corner of the garage. She shuffled down the two stairs to the cement pad. "But I don't understand."

"Did I not mention this on the weekend at some point? Marisol was eyeing this dresser. I'm going to refinish it for her. A surprise. And given I can't exactly work on it in my apartment..." He motioned to the empty space next to her SUV.

"Oh, good grief." Her sigh was epic, but she hoisted herself onto the tailgate and gave him a hug before shooing him to the ground. "During what spare time? I thought you were meeting with the contractor and working on your website this week."

"I am. I'll just live with less sleep for a while."

She made a face, but was too busy grumbling about heavy old dressers to reply.

Once they had the wooden behemoth off the truck and onto an old drop cloth, she grabbed him by the elbow.

"I don't want her to get in the way of your plans. You've worked too hard to have your focus divided."

"Maggie." He raked his free hand through his

hair. "It's not about her. It's about becoming a father. And doing that right."

She blanched, stricken.

"Hadn't thought of it that way?" he murmured.

"Not exactly." Her lower lip wobbled.

Something he'd seen far too many times over the years. Maggie liked to pretend that their parents' "we only pay attention when it suits us" routine didn't bother her, but wet eyelashes didn't lie.

"I want to do this right," he repeated.

"You will."

Doubt crawled up the back of his neck. Showing Marisol she could trust him was no small feat. Nor were the more tangible concerns. Balancing his training business and his tech job, finding a new place to live, affording it all… There were too many variables. But he didn't want to give Maggie another reason to worry about Marisol and him. She needed to hear all the things that were going right.

He stepped back and started examining the dresser's finish. Sanding sucked ass, and getting the glossy varnish off was going to take a lot of it. "Dinner last night went well, you know." He'd put forward the invitation, expecting Marisol to make her usual excuses. But for once she'd said yes.

"Yeah?" Maggie sounded entirely unconvinced.

"It was absolutely—" he scrambled for the right word "—normal. Unremarkable, almost."

Except for how much he'd wanted to have Marisol

in his bed rather than sitting in his armchair with a tea in her hand. Though the fact she'd accepted his invitation and they'd had a quiet evening was a step forward.

"You hooking up with her again?" Maggie asked.

"Not that it's your business, but no." He pulled the dresser drawers out and stacked them next to the main frame.

"Huh. I'm kinda surprised by that."

"She doesn't want to risk things not working out between us," he admitted. He hadn't wanted to get into it, but keeping it all inside was too hard. He and Maggie had always been confidants. He'd have loved to be equally close to his half sister, Stella, but she'd always kept a wall between them.

"Logical." A note of appreciation colored the word.

"Probably." Frustrating, though. Marisol hadn't stayed late last night. She'd been legit tired after a long day at work. And once she'd gone, he'd taken a cold-as-hell shower.

But though he'd had to work to keep from touching her, avoiding small displays of affection as much as anything sexual, having to focus on talking had been nice. She'd mainly discussed her dissertation and classes, and he, his plans for construction and course offerings. And damn, she'd looked right in his space.

Not long from now, there'd be a tiny human joining them.

It still shorted out his brain, acknowledging that.

"I'm thinking of checking out Gertie Rafferty's house on Ponderosa tomorrow over my lunch break. Decent yard, three bedrooms."

Maggie gnawed on her lip. "Space doesn't mean love, Lach."

They both knew that. Their parents' house in Chicago was massive. And entirely devoid of real love. "I'm not going for a McMansion, Maggie. I just need more than five hundred and fifty square feet. For the baby."

And for Marisol.

He'd agreed to keep things platonic. But his heart still held out for that changing in time. One reason he'd been so happy to have last night's dinner be re-laxed and easy. If Marisol saw that they clicked in more ways than just sex, she might start to soften her stance on getting closer.

"Babies don't take up much space, Lach," Maggie said.

No, but his pride did, apparently, because no way would he cram a crib in underneath the TV mounted to the wall by his bed. "It's a happy medium, Mags." He snapped his fingers. "I hear about the Backcountry International grant sometime this week. Then I'll be able to breathe easy."

"What if you don't get it?"

"Hold your tongue." He sent her a teasing grin. "I will. It's all but a formality, given how I saved their ass by taking the traveling position this winter."

She smiled, but her deep breath echoed the apprehension he'd been living with since he'd started signing contracts with people to build the barn.

Hoisting his box of supplies from the truck, he took out two sanding blocks. "Here. Take out your worries on some ugly varnish."

Chapter Eight

On his lunch hour the next day, Lachlan left Fudge under Evan's watchful eye, hopped in his truck and headed for Ponderosa Street. His route took him past Marisol's apartment, and her car was in the parking lot.

He pulled in to a visitor spot and dialed her up on his cell.

"Hello?"

"You're home."

"How do you know?" she asked warily.

"I was driving by—I'm on my way over to check out a house… Want to come along?"

"You want my help picking out a house?"

"I could use a second set of eyes. Are you busy?"

"I've been staring at the same paragraph for the last two hours," she said with a yawn.

"You need a break, then."

She sighed. "I really do. But I'm not dressed to go out."

"Oh." He checked the clock on the dash. "I need to be there in seven minutes."

"God, you like giving a woman some real lead time."

"I—It was a spontaneous invite." More like her inevitable refusal was easier to take if he could blame it on not giving her any warning versus asking in advance and having to wonder if she just didn't want to spend time with him.

"Let me see what I can do. I'll be down in a few."

He stared at his phone. Had he heard that correctly? But she'd already hung up.

True to her word, she exited the building three minutes later. She had on leggings and a loose top with a wide, asymmetrical neckline. Her hair was up in a messy bun.

Her academic-on-a-writing-tear look only intensified the urge to wrap his arms around her. He hopped out and went to the passenger side to give her a boost.

"Thanks." She smiled, lips bare of their usual gloss. Actually, her whole face was makeup-free. Goddamn, she looked kissable. Natural sexy.

He swallowed down the urge to lean in. "Thank

you. I'll make it up to you. If you want to use any of my contacts in the training world, let me know."

"I don't know, Lachlan." She gripped her purse strap with both hands and stared at her knuckles.

"Just think about it. It might help."

"Okay."

Going back around to his side, he got in, started the car and headed toward the rental. "I was thinking about what you told me about your study. That you're trying to clarify the factors that impact canine empathy—"

"If canine empathy exists at all," she cut in. "Still hasn't been proven."

"Scientifically? Maybe not. Practically? You'll never convince me it doesn't."

"Well, that's what I'm trying to do. See if the science will back up the practical."

"What about narrowing down your test groups even more, then?" When she'd explained her study to him over dinner two nights ago, she'd talked about having groups of mixed breeds. "Separate them out. By breed, by type of training. Take Labradors, for example—test a group of working Labs, a group who aren't working and a control group, whatever that would look like."

"The problem is, breed or working or whatever, when dogs are exposed to a situation where they're tested to see if they respond to distress, we can't know for sure why they do or don't go to their owners or handlers. It might be empathy, but it could also be loneliness or curiosity. A hope of getting dinner."

"What about changing up the sounds, then? Some distress, some not."

"I thought of that. I thought of all these things. But my previous advisor wanted me to stick close to a study that's already been done. Part of the reason I was happy to switch schools—I never worked well with that guy."

"Now that you're with someone new, you could try again."

"I could." She peered out the window as he slowed to a stop at a curb of a quiet residential street a few blocks from her apartment. "I'm nervous to change things up given my tight timeline."

He got out and opened her door for her. Squeezed her hand in reassurance as he helped her down. "It'll be the next couple of years of your life, though. Not to mention your name on a study. If you've thought of all these things and had to argue yourself out of pursuing them—maybe there's something to that."

"Maybe." She straightened her shirt. Her expression went from contemplative to charmed as she took in the olive green split-level house with a cheerful border of bedding plants. "Oh, Lach, it's adorable."

Satisfaction spread through his stomach. "Glad you think so. Come on, Mrs. Rafferty will be waiting for us."

"Ah, you caved to her offer, did you?"

"We'll see. She's persistent." He snorted at the understatement. "I'm sure she's learned everything from your shoe size to the way you take your coffee by now."

"Comforting."

"Just means you've been accepted by the old guard." Lach palmed Marisol's lower back as they traveled the cement path bisecting the lawn and went up steps to the stoop to knock on the door. "I can tell she likes you."

The front door swung open. "Of course I like her! She caught your eye, didn't she?" Mrs. Rafferty exclaimed.

Ah. Their voices must have traveled through the living room window, which was open a crack.

"Gertie, we're not a couple," Lachlan reminded the older woman as she waved them inside the front entrance and into her empty living area.

"That's what they all say, dear, but you're house hunting together." A brow arched over her Ruth Bader Ginsburg-esque glasses. She had on a T-shirt and long shorts, and from the dirt smudged on the hem of her top, he suspected she'd been gardening.

"I want Marisol to be comfortable with the house where I'll be living with our child."

Comfortable enough to want to move in.

Good grief, he was getting ahead of himself.

"I brought up four kids and a grandson here. It's

well loved. Raising Ryan, well, you know…" She took a deep breath.

He smiled sympathetically. Ryan Rafferty defined "upstanding county sheriff" now, but he'd been a hell-raiser in his younger days. With Lach's older sister Stella, to be specific. Talk about a love that flamed out. Stella still wasn't over it, as far as Lachlan could tell. The rare time they talked, she didn't bring it up.

"I wouldn't rent it to just anyone," Mrs. Rafferty said.

Marisol reached out and touched the older woman's arm. "We'd take—I mean, Lach would take good care of it."

We. Damn, that sounded good coming from her pretty mouth.

"How about I show you the master bedroom, first?" Gertie's eyes twinkled as she glanced meaningfully between Marisol and him.

"You're incorrigible," he scolded gently.

"That I am." She headed down the hall, motioning for them to follow.

He didn't need to see the bedroom to know he'd picture Marisol in it for as long as he lived here. And he would live here. He'd scrimp and cut corners with his monthly budget to make the rent on this place. Spending so much of his life in the bush relying on both his and Fudge's instincts meant he was willing to trust how right this felt in his gut. But Mrs. Rafferty seemed so amused and nostalgic by taking them around and telling stories about her life in the house that he stayed until the last possible minute, scribbling out a check for a security deposit on the fly.

"Take me to the office with you," Marisol said once they were in the truck. "I'll walk home. I need to move before I dive back into my research."

"Sure."

She crossed her arms over her chest and stared at the floorboards. "It's a good house, Lachlan."

"Agreed."

"You're sure it's not too much?"

She probably meant space, not money. But he bristled at the question. "It's just right."

"You have a lot on your plate. I'm sorry this is complicating your life."

He pulled into the clinic parking lot and braked hard. "We're both responsible. And we're both doing what we can to manage. Why are you apologizing?"

Apologizing, and withdrawing. He could feel her pulling away.

"I don't know." She shook her head. "I guess I'm used to feeling at fault for things going wrong in a relationship."

"We don't have a relationship, Marisol. Not the kind where things can go wrong, anyway."

Her regretful gaze cut deep. Christ. Why was she looking at him like that? With just enough doubt to make him hope there was a chance? Maybe he shouldn't have put it that way. Maybe he should keep his mouth shut about relationships in general.

"Right," she said.

No, it wasn't. Nothing about this was right. But he'd promised he wouldn't push, so he wouldn't. If he wanted to earn her trust, he needed to keep his word on that. And once he'd proved he had her back, then he could work on reminding her of how perfect it had felt to fall into a kiss on the side of a dusty road.

When he circled around the truck, she flung her door open and shook her head. Gripping the door tightly, she climbed down. "I can do it myself."

"I know. But there's nothing wrong with getting a hand now and then."

"I guess."

Had two less convincing words ever been spoken? Frustration ripped through him and he pointed her in the direction of her apartment. "You know the way?"

"For sure."

I can do this without you, in other words.

That applied to more than just climbing out of trucks and street directions. What was it going to take for her to be willing to be actual partners?

He stomped into the clinic, steps echoing on the tile loud enough to turn heads in the waiting room. His phone vibrated in his pocket and he stopped in the middle of the hallway to check it, on the off chance it was Marisol.

An email alert was on the screen. From Backcountry International. His heart skipped a beat. Things hadn't gone well on a personal front today, but maybe some business success would soothe the earlier sting.

He pulled the message up on the screen.

Dear Mr. Reid,

We regret to inform—

The rest of the words blurred and his gut took a nosedive. No damn way. He wasn't the recipient? What?

Bile rose at the back of his throat. The number he'd just written on the check to Gertie Rafferty, and the extra rent he'd be paying every month added to the loss of zeros from the grant...

He swore.

A throat cleared behind him. His sister. "Thought I talked to you about keeping your language clean around this place in case there are patients nearby."

He passed her the phone.

Her expression fell. "Oh, Lach. I'm sorry."

The second time a woman had apologized to him for something out of her control today, but this one felt more sincere. He shrugged. "I'll figure it out."

"How? We're both tapped out."

"And I just stretched myself further today."

She grimaced.

"I know." He matched her expression. "I'll try the

bank again. And if that doesn't work, I could call Mom and Dad, I guess."

"Seriously?"

He closed his eyes. Being indebted to his parents? Feeling like he was at their beck and call, like he owed them after spending so many years blessedly free of their machinations? "No, not seriously. I'll have to find another grant. Or delay."

"But you have a schedule with the contractor."

"I do." He shook his head. Delaying wouldn't work. His contractor had a job lined up right after his project. "Family might be the best option, though, and Mom and Dad aren't the only ones in our family with money. I'll give Stella a call."

Their hedge fund managing half sister hated everything to do with Sutter Creek, but she understood vocational dreams. Maybe she'd float him a loan.

He waited to call until around six, when he was over at Maggie's putting the first coat of paint on the dresser. Stella picked up after a few rings.

"Hey there, errant youngest child. Has Grams's ghost started to haunt you for having a baby out of wedlock yet?"

He snorted. "No, but Gertie Rafferty's doing her best to pick up the slack."

Stella paused, and he kicked himself for bringing up her ex's grandmother. Ryan Rafferty was a no-go subject with his sister.

"I was kidding, Lach," she finally said. "And don't listen to Gertie. No way should you consider marrying this woman."

"She's not 'this woman.' She's the mother of my child. And I'm not trying to marry her." *Not yet, anyway.* "But I do want to date her. Get to know her better."

"You obviously know her in some ways," she said dryly. "And you *don't* know how to use a condom."

"Jesus, Stella."

"What?"

"You're not exactly one to give a sex-ed lecture." He wasn't the only Reid to have an accidental pregnancy on their record. Stella had gotten pregnant the summer after her senior year but had miscarried fairly early on. He never had pieced together if she'd told Ryan. He'd been sent to a ranch across the state after getting in trouble with the law. And she refused to talk about it, especially since Ryan had returned and was now the town's prodigal son instead of the rabble-rouser he'd been before he left.

Her stony silence dragged on far too long for comfort, until she finally said, "So you're calling just to be your usual pain-in-the-ass?"

"Sort of." His stomach jittered. *It'll either be yes or no. Might as well get it over with.* "I need you to invest in my business, Stell."

She laughed. "Put money into Sutter Creek? Yeah, right."

He sucked in a breath. Sure, she had never professed love for the town. Outright tore the place down, more like it. But he'd have thought her feelings would be swayed by the fact this was his dream. "It has nothing to do with Sutter Creek. It has to do with me. With what I've been working toward since I was a teenager."

"My life is in New York, Lachlan. You're not going to pull me back there. You and Maggie have been trying to get me to come home, to tie me to that town for years now. It's not going to work."

"I'm not—" Stifling a groan, he released a desperate gulp of air. "Stella, that's not what this is about. Whatever past you have with your ex is unrelated to my business."

"And my feelings toward the town have nothing to do with Ryan effing Rafferty."

Pointing out that gargantuan lie would only piss her off more, so he modulated his tone and said, "This is really important to me."

"I'm sure it is. Send me your business plan, I'll take a look. But I'm not dropping cash on anything to do with that godforsaken place."

Okay, then.

Hopes dashed, he was no longer in the mood for chitchat. He cut the call short and sat down on the drop cloth. Fudge cocked her head at him, a classic pointer forty-five-degree-angle "what's up" tilt, and trotted over from the dog bed to sit in the crook of his crossed legs. He wrapped his arms around her and nuzzled behind her ear.

"Such a good girl," he mumbled into her short fur.

She flopped against his chest and stuck her cool nose under his jaw, licking him until he laughed.

"You think you can fix everything, hey, dog?" He wished life were so easy as chew toys and dog biscuits.

But no, Fudge's life wasn't that simple. She did amazing work in the bush and the snow. And he wasn't going to bother being modest—he was a hell of a handler and teacher. He couldn't give up on his dream. But he needed to figure out a way to compromise, somehow.

If Stella wasn't going to help him, he might have to call his parents, after all.

He shuddered and scratched Fudge's belly. Last resort. Maybe the bank would hear him out, save him from depending on his parents in a way he'd promised himself he'd never do.

Chapter Nine

"I'm sorry, Lachlan. My hands are tied. If you had more equity, I'd be able to extend your line of credit. But I can only do so much, even with Maggie cosigning."

Lachlan's neck burned and he stared at a point over Lena Wilson's shoulder. The bank manager's dark brows crinkled in apology.

"I'd have hoped the quasi-family connection might tip the balance..." Lachlan trailed off. Evan was engaged to Lena's son Deon, a physical therapist in town. Lachlan rock climbed with the couple on a regular basis.

Lena pressed her lips together, and faint wrinkles marked her rich brown skin. She shook her head.

Disappointment flooded in, along with a hell of a lot of embarrassment, and he heard the voice of his father in his head. *Being a vet tech, son? Working for your sister? You're really going to make enough doing that?*

Clearly, his dad had been right. And it wasn't like he'd be raking it in with his training facility, either. His business plan was solid, would eventually build up to the point of him making a comfortable salary, but Stella would always hold the "most successful sibling" title.

Straightening, he tapped both hands on the desk and forced a grin. "Had to ask. Thanks for the meeting."

"Wish I could do more, Lachlan. It's as much about Maggie's student loans and mortgage as it is about your lack of assets."

Funny, knowing Maggie had her own financial burdens didn't make his any easier to take. "Not a problem, Lena."

"The glucosamine supplements you recommended for Grover seem to be helping with his arthritis," she offered, guilt plain on her face.

"Glad to help. I'd better get going."

He sped out of the bank and hung a left onto the sidewalk, busy with the usual Friday-afternoon-in-the-summer crowd. His father's opinions on his job and his upcoming bills buzzed in his mind, persistent mosquitoes of doubt. It took accidentally bumping into a tourist to force him to pay attention. He apologized and paused, glancing around.

He stood in front of the town's little library. He'd managed to speed-walk two blocks without really noticing where he was going.

A familiar face emerged from the glass doors of the quaint building. Caleb smiled and raised a hand in greeting, then readjusted a New York Islanders ball cap over his black-brown hair. "Lachlan. You okay? You don't look— It's not Marisol, is it? If she needs to come see me before next week's appointment…"

Lachlan shook his head. "Nah. Just got—" His embarrassment hadn't faded enough for him to admit his financial failings to his friend. He cleared his throat. "Doesn't matter."

"I heard you're renting Gertie Rafferty's place." He punched Lachlan lightly on the shoulder. "Stole it out from under me. It would have been perfect for my brother—he and my niece are moving to town next month."

"Ah, sorry. But I need the extra space, and Gertie seemed intent to be either my matchmaker or my landlord. Maybe both." His gut crawled at the thought of the rent check. "And Marisol liked the look of it."

Caleb's brows rose. "She's moving in with you?"

"No." Christ, what was about today, reminding him of all the ways he was falling short in life?

Stop whining. Find a solution.

"Didn't mean to snatch your brother's house away, though." He slapped on a genial expression.

"Enh, Garnet's playing real estate agent for them. She knows the area better than I do." Caleb cleared his throat. "Oh, question for you—I'm thinking of getting Garnet a dog for her birthday. Any opinions on breeds?"

Lachlan laughed. "Too many to properly run through on the sidewalk. Give me a call this weekend—I have a list of shelters in the area, or breeders if you're wanting to go purebred."

"We'll be coming to you for obedience training, for sure."

"Thanks, I—" The words clicked in place. "Obedience training. Crap. I've been so distracted since I left the bank that I forgot I need to boot it back to the clinic for my evening classes."

Caleb gave a two-fingered wave. "I'll call you."

"Do that." He jogged off, thankful both for his friend's faith in his skills and for having something to pour his attention into tonight.

Now that the bank had said no, he had some tough decisions to make about whether to call his parents or not. And he was A-okay with a few hours where he had an excuse not to choose.

"This is a good concept, Marisol."

Marisol's advisor, Dr. Jennifer Wiebe, tilted back

in her desk chair. She plucked a pair of horn-rimmed reading glasses off the top of her blonde head and peered at Marisol's draft. "It's not what we discussed previously, but I think there's more opportunity for discovery. It'll provide you with a challenge." Her gaze dipped to Marisol's baby bump and her lips thinned.

Marisol didn't like the look of that face. She inhaled, trying to slough off the feeling that the tall bookshelves lining both sides of Dr. Wiebe's office were closing in on her. "I sense a 'but' in there."

"Are you sure you want to take on something with a larger scope? Your previous idea had merit, and this might not be the time in your life where you want to complicate things further."

"Oh." Yeah, that one had come up before. Her advisor in Vancouver had had no qualms opining that a new mother had no place in a doctoral program. But she'd hoped working with a female professor would mean not facing as many preconceived notions. "Given how much support I'm getting from my family and Lachlan, I feel I'm up to facilitating a more involved study."

"Lachlan. I know that name."

"He's a SAR dog handler on Sutter Mountain."

Dr. Wiebe nodded. "Right. That's it. He teaches classes locally from time to time. Smart guy when it comes to dogs. He's your partner?"

Marisol bit her lip, contemplating how to phrase

it. "Yes" hovered on the tip of her tongue. And the yearning for that to be so shifted the shelves toward her again until the truth squeezed out. "He's the baby's father." When that didn't seem to faze Dr. Wiebe, she continued, "Encouraged me to suggest this change, actually."

Her advisor nodded thoughtfully. "Good to have some flag wavers in your cheering section. Just make sure the changes you're making are going to benefit you, as well as the research. You don't want to burn out. Or take on too much and have to quit."

"What happened to publish or perish?"

"That's true, too." The other woman's resigned smile did nothing to convince Marisol she'd picked a sensible career path. "You really have to love the research, as well as your field of study."

"I do. Ever since I was a kid, I loved to figure out what made people tick. And then when I took a senior-level psych class focusing on dogs, well, I was a goner." She'd needed something to throw herself into—it may have been a year after her miscarriage and divorce, but she'd still been grieving. And she hadn't been willing to occupy her time with a relationship. She'd been too busy paying off her ex's debts to even casually date.

"Well, I look forward to seeing what you do with this. I'll see you next week, and you can show me a more fleshed-out draft."

Marisol nodded and gathered her things. It was

time to get home and thank Lachlan for encouraging her not to put limits on herself.

Say, like I'm limiting things with him?

The question followed her back to Sutter Creek. But taking risks in academia and repeating mistakes from her past couldn't be compared. *And comparing Lachlan and my ex is starting to feel all kinds of wrong.*

He'd be excited about her news, not solely concerned about his own career like her ex had been. She drove past her own apartment, continuing on to the clinic where Lachlan was running his bi-weekly Friday-evening puppy-behavior classes. She wanted to see him. To say thanks. But also to see if her heart skipped when she saw him.

A skipping heart doesn't guarantee longevity, idiot.

When she pulled up, Maggie was out front watering the flowers. She still wore her scrubs. Fudge was sacked out on the sidewalk nearby. Such a lazybones for a pointer. But Marisol had seen Lachlan putting the dog through her paces, and had been damned impressed. Both by the dog and her handler. Fudge was just efficient, conserving effort wherever possible.

Marisol yawned. She'd probably do well following the dog's lead when it came to energy austerity. The deeper they got into summer, the more she felt like a sloth.

She parked and hoisted herself from the driver's

seat. The dog's head perked up, and she bounded to her feet and came over for a scratch.

"That looked difficult," Maggie commented.

"What, petting the dog?"

"No, getting out of your car." For once, Lachlan's sister's teasing was affectionate.

With a conceding laugh, Marisol motioned to the hose. "Want me to finish up so you can get out of here? I came to see Lach, and he still has fifteen minutes left in his class, right?"

"He does." Reluctant appreciation crossed Maggie's face, and she passed over the nozzle. "I'm going to take you up on that. I haven't eaten in ten hours."

"I need a bite to eat, too. If you don't mind waiting for Lach, want to get pizza and take it back to my place?"

"I—" Maggie crossed her arms, losing a fraction of the stiffness that had marked her posture since the moment she'd opened the door the first day Marisol came to the clinic. "That would be really nice."

"I shouldn't assume he'll want to come, I guess."

"Are you kidding? Of course he will."

Marisol gave Fudge a drink from the hose before turning the stream on the petunias. No doubt Maggie was right. And she knew full well she was projecting her own hesitance on to Lachlan.

"Seriously, what else does he have to do?" Maggie said. "To prove to you he wants to be with you?"

Okay, so Maggie saw the projection, too. Or at least the hesitance.

"He—" Marisol swallowed, unsure of how to admit the truth. There wasn't anything Lachlan had to do. He'd checked off a whole lot of boxes—taking her on dates, making sure she was comfortable, giving her space, rescuing her from the side of the road. And the fact she couldn't bring herself to believe he'd keep doing it…

That was on her, not him.

"Nothing," she whispered.

"What do you mean, nothing?" Maggie's eyes flashed. "How can there be nothing? It's not a case of you not being into him. The two of you look like Fudge when the treat jar's up on a high shelf. Drool included."

"Maggie." Had she been sitting, she'd have brought her knees to her chest, a physical wall between herself and Maggie's overly correct observation. *Yeah, right. As if I could pull my knees anywhere close to my body at this point.* She settled for crossing her arms. "Full honesty—your brother is incredible. He's a narwhal."

Maggie drew back as if Marisol's sanity were in question.

Hell, maybe it was.

"A narwhal? What are you talking about?" Maggie asked.

"Just as magical as a unicorn, but 100 percent more real."

Maggie's expression darkened. "Come on, Marisol, you're an academic. There's no such thing as magic, not in a relationship."

Hearing her own cynicism coming from someone else hit a raw spot at her core.

It's not cynicism. It's self-protection. And necessary.

She forced a smile. "Well, no matter what, understand that I see his value. And his innate goodness."

With a nod, Maggie made it clear she wanted a subject change. "I'll head home and shower, and will meet you at your place in a half an hour. Get Lach to text me if you decide on something different."

Marisol waved a goodbye, then spent a few minutes finishing up the watering. She was winding the hose around the spool bolted to the side of the building, intermittently tossing Fudge's tennis ball, when the members of Lachlan's class passed by. The puppies bounced on their leashes, trying to say hello to Fudge, who tolerated the attention with the pointer equivalent of an eye roll. Marisol bent to greet a particularly adorable King Charles spaniel, and regretted the motion. Standing from a squat was not the fluid movement it had been in the spring.

A hand extended down to her, and she glanced up at Lachlan's amused face. Silently taking the offered lift, she stood. It would be so easy to keep her hand in his. Would feel so right. The urge struck never to let go.

A jolt of fear followed.

She broke their grip, and disappointment flickered in his eyes.

"Didn't expect my two favorite ladies to be waiting for me," he said.

God, he looked edible. His hair was mussed, and what looked like a muddy paw print marked one of the legs of his khaki shorts. And his chest was a thing of wonders, broad under his navy polo shirt.

She really missed touching that chest.

"I—" *I wanted to see your face? To apologize for being romantically stunted?* Yeah, no. "My advisor liked the new direction for my dissertation. It's going to be under the wire to polish everything in time to present my prospectus to the committee, but I'm excited to try."

"That's great, sunshine."

"And Maggie's going to meet us for pizza at my place in fifteen minutes."

His smile grew wider.

"It won't take that long to get home. Want to show me this barn you're renovating?"

And there went his smile.

She cocked her head. "No?"

"Not today." He jammed his hands in his pockets. "Let's head to yours. I'm starving."

A few hours later, Maggie had come and gone, having expressed teasing thanks for being a vegetarian because it meant not having to eat the pineapple on the Hawaiian pizza Marisol insisted on ordering. They'd found common ground with the artichoke, olive and goat cheese special, though, and had ganged up on Lachlan when he'd complained that it needed sausage. Marisol had enjoyed the evening and was glad to have had time getting to know Maggie, but it was easier to relax with just Lachlan. After a long week at school, she needed the time to wind down.

"Dinner was nice," she said to Lach, who was stretched out on one end of the couch with his feet up on the coffee table and fingers linked over his flat abs.

"Yeah, Maggie's warming up to this."

The couch was small enough that when he reached over, his knuckles brushed her belly, sending a wave of longing through her.

It's just sex. I've always been attracted to him.

He turned his hand over on her stomach and drew a slow circle with his palm.

Heat fisted between her thighs, a reminder it had been over seven months since anyone other than she had touched her anywhere intimate for pleasure's sake. Not the longest of dry spells, but she was feeling it more than she had even when she'd gone years between relationships. Maybe it was the proximity to Lachlan. Maybe it was biology. Between being meticulous about nutrition and monitoring exercise and enduring pelvic exams, pregnancy was doing its best to convince Marisol her body was for medical science only.

Well, she was not a host, damn it. And Lach had been the last man to settle his hands on her, to caress her to the brink.

To send her over.

He could do it again.

Not that he'd want to—she wasn't exactly feeling her most attractive.

He'd cherish me.

Impossible to avoid the truth of that.

She'd caught Lachlan's glances, appreciation and curiosity and downright hunger. It flashed on his face now, as if he was struggling to suppress it.

She was scrambling for something to say when the baby kicked. Right against his palm, hard enough he couldn't have missed it.

Wonder overrode the desire in his expression.

She grinned. "Felt that one?"

"I cannot get over how awesome that is."

Her heart bloomed. Sharing moments like this— she was starting to crave them, depend on them.

But it wouldn't happen often, not if they were living apart and coparenting. It would be a lifetime of phone calls and drop-offs and only catching half of their kid's life.

That didn't sound like protecting herself. It sounded miserable. Why would she be okay with missing out on so much? With both the baby and with Lachlan?

Because I'm afraid to take a risk.

Oh, man. Did she really want to let her past have that much control over her future? She didn't know how much she could change her thoughts and feelings. But to get to share Lachlan's joy more often—it might be worth trying.

She shifted closer, turning on the couch and crossing her legs. Taking his hands, she put one on each side of her belly. "She should move again soon."

"Are you hoping for a girl?"

"No. I just like it better than 'it.'"

"Me, too." His hands pressed a little harder and he trained his eyes on hers, all the seriousness in the world written in his rich brown gaze. "We never did ask Caleb about the sex. Maybe we could get him to tell us at the next appointment. I'd love to know what color to paint the bedroom. Bedrooms, I mean."

Two bedrooms.

That didn't sit right, not anymore. They could made things work as coparents, she had no doubt. But maybe...

"I want to try, Lach," she blurted.

"Try...to find out if we're having a girl or a boy?"

She couldn't blame him for his confusion. It was admittedly an about-face.

Putting her hand to his cheek, she shook her head.

Her pulse picked up, hammering at her throat and in her ears. "No, try being together."

His lips parted, and his pupils swallowed his irises.

But he didn't respond.

Oh. Oh, no. She'd waited too long, misinterpreted his feelings... She tried to pull her hand from his face, but he trapped it there with his fingers.

"Don't withdraw, Marisol. But for Christ's sake, give me a second."

She swallowed the lump of panic forming in her throat. "Did I read you wrong? I thought that's what you wanted."

"It is. I want to be with you. Hell, I plain want you." His Adam's apple bobbed. "But it's a big pivot for you. I don't want to take the next step unless you're sure. We both know there's more on the line than our feelings."

Doubt squeezed her chest. "You don't think it's worth trying? If it doesn't work—I'm sure we could be grown up about it. Put aside any personal differences for the sake of the baby."

"That's a lot of ifs. You were scared of the ifs."

"I know. But I think that's the best I can do right now. I want to believe we can make it." She lifted their linked hands and kissed the knuckle of his thumb. "But I've been conditioned not to believe I can do this. Not to be able to trust."

"I—"

She held up a palm, saving him from having to defend himself. "I objectively know you're trustworthy, Lachlan. It's convincing my animal brain of the same."

He raised an eyebrow, and a hint of a smile flickered at the corner of his mouth. "So you need to train yourself to be part of a pack again? Because I have some expertise there."

"Oh, good grief." She swatted his forearm. "We're not dogs."

"I'm just teasing." He full-on grinned. "Okay, so set out the training ground rules—"

"Lach!"

He laughed, a hearty vibration that shook free all her excess tension. "Tell me what you need, Marisol. What you want, and what you don't want."

Sweet Mary, did he know how hot it was to have it all laid out like that? Desire pulsed at her core, intense and knotted in an unfamiliar way. It appeared her hormones were good for something other than making her weepy.

She brought his hand to her lips again and gently bit the tip of his thumb. "I'm all for being clear on our relationship dynamic. But I'm having a hard time thinking at all right now."

"Yeah?"

The low rasp teased her core and she nodded, squirming against the couch.

The soft cushion was a pathetic substitute for his

body. She knew how good he felt. They'd done this before.

But you weren't eighteen zillion months pregnant at the time.

He slid a hand down her hip and cupped her rear. "So what are you thinking of?"

"You."

"Me, too. Specifically, you climbing into my lap. Enjoying me instead of whatever's putting that little smile on your face."

Cocking a grin, she said, "When you put it that way…"

"Come here, sunshine. I feel like I haven't held you for years."

She rose on her knees and straddled him as gracefully as she could. "You kissed me less than a week ago."

"Remind me."

Her round belly bumped his flat one. Who cared? The friction between them brought any overthinking to a screeching halt. God bless whoever had invented leggings. Every hard inch of him tantalized her sex, making promises she knew damn well he could keep.

"I want you to kiss me again," she said. "But this time, I don't want you to stop."

Chapter Ten

Lachlan wanted nothing more than to please her. Preferably for the rest of their lives, but he'd start with tonight. She wiggled in his lap, feminine heat against his erection. Four too many layers of fabric lay between them, reducing the delicious friction. He let a groan rumble out, and tilted his hips. He splayed his hands into her hair and ran a thumb on her lower lip. "Not stopping… Little easier to do on a couch than pressed up against your car."

"Come now." She nipped the end of his thumb, sending a thrill through his body. "Making out on the side of the road was hot. Admit it."

"Never any doubt there. But this is even better."

He kissed her. Slow and needy. The last time they'd had sex, they'd been in a haze of passion. On the clock, pressed to cram as many seconds in as possible before she had to head back to Vancouver. Now, who knew how long he'd have to kiss her? To savor her honey taste and enjoy her curves under his palms.

Hell, worship her curves. He full-on intended to prolong this, for as much time as he could. Both pleasure tonight and some sort of commitment going forward.

But was it right to sink into that pleasure without figuring out the latter?

He pulled back, tracing a gentle line along the collar of her short-sleeved, checked shirt. The long hem dipped below her hips, and he teased it up a little. Every aroused cell in his body protested at the easy pace. *She matters too much to rush. Take it slow.* "You really want to make a go of this, sunshine?"

She tugged her lower lip between her teeth, and one of her eyebrows crinkled. "You don't?"

"I do. Very much. I just—" *I don't want to end up with my heart broken* "—trust is a deal breaker for me. It has to be at the center of a relationship."

Both her palms landed on his chest, and she stared at the diamond shape formed by her thumbs. "I want to trust you."

Her mouth pressed into a line, tense at the corners.

And he'd kiss her until she relaxed, the minute

he was able to convince himself that "want to trust you" was enough of a guarantee.

But the tension fell into sadness before he could get his thoughts in order.

"You're right, I'm being unreasonable," she said.

"Hey," he said, tipping up her chin with a finger and brushing his lips against hers. "I think you're attributing something I didn't say to me. I don't think you're being unreasonable."

"Except…"

"You're protecting yourself, our baby, too. I admire that. But you need to know something about me." He glided his hands down her sides, settling them on the sexy flare of her hips. "I want to protect you, too, Marisol. And our baby. And whatever feelings we have for each other."

She smiled, sheepish and vulnerable. "I'm not quite sure what they are, but there are a lot of them."

"Me, too." He *could* put a name to them, but she wouldn't appreciate that, not if she was still unsure of her own. But her admitting she had feelings? That'd do for now. He flicked the top button of her blouse open and sneaked the cotton to the side, laying a strip of kisses along her collarbone. She let out a soft "oh."

"If memory serves, the bedroom is about ten steps down that hall," he said.

"Give or take."

"Good way of putting it. I think we should give *and* take." He continued his ministrations up her neck, then slid a hand under the thin cotton of her blouse, pushing the fabric up, trailing his fingers along the taut skin of her belly.

She gasped again, surprise instead of pleasure.

"What?" he asked.

"It's different."

"Nothing wrong with different." He shifted his hands down and caressed her hips again, holding her still while he thrust up a little. "I'm liking different."

"Me, too," she breathed.

He moved to pick her up, but she scrambled off his lap. "No hoisting the pregnant lady."

"I wouldn't exactly call it hoisting," he said, spooning her in a standing position. He teased his fingers low on her hip with one hand and the underside of a covered, full breast with the other.

Yep. Definitely needed to try this with clothes off. God, he loved her body. And he wanted to remind her of that, one slow touch at a time.

She sagged back against him and tipped her head back against his chest. "Don't suppose I could convince you to slide that hand a little to the right."

"You very much could, but let's do that on a bed."

He nibbled on her neck as she led the way to her room. She threw out an arm as they passed through the doorway, swatting the light switch.

The spare decor smacked of her having been working all hours since she arrived. A stack of texts and notebooks teetered on her one bedside table. A mountain of pillows formed a wedge in the middle of the otherwise unadorned bed. She had a duvet printed with big squares of blues and purples, and none of the fussy throw pillows some of his past girlfriends had decorated with.

She closed her eyes and scrunched up her nose. "I have to be kinda elevated... And I need support under my stomach otherwise it throws my back out." She swore under her breath. "Okay, so this is why people stop having sex in the third trimester."

"Not everyone, you know that." He scooped her up and placed her on the bed against the pillows. "But if you're not comfortable, we can do other things."

"Oh, no." Shoving the pillows to the floor, she took him by the shoulders and gave a playful tug and shove, until he was on his back on the soft mattress. "I want very specific things, Lachlan."

"Such as?"

A smile softened the lines of self-conscious concern in her brow. She lowered her lips, kissing him, all languid pleasure and sweetness.

"I'll have to be on top," she whispered into his ear, flicking the lobe with her tongue.

Need licked through him. "After eight months without you? I'm not picky, Marisol."

"We should start by getting rid of a few layers." She scooted off the bed and slipped out of her leggings and panties, then knelt next to him. Her speedy removal of his belt, shorts and boxers made him laugh.

"I haven't lost my touch, have I?" she said, a pout edging her lips.

"I just didn't expect to Donald Duck it," he teased.

"What?"

"Tops on, bottoms off," he explained.

"Pants are overrated." With a cheeky smile, she ran a hand up his thigh and traced a slow line next to his erection, just brushing the sensitive skin with the back of her thumb.

Breath shuddered from him, rough in his throat. "So are shirts."

He propped himself up on an elbow and reached behind his head, grabbing a handful of his polo shirt and shucking the fabric off and onto the floor.

Appreciative eyes scanned his naked body, and her lips parted. She settled her hands on his chest and commenced a leisurely exploration. "You're too hot for your own good, Lachlan Reid."

"And you're too clothed, sunshine."

"I figured you'd want to take care of that."

"Mmm, I really do."

She climbed onto him again, and the sheer delight of her skin against his tore another guttural noise from him. He hadn't been a monk while he was overseas. But nothing about a quick fling in a hotel room could even approach what he had with Marisol. The perfect fit of their bodies, sure. Her heat, her wetness tantalized and made sweet promises of the ecstasy to come. But it was the way joy flooded him when she graced him with a smile, too. And the deep, instinctual need to hold her, to help her, to love her.

He traced a finger along her throat until he got to the V of her blouse, and he untied the belt below her breasts, then teased open the buttons.

She tugged her lip with her teeth as he traveled down, revealing a trail of soft skin.

"Don't be nervous, Mari. I don't have any expectations, beyond taking you out of your head and into whatever pleasure we can find together." He pushed her blouse off her shoulders and discarded it. Stroking her lips with his thumb, he tilted his jaw. "Kiss me. I want to taste you again."

Anticipation flirted at the corners of her mouth, and she leaned in. Yeah, that was what he needed. The flavor of mint tea flooding his tongue, her mouth driving him to distraction. With a circle of her hips, he lost his mind a little more.

He needed to do the same to her.

A palm to her breast, a thumb swirling her nipple, and she ground into him. He dipped his head, sucking the bud between his lips, smiling as she whimpered and writhed.

His body ached with the need to fill her, but he wanted to draw out her sweet response further, take her to the brink. Sliding a hand between their bodies, he swirled a thumb on her sensitive flesh and teased her sex with his fingers.

"Not enough," she said, panting, nails digging into his shoulders.

He slipped his fingers in farther and released her nipple, finding her mouth again and kissing her until his body shouted that he was getting close to losing control.

"I'm—I'm almost—" she pressed her core into his hand "—but I need—"

Yeah, he needed, too. He shifted his hand away and gently nudged her opening, then thrust in, just a little. "Tell me what works. If we need to adjust."

"Mmm, how about—" she slid to the base of him "—yeah, that."

He let her set the pace. Tentative at first, getting attuned to each other, but then edged with abandon as she tossed her head back and moaned.

"So close. You… You feel…"

Need pooled at the base of his spine, threatening to break loose. He gritted his teeth and tilted his hips, earning a cry of pleasure.

"Oh, there—" Her words turned nonsensical as her mouth went slack and her eyes closed. She pulsed around him.

The rhythmic release pulled his own from him, taking him down, surrounding him with a sense of completion.

Yeah, that's love, buddy.

He choked back the need to pass that along and lost himself in the fulfillment on her face and in his veins.

After long minutes of snuggling, he got cleaned up and then spooned behind her, hugging an armful of warm woman and pillows. "Comfortable?"

"I am."

He felt her muscles give, that point of relaxation where she wasn't holding anything to herself anymore; she was leaning entirely on him.

He wanted that level of surrender emotionally, too. He'd seen what walls and clawing back trust and intimacy did to a relationship. Marisol's claim that she wanted to trust him did soothe his worries, but it wasn't enough to build on. They'd have to work on that, develop more of a foundation before he would feel secure.

"At first, I didn't think us being together would be good for the baby," she said. "I was focused on what would happen if we broke up. I was *expecting* we would break up. My marriage…it sucked the trust out of me."

He tightened his embrace and kissed the back of her head. "I know."

"But I'm starting to wonder—what if we didn't break up?"

"I like the sound of that one better."

"It's not just about my trust issues, though. I'm worried about being able to do everything. Balancing my degree and parenting, and add a relationship to that? I worry about screwing up and neglecting something."

His chest clenched. Now was not a moment to get into a spiral of memories of his father missing his graduation. Of trying to emotionally support his sisters but worrying he wasn't doing it well enough. "My parents are workaholics. But I don't see you doing that."

"I'm stretched pretty thin. And so are you. How would we make a relationship last, Lach? At some point, one of us will fail."

He had to take a deep breath to keep his desperation to convince her out of his voice. So much for a languid, post-sex cuddle. "It's not about one person failing. It's about working together. Communicating. Finding a balance and allowing that balance to shift when necessary. We can do that. If we keep talking to each other."

She shifted around to face him. Doubt and hope warred in her green eyes. She bit her lower lip, releasing it when she brushed a kiss across the corner of his mouth. "And that's all you'd need at first? Talking and finding a balance?"

"At first, yeah."

"Okay. We can try that." She stroked his chest with a lazy hand. "I missed this. I… I really like the idea of being with you."

He nodded, ignoring the pang in his heart that

warned him it wasn't enough. Because it was, for now. Sure, "loving you" would have been preferable. But he'd take "being with you" in the interim.

Lachlan fussed around the edge of the painted dresser with a sheet of sandpaper, looking for a just-right level of wear. He'd taken three weeks of mixed emotions out on the piece of furniture. So many fantastic little moments with Marisol—laughing as she tried to teach him how to make schnitzel, buying necessities for the baby, hand-in-hand walks along Moosehorn Lake—tangled up in the fear she was still holding back. Plus his continued frustration that no magic solution had come up as an alternative to calling his dad. At least he had a beautiful project to show for all his internal debating. He was hoping to take the dresser over to Marisol's tonight, had enlisted Zach's help for the heavy lifting.

He texted Zach to let him know it was time to meet in Maggie's garage, but before he could put his phone away, it rang. The picture he'd taken of Marisol snuggling with Fudge on the weekend popped up on the screen.

"Hey there, ready for me to come over?" he said, flicking the call to speakerphone so he could keep adding finishing touches to the antiquing.

"Uh, no." She sighed. "I'm still at school. I had to fill out some paperwork I wasn't expecting, and got stuck in a meeting with my advisor. I'm not as far along on my research as I'd intended to be today."

"It's eight o'clock." Jesus, she should be in her pajamas with her feet up. Preferably cuddling with him on her couch. Not still hunched over her desk, almost an hour's drive from home. "Have you had dinner?"

"I ate." Her tone bristled with warning. "I'll be home when I'm done. And I can take it slow in the morning—I don't have to come in to the office tomorrow."

"Is there anything I can help you with? Proofreading? Combing through journal articles? Grading papers?"

"You can't do my job for me, Lach! Sweet Mary. Worry about your own projects."

"Oh, I am." His follow-ups with the organization who'd denied him the grant, asking about further funding, had been met with apologies and zero success. He was seriously running out of options to pay his contractor's bill. Not that he was going to worry Marisol with that—she had enough going on. He wasn't going to add his own concerns to her mountain of stress.

"I just want to help," he continued.

"I have to do this myself."

"You are. Nothing wrong with asking for a hand, though."

She humphed.

And his words smacked him upside the head. *Time to take your own advice much?*

His stomach rolled. With Stella and the rescue organization turning him down flat, and his options with bank financing tapped out, maybe it was time to call his parents.

He shook his head. Not tonight. Tonight, he'd focus on Marisol. "Does your brother have a key to your place?" Marisol hadn't yet offered him one, and he hadn't pressed her.

"Yeah, why?"

"I have something I need to drop off. And I'll bring over a lasagna, and we can have a very late dinner when you get home."

"I *ate*."

"Cafeteria food doesn't count. Make you a deal—I won't give you a hard time about staying as late as you need to as long as you're okay with Fudge and me being your greeting party when you get in."

"I—" She exhaled. A whole lot of longing rode that breath. "I love the idea of you being home when I get there. No lasagna. Really. But definitely you."

"Mind if I stay the night?"

"I'd mind if you *didn't*. I'm going to hang up now, though. Otherwise it's going to be tomorrow before I get home."

He hated the idea of her driving home that late. *But if she's going to trust me, I have to do the same.* "See you when you get there."

Shortly after he hung up, a truck rumbled down the street and a door slammed. Lachlan peered around his own pickup.

Zach loped toward him, progress slowed partway up the short driveway when Fudge wiggled over and demanded love.

"What are you having me do again?" Zach called, turning the dog to a limp noodle with some solid belly rub skills.

"Lifting. I need to get this dresser into your sister's apartment."

Zach joined Lachlan in the garage and let out a low whistle. "Nice work."

Lachlan rubbed the back of his neck. "Marisol fell in love with it, but wanted a different paint job. It was worth a few late nights."

With a knowing look, Zach rounded the dresser and gripped one side. "My sister's fallen in love with more than a dresser."

"News to me." The complaint grumbled out of him before he could stop it.

They hoisted the dresser up and set the front feet on the edge of the truck bed.

"Shouldn't be," Zach said.

Hope zinged through Lachlan's limbs. He fumbled, almost losing his grip on the dresser. "What makes you say that?"

"The fact she's let you in as much as she has.

Normally, she closes herself off entirely. What, you don't see it?"

The dresser screeched as they pushed it into place. Lachlan slammed the tailgate shut. He wished he were half as convinced as Zach. "I don't know what I see, man."

Fifteen minutes later, they had the dresser loaded into the second bedroom at Marisol's.

"Looks awesome," Zach said appreciatively.

It did. The white of the dresser, lovingly distressed in places over the last few hours, complemented the pale yellow walls. Marisol had decided she didn't want new paint, and she'd made the right call.

"Now I just need Marisol to get home from work so I can surprise her."

Zach headed for the kitchen, and Lachlan followed. It felt a little odd to be in Marisol's place without her, even with permission. At some point he'd relax.

Not until you feel like she's fully let you in.

"You two are something else," Zach commented as he pilfered a soda out of the fridge. "You're procreating, but you haven't exchanged keys?"

"We haven't needed to yet. I'm sure we will when it's necessary." Though the idea of achieving that level of intimacy with Marisol appealed so damned much.

"But you're together?"

"Yes?" They'd spent every second night together

since last Friday, so that part seemed back to normal. But his need to hear an "I love you"—to be able to say it to her—was reaching embarrassing levels.

"Convincing." Zach flopped on the couch and cracked open the can. Fudge followed, draping her head across Zach's knee and giving him longing "pet me" eyes. He gave in to the begging and stroked the dog's ears. "Look, take it from someone who's with a person who had skyscraper-high walls—it's an effort to break through them, but it's worth it. *She's* worth it."

"I know she is."

"Some of our family gave Mari a really hard time when she got divorced. Didn't think she tried hard enough, even though her ex was to blame. She was too embarrassed to tell anyone except our parents and sisters how badly Glenn had screwed her over financially, so some of our aunts and uncles tried to imply she was immature."

Lachlan raised a brow. She'd only hinted at trouble with money when they'd talked about it, so it seemed she still wasn't thrilled to hash out the specific details of her divorce. He sat on the other end of the couch and patted his leg to call the dog over. She obliged, and he dug his fingers into her soft neck fur. "I'll do what I can to win her over. But I wish she'd let me help her more often."

"Oh, good luck with that. And I'd love to have

some advice for you, but I'm not going to pretend to understand Marisol."

Lachlan shrugged. He didn't need advice. He just needed time. "Understanding Marisol isn't the issue. The complicated part is convincing her I get why she protects herself, and showing her I deserve to be let in."

"Supporting her at work helps. She's mentioned that you're cool with her juggling her time. That's something the jackface she married didn't get. He was all about himself. Dumped all his problems on her."

"Good to know." Especially good to be validated in not bringing up his financing troubles with her. He'd figure it out.

Swallow his pride, more likely.

"But don't be freaked about getting together with a kid. Cadie and I managed, and Ben was almost a year old."

"I'm not the one you have to convince." He cleared his throat. "She's coming around, though."

By the time Marisol's key snicked in the lock, Zach was long gone, having headed home to Cadie and Ben and all the love a guy ever needed in the world. Lach couldn't help the bolt of jealousy stiffening his spine.

Nor the irritation when he checked his watch and saw she'd beat midnight by only a few minutes.

He flicked off the television and followed Fudge

to the entryway. "Hey there, Cinderella. Pretty damned close to pumpkin time."

Weary circles smudged the skin under her eyes. She dropped her purse on the ground, gave the dog a cursory pet and fell into Lach's offered embrace. She smelled of flowers and something not quite her… Old books? He tightened his embrace, trying to hold her up to help support her back. "You close down the library or something tonight?"

"Guilty."

He reined in the impulse to call her out on pushing herself too hard. A hundred and one parent-to-be blog articles mentioned pregnant women often got treated like they were incompetent, and he didn't want her to think he believed she didn't know what was best. "Let me know what I can do to help, sunshine."

"I'm not going to put you to work doing research for me."

"I would if you wanted me to."

She sighed, and sagged a little.

"I have a surprise for you," he said.

"A naked surprise?" Her yawn contradicted the heated curiosity in her words.

"Not yet. Something in the baby's room."

A twinge of pain crossed her face. "Just let me stretch out my hips first, okay? Driving is killing me. Glad I don't have to go in tomorrow."

"Want me to make you some tea? I boiled the kettle a bit ago."

"Mmm, yeah. Ginger, please."

He dragged the pad of his thumb along her lower lip, followed the caress with a nip and a kiss. "I like that flavor on you."

She dug her fingers into his hair and kissed him back. "Coming home to you is fun."

"That's the idea."

Leaving her to stretch in the living room, he ducked into the kitchen, reboiled the kettle and poured her a mug. The occasional glance of her easing into yoga poses on the floor through the cutaway in the kitchen wall warmed his belly. Making tea, everyday routines, being home with each other—this was what love was supposed to be. What his parents didn't have, and what he'd fight for.

He brought the mug into the living room.

A soft snore sounded from the floor.

He huffed out a laugh. So much for tea and surprises. Fighting the frown pulling at his mouth, he put down the mug and knelt next to her on the navy throw rug. She lay on her side, lashes brushing her cheeks and hands fallen to the ground by her knee. She'd conked out midstretch.

Those blogs could go screw themselves—she was working too hard.

"Sunshine?"

She didn't stir.

Fudge stared at him from her tight ball next to the couch, a look of pointer disdain over not being on her own bed after 9:00 p.m.

"Cuddle up, buttercup," he said to the dog. "You've had worse."

Way worse, really. They'd spent many a night together out in the bush or in the snow, not sleeping at all. Being cozy at Marisol's was not a hardship.

Even so, he couldn't completely erase the disappointment that he hadn't been able to show her the dresser.

He lifted her and carried her to the bedroom. Tonight, he'd have to be happy spooning with her. Hopefully they'd wake up in the morning with enough time for a surprise—and for him to express his concern over her late nights—before he had to go in to work.

Chapter Eleven

Something was brushing her cheek, but Marisol's eyes refused to open.

Soft breath caressed her ear, then another teasing touch.

Lachlan. His mouth, to be specific.

And she was surrounded by pillows and blankets and his delicious scent.

"I'm not on the floor," she slurred, tongue refusing to wake up, too.

"I moved you last night." His voice came from somewhere in front of her. The edge of the bed, no doubt.

She was too tired to open her eyes and confirm,

though. She tucked the feather-filled duvet closer around her chin. "Thanks."

He stroked her hair back from her forehead. Felt like she still had in last night's ponytail. *Whatever*.

"I have to get to work. The contractor's breaking ground today." He sighed. "Check out the baby's room when you get the chance. I left you something. Hope you like it."

"Mmm. But... Snuggles." Oh, God. She needed at least five more hours in this bed. She might have overdone it a little last night.

"I wish." He ran a hand on her shoulders, over the covers. "You'll sleep better with me gone, anyway."

"So not true."

He chuckled and kissed her again.

"Bye," she mumbled. "Have fun with the contractor."

She drifted back into sleep.

By the time she woke up again, not even her black-out blinds could keep out the summer sun. Cursing being pregnant in the hottest weather of the year, she dragged herself from the mattress and hurried to the bathroom.

Lachlan had said something about a surprise, and now that she no longer felt like she'd been hit by an exhaustion truck, she shuffled toward the baby's room.

Furniture lined a wall, no longer just the crib.

Wait…was that the dresser from the antiques store? But it hadn't been white—*Oh*.

She covered her mouth with her hands and let out a squeak. When had Lachlan done this?

Probably on one of the nights I was working late.

Tears pricked her eyes. She skimmed a palm along the impeccable, perfectly distressed paint job, emotion swelling in her throat and at the back of her nose.

Good grief, hormones. It's just a dresser.

But it wasn't. It was him listening, paying attention, using his limited time to do something really sweet for her and the baby. And on a week where big things were happening at his expansion, too—construction starting today was no small thing.

And she'd been so focused on her own life, she'd barely acknowledged what was going on in his. Ugh. That was exactly how her ex had treated her when they'd been married. No way would she do that to her partner, romantic or otherwise. Curling up with the journal articles she'd printed off at school yesterday could wait a few hours. She had to go say thanks in person, and commemorate the first day of the next step in his career.

After showering and throwing on a lightweight pastel blue dress that nipped in just right under her breasts, she walked to the pie place and picked up enough lunch for everyone at the clinic. The bakery was just across the street, so she queued up with the noon lunch crowd.

A throat cleared next to her. "You're looking ready to pop, dear."

Internally rolling her eyes at the comment she got about eight times a day, she turned to Gertie Rafferty and smiled. "Another month to go yet."

"Well, enjoy the time. You won't sleep a wink for months after the baby comes."

"Mom!" called the woman behind the counter. "Don't exaggerate!"

Gertie harrumphed, and they moved forward a few feet. "Well, you know what I mean."

She did. Between school and the baby, she doubted she'd sleep for years, let alone months.

You will if you let Lach do his share.

Right. Needed to get better at that.

"Thanks for the advice, Mrs. Rafferty." Marisol forced another smile. "What's your recommendation for a cake?"

"Nancy, do we have Creamsicle cupcakes today?" she shouted toward the counter.

"Yes, there are a half-dozen left."

"Go for those, then." Mrs. Rafferty's gaze dropped to Marisol's hand, which she was desperately trying to use to support her aching back. "Stiff, dear?"

"Yep," Marisol said, digging her fingers into a knot.

"Well, make sure to let Lachlan do the heavy lifting when you're moving into the house this weekend."

"I'm not moving into the house with him."

"Whyever not? His grandmother taught him right—he's a caretaker." Mrs. Rafferty pressed her lips together. "A good man like that, if you don't snap him up, someone else will."

Jealously streaked up her spine. "Oh, no one else is going to snap him up, I'm just not… I mean, I need some more time."

An age-spotted hand landed on Marisol's belly. She flinched at the uninvited touch.

"Time's a-wasting," the older woman said.

"Mom, can you go switch the bread from the proofer to the oven for me?" The full-figured woman behind the counter sent Marisol an apologetic look.

With Mrs. Rafferty off on what Marisol assumed was busywork, she took a deep breath. A few minutes later, cupcakes in hand, she set off on foot for the clinic. She could handle walking a couple of kilometers. It would be good for her.

Halfway there, she was gritting her teeth, holding her hand under her belly with one hand and gripping the bag of food with the other. The baby had a way of shifting around that irritated her sciatic nerve. And her back was already throbbing. Her Braxton-Hicks were off the charts today—her stomach had been tight since she got out of bed.

Which means taking it easy.

Okay. She'd see if Lach could run her home after lunch, provided he'd driven instead of riding his bike. But she could make it six more blocks, damn it.

By the time she pushed the door to the clinic open, she was full-on wilting from the exertion and the midday sun. Fudge ambled to her side and nosed the bag of food.

"Not for you, sweetie."

"How about for me?" Evan said, eyes fixed to his computer screen and hands flying on the keyboard.

"Maybe, other sweetie."

He finished with a flourish and pinned his gaze on her. "You walked here?"

"I needed to work the kinks out."

He arched a brow. "What, Lach isn't taking care of that for you?"

"Ugh," Maggie interjected, coming out of an exam room. "Place of business, Ev."

"Yes'm," Evan said, then winked at Marisol. "Lach's on lunch in a few minutes. But that smells like Aussie pie, so if you want to leave any of it here…"

She plunked the bag on the counter and handed him a take-out container. "Two pepper-steak pies—one each for you and Maggie."

"Good guess." Maggie smiled. "Lach's office is open—set up there if you want."

"Thanks." She shifted her feet, then winced as her back twinged. Ugh, why wasn't her heart rate going back to normal now that she'd stopped walking? Her head spun a little, and she gripped the counter.

Maggie rushed in behind her and braced her. "You feeling okay?"

"Guess I need to eat."

"Come with me."

Within a minute, Marisol was sitting in Lachlan's desk chair with a pie in front of her and a fork in her hand.

Maggie stood next to her, hands on her hips. She took one of Marisol's wrists and checked her pulse. "Eat."

For once, being told what to do didn't chafe. Her hand shook as she brought a bite of pastry to her lips.

"More," Maggie ordered. "Your heart rate is high."

"I know. I'll eat. Promise. You don't have to hover."

"Yeah, I do. Until Lach's done with the contractor, anyway. Actually, never mind that. He should be here."

This visit was supposed to be about him for once, though. "Don't—"

But Maggie was already holding her phone up to her ear.

Lachlan surveyed the outside of the old barn as the construction workers prepped for knocking down non-weight-bearing interior walls and for fixing the crumbling foundation. Stacks of two-by-fours, rebar and a small backhoe took up the space where an old dog run had been. Instead of satisfaction, his veins popped with anxiety. All these people were going to need to be paid, and he was still short.

"Lach." His contractor, Alejandra Brooks Flores, one of his friends from high school, loped over. She wiped a bead of sweat and a strand of curly hair from her tawny brown forehead. "This is going well. But about your bill—"

"Ran into a little glitch, Aleja." Hell, between the grant failure, his rent hike with his new place and Stella being obstinate, it was a few glitches. "But it'll be taken care of. I'll make a call today, and the money'll transfer by tomorrow morning."

Aleja grinned. "Good man."

Turning away, Lach pulled his cell phone out of his pocket and cursed as he entered his dad's office number.

It rang twice before the receptionist answered. "Reid, Reid, and Travers, how may I direct your call?"

"Gregory Reid, please."

"Oh, I'm afraid—"

"I'm his son. Please put me through." His dad would be pissed about the interruption, but it couldn't wait.

"Yes, Mr. Reid."

A few seconds of elevator music, and a click sounded. "Lachlan, what's this about? I'm in the middle of a meeting. Is this about the girl you knocked up?"

"For Christ's sake, Dad—" *easy, killer, you need him on your side* "—I mean, insert 'woman' and 'having a baby with' into that sentence, and yes, that's part of the reason I'm calling."

Muffled words filled his ear, then a pause. "Okay. Bruce is going to give me five. Shoot."

Every muscle in his body went tight, hating the words that he was going to have to force out. "I need a loan."

"For what, to pay off the chick?"

"No," he snapped. "She's my partner, not a 'chick.' And I'm not paying her off. I'm going to build a life with her."

His father made a derisive noise. "Is she going to be an asset to your business?"

"She's in the same field, but she's got her own career trajectory. I didn't mean partner in that way."

"Well aware, son. I just don't see the point to a relationship if there aren't benefits elsewhere."

No, you wouldn't. Lach's stomach lurched. "The baby's meant an increase in expenses, and—"

"You shouldn't have to shoulder that burden if you didn't have a choice in whether to keep the kid."

The lurch turned to a full-on retch, and he swallowed acid. "I'm fully in support of Marisol's choices. I'm damned happy about fatherhood." He didn't bother to ask if his dad cared about becoming a grandfather. He knew the answer. "But I needed to upsize from my apartment, and lost out on a grant that was going to float a good chunk of the renovation on the barn. And I've maximized what I can get from the bank already, given my limited equity."

"How much do you need?"

He named the number, shame cold and slimy on the back of his neck.

"It'll be in your account by this afternoon."

Selling his principles shouldn't have been that easy. He rubbed his burning throat. "Great."

The line clicked, and he stared dumbly at the screen.

His sister's name and avatar popped up immediately, which—what the hell? Since when did she call him from inside the building?

He tapped the screen to answer. "Feeling lazy today?"

"Marisol needs you," she snapped. "We're in your office."

The concern marking his sister's words had his stress levels rebounding. He strode toward the back door. "What's wrong?"

"My guess is blood sugar. But she just doesn't look well."

"You're the doctor."

"And my professional opinion, given I'm licensed to treat Fudge, not your girlfriend, is that you take her to see Caleb."

Lach strode past the staff room and into his office, switching places with his sister at Marisol's side. "Thanks, Mags."

"Of course." His sister left quietly.

He knelt, heart in his throat. His first aid training had him reaching to take Marisol's pulse.

Her pink, sweaty face scrunched in apology. "Sorry," she mumbled around a bite of food. "Didn't mean to interrupt."

"What happened to taking it easy?"

"It was just a walk. Seriously." She grimaced, and put a hand to her belly.

"Talk to me, Mari. Are you cramping?"

"No. It just feels like bad Braxton-Hicks."

He fumbled in his SAR backpack for his blood-pressure cuff. Strapping it on her and jamming the earpieces of his stethoscope into his ears, he studied her face. The lines by her mouth suggested something between discomfort and pain.

He read the number on the dial. Oh, Christ. Way too high. Swallowing, blanking his face, he leveled her with a look. "Have you had enough to eat? We need to go see Caleb."

Her face fell. "But I brought cupcakes. And lunch."

"And one-sixty-five over a hundred says we're going to the doctor."

She blanched. "I— Okay. Cupcakes can wait."

Chapter Twelve

Marisol lay back on the angled hospital bed and squeezed her eyes shut. Lach sat next to her, holding her hand as he had been doing for the past couple of hours. When she'd called Caleb's office to check if he could see her, the receptionist had told her to head for the hospital. Which they had, but of course now it was a whole lot of hurry-up-and-wait. A belt circled her waist, monitoring any contraction activity. The nurse had come in periodically to check her blood pressure and to administer medication.

Her back spasmed again, followed by her belly clenching, and she tucked her knees up to alleviate the pressure. Oh, God. What if she was in labor?

The baby couldn't come yet. She wasn't full-term. And she wasn't done her prospectus. Hell, her presentation wasn't happening for another two weeks. Maybe she could convince Dr. Wiebe to let her move up the date… But how could she get ready in time?

She swore under her breath.

Lach brought her hand to his lips and pressed a kiss to her knuckles, glancing at the clock on the wall. "I'm sure Caleb will be here soon, sunshine."

Heat flooded her cheeks. She'd been caught up in worrying about her prospectus, which wasn't exactly the priority right now. Sweet Mary, was she ever going to be worried about the thing she should be worried about?

"I'm sorry," she whispered.

"Hey." Lach put a hand on her stomach. Unlike when Mrs. Rafferty had touched her earlier, his caress anchored her. Made her believe for a few seconds that everything would be okay. "Just breathe. Let the meds do their thing. There's nothing to worry about."

"Liar."

"Marisol. It's all stuff we can manage. We just need to talk to each other." Guilt flicked across his face. "And I need to support you wherever I can. Let's be honest—it's mostly your show. But I can be your assistant director."

"But—"

"Knock, knock." Caleb's voice came from outside the curtain. Metal zinged as he pushed the fabric aside to let himself into the space, then closed up the gap for privacy.

He wore a measured, serious expression on his handsome face, and she didn't need to see the lab coat hastily thrown over his polo shirt and khakis to guess he hadn't expected to come to the hospital today. The golf pencil tucked behind his ear broadcast that little fact.

Guilt oozed through her gut again. "Caleb, I'm—"

"Marisol. Glad you came in." He picked up the paper strip hanging from the machine monitoring the baby's movement and examined it. "What's shaking?"

Lachlan sat straighter and gave a rapid-fire description of the last couple of hours, down to the individual results of all the tests the nurses had done.

A month ago, she'd probably have been bothered by him jumping in. Now, all she could do was say silent thanks he was there, because she'd been too worried to absorb half the things he just belted out. Maybe there was something to this teamwork thing, after all.

Caleb frowned at the jagged lines on the output strip, and then on something on his phone. "Were you or any of your siblings premature, Marisol?"

"Luisa was, I think. Why? It's not genetic, is it?"

"Might be." Caleb shrugged. "Studies are still

inconclusive, but my gut tells me there's something to it."

She muttered a curse. "Am I in labor?"

"Not yet."

"My back is killing me today."

Caleb glanced at her stomach and hovered a hand by her navel. "You okay with a quick exam?"

She nodded.

He manipulated around her abdomen with gentle fingers. "Yeah, the baby dropped. Shifted things around, no doubt."

"Awesome. Maybe that walk today wasn't such a good idea."

He shook his head. "Gentle exercise is a good thing. I'm not seeing any signs of preeclampsia—no need to panic here."

She exhaled.

"Talk to me about your stress levels."

She snorted. She couldn't help it.

Exchanging a look with Lachlan, the doctor took the plastic pencil from behind his ear and fiddled with it. "What hours are you pulling at school these days?"

Damn it, nothing got past this guy. "Six to twelve hours a day."

"Six?" Lachlan muttered.

"Twelve," she admitted.

"Cut it in half," Caleb said.

"But I still have another week of summer session. And my prospectus presentation is scheduled in two weeks."

"And I just had to medicate you for high BP. So for those other six hours, I want you legitimately relaxing. Doing schoolwork on your couch doesn't count. Short walks are fine. If I catch you helped with moving *anything* of his—" he jerked a thumb in Lachlan's direction "—into his new place this weekend, I'll put you on full bed rest. Nor do I want you doing housecleaning at your place. Make Lachlan do the dishes and the vacuuming."

The thought of Lachlan standing at her sink made her smile. Mainly because she pictured him from the back, and the man had shoulders that would rival a Marvel character... "What about sex?" she blurted.

"Marisol, don't worry about that," Lach whispered.

"Should be okay," Caleb said. "Lay off any acrobatics, though."

Lachlan reddened a little. "Seriously, we can take a pause."

"We can?" she whispered to him.

"No need," Caleb said. "Physically, it's not going to cause harm, and emotionally, it relieves stress and builds bonds. All good things. School's another story, though. Talk to your advisor and whoever's in charge of your class scheduling. Make sure they understand you have some health concerns."

Awesome. Just the conversation she wanted to

have with Dr. Wiebe. She was so falling into all the stereotypes about women in graduate programs that she'd battled with her previous advisor.

"But you can leave for today, as soon as the nurse comes and detaches you from all the wires. Come see me at the clinic tomorrow, okay? I'll be working my usual Friday hours. I need to monitor how you're adjusting to the meds."

Tomorrow she was supposed to be at the university for the day, but she held her tongue. "Okay. Hopefully this one behaves overnight." She spread her fingers under her navel. "Oh! Caleb?"

"Yeah?"

"Do you have access to all my records here?"

He nodded.

"Do my ultrasound results have the sex on them?"

A grin brightened his face. "What, you want them?"

"Definitely."

Lachlan leaned an elbow on the bed and linked fingers with hers.

"I don't need to look. I remember," Caleb said. "When I saw the note, I thought to myself that it would've been fun for Cadie and Zach's kid to have a little boy cousin who'd look up to him—"

"A boy?" Marisol interrupted, heart swelling.

Caleb shook his head. "Would *have* been nice. Except you're having a girl. I'm sure she'll still hero-worship Ben, though." He reached over the bed to clap Lachlan on the shoulder. "Good luck, buddy. I'll babysit for you now and again."

"A girl," Lachlan croaked.

"Either would be fine," Marisol said hurriedly.

"Of course it would be. Doesn't make hearing it any less magical, though," Caleb said. "I'll see you tomorrow. I'll get my receptionist to call you with the time."

He scooted out of the curtained space.

Marisol covered her face with her hands and sank against the stiff hospital pillow.

"Lachlan," she said, unable to put much volume behind it.

"Mari."

She blinked at him. And she hadn't put much thought into him using the nickname, but it had an intimacy infused into it. A familiarity. Pretty much only her family called her that. Were they family now?

We will be if I can move past my damned issues.

"God, you're beautiful." His mouth crooked, and the muscles of his hand tensed against hers. He closed his eyes for a second. "A girl. It—it makes absolutely no difference in the world. But it's still the best thing I ever heard."

"It is."

He leaned in and kissed her. "Thanks for taking good care of her."

"Am I?" she croaked.

"You heard Caleb. She's healthy. And once you talk to Dr. Wiebe, tell her you need to ease up some, you'll be healthy, too."

She bit her lip. Mrs. Rafferty's assumptions from this morning filtered through the stress of being admitted to the hospital. *He's a caretaker...* He was that. And with all he had going on, it would be a hell of a lot easier for him to take care of her if they were living in the same place. "Maybe, I mean, what do you think..."

He raised a brow. "Going to finish that thought?"

"It would be easier on you if we were living together."

A slow, easy smile spread on his lips. "I don't know about easier, but it would be damn nice."

"That way you wouldn't be doing two sets of dishes. I mean, if we were going to follow Caleb's orders."

"We're following Caleb's orders," he said gruffly.

Panic clenched at her chest. *He likes the idea now. Until being with me gets in the way of his commitments and goals.*

Her ex's words.

Ugh, why did they still have their claws in her psyche? But...with all Lachlan had going on, and with her schooling, the possibility of ending up in the same miserable place seemed far too probable an outcome. "It would just be temporary. I—I'm not ready to live with someone full-time. But as long as Caleb expects me to be so damned helpless..."

His smile faltered. "*Mi casa es su casa.* Or how-ever you say it."

"You'd have to ask Zach. My Spanish conjugation skills are abysmal."

He squeezed her hand. "My apartment is a bit of a disaster—half in boxes, half not—so why don't I stay at your place for the next couple of nights, until we can move in on Saturday?"

"Sure."

"Marisol?"

Huh. He was back to her full name, and for some reason, that didn't sit right. "Yeah?"

"Whatever's putting that fear in your eyes? And has you thinking temporary instead of long-term? I hate it. I want you to feel so loved that you forget what it was like to fear."

"I—"

"Don't say anything back," he interrupted. "It's not going to feel right if you do."

"Oh—okay." So she did all that was left without words, and kissed him until the nurse came.

Kissing him was enough to make her forget a lot of things. Her worries about school. Her doubts about being a good mom. Hell, her name, age and phone number.

But the memory of lying in a bed much like this one and being alone? Of watching her ex walk out the door, and finding separation papers on the kitchen table when she got released from the hospital after being discharged?

Even Lachlan's arms around her couldn't make that go away.

"Marisol? Sweetheart?"

Lachlan's words filtered in to her awareness, along with a gentle stroke along her face.

"What—is it time to get up?" she mumbled, cracking open one eye. The dark room suggested otherwise. Though with him moving this morning, they hadn't planned their usual Saturday sleep-in. "You're getting up this early to move?"

"Moving's going to have to wait. I got a SAR call. Might take a while. I'll text when I can."

Worry pinched her stomach, and she sat up. "Be safe, okay? And tell my brother to do the same."

"Will do."

There was no falling asleep after that, so she got up and did an hour of yoga, then dug into a few hours of polishing her proposed study.

She was right in the middle of calculating statistical variances when her phone chimed.

Time to take a break, sunshine.

She gritted her teeth and checked the clock. Past noon. Her heart sank. She had so much left to do, but Lachlan was right—she'd hit her limit for the day.

An afternoon of boredom stretched ahead. She didn't want to push it with being too active, but what else was she supposed to do with a day where neither Lachlan nor Zach was available? She'd already made cookies yesterday, and she didn't have another doctor's appointment until Monday…

Um, make other human contact?

Maggie would probably be at the SAR call, too, though. As would Garnet James… But Cadie would probably be free. She didn't usually work Saturdays. Maybe Marisol could go chill in Cadie and Zach's backyard.

Cadie answered on the third ring, a little out of breath. "Hello?"

"Hey, uh, did I interrupt something?"

"Just my frustration. Zach needs me to deliver his spare hiking boots out to the base camp, and Ben's decided today's the day to have a monster nap."

"Want me to take them?"

"Oh." Cadie paused and hummed. "Well, it's not an emergency. Hence me not waking Ben."

"I'm free. And bored. I was calling to see if you wanted to do something."

"I'd love to. But yeah, if you're willing to play courier, your brother would owe you. You can take his truck—he got a ride out with Lach and Maggie. And then you can come back and hang out while we wait for the call to end. Sounds like it might be a complicated one."

"Complicated as in dangerous?"

"No, a small plane went down in the middle of the bush. Multiple casualties."

Her heart clenched. "How awful..."

"Pretty much. Don't worry, though. The SAR team is safe enough. It's just ugly for them."

Pinching her phone between her ear and shoulder, she grabbed her purse and slid into her shoes, then snatched the container of cookies she'd baked. Sugar was always appreciated. She remembered that too well after helping support the rescue crew after the avalanche Zach had witnessed. She headed for her car. "Always amazes me Zach's able to get back out in the field after what he went through."

"It helps him, I think."

"So do you, Cadie."

"I try."

"He's lucky." Unlocking her car, she got in. "I'll see you in a few."

After making her way to her brother's place, retrieving his boots and switching vehicles, she followed the directions Cadie gave her to get out to the operations base. The forty-five-minute drive around the backside of the mountain gave her way too much time for her thoughts to drift.

Cadie was lucky to have Zach, and vice versa. They'd both managed to get through a horrific situation, worse than what Marisol had ever dealt with.

So why were they able to move on, and she wasn't? What was wrong with her?

She bumped along the gravel road, but even the rough ride couldn't jar her doubt.

The SAR unit was set up in a small clearing on the side of an old mining road. Thick trees lined the grassy patch. A couple of tents like the ones soccer teams used for sideline shelter and a circle of various law enforcement vehicles made up the makeshift command center. The county's incident control vehicle buzzed with activity. She pulled in next to Lachlan's truck, parked among a half-dozen personal vehicles.

Grabbing Zach's boots, she carefully navigated the rough terrain. She hadn't been thinking. Her Toms were not the best shoes to be wearing on bumpy ground. Approaching with caution—she didn't want to get in the way—she spotted her brother among the four people surrounding a folding table. The group was poring over a set of topographical maps. Her brother wore technical pants and a SAR-emblazoned T-shirt, but the others were uniformed. Two police officers and a federal official, by the colors and letters on their jackets. Their backs were to her.

"Zach?" she called when she was a couple of yards away. "I come bearing footwear. And junk food. Lebkuchen."

He turned, and his green eyes lit. "Mom's recipe?"

"Of course."

"Since when do you make those in the summer?"

"Since I was climbing the walls yesterday afternoon." She took a last few ginger steps across the pitted ground and handed him his boots and the plastic container. "Nothing wrong with a little Christmas in August."

"Truth."

She backed away. "I don't want to interrupt."

"You're not." His face sobered, and he put the cookies on the table. Then he grabbed a clean pair of socks from his pocket and bent over to change his shoes. "The team reached the wreckage a few hours ago. No survivors. So it's a recovery mission at this point, and then these guys will be on deck for the investigation." He jerked a thumb at the team of officials.

"Are you heading into the bush again?"

He shook his head and tied his laces. "No. But I landed in a creek earlier and my feet were wet, and I was an idiot and didn't have my spares with me. Thanks for the fresh change."

"Cool. I should go, though."

"Or pull up a chair. Lach'll be back in an hour or so. He'd love that—you can leave my truck for me, and he can return home early. He's bringing Fudge out now, so he's all done for the day. But being incident commander, I need to stick around longer, as does Maggie. She's on one of the extraction teams."

And someone would have to be called, told their

loved one wasn't coming home… Tears stung the corners of her eyes.

Zach squeezed her shoulder with one of his big mitts. "I know. I do this because it's necessary, not because I enjoy it. Lach would probably say the same."

She'd never asked, and guilt twinged in her belly. "Cookies don't seem like enough."

He lifted the lid off the tin and grabbed a cookie, then popped it into his mouth whole.

"It helps," he said, chewing.

After texting Cadie to say she was going to stick around the SAR site for a bit, she kept to the sidelines for the next forty-five minutes. Her brother and his colleagues fascinated her—the radio calls and strategic discussion were a far cry from anything she ever dealt with at school.

Just when she was starting to worry she was in the way, a small group of people emerged from the bush ten yards away, led by Fudge in her red work vest. She was favoring her right foreleg, which had a white bandage wrapped around it. Concern pinged through Marisol as she watched the small group cross the clearing. The dog's drooping ears matched the solemn expressions of the three people who followed her.

Lachlan's included.

They locked eyes and he picked up his pace.

Damn. Normally he smiled when he saw her. Not

that she would have expected it, not after what he'd been dealing with on the rescue. He was hurting.

Fudge came to her first, sniffing her hand and nosing her thigh.

"Probably wants a cookie, too," Zach said lightly, snitching another from the stack.

Marisol knelt on the ground and put her arms around the dog. "I bet she earned one. Hey, baby. Tough day, huh?"

"Brutal," Lachlan rasped. "I could use one of those. The hug, not a cookie."

"I dunno, the cookies are pretty awesome," Zach mumbled around a full mouth.

Letting go of the dog to reach out for a hand up, Marisol looked up at Lachlan. A scrape marked his stubbled cheek, and he had a few tree needles in his hair. A rip marred the sleeve of his navy SAR T-shirt. He quickly linked fingers with her, and took her into his embrace the second she stood.

She clasped him to her as hard as she could given her belly was crazy in the way. An odd mix of smells came off his shirt—fresh air and pine, but fragments of acrid smoke. Sweat, too.

She brushed at a dirt streak on his forehead. "You look a little worse for wear."

"Some of the trees around the crash site were unstable. I caught a skinny one right before it fell on Fudge. It nicked me a little. And as she jumped out of the way, she cut her leg on a snag. I need to take her to the clinic, clean her up. She'll need a few sutures."

"You can do that?"

He stiffened.

"I didn't mean skill-wise. I just wasn't sure you were licensed for that."

Relaxing, he nodded. "Regulations are pretty vague in Montana. As long as Maggie clears it, I can do it."

"I brought Zach his truck—he said he'd take Maggie home, and you and I can head back into town together."

Closing his eyes for a second, he nodded. His throat bobbed. "Man, I need that. Thank you."

After a little paperwork and signing out, they made their way to the truck. He got Fudge settled in the passenger side of the crew cab. The dog gave Lachlan an extra lick. If Marisol's test subjects were as in tune to their people as Fudge was to Lach, she wouldn't have trouble proving her hypothesis at all.

She climbed into the front. She leaned to close the door, but he put out his hand. He reached under her seat and slid her backward.

"Shift over?" he said.

She did, rising awkwardly onto the console with one hip. He climbed in behind her and pulled her sideways into his lap. Her legs hung out the open door.

"I just need to hold you. Bear with me for a second."

He dropped his forehead to her temple and inhaled, chest hitching unevenly.

"You can have more than a second, Lachlan."

"Thanks." He sniffled. A tear dripped onto her ear.

"Oh, love." She turned her head and wiped the wetness with her thumb. His whiskers were rough on her skin—figured he hadn't shaved this morning, he'd probably shot out of bed. "It's okay to need time to process. Good, really. A lot of first responders bottle things up and end up the worse for it."

His lips twisted and he glanced to the side.

"I don't think I saw my ex cry once. And let me tell you—anytime I see a difference, I jump for joy." She kissed his cheek softly. "Figuratively. No way am I risking jumping right now. My water might break, for God's sake."

He chuckled, and he let go of her to press the heels of his hands into his eyes. "Don't think it works that way, sunshine. That baby's not coming out until she's ready, no matter what gymnastics you do."

"She can stay put for now. I'm not ready for her to be an outside-baby yet." School was counting on the baby not coming early. But the mountain of work she'd left behind didn't seem quite as pressing as it had a couple of hours ago. Not in the face of plane crashes and Lachlan's tears.

He sniffed again and dropped his hands from his eyes. One clasped her shoulder, and one rubbed her side, right under the empire waist of her cotton spaghetti-strap top. "What's the line from that Christmas movie? The one with Jude Law? 'I'm a weeper?'"

"Aw, *The Holiday*? I love that movie." And it was cute that he knew it that well.

"So does Maggie. You can watch it with us this year. We always have movie night on Christmas Eve."

Making plans that far ahead sent a rush of concern through her, but she ignored it. "That sounds really nice. And we'll have a tiny human with us, too."

"We will." A smile broke through, brightening his face for a second before it turned sheepish. "Sorry for falling apart on you."

"Don't apologize." Her own emotions swelled, pressing against her throat. Not sadness, though, or trauma—just love. "I like being candid together. I haven't had this before."

"Then you weren't loved right."

"I know."

"Stands to reason you shouldn't base your beliefs about relationships on that experience, then."

"I see we're in the 'real talk' segment of today's show." The joke flew out. A defense mechanism, obviously. She saw that.

So do something about it. Don't give in to bad habits.

He raised an eyebrow. "You're deflecting."

"I know," she repeated.

His gaze searched her like she was transparent, like he could see into her cracks, into the parts of her that she pretended didn't exist.

"I'm trying to look at us differently." Her throat went dry. "I'm working on it."

He raised his eyebrows. His head fell back against the headrest, a hint of doubt marring his brow. "And how's that going?"

The urge rose to clam up, to shove down the words. But that was old wounds taking control. It was time to try something new. Her heart accelerated to a sprint. "I—I'm falling in love with you."

His mouth gaped.

"You're catching flies," she said softly, then kissed him.

Threading his fingers into her hair, he murmured his happiness.

Their tongues tangled, a hot press of lips and breath and drifting hands. Didn't take him more than a second to discover she had a skirt on. His fingers slid up the inside of her thigh.

On the side of the road, in sight of her brother and a half-dozen SAR people.

She pulled away. "I want you to go there. But just not here."

"Good point. Also, I need to clean Fudge up. But after that... I will finish this."

"I'll hold you to that."

Chapter Thirteen

The August sun was just rising above the trees on the highway as Marisol drove in to Bozeman to teach her Thursday morning class. The days since the plane crash had been busy, but she'd followed the rules. She'd lifted nary a box while moving both Lachlan's stuff and some of hers to his new house on Sunday. She'd kept her work hours to exactly six hours a day, and she'd managed to put her feet up for a lot of her off time. Her Monday and Wednesday appointments with Caleb had rewarded her efforts—he was pleased that her blood pressure was in a healthier range.

And getting to spend evenings with Lachlan, having him cook dinner and be her pillow while they watched Netflix before bed…

Don't get used to it. This didn't work the first time you tried it, so why would it work now?

And it wasn't just her heart on the line—she had to be cautious for the baby's sake, too. She wanted to believe the counterarguments—she was older, Lach wasn't a world-class douchecanoe—but her amygdala was definitely stuck in a fight-or-flight response. Heavy on the flight.

She swallowed, fighting the dryness in her throat. Having an after-class meeting scheduled with Dr. Wiebe was only contributing to her anxiety. Her advisor had been away for the week, so Marisol hadn't been able to talk to her about her health issues. She was not looking forward to explaining why she was having to limit her hours.

Once she made it to campus and settled in to handling her class, she pushed those worries aside for a little while. Her students were a good distraction, stressed as they were about their imminent final exam. Counseling others served as a nice diversion from thinking about her meeting, but eventually the classroom emptied out and she no longer had the excuse to delay.

She made her way to the neighboring building and up to Dr. Wiebe's office.

"Marisol. How's teaching going?"

"Well. I'll be honest, I think I'm more suited to teaching than to the publication side of professorial work." She took a seat in one of the chairs set up in front of the heavy antique desk.

Dr. Wiebe scrunched her nose, causing her wire-frame glasses to slip down. She pushed them back into place with a finger. "You'll have to find a balance. Can't do one without the other."

"I know. And don't get me wrong—I'm excited about taking my research in a new direction. Last night, I experimented on Lachlan's dog, just a test run, not to standards of course, but she responded exactly as I anticipated."

"You can't base results and hypotheses off a human-dog team to whom you're close, Marisol."

"Obviously, but Lachlan was giving me a hand compiling my annotated bibliography, and then was reading through my proposed study, and—"

"Nor can you have people do your work for you."

She sat back in the chair. "I wasn't, I—"

"Lachlan Reid is well-known in the SAR community around here and if the rest of the panel gets the impression he's collaborating with you on work that's supposed to be done individually that could compromise your success."

The reprimand bit in, and the edges of her eyes stung.

Deep breath. Do. Not. Cry.

Once she was sure she could speak steadily, Marisol said, "I would never be dishonest about my work. I also think he is an excellent resource. As well, I've been told I need to cut down my work hours before the baby comes. And given I have to teach, and I have to get my prospectus polished, I accepted his offer to help. He was just typing out my notes verbatim."

Dr. Wiebe crossed her arms. "Well, be very careful about what you mention in front of the committee next week."

"I will," Marisol promised quietly. She'd come too far to compromise her success now, so she'd watch every word she said. And to be on the safe side, she'd watch how much she involved Lachlan in her research, too.

Tick. Tick. Tick.

Okay, that clock was going to have to go. Marisol had brought the wall-hung timepiece with her from her apartment and had put it up in their new living room, explaining it was an heirloom her great-grandmother had sent her from Germany, but the thing was loud as hell. Plus, every tick reminded Lachlan that she still wasn't home yet. The minute hand traveled from five thirty to six, and he got antsier by the second. Unpacking his remaining boxes did zip to quell his jumping nerves. Where was she? She'd left for Bozeman before 9:00 a.m., and she still wasn't back yet? Nor was she answering her phone.

He was three seconds away from hopping in his

truck and driving her usual route when the front door opened.

"Lach?" Her voice wobbled.

He took a deep breath and put down the hammer he was using to hang a picture above the mantel. "I'm in the living room."

She trudged up the half flight of stairs from the entrance to where he was, holding up a hand. "I know, I know. I broke the rules. But I had a bitch of a meeting with Dr. Wiebe—she chewed me out for letting you get too involved with my research—and I was on a tear, getting about twice as much done as I normally would."

"Marisol…" His throat squeezed at the thought of what could go wrong if she didn't follow Caleb's orders. Premature delivery… And God forbid she develop preeclampsia.

"Don't say anything. You don't need to. I know. Look, I'll go to bed extra early. Watch me." She walked down the hall, fists digging into her back as she went. The bedroom door clicked shut behind her. One loud sob penetrated through the barrier.

Well, crap.

Following, he quietly entered the room. She lay on the bed on her side, shoulders shaking. He'd used some of his ill-gotten loan from his parents to buy a king-size bed, so there was plenty of room for him to curl up behind her. And given he'd pay off the money with interest, he didn't have to feel that awful about having borrowed the cash.

As if.

Okay, fine. He contemplated punching a hole through the wall every time he thought of it. But coming home to this house, having the space to properly raise their kid, made it worth it.

So did coming home to Marisol.

For now. Until she decides she doesn't need to live here anymore.

His fist itched to connect with drywall over that, too, but instead, he spooned her back and looped an arm around her belly. She shuddered in his embrace, her sobs now silent.

"Talk to me, sunshine."

"I—I know I sc-c-rewed up, o-k-kay?"

He wanted to say something soothing, but he knew whatever he said would come off as a lecture, so he just held her closer to his body.

"I'm ju-just so a-af-fraid."

That knocked his temper down by a few degrees. "That you won't get your prospectus done? But you're so close."

She curled into more of a ball. "I'm behind where I should be. Next Friday... Oh, God. And Dr. Wiebe wanted help with a journal article today—she was already so disappointed with me, I couldn't say no."

"Yes, you could have," he said quietly. "Does she not understand doctor's orders?"

A long minute of silence stretched between them.

"What if I can't do it?" she whispered.

"You have eight more days. You've got this."

"No, the whole thing. My degree. Being a mom. Being a good girlfriend."

His arms tightened of their own accord. "We just need to stick together."

"Me working with you is what set Dr. Wiebe off in the first place."

"What, me playing secretary?"

"And me experimenting with Fudge."

He swore. "Academia is a piece of work."

She sniffled. "And it's my life, Lachlan."

He spread his hand on her stomach and held in a "so's this."

"She warned me I'd have to be really careful."

"Funny how she's all over you being cautious with your research but not with our child," he grumbled. Crap. Probably should have kept that one in, too.

A snort, somewhere between agreement and protest, puffed out her nose.

"Even if I can't involve you in my work, that doesn't change what I agreed to. I want to be your partner, Lachlan. It feels like…like we're a family."

"I— We—" He wasn't sure how to voice the swell of hope pressing against his chest, clogging his throat. Holy crap. He'd gone his whole life trying to piece together some semblance of family. Always feeling like people were water through his fingers—

his grandmother dying, his grandfather moving to Arizona, his parents being useless. Stella, off in New York. Leaving him with Maggie and Fudge and some close friends. But one word from this woman and the brass ring he'd been grasping for was finally staying in his grip.

He kissed her hair, then brushed the thick strands aside to nuzzle behind her ear. "I love you, Mari."

She reached back and awkwardly stroked his cheek. "I love you, too."

"Since when?" he teased.

"Since you showed me you're a good man. Easy to be around." She giggled. "And kinda nice to look at, too."

He laughed. She'd spilled a lot of herself tonight—he didn't mind being a little lighthearted. "Mmm, I knew it was about my pretty face."

She swatted his hip. "You're right, you know. About being a team. About working together. I'd forgotten how to do that. Still feeling shaky on it, really. But I have faith we can handle anything that comes our way. You're not my ex. I can trust you. And I'm not the person I was when I was with him."

And the very bed we're lying on is proof I haven't been as honest with you as I've professed to be. He had to tell her about the loan, explain that using his last resort meant getting to care for their baby and to keep his business, and so long as he wasn't indebted to his parents for eternity, he'd learn to deal with having to go back on promises he'd made to himself. Better she find out from him than from someone else. Nothing stayed quiet in Sutter Creek.

But she'd already had a rotten afternoon—he could wait to tell her. He'd find a day when the weight of the world wasn't crushing her to the mattress.

"Sure you don't want to have dinner?" he asked. "You're just going to go to sleep?"

"Well… Oh, hey!" She grabbed his hand off her shoulder and placed it on the underside of her stomach. The pop against his palm made his heart skip a beat. "Did you feel that?"

"Very much." Throat thickening, he swallowed. "Our daughter, throwing elbows."

She laughed and nestled closer to him. The scent of cherries and chocolate curled into his nostrils. He loved that smell. Wanted it on his sheets indefinitely.

His body responded, groin thickening. He sneaked his hand down until his fingers teased the top of her mound through the fabric of her dress.

The wiggle in response had him hard as a rock. "Delay dinner, then?"

"Definitely."

Now that Marisol had released the pressure valve with a good cry, other priorities were making themselves known. Mainly how Lachlan's hand would really be put to much better use a few inches lower instead of resting just above the money spot. And over her clothes, no less. That needed to change.

She took his hand and used it to nudge her dress up. Heat trailed in the wake of the skimming touch. She sucked in a breath.

He chuckled. "I see where you're going with this."

"Yeah? Do you want further direction, or can you take it from here?"

His thumb rested along the edge of her underwear, right in the crook between thigh and pleasure. "Let's go with column B."

"Mmm, I'm a big fan of either."

With a single fingertip, he explored and teased, setting her aflame as he dipped in and around the stretchy lace. "These are pretty. But they're really in the way."

He eased them down, and she kicked them off. Tilting back against him, she opened her legs wider.

The message was obviously clear, because he stroked her sensitive flesh, tracing swirls.

Her hips rose off the bed and she moaned. *Sweet Mary.* This man, he helped her forget everything, distilled life down to a simple but complex knot of need and love.

And when he thrust a finger deep into her wet heat, she went over the edge. She rode his hand, rode the pleasure, the release.

His lips pressed softly along the edge of her ear.

"Do you want to make love this way? Or do you want to be on top?"

Having him at her back, supporting her and cherishing her, filled her soul as much as quenching her desire. His hard length pressed against her ass, promising more of the ecstasy still lingering in her veins.

"Yeah, let's try this way," she said.

He stroked her sex again, sending a wave of anticipation through her. "You feel ready."

"I *am* ready."

He reached between them and fumbled with his belt buckle. He shoved down his pants and boxers. His arousal singed her skin, a brand at her back. He stroked her inner thigh, nudging her to widen. With a swift, gentle thrust, he filled her.

Limited a little by the position, she tilted her hips to let him in deeper. Wow, the angle. Pleasure blossomed through her core. "Lach, that's— You're— Oh, sweet…"

Groaning, he cupped one of her breasts, toying with her nipple through her bra and dress.

"I didn't even undress you properly." Amusement layered over a hint of embarrassment in his voice. He set a slow, sensuous rhythm that had her struggling to follow his words. "Badly done on my part."

"As long as you keep doing that—" she covered his hand over her breast, tightening the caress "—I'll forgive you for anything."

He froze for a second, then sped up, rocking them

together. His hand skimmed over her belly, and she shivered when he reached the raised hem of her dress and the bare flesh below. Torn between tipping toward his body and his hand, she groaned.

"Don't tease me," she panted. She hooked her foot over his leg and arched backward.

"Fine line between teasing and pleasure, sunshine." He touched her mound, slicked his fingers between her folds. Being full of him, and having him graze her tender arousal, broke the dam within her.

She swore, moaned his name, ground back and clamped his hand between her thighs, stealing every last moment of bliss. He thrust long, finding his own satisfaction with a shout.

Aftershocks pulsed in her limbs, and she went limp, letting her raised leg flop to the mattress. "Lachlan."

He murmured something crude against her hair, then stroked her hip. "Damn, that was… We're too good at this. Must be why we got lucky, made a baby."

No, we were just stupid and didn't follow the damned directions on the condom box. But she couldn't bring herself to correct him.

Because he was right. They were lucky.

Rap rap.

Marisol blinked, registering Lachlan's empty side of the bed. Right. He'd muttered something in her ear about taking Fudge out for a run after the last time she'd gotten up to use the washroom.

Rap rap rap.

Had he forgotten his key? Or was Mrs. Rafferty dropping by to make sure they were watering the petunias?

Wincing as her hips pulled with morning stiffness, she tied her thigh-length summer robe over her tank top and the pair of pajama bottoms she'd borrowed from Lachlan, and walked down the hall and the stairs to the front entrance. Electrical jolts snapped through her pelvis as she navigated the steps.

"Ow," she muttered. God, stairs sucked.

Another knock rang out, and she turned the knob. "Yeah, yeah, I'm moving as fast as I can. Did you forget your—"

Oh. Not Lachlan. A middle-aged couple stood on the stoop. The woman was the spitting image of Maggie, except her blond hair was longer and pinned in a sleek French twist. Her crisp, sleeveless red dress hung on her slender frame. Clearly designer made. Or custom, going off the clothes of the man next to her. His gray summer suit screamed bespoke.

He had light brown hair and Lachlan's eyes.

She did a double take. No, not the same. Lachlan's eyes danced with life and humor, and this man's brown irises looked like they hadn't sparkled in decades.

"Um, hello. You must be Lachlan's parents." She smoothed a hand down her robe. Her cheeks heated.

"You're living with him?" his mother said, mouth screwed in a sour bud.

He hadn't told them they'd moved in together? But…

No. Be calm. He's not close to them. From what he and Maggie had implied, the relationship was downright antagonistic, in fact. But without actual instructions, she was flying blind, and she seriously doubted he'd want her to leave them out on the porch.

"Yes. Um, it's nice to meet you. I'm Marisol. Come in?"

"Sure," Mr. Reid said, broaching the landing as Marisol stood to the side and held the door open. "Might as well see what my money's paying for."

Marisol blinked in confusion. His money? That couldn't be right.

But Lachlan's finances weren't her concern, so she followed his parents up the stairs, gripping the railing for support. Good lord. She'd never felt less graceful in her life, and compared to Lachlan's elegant mother… Quite the first impression she was making.

"Can I get you anything? Lachlan just moved in— well, me, too," she corrected. "But I could get you tea or coffee."

"You don't need to get to work?" Mr. Reid asked as he ran a hand along the back of the couch her brother had told them to bring over from the apartment. Mrs. Reid stood in the center of the sparsely appointed living room, scowling at the framed, vintage ski advertisements Lachlan had hung yesterday.

"I—" She took a deep breath. "I'm only working six hours a day until the baby's born. So I'm heading in later this morning."

He glanced at her stomach. "Not that it's a reason to be less productive, but you look like you should have given birth two weeks ago."

"But—" Irritation erased any patience she might have clung to. If one more person made a comment about her pregnancy, she'd lose it. But this man doing it, showing zero interest in the fact she was carrying his granddaughter, didn't raise her ire. Sadness washed over her. Lach wasn't kidding when he'd called his father an asshole.

She straightened. "You're going to be a grandfather, and that's all you're going to say?"

"I never was much for babies," he said, voice blasé.

Marisol's jaw dropped, and she looked over at Lachlan's mother, who had pulled out her cell phone and was studying the screen. A wave of gratitude rushed through her for her own parents, who couldn't wait for the baby to be born, even though they didn't live close by. They'd have to do grandparent double duty—her daughter sure wasn't going to get much affection from this pair.

And Lachlan, growing up with this? Her heart ached for him, and she wanted him to be back from his run so she could hug him and assure him that his parents being pricks didn't need to affect his life anymore.

Nor would it impact their daughter. There was plenty of love coming the baby's way, with or without these people. But still, how could they not be interested in their grandchild? "You can't mean that. Not really."

"Talk to me once the kid's old enough to go to law school. Maybe it'll be smarter than my own children and will want to take over the family firm."

"Dad!"

Marisol startled at Lachlan's voice. She turned to face him. He stood at the top of the stairs. His eyes flashed with temper and his hands gripped Fudge's leash. The dog strained, seemingly torn between getting to Marisol and glaring at what she perceived as intruders.

Lachlan didn't seem too eager to call off the dog. He was still breathing heavily from his run. His sweaty shirt molded to his chest. Which, despite the awkward company, she could still appreciate. Those muscles were probably 65 percent responsible for her being weeks away from giving birth.

"I didn't hear you come in," she said, closing the space between them and laying a calming hand on Fudge's soft head.

"You left the door open, sunshine," he said, closing the space between them. He kissed her forehead and slung an arm around the middle of her back. He leaned to her ear. "What did he say to you? Besides the bit about law school? You're pale."

"Nothing that needs to be repeated," she murmured back. "Just enough for me to understand that he's not marking the baby's due date on the calendar."

The corners of his mouth tugged down.

"Lachlan." She'd do anything to erase that sadness. She stood on her toes and kissed him. Salt from his sweat stung her mouth. "I love you."

He dropped his forehead to hers for a moment, then sucked in a breath.

"I don't get why you're here," he said to his parents.

His dad looked around the room. "Enh, I paid the rent on this place, didn't I? Thought I'd come see it, and then you can run me through your plans for the expansion. I want good return on my investment."

Investment? Marisol blinked. Lachlan had funded his business through savings, grants and a bank loan, so why would his dad be loaning him money, calling himself an investor?

Unless he lied. Had he lied just like her ex, borrowing from places and digging himself further into the hole?

Nausea lurched in her belly.

"What does he mean?" She dug her fingers into Lachlan's forearm.

Lachlan cringed, his mouth slackening.

"Oh, so you haven't shared that with her. Not that close, are you?" His dad laughed. "First smart thing you've done in months, son."

Marisol's face went numb. Lach's arm muscles were concrete under her grasp, his expression walled off. What the hell was going on? She needed to know, but not in front of these stiff people, in front of his dad, who was nodding at Lachlan in the only display of fatherly pride she'd seen since the Reids arrived. She yanked him down the hall, moving faster than she had since the baby dropped.

"Slow down, Marisol."

"No damned way." She ushered him into the bedroom and crossed her arms. Her heart threatened to beat out of her chest. "What did he mean, *investment*?"

Chapter Fourteen

Lachlan held up his hands as Marisol stared him down, her eyes flashing green fire.

"I just wanted to reduce your stress…" he protested.

Weak, Reid. Weak.

"Making unilateral decisions does not reduce my stress, especially from someone who's been preaching teamwork to me."

An understatement. He'd worked himself into a no-win situation. No way to lie. But honesty would lose her, too. Goddamn it. Why had he kept this from her?

Except, had there been another way to keep her

in his life and go forward with the expansion? "You didn't want me to compromise, but when that grant flopped, I didn't see another way to secure financing. Stella wasn't willing, and the bank was tapped out."

"So you made a deal with the proverbial devil? For the baby?"

"And you. I wanted it all, Marisol. And this was the only way to do it."

She wrung her hands. "You didn't talk to me."

"I didn't want you to worry."

"No, you thought I'd say no. You knew I'd be sensitive about money because of me and the baby, both from the perspective of having to borrow more *and* having to borrow from your parents, who you clearly don't want to be associated with."

He swallowed the self-protective urge to minimize, tell a half-truth. "Yeah, some of that, too."

She sat gingerly on the edge of the bed. A breath shuddered from her lungs. "I—I can't trust you if you're going to hide big things, Lachlan. I can't be with someone who's going to lie about money. You knew I didn't want you to alter your business plans. And is there any other way to define you taking a loan from your parents? Everything you've told me about them points to a bad situation, where they'll expect things in return from you, things you'll resent."

"Yeah, but it's a necessity."

"I didn't want this to change.your life." Her misery made his chest ache.

And he couldn't help the disbelief rising to meet it. For someone who studied psychology, she sure didn't acknowledge her own compartmentalization around this. "Okay, how could a baby *not* change my life? And the loan was my way of keeping all the balls in the air."

"But it meant hiding something from me, and going back on something fundamental to you. Something you're clearly not happy about."

His jaw locked, and he forced it to relax. "I didn't like keeping secrets. But borrowing the money? I'm fine with it."

Or he would be, once he paid his parents off.

"You're lying again."

"Marisol… This was the best I could come up with."

"The best was supposed to be us, being open, letting each other help. It can't be a one-way street. I did that before—me being the giver, not being honest about my needs. And it was a disaster."

"This isn't the same—"

"I can't deal with this this week. I have limited time enough, none to spend on being up in my emotions." She got her suitcase from the cupboard and put it on the bed.

"You're leaving?" His stomach soured. "We can work through this—"

But the words he'd been saying to her for a couple of months didn't feel as convincing this time.

"Not today, we can't."

"Marisol, the baby's due in three weeks. You can't just walk out…"

She threw her dresses into the suitcase. "I have to."

"I get I screwed up. But I don't want you to be alone—"

"It's easier when I'm alone."

He reeled from the gut punch.

"I'll wait until your parents are gone. Then I'll head back to my place."

"But Zach and I were going to move the nursery furniture over."

"I'll call him and tell him we're waiting."

"For how long?" he croaked.

She wiped a hand along her wet cheeks, but when he motioned to comfort her, she backed away, clutching a stack of T-shirts to her chest. "When I figure out if I can trust you again."

"You're an idiot." Maggie finished administering anesthesia to the Jack Russell terrier lying between them on the hydraulic operating table, then reached up to smack Lachlan on the back of his head. "Why weren't you honest?"

"Waste of a perfectly good glove," he said, raising a brow at her hand.

Maggie growled, tearing off the blue latex and throwing it in the waste disposal. She yanked on another glove. "Haven't you been lied to enough by Mom and Dad to know how much of a problem it is?"

"Thought you didn't think relationships were worth it," he grumbled, avoiding the truth nestled in her question.

"I don't. But you started one with the mother of your child, so fix it." She pointed a syringe at him.

"Could we have this conversation when you're not holding a sharp implement?" He busied himself clipping and disinfecting the dog's rear leg. The terrier was a leaper, and had managed to land the wrong way while catching a Frisbee. She had a fractured tibia to show for her efforts. Lucky for the dog, Maggie was a wizard with external fixation.

Prior to being put under, the wounded dog's eyes had flashed with panic.

Like Marisol when she'd faced down his parents. Wounded. Panicked.

And his parents might have been the catalyst, but he was the cause. Lying to her about money *was* way too close to her ex-husband's actions for comfort. He knew she was particularly fragile because of that experience. And he'd still thought he knew best and made the exact wrong decision.

Bending his head, he gripped the edge of the operating table and resisted the urge to flip over the tray of the pins and struts they'd use to immobilize the dog's limb. "I'm no better than they are, Maggie. Telling myself I could make a relationship work as long as I was a team player—clearly, I don't know a functioning partnership from a damned hole in my head."

Maggie stared at him. "I thinking the hole's in your heart."

He barked out a laugh. "Christ, corny much?"

Her hands dropped to her sides. "I know I wasn't super supportive when Marisol came to town. But she's good people. And if you're going to be naive enough to risk being flayed open for someone, then don't mess it up."

"I already did," he said quietly.

And flayed was about right.

He swallowed bile. "I don't think I can make it right, Mags. I lost her trust. Pretty fundamental."

Maggie raised her chin and glared at him before studying the X-ray illuminator. "Figure it out."

"I—" He swallowed. "Aside from the honesty fail, she's pissed I borrowed money from Dad. Hell, *I'm* pissed I borrowed money from Dad. But there was really no other way. Can't get the honey back in the jar once it's spilled."

"Remind me what Stella said when you asked for a loan?"

"Something about never investing in Sutter Creek. I can't remember her exact words."

Maggie's eyebrows wrinkled. Guaranteed she was

frowning under her surgical mask. Shaking her head, she started muttering to herself about clamps and drill bits.

He waved a hand at the equipment he'd prepped. "All there."

She glanced at the tray, then back at him. "We need to talk to Stella again. She needs to understand how important this is."

"It's my crap to shovel."

"Not entirely. Your business is intertwined with mine. And I wish I had the ability to foot the bill for you, but I'm stretched as much as you are."

She was right. His business did impact hers. Not to mention affecting his dreams, and the baby, and Marisol... And his borrowing money from his parents had screwed up way too many parts of his life. "You think going back to Stella's worth a shot?"

"Isn't getting Marisol back worth trying anything?"

Well, when she put it that way... "Touché."

They finished the surgery and a couple of other appointments, then set up his laptop in the staff room and both pulled up chairs.

"Ganging up on me for some reason?" Stella asked when she answered their Skype call. Judging by the buildings of midtown Manhattan glittering outside the window behind her, she was still at the office.

"Little bit," Maggie said with a shrug.

"Well, get to it. I'm finishing up a quarterly report for one of my boss's closest clients, and the numbers aren't lining up. And I'd like to set foot in my apartment before it's technically tomorrow."

Lach frowned. Stella was no stranger to stress, but the strain on her face was tenser than usual. "We called about me, but if—"

"Then keep it about you, little brother."

He exchanged a questioning look with Maggie, who shrugged again.

"I've screwed things up with Marisol—"

Stella snorted, and he shot her a glare.

"Thanks for the support, there, sis," he said.

"Not even you, with your sunshine-and-roses exterior, can make love work, Lach," Stella said. "Someone's always bound to screw up. Bound to leave the other behind."

He swallowed. Dealing with his sisters' old issues made it hard to hold on to any sense of hope. "Well, my love life isn't what's up for debate here. It's about my business. Which impacts Maggie's. I made a stupid move, taking a loan from Dad, and I'm regretting it. I can't live the next five years knowing I owe him money." Knowing Marisol would resent his decisions, too. "Stella, I need you to reconsider."

"Considering you didn't take me up on my offer to look over your business plan, I don't *need* to do anything."

"His business plan is fine, Stella." Maggie crossed

her arms. "But he'd been essentially guaranteed that grant. It's not his fault he counted on a promise that got broken. Surely you have a little sympathy for someone being the innocent casualty of a liar."

Stella's mouth gaped for a few seconds. "Are you talking about Mom and Dad, or Ryan?"

"Take your pick," Maggie said.

"Harsh, Mags," Lachlan murmured. Using Stella's past as a weapon didn't seem fair.

"No, Lach, it's not. You've worked really hard on this. And borrowing money from Stella would get you out from under Dad and Mom's thumb, and would let you follow through on your obligations to Marisol—"

"The baby's not an obligation," he said. Bracing his knees on his elbows, he dropped his head into his hands. "Neither's Marisol. I love them."

Stella's sigh passed through the speakers, and he looked up sharply. Her lower lip was wobbling. She coughed.

"You're really wanting to make a go of this?" she asked.

"I've been working toward owning my own training facility for—"

"No, with Marisol."

"Of course I do. She's the mother of my child, Stell. She should be the center of my world." Granted, she wasn't clamoring to fill that role. But if he managed to fix his financial issues, maybe she'd see that he'd learned from his mistake.

Stella's face crumbled. "Okay. Sure. I'll loan you the money. Text me the amount you need."

She disconnected, but not quick enough to stop them from hearing a big sniffle.

Lach winced. His sister's misery squashed any joy he should have felt over the money.

Maggie whistled low. "And you were accusing *me* of being harsh. Reminding her how she *wasn't* a priority for our clown of a sheriff? Ouch."

"That's not what I was meaning to do. I was just telling the truth." Lachlan shook his head. "And we don't know the whole story about Stella and Ryan. Plus, you and I both have to work with him on every SAR call. Best we not call him a clown, don't you think?"

"He broke our sister's heart, Lach. I can call him what I want. Just not when he's my superior." Maggie made a face, then nudged him. "You got your money. Shouldn't you be smiling?"

"Yeah, I should. But I haven't seen Stella cry in years." Not since he'd comforted her after her miscarriage. Dread spread through his chest. "What if, even with the money, I can't fix this? Look at our sister. Some hurts are too deep to mend."

Maggie hooked her heels on the edge of the chair and hugged her knees. "You know, I don't ever see wanting to put myself out there. Ending up like Mom and Dad… I don't fool myself, thinking I could have what Grams and Gramps had, or what Gramps found with Carol. I'm not charmed like him. But you—I thought you were."

"I thought I was, too. I figured as long as I emulated him, I could have what he had."

"And you honestly think that over fifty years, he and Grams didn't have any trust issues? Because I'm betting if you called him, he'd tell you otherwise. You've done what you can here, Lachlan. You're going to use Stella's loan to sever things with Dad. Prove to Marisol you did the work. That you'll keep doing it. For heaven's sake, one of us should end up happy."

"You can, too, Maggie."

She shook her head. "Be happy for all of us, okay?"

He took a deep breath. Maybe his sister's blessing would bring him some luck. One call had gone well; he needed the next one to be even better.

"All right, I'll see if I've done enough."

He went to his office and pulled out his cell.

No answer. Crap. Impatience bubbled in his veins. Was Marisol screening his calls? Maybe text would work.

Sunshine, we need to talk.

The sent message glared at him in its insufficiency.

You were right about the money, about me being dishonest, and I'm truly sorry. Please call me.

She didn't.

His heart sank further and further as he made his way back home. It was Monday—she'd be working from her apartment.

Want to go for a walk? he texted.

He heated up a serving of lasagna from the freezer and scarfed it down. Still no response.

Ready to crawl out of his skin, he tried again. Coffee? Decaf, in solidarity?

Three dots popped up on the screen.

And hope fluttered in his chest.

I'm napping. And you're really crappy at keeping things just about the baby.

She was right on that. I've made some changes. I need to talk to you. Come and get some fresh air.

More dots. I don't know, Lach.

Desperation filled him. Exercise is about the baby.

He flopped down on his couch. The silence raked across his brain. Hell, he'd take her stupid noisy clock over the agony of nothing. She was giving him enough time to knit a pair of socks in between each reply.

Maybe tomorrow. I'll text you if I have time to meet up.

Goddamn it. Failure sank heavy in his stomach.

He shoved it away. Her answer wasn't a no. He'd cling to the possibility until she made up her mind.

His phone didn't buzz the next day. He got up-dates from helpful pet owners for two days run-ning—*Marisol's been in the bakery* and *ran into Marisol at the library* and *pretty sure I saw your girl walking down by the creek yesterday*—but nothing from the woman herself. Thursday morning, when he and Fudge were in the middle of nowhere run-ning through training exercises with the SAR team, he finally got a message.

I'm taking the afternoon off. Figure I'm better off going in tomorrow having cleared my mind. Cram-ming never works for me. So I'm free if you're still wanting to talk.

He swore to himself and kicked a rock on the side of the dirt road. Of course. The one day he was doing something he couldn't get out of. It was 9:00 a.m., and they had at least eight hours in the bush today.

Dinner? I'm at SAR training today.

No, I'm busy tonight.

"Why the long face? Good grief, you and Marisol have twin frowns," Zach said, prepping ropes for a climbing maneuver.

"I screwed up, and she broke things off."

When Zach stayed silent, Lachlan couldn't help letting the rest spill out.

Zach whistled low.

"What, she hadn't told you?"

"She's been speaking in one-word sentences all week."

Well, damn. She was either stressed or upset, and he couldn't do anything about either, not until she asked for his support. He inhaled a long stream of forest-scented air, trying to soothe his rising concern. "Not being available today is *not* helping my case."

Raking a hand through his hair, Zach said, "I'd invite you over for dinner, but she knows you're welcome to join us and that she could do the inviting."

"What, she's eating with you tonight?" That would explain why she was busy. But it stung that she hadn't invited him along.

Why would she? You lied to her.

He let out a string of profanity.

Zach nodded. "She had family interfering enough in her marriage. She'd kill me if I all of a sudden started putting my nose in your business."

"I get that. And you're right—she would have invited me if she wanted me there."

Fudge, wearing her vest, stared at him expectantly.

"Any bright ideas, girl?"

She dealt him a doggy frown.

"Thanks for the optimism."

Though he couldn't say he was having any more success at clinging to hope.

After finishing his SAR session, he ripped by the clinic so that he could admire the setting foundation of the barn.

God, it was so much better now that the project wasn't tainted by his parents' involvement.

"Great work, Aleja," he said, nodding at his contractor, who was packing up for the day.

Her dark brows narrowed. "You sure? You don't look happy."

"I'm not, but it has nothing to do with the barn."

Well, it had a lot to do with this place, but not in the sense of Alejandra's crew's efforts being substandard.

She hummed knowingly. "Heard you broke up with your girlfriend."

"You did?"

"Gertie Rafferty was talking to Nancy about how she'd lasted less than a week in the house. I was in the bakery and couldn't help but overhear."

He cringed. Hopefully Marisol didn't learn about

the gossip. She'd always seemed bothered by the speed at which news flew around Sutter Creek.

Fudge bounded up to him, swinging her Kong and begging for a throw. He caught her by the collar. "Come on, doggo, you'll get a nail in the foot if you're out here. See you later, Aleja," he said, leading the dog back to the clinic.

"Later. You know," she called, "sorry's usually a good place to start."

"Tried that," he gritted out. The door slammed shut behind him. He apparently hadn't said sorry in the right way, though.

Or maybe sorry wasn't going to be good enough—

His cell vibrated in his pocket, jarring him from his depressing conclusion.

Maybe it was Marisol, needing something before tomorrow's presentation.

He scrambled to answer, fumbling as he yanked it from his hiking shorts. The words *Gregory Reid* shot down his hopes.

He answered with a sigh. "Dad."

"What's with the bank transfer from Stella, son?"

He gritted his teeth. "Suited my needs better."

"Something to do with the woman I met last week?"

His phone squeaked as he gripped it. He wasn't dignifying that with an answer.

"Don't let her dictate your life, Lachlan. Tell her

how things are going to go. Pursue her, if that's what you want. She's hot enough. But don't be a loser. Take charge."

Rage cascaded through him, momentarily muting his need to roar a reply. A buzzing filled his ears, drowning out the usual aural debris of the clinic. His vision swam. *Deep breath. Take one. Now.*

He did.

Then another.

It didn't lower his blood pressure, but it loosened his tongue.

"I'm not a loser," he asserted. But taking charge, bullying, wasn't the answer. His father's advice hammered home one thing—how pursuing someone after they gave a clear "no" quickly became a lack of consent.

"That's more like it," his father said.

He cleared his throat. He was only going to say this once, and then intended to go a long, long time before speaking to his father again. "I'm not going to be a dictatorial bastard, either. If she just wants to be friends, then I'll respect that. I'd rather be alone than be like you."

Heart clamoring, he hung up, then shut his office door and let out a growl of frustration. He would respect Marisol's wishes. Hell, with how he'd hidden things from her, he'd count himself lucky if she was willing to maintain a friendship.

Living without her would hurt. Every day.

But she'd set a clear line, and he'd crossed it.

It was time to stop asking for forgiveness, and to accept the limits she'd set.

Chapter Fifteen

Had Marisol known dinner was going to involve her brother studying her like a mountain face ready to be prepped for avalanche blasting, she probably would have stayed home.

Liar. Being alone this week has been the worst.

The worst, maybe. But necessary.

A tiny hand smacked her arm, leaving a smear of barbecue sauce. "Ana-ma-ra." Arresting blue eyes latched on to hers, dragging her into a vat of irresistible toddler charm.

"Ben-Ben," she cooed. She tickled him under the chin, earning a smile.

Okay, seeing this little gem was worth Zach's

scrutiny. But seriously, the back of her neck was crawling.

"Stop giving me the hairy eyeball," she insisted, cramming a bite of coleslaw into her mouth.

Everything tasted bland tonight. Her taste buds' fault, not Cadie's.

"You're not happy. Which means I'm not happy," he said quietly.

"After tomorrow, things will be fine." She tugged down the hem of the maternity tank blouse that Cadie had lent her. No way would Marisol be able to get her assets into skinny-minnie Cadie's clothes normally, but maternity ones fit fine, and having something new was a nice distraction from feeling like she couldn't possibly get any bigger.

If only she had a distraction from her brother.

He eyed her suspiciously. "Things will be fine? Really? I get you'll have successfully presented your prospectus, but then—"

"I *might have*, you mean. It might not get approved." She twisted her hands around her paper-towel napkin.

Zach scoffed. "Stop with the self-doubt. And don't try to avoid talking about Lachlan. You're going to live the rest of your life loving the guy, keeping him at arm's reach, because you might get hurt?"

Oh, probably. A lump filled her throat. "I did get hurt."

"Glenn was a long time ago."

She heated with irritation at the mention of her ex's name, one she purposefully kept herself from thinking.

"I don't mean Glenn. I mean Lachlan. He lied." *Just like Glenn.*

"I know he did."

"Why would you want me to be with another selfish prick?"

"There's a big difference between your ex-husband setting creditors on your tail and Lachlan keeping secrets in some misguided attempt at sheltering you. And he knows he screwed up. He's trying to make things right."

"He is?"

Maybe that was what he'd meant by "changes" when he'd texted her on Monday.

Zach put his fork down and glanced at Cadie, who paused in scraping some cut-up carrots onto Ben's plate. "He didn't tell you?"

"We, uh, haven't found a time to get together that worked for both of us." Oof, that was stretching the truth. Lachlan *had* tried, but she hadn't agreed to meet up. Not until today, when she'd known he had training. Okay, fine, she was being a bit of a pill. But she didn't owe him a conversation.

Her brother arched a brow. "He and Maggie convinced Stella to cough up the money he needed. He paid his dad back. He won't be indebted to that jerk, so don't worry about that interfering in your relationship."

A metallic tang hit the tip of her tongue, and she released her teeth from where she'd dug into her lip. *Oh, wow. He did that for me.* She stroked her bump. *And for you.*

Zach and Cadie exchanged another knowing look, then turned their gazes on her. Marisol glanced at Ben instead. Her nephew was making some solid dinner-plate art, but his parents didn't seem to notice.

"Love's a big step. We both know that," Cadie said. She smiled at Zach, blue eyes crinkling. "But don't you think it's worth it?"

"I—" Telling her brother's fiancée that love hurt too damn much seemed like preaching to the choir. Cadie had been widowed, for God's sake. She knew. It was written in the tilt of her dark head, the sad creases that marked the corners of her eyes despite the happiness curving her lips. So how was she sitting there, looking at Zach as if he hung the moon—and Marisol had lived through way too many brotherly antics to believe that entirely true—risking the pain again?

"I don't know," Marisol admitted. She growled to herself. Her emotional tank was sputtering, had been hovering above E for days. Did this seriously have to be happening now? She really needed a clear head for tomorrow's presentation. "I let a relationship interfere with my education before, and if you think I'm going to let that happen again—"

"Is Lachlan not supporting you getting your degree?" Zach asked.

"No, but…" But spending so much time thinking about him, about how she'd rather have him by her side, was sure as hell getting in the way of her focus.

It's only getting in the way because it's wrong to be apart.

She stabbed a carrot with her fork. The tines screeched across the plate. Damn it. Being without him *was* wrong.

And he was trying to make things right. He'd screwed up, but his heart had been in the right place, wanting to mesh both her needs and his dreams… and now, persevering to fix the trust he'd broken.

Glenn had never done that.

He'd blamed her for getting in the way of his ambition and then hit the road at her lowest point, left her to grieve alone and to scramble to pay their bills. She hated the thought of being so naive, so open again. Could she trust Lachlan to be different?

No definitive answers came from the rest of the evening with her overly in-love brother and his fiancée.

Snuggled in bed a few hours later, feeling the lack of Lachlan's company as if an abyss had formed on his side of the mattress, she picked up her phone.

Can we meet up tomorrow? Maybe before I head in to school?

He didn't reply right away. Maybe he was already asleep...

She was about to drift off when a reply chimed.

Focus on polishing your presentation. Maybe we'll talk after.

The command walloped into her, and her hope dissipated. Why had Zach been so certain Lachlan wanted to fix things? If that was correct, Lach would have been as eager to meet up as earlier in the week. Had he changed his mind? The question kept her tossing and turning, long past when she should have fallen asleep.

Lachlan trudged along the university sidewalk, gripping an overlarge bouquet of flowers. He'd agonized over these suckers. Sunflowers and gerberas, greenery the same color as Marisol's eyes.

I'm a freaking sap.

And he wasn't going to pursue her anymore. Didn't deserve to. So after today, no more flowers. Not ones that carried symbolic meaning, anyway.

He switched hands. The cellophane wrapper crinkled, competing with the chatter and guitar chords drifting from a group of students hanging out on one of the university's grassy ovals. His stomach was jittering too hard to let him enjoy the late August sun on his skin or the clever fretwork of the musician. He hadn't seen Marisol since she'd walked out on him. Hopefully after today, with her presentation behind her, she'd be willing to spend time with him in addition to the big events of their life. He'd gotten way too attached to the idea of trying out her new jogging stroller together on the trails in the area. Would "friends" allow for that? Or were they destined to become casual acquaintances who happened to share a kid?

Frustration layered on top of his nerves. Wouldn't she miss—

No. This wasn't on Marisol. She had major trust issues thanks to her scumbag of an ex-husband, and Lachlan had lied anyway. Of anyone, he should have known the inevitable outcome of that. So add inconsiderate to his list of wrongdoings. Aside from congratulating her today, he needed to assure her that he understood her decision.

He'd always regret it. Would never get over the yearning.

But he wasn't going to barge through life like his father, oblivious to the pain caused by his mistakes.

The three-story building loomed large in front of him, the reddish brick a sharp contrast to the green of the oval's foliage. Next summer, he'd have to pick

Marisol up from school now and again, bring Fudge to chase her Kong on the lawn while the baby toddled…

She might not want that.

His chest tightened and he took a deep breath as he entered the building.

After climbing the stairs and ascertaining from the department's receptionist that Marisol was in a conference room down the hall, he registered how unsuited the building was for waiting and stopped short at a T junction. What was he going to do, hang out like a heartsick creeper next to a doorway?

I'm not too far off heartsick.

No, more like smack in the middle of it.

Rubbing his chest, he glanced down each wing of the hall. He could go back to the receptionist and ask about waiting in the office Marisol shared with another PhD candidate, but if she was feeling at all protective over her space—

A door flung open about ten feet to his left. He jumped and looked in the other direction, pretending to be studying door numbers lest one of Marisol's coworkers catch him lurking.

"Lachlan?" Strain rent Marisol's voice, and he turned. That tone of voice had alarm bells clanging in his head.

Damn, she must be so stressed—

But the tension around her mouth spoke to pain, not worry. He narrowed his eyes and did a visual scan, checking her color and for sweat or pallor. Other than her tight jaw, she appeared okay.

Instinct pricked at his neck. He'd been on too many SAR rescues to ignore even the most minor signs of distress. "Is your back still bothering you?"

She sloughed off the question with a careless wave, but her jaw clenched again. "What are you doing here?"

"I came to congratulate you on being finished." He lifted the flowers in a feeble motion and stepped closer.

"I'm not done yet. Hit the halfway point and asked for ten minutes to stretch my legs," she said, teeth gritted. Her mouth flattened even more.

"Marisol, are you in pain?"

"Sort of." Her hands splayed against the underside of her belly and she sucked in a breath.

Her bump looked even lower than it had last week, and he wanted to stand behind her, hold up some of the weight for her like he had a few times.

"Is she sitting on your sciatic nerve again?"

Her jaw clenched, and she shifted her weight from side to side a couple of times. "Something like that."

She bent over, putting her hands on her thighs and doing a modified cat stretch from one of the yoga videos he'd watched her work out to. Helplessness washed over him. Goddamn it. Respecting her boundaries was one thing, but standing idle while she was hurting because their baby was head down and two weeks from—

Wait. He strode to her side and gently laid the flowers to the side of the hallway. He rubbed her lower back with one hand and bent down a little, cupping the other hand under her stomach. Her stomach competed with her back for the more rock-hard designation.

"Marisol…"

She dropped the side of her head against his chest and let out a strained, "Yeah?"

"You in labor, sunshine?"

"No!" She backed up the denial with a vigorous head shake. "I can't be. I'm in the middle of my presentation."

Somehow her stomach tensed even more under his palm, and she whimpered and turned into him, burying her face against his T-shirt. Her nails dug into his arm.

Ow. That was going to leave a mark.

But it was nothing compared to what she was about to go through, so he kept his mouth shut.

He tightened his hold on her, bracing one arm across her back and continuing to rub the base of her spine with the other, taking a quick glance at his watch. If this was what he thought it was, one of the only things he could do was keep track of the time. "How often are you having contractions?"

"Do we have to call them contractions?"

"I can't answer that for you. But this seems like more than Braxton-Hicks. Has your water broken?"

"No."

"Good, good." He took a relieved breath. "Okay, then. Let's come up with a plan."

"I had a plan! And I failed at it. I was stupid to think I could do it all," she cried. "God, I didn't manage to do any of it. I was crazy to think I could be a good parent and get my degree. And then…then I lost you…"

"Hey." Man, they had two different opinions on why a relationship hadn't worked between them. "That's just pain talking. I was the one who screwed up our chances. And you are going to be just as good of a mom as you are a student. As long as you're okay with a few detours and unplanned stops, you'll definitely get everything done." He wasn't going to add another failed attempt at a relationship to that list. She deserved better than what he could give. "Take a breath for me, okay?"

She did, and a little of the tension around her spine loosened.

"I suck at detours," she griped.

"I dunno, they bring some pretty awesome things." Would bring them a baby over the next day or so. His heart swelled, clamored to get her into the car and to the hospital. *Slow down.* His SAR training had his senses on alert, but it wasn't panic time yet. "You have about six minutes left in your break.

Let's just stand here, see how you're feeling once that's up."

He braced himself against the wall and took more of her weight. His pulse raced, but not as fast as his thoughts. Depending on how far apart her contractions were, it might make more sense to stay in Bozeman to go to the hospital—did Caleb have privileges there? Pretty sure he did... It'd avoid the forty-minute drive to Sutter Creek, though none of Marisol's stuff was here. Unless she had her bag in the car? Maybe they would drive back, and Zach or Cadie could meet them at the hospital with whatever she didn't have with her. She'd mentioned packing one the other day... Which would have stuff in it for the baby, who was about to arrive.

Panic exploded in his brain, and he bit his lip to suppress the shivers that raced down his limbs.

"You're thinking too hard," she mumbled into his shirt.

"Sure, but we're about to meet our daughter, here. And I want—" He stopped himself before he blurted out the lengths he'd go to keep Marisol in his embrace for the rest of his life.

"I'm not in labor," she insisted in the most unconvincing tone he'd ever heard. "You won't need to play doctor."

"Not intending to." He'd have her at the hospital far before the baby made her entrance.

She sucked in a breath and peeled herself from

his chest. Her determined gaze met his. "I only need another hour. I'm going to walk in there and—" Her eyes slammed shut and she bit her lip hard enough to turn the skin near her teeth white. Supporting her belly with her hands again, she breathed deeply through her nose.

He checked his watch again. "That was about five minutes, Mari."

Her nod was tiny, but was enough of an admission for him. "Want me to come in with you, be with you when you talk to the panel?"

"Just need a minute," she said around her sucked-in lip. "I can do it."

"I know you can. But do you want support?"

She released her lip and a low click of a breath. "I do."

Relief flooded his limbs. At least there was something she'd let him do for her.

Small potatoes next to how badly he'd failed at loving her. *And if I do that with our daughter...*

He swallowed. Okay, so she wasn't the only one going through a crisis of confidence.

For Christ's sake, today is not about me.

He refocused on her body language, waiting for the contraction to pass. After a few seconds, her shoulders relaxed and a serene expression crossed her face.

"That one all done?"

She nodded.

His heart swelled with admiration and he brushed his thumb down her cheek. "You are so strong."

"I hope so."

Another doubt slammed into him. "Do you still want me as your labor coach? Or do you want me to get Cadie?"

She barked out a laugh. "You did this, buddy. You get to suffer through it, too."

Straightening, he sent her an encouraging look and motioned for her to lead the way. He had the rest of his life to use his paranoia over treating people like his father did as motivation to be different, to be a good parent to their child and have a healthy co-parenting relationship with Marisol. And his doubts could piss right off for the rest of the day—they had a baby to welcome into the world.

Chapter Sixteen

You are so strong.

 You are so strong.

 In the throes of another contraction, every muscle in her body consumed by the rhythmic, racking tension, Marisol mentally recited Lachlan's words like she had been for the last six hours. The mantra had kept her going for a while, but the longer it took to get to ten centimeters, the harder it was to believe it.

 "Painful isn't enough," she said, panting as the contraction passed. The way they'd been going, she had all of forty-eight seconds before the next one would arrive.

 "Huh?" Lach gripped her hand, confusion written

on his face. His hair stuck up in about eight directions, and he was wearing a doctor's surgical shirt because she'd thrown up on him an hour or so ago.

"Painful isn't a big enough word."

His brows drew together and his mouth went loose. "Sunshine…"

She let her head drop to the pillow. She'd had all these big ideas about laboring in the tub or walking around, but the minute she'd arrived at the hospital after forty agonizing minutes in the car—why again had she insisted the hospital in Bozeman wasn't good enough?—all that had worked for her was lying on her back on the inclined hospital bed, contradicting every bit of labor advice she'd read. Whoever had convinced her that doing this without an epidural was a good idea could go suck a sewer pipe, too. "I can't do this."

His grip tightened. "You're so close. You know what Caleb said. Transition's super intense, but it'll lessen off once you can start pushing."

"I'll show you pushing," she snarked, lightly shoving his chest.

"I'd do this for you if I could," he whispered. "I wish it didn't have to all be you. But this is the only time it will be, Marisol. I don't blame you for not trusting me, but know that when it comes to the baby, I will fully take on my share—"

She squeezed his hand and caught him wincing.

He couldn't take on her pain, though. If only. How much *longer*—

A wave swelled. There were no words for it, for the consuming intensity. Agony didn't cut it, because it wasn't suffering, but she sure as hell wasn't able to ride on top of it. The doula she'd worked with in Vancouver had been so full of—

"Marisol, are you pushing?" A nurse—Fiona?—materialized at her side, all encouraging smiles and perfect lipstick and decidedly not dripping with sweat.

Marisol squeezed her eyes shut. *Right. Don't push. Don't.* "Trying not to. Can't…help it."

"Let me check you." Fiona did a quick internal exam. "No wonder you're pushing. You're fully dilated." Pressing the call button, she smiled at Marisol. "Someone's ready to be born."

Gulping air, Marisol clung to her few seconds between contractions. "Pretty sure she's been ready since she forced me to leave my prospectus presentation."

"Babies are notorious for not cooperating."

"Mmm." The committee would have a good story to toss around the department staff meeting tomorrow.

And she didn't care one iota.

The baby was what mattered. Getting her out, specifically, but more than that. She'd come first. Every time. As would the man crouching by her side, letting her squeeze the stuffing out of his hand. She flopped her head to the side. "I love you."

An impossible amount of hope blossomed on his face. He kissed the back of her hand. "I love you, too. Focus on pushing, okay?"

As if she could do anything but.

Her stomach started to tighten, tighten, tighten, an unforgiving vise that tunneled her vision. She yelped, then flattened her feet against the bed and bore down. Yes. Relief. Intense, still, but purposeful—

"Whoa there, Marisol." Caleb's voice soothed and warned simultaneously. "You're going to hurt yourself if you try to push that way."

One day, she might care that the man who she ran into at SAR events had seen every part of her that mattered exposed, with a baby stretching her body into shapes it would probably never recover from, but today was not that day. "Ca-leb," she panted. "Get her out. Please."

"'Fraid that's a joint effort. But I'm here to help."

She growled. "I feel worn-out and I haven't even started."

"Let's be efficient, then. Lachlan's going to help Fiona support your legs, and you're going to push using your pelvic floor, okay? Remember talking about that?"

"Yep."

She lost herself in Caleb's instructions, in focusing on muscle groups, on trying to get above the magnitude of each contraction.

"Hold there, Marisol," he said. "Baby's crowning. Almost done."

"Oh my God! Hold? How?" She swore. "This is the worst!"

"Do you want to try visualization again?" Lachlan asked quietly.

The entire lower half of her body was on fire and he wanted to talk psychology? What the hell? "How about visualizing my fist in your face?"

She'd have to complete her PhD without using any psychological terminology, because labor had ruined the words for her.

"Do you want to touch the baby's head?" Caleb asked. "Help guide her out? Lachlan, you watching?"

"Hard not to," Lachlan said in a strangled voice.

"One more push, maybe two."

Mary, mother of God, this was happening too fast. Her eyes stung as she fought the hot pain. But her baby's head? Yeah, she wanted to feel that. Proof this would be over and with one more push—

She reached down, and Caleb guided her hand to the little patch of scalp, like a peach, almost, a peach that felt way damned bigger than a peach as another contraction hit and she pushed and there was a head, and a blur, and she was lying skin-to-skin with a wrinkly pink human on her chest.

"Ohhhhh, hello," she cooed. The baby squinted

and squawked, and Marisol instinctively shushed her. Her breath caught, a rush of indescribable connection consuming her soul. The intensity of labor had nothing on the immediate, vehement attachment to the tiny being with the little rosebud mouth and a heck of a mop of dark hair. *Oh, wow. Wow.* Textbooks did not lie about the hormone surge, the bond that followed childbirth.

Lachlan slid an arm behind her and settled his free hand on the baby's back. Fiona slid a warmed flannel blanket between his palm and the baby, and a flash of disappointment crossed his face.

"Once I've tried feeding her and they've cleaned me up, you can try skin-to-skin, too," Marisol whispered.

"Whatever works for you."

She cupped his cheek. "This works for me, Lachlan."

"Let's talk when you're not swimming in oxytocin, okay?"

Too much self-doubt swam in his eyes for her to be mad at his assumptions that she was making decisions because of hormones.

The next hour melted into two as she dealt with the third stage of labor and tried nursing for the first time under Fiona's watchful eye. After, she put on some comfy jammies and called her parents to tell them that no, she hadn't completed her presentation, but yes, they had a healthy six-pound-ten-ounce granddaughter. Lachlan sent a group text with a picture to his sisters, and then forwarded it on to Zach with the instructions to pass it on to the rest of the Cardenas clan.

"Your turn, I think," she said, once they were finally alone in the room.

He pulled the rocking chair over and stripped out of his shirt, then gingerly lifted the baby off Marisol's chest and sat, settling the infant against his skin.

Ohhhh. Yep. Strong man, teeny baby. The "mommy porn" hashtag made so much more sense now. She rolled onto her side, hissing as her abused body adjusted to the new position.

"Once they release us, I don't want to go back to my place by myself," she said quietly. "I'm too sore." Tears pricked her eyes. "Emotional, too. I don't want it just to be me and the baby."

"I can sleep on the couch for however long you need. And she needs us to pick a name. Feels wrong calling her 'the baby.'" Amazement crossed his face as he touched a fingertip to their daughter's nose.

"We will. But it feels even more wrong that we're not together in this, Lachlan." The need to convince him clogged in her throat. "I don't want you to sleep on the couch. Now that she's here—I know I can do this. *All* of this. My program isn't going anywhere. They're being flexible for me. And if I don't climb the ranks of academia as fast as I'd anticipated, well, so be it."

"It's too soon to make decisions, Marisol." Frowning, he shook his head. "I messed up. I—I hate what I did. Even though I thought I was doing the right thing… I've been treated like that before."

"I know you have. That's why you feel bad about it." She inched closer to the edge of the bed and reached out to touch his shoulder. Warm skin flinched under her palm. "We can make this work, Lachlan. I need you to trust me."

Trust me.

He'd been preaching that to her for months. Objectively knew he could. So what was with the wariness running through him? When all he should have been feeling was the all-encompassing love that filled his throat every time he looked down at his sleeping daughter?

Oh, right. Because he hadn't practiced what he preached and then ended up failing her. And if loving someone meant not honoring their limits and being dishonest, then it wasn't something he deserved.

He inhaled, struggling to form the words. "I pushed too hard. To the point you were committing before you were ready. That's not love, Marisol."

She stroked his cheek. "You're not pushing me now."

"Well, no. I'm not going to do that anymore—"

"And I'm still here. Still wanting this."

Hope blossomed and he shoved it down, studying her. She blinked long, betraying her exhaustion. She'd essentially just run a couple of marathons back-to-back. But serenity marked her weary smile. Spoke to a truth, as if she'd discovered another layer to reality.

The baby snuffled on his chest. How was it possible to feel like he'd known her for his whole life after knowing her for a couple of hours? Warmth spread through him, real and pulsing. Love, for the baby. For Marisol.

But if he screwed up again... Hurt her again...

A series of alarms sounded from the nurse's station down the hall, echoing the warning in his head. He wanted to hope, but it wasn't about trusting Marisol. He had to trust himself that he wasn't going to screw up again, and that she wasn't feeling obligated because of the baby...

"I still want you, Lach," she continued with emphasis. She reached over and stroked the baby's back. "Us."

"I want to love you more than anything." He swallowed the lump in his throat. "But I can't handle taking the chance that I'd walk over what you need."

She scoffed. "Am I a pushover, Lachlan?"

"No, but—"

"I know what it's like to be in a relationship with someone who doesn't have any regard for me and my needs. And this is not it. Also, if you overstepped in the future, you can trust that I'd call you on it if you did. Yeah, I don't like that you didn't tell me about the money. But I believe you'll be honest in the future. I don't mind that you pushed for us to be together. You forced me out of my comfort zone. That was healthy. And I need to remember you're not… him. My ex. It was unfair of me to put his history on you."

"Was it? I lied to get what I wanted."

"And I've forgiven you for that. You found a different solution for your finances, and you're here. Look at what we just did—"

He shook his head. "What you just did."

"No, what *we* did. We were a team. You were right about that—we can do whatever we put our mind to as long as we stick together. I just pushed a human out of my body without drugs, for heaven's sake. Figuring out work and parenting this amazing human and loving you? I can do that, too."

She eased herself backward on the bed, the evidence of her superhero status written in every tug and pull of her mouth.

Concern panged through him. "We should get you more painkillers."

She patted the space she'd cleared on the bed. "In a minute. Come here. Family snuggle."

"Family." He rolled the word around on his tongue and settled in next to Marisol. With one hand holding the baby to his chest, and one around the woman who'd brought her into the world, could life get any fuller? He sure as hell couldn't love them any more than he already did—

So reach for it. She was telling him she wanted this. He'd been intent on believing her when she *hadn't* truly wanted it—why couldn't he believe her when she did?

"I'm not sure I deserve the two of you," he mumbled.

Soft lips pressed against his bare shoulder. "You so do, my love."

"And you're not afraid anymore? Your ex screwed you over but good, and then I piled onto it—I get why you were wary."

She smiled softly and laid her head in the crook of his neck. "We're both going to make mistakes, Lachlan. But we'll fix them, too. And no, I'm not afraid anymore. Would a fearful woman ask you to marry her?"

"Well, no, but you haven't asked me, so that's moot."

"I just did."

His pulse seized. "Pretty sure it was a rhetorical question."

She poked him between the ribs. "Do you want it to be rhetorical? Because if you do, tell me so I can pretend that's what I meant."

"I don't want that at all. I want to be a family. Want to marry you."

Her mouth quirked, wobbly smile solidifying with

joy. Tired joy, but joy for sure. "I proposed without a ring. Badly done of me."

"You gave me a baby. That'll do."

"She will."

But it wouldn't be enough for Marisol. She'd need an engagement ring. And he knew the exact right one. "Given we're full up for novelty today, I'm not feeling the need to be secretive—I'll call my grandfather, ask him where Grams's engagement ring ended up. He probably has it tucked away somewhere."

"That'd be lovely." Her face was tucked against his chest, but her soft tone made her happiness clear. "What about her name?"

"Grams's name? Laura? What about it?"

She chortled, then groaned. "Laughing…oh, it's no good."

"I bet. But what's so funny?"

"I was suggesting we use your grandmother's name for the baby. It's pretty. Laura Reid Cardenas, if that works for you. Maybe with Marisol as a middle name. My parents didn't stick with the paternal and maternal naming custom, but I think I'd like to."

"Sunshine, given what I just watched you do, I'll bow to whatever choice you make. But using my grandmother's name…" His voice cracked, and he gave her a sheepish smile.

"I'll take that as a yes," she murmured.

He coughed to clear the swell of emotion. "To Laura. And to being a family, and to a lifetime of loving each other—it's all a yes."

Epilogue

Marisol moved the cursor, ready to press Send on her last round of revisions. Could four years of work—thirteen, really, if she included her bachelor's and master's degrees—be distilled down to one tap on a touch pad? Her hand hovered over her laptop, and her heart thudded in her chest.

Footsteps sounded from down the hall. She'd been revising and editing at the training facility lately, a desperate attempt to see her husband and daughter for more than an hour a day. Laura's preschool was only a block away, so Lachlan usually picked her up after her session and brought her back to play with the dogs. And family time aside, she got more done in Lachlan's office than she did at the house, which they'd recently purchased from Gertie Rafferty. No end to the make-work projects there. She'd be juggling teaching and renos and family this summer.

A smile spread on her face at the prospect.

"Mari?" Lachlan's voice floated from the direction of the footsteps, and he appeared in the doorway. Too handsome for his own good, this man. And he was all hers, from his six-ways-to-Sunday hair to the polo shirt that stretched oh-so-fine across his pecs to the puppy prints marking up his shorts.

Heat settled in her belly. They'd have to celebrate tonight...

Her gaze fell to his hands. Seemed like he was on the same page—a bottle of sparkling wine dangled from one hand and two glasses threaded between the knuckles of the other.

Not the kind of celebration she was up for. Nerves jumped in her stomach, and she put a hand to it.

Crap, she'd have to make excuses somehow.

Or fess up about my suspicions...

"All done?" he asked.

"Almost. Just need to submit it via the portal."

He grinned and walked around the desk. Perching on the edge with his legs stretched out, he put the bottle and glasses down. "Submission anxiety?"

"Little bit."

"Need a kiss first?"

She tapped the send button. "No, I need a kiss now that I've done it."

"You *did* do it, sunshine." His smile spread even wider, and he caught her fingers and tugged her up. "Dr. Sunshine, I should say."

"You *should*. I busted my ass for that title." She settled in the V of his legs and brushed her lips along the tickly soft hair on his jaw. He'd grown a short beard the winter after Laura was born, and she refused to let him shave it.

"I will. Often as you like. I'm so proud of you." His lips sealed over hers, a vow of a kiss. "And maybe life'll settle down a bit now. We'll take a bit of time to enjoy what we've worked for."

Yeah, about that "time." Her mouth went dry, and she couldn't stop her eyes from widening.

He cocked his head. "What?"

"As if Laura will let us settle down." *Not to mention...*

His brow furrowed. "Where *is* Laura?"

"You didn't leave her with Maggie?"

"No, I thought she was—" His head swiveled toward the little activity table set up in the corner across from his desk, next to Fudge's dog bed. The dog, gray around the muzzle now, was snoring away, unaware that the small human who lovingly tormented her had gone missing. "Damn, should have realized it was too quiet."

They rushed out of the office and down the hall, through the indoor ring where Lachlan led obedience and indoor training classes.

"Laura?"

"Lolo?"

As long as she was inside, there wasn't much she could get into, but she was starting to figure out doorknobs. Normal safety concerns aside, there was a heck of a junk pile out back that Lachlan used for search training.

Opening and closing doors to the bathroom and the sole classroom, they quickly discerned their four-year-old wasn't in the building.

Lachlan swore.

"Maybe she *is* with Maggie," Marisol suggested, heart rate picking up.

They tore from the building and along the walkway that connected the vet clinic to the training facility. She scanned the cement-and-grass area between the two buildings. Empty. Silent, too. Maggie only had a senior spaniel in her care at the moment, as well as a Labrador puppy that a family had decided they couldn't handle. The normally noisy kennel—

"The *kennel*," she said, slowing. "She's your kid. We should have looked there first."

He shot her a wry smile. "Just my kid?"

Tipping her head in a guilty-as-charged admission, she pushed open the door that led to the dogs.

Between the two rows of small pens and kennels, a metal-fenced play area was set up. If Laura was anywhere, she'd be— Yup.

A tiny human body was curled up with a tiny canine body on the thin foam dog bed. Relief poured through Marisol, and she grabbed Lachlan's hand.

He squeezed. "Sound asleep. Guess she hasn't totally grown out of naps."

Brown curls askew much like her daddy's sandy blond ones, Laura clutched the twelve-week-old lab to her chest. Marisol's throat ached at the cuteness.

"Wake up, baby bear," she murmured, opening the enclosure.

Laura's eyes fluttered open, arms tightening around the black-furred puppy. "I closed the gate, Mama."

"I know. But Mommy and Daddy didn't know where you were. We were scared."

"Vader is scawed, too, Mama. He's awone." Her little lip wobbled.

Oh, God. Laura had skills. And Marisol had at least fourteen more years of being equal parts charmed and suckered in by that epic pout.

Lachlan entered the enclosure and knelt, stroking a hand on Laura's head and then the puppy's back. "Vader, huh?"

Laura nodded solemnly.

"We can't name him, Lolo. He's not ours," Lachlan picked her up and stood. "And he won't be alone. Auntie Maggie is taking him home tonight."

"He could come to our house." She nuzzled into his neck and sniffled. "Peez, Daddy?"

Lachlan's gaze locked on Marisol's. A "helpless to withstand the tears of his daughter" kind of look.

"Oh, no," Marisol said. "We can't."

"Fudge is nearing retirement, Mari." His mouth turned down at the corners. "I've spent some time with this guy this week. He has potential."

Her heart panged. Lach wasn't the only person in the family who couldn't resist the sadness of a loved one. "But I *just* finished…"

And I think we're going to be mighty busy with someone else.

It seemed their somewhat lackadaisical attention to birth control over the past couple of months had had its effect far sooner than they'd expected it would. She couldn't drop that on him here, though, not with little ears on the alert. They'd need to decide when and how to tell Laura.

"I know, we'd thought we'd slow down a bit," he said. "But maybe we should do the opposite. Our family could grow by one?"

She glanced at the puppy, who was awake and had started attacking Lachlan's shoelace.

"He looks like a sweetheart. And I know you're close to needing to train a new dog. But…" She tilted her head and splayed her hand below her navel.

His jaw dropped. Joyous realization spread on his face. He shifted Laura to his hip and held his free arm open.

Marisol snuggled close, breathing in the soothing scents of Lachlan's soap and Laura's shampoo and puppy.

"You sure?" he choked out.

"No test yet."

"You need one to know?"

"Not really. I know."

"I love you, sunshine," he murmured in her ear. "And don't worry. We've got this."

Her heart settled. Lachlan trained dogs better than anyone she knew. He wouldn't take on a puppy if he didn't truly believe they could manage. And as for a baby… A second child was obviously more complicated than an only, but it wasn't like when she was pregnant with Laura. They had a foundation now. Were ready to keep building on it.

She rose on her toes and whispered, "Looks like we're growing by two."

* * * * *

COMING SOON!

We really hope you enjoyed reading this book.
If you're looking for more romance, be sure to
head to the shops when new books are
available on

Thursday 26th
June

To see which titles are coming soon, please visit
millsandboon.co.uk/nextmonth

MILLS & BOON

Coming next month

CINDERELLA'S NEW YORK FLING
Cara Colter

The sales assistant, Meredith, swept up all the clothes and left them.

"I feel like Cinderella," Jessica said, sinking into the chair beside him. The dress hitched up on a slender leg. He tried not to look. Failing in that, he tried not to be obvious about looking.

"But it's just about midnight. The glass slipper falls off, and I see what it all costs. I probably can't even afford one thing from here."

Jamie looked at his watch so she wouldn't see the pleasure in his eyes that he was going to play a part in her fairytale.

Not the prince part, of course. Though something about seeing her in all those clothes could tempt any man to play that role, even one as cynical about fairytales as him.

Meredith came back. She held out a piece of paper to Jessica.

Jessica took it, looked at it, and blinked. "Oh," she said. "It's so much less than I expected. Still, I don't need two skirts. So, I should probably take out the pencil-line one and keep the navy slacks."

Meredith snatched the paper back from her. "I forgot to add our preferred customer discount."

Jessica took back the paper with the adjusted price. Her mouth fell open with shocked surprise.

"Alright," she cried, beaming, "I'll take it all!"

As Meredith handled the transaction – giving the one

bill to Jessica and putting the real amount on Jamie's credit card, Jamie realized this was probably the most duplicitous thing he had ever done. But Jessica was absolutely radiant.

"I'll pay you back, of course. The insurance representative said I'll have some money by this afternoon."

How could something feel both so very wrong and so very right at the same time?

When they left the store, Jessica was wearing the brand new sundress. Jamie couldn't help but notice that, in a city where no one paid any attention to anyone else, Jessica was receiving subtle – and deeply appreciative glances – from the men of New York.

A man on a construction site whistled at her. Jamie threw him a warning glance, and then noticed Jessica was blushing as though she had been propositioned.

How could he turn her over to an assistant when it was so complicated? Jessica now looked like a sophisticated woman of the world. But she was the furthest thing from that. He couldn't just cast her out on her own. A still small voice, somewhere in the region of his heart, whispered to him, *admit it, pal, you don't want to.*

Continue reading
CINDERELLA'S NEW YORK FLING
Cara Colter

Available next month
www.millsandboon.co.uk

LET'S TALK
Romance

For exclusive extracts, competitions
and special offers, find us online:

 facebook.com/millsandboon

@MillsandBoon

@MillsandBoonUK

Get in touch on 01413 063232

For all the latest titles coming soon, visit
millsandboon.co.uk/nextmonth

JOIN THE
MILLS & BOON
BOOKCLUB

* **FREE** delivery direct to your door

* **EXCLUSIVE** offers every month

* **EXCITING** rewards programme

50% OFF
YOUR FIRST
PARCEL

Join today at
Millsandboon.co.uk/Bookclub

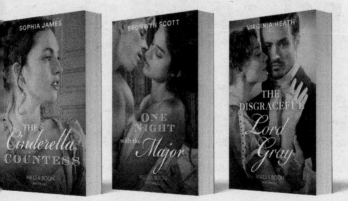

MILLS & BOON

THE HEART OF ROMANCE

A ROMANCE FOR EVERY KIND OF READER

MODERN

Prepare to be swept off your feet by sophisticated, sexy and seductive heroes, in some of the world's most glamourous and romantic locations, where power and passion collide.
8 stories per month.

HISTORICAL

Escape with historical heroes from time gone by. Whether you passion is for wicked Regency Rakes, muscled Vikings or rugg Highlanders, awaken the romance of the past.
6 stories per month.

MEDICAL

Set your pulse racing with dedicated, delectable doctors in the high-pressure world of medicine, where emotions run high an passion, comfort and love are the best medicine.
6 stories per month.

True Love

Celebrate true love with tender stories of heartfelt romance, f the rush of falling in love to the joy a new baby can bring, and focus on the emotional heart of a relationship.
8 stories per month.

Desire

Indulge in secrets and scandal, intense drama and plenty of si hot action with powerful and passionate heroes who have it all wealth, status, good looks...everything but the right woman.
6 stories per month.

HEROES

Experience all the excitement of a gripping thriller, with an in romance at its heart. Resourceful, true-to-life women and stron fearless men face danger and desire - a killer combination!
8 stories per month.

DARE

Sensual love stories featuring smart, sassy heroines you'd want best friend, and compelling intense heroes who are worthy of
4 stories per month.

To see which titles are coming soon, please visit
millsandboon.co.uk/nextmonth

JOIN US ON SOCIAL MEDIA!

Stay up to date with our latest releases, author news and gossip, special offers and discounts, and all the behind-the-scenes action from Mills & Boon...

 millsandboon

 millsandboonuk

millsandboon

t might just be true love...